Praise for
The Black Phantom Chronicles

Esther Wallace has created an interesting world with deep characters who drew me into their story. She weaves a tale of hope, even in the midst of severe conflict, and shows how one person can truly make a difference.

- Suzanne Hartmann, co-founder of Castle Gate Press and author of the *Fast Track Thiller* series

Hold on to your seat! *The Eternal Struggle* immediately draws the reader into the action. The dire situations of the two main characters—Valoretta, Queen of Mira, and Arnacin of Enchantress Island—are clearly portrayed as the action alternates between their evolving parallel perils.

Wallace is a solid storyteller. Her ability to maintain the period dialogue adds charm to the reading that frames the action in an unusual fantasy world of old. The characters peopling this world are clearly drawn and compelling.

– Andrea O'Connor

Esther Wallace is a tenacious writer who will break your heart with her characters and their journeys. Her debut is a high-stakes world filled with fierce and philosophical hearts.

– Stephanie H. Warner, writer and author

The Savage War is an ingeniously plotted novel that is fast-paced and filled with action and focused scenes. There is a kind of ritual that opens the narrative, establishing a custom that is passed from father to son, allowing readers an idea of a tradition that reflects the setting in which the story takes place. Arnacin is a young protagonist who grows in wisdom, but he is a character that has internal battles of his own. I loved the way the author allows his humanity to come out in the narrative, a personality that is characterized by "humility, compassion, and intense feeling of responsibility" and these are the values at the center of the internal conflict when he has to make difficult choices. *The Savage War* is well written with a vivid setting; deft and balanced, and featuring characters that are interesting and real.

- Readers' Favorite, 5-star review

The characters in *The Savage War* were well thought out with unique personalities. The protagonist was wise with sharp instincts and values honor above all else. The reader can feel how torn he is when he has to make those hard decisions.

– Eileen K. Copeland

The Savage War is definitely packed. (But do buckle in for the long ride, because it is definitely worth it.) There is a lot going on by way of story, themes and thought-provoking moments. I especially love Anarcin's willingness to see the conflict from all sides, to ask the hard questions, and do what he feels is right despite opposition.

– M

The Savage War is ideal for fans of G.A. Henty and R.A. Ballantyne. It's intentionally written in an older style, evoking classic adventure/fantasy authors. The characters are charming and the imagery evocative.

– CT Reader

Many books of epic medieval fantasy clamor for attention in the market today. But few of them manage to retain a balance of majestic tragedy with the themes of honor and nobility, a balance which characterized similar novels of a bygone era. [In *The Savage War*,] Author Esther Wallace tells a story about a young man who feels called to an adventure away from his idyllic homeland, where he eventually discovers a nation torn by war. Arnacin's sense of honor compels him to take part in the conflict that, over time, threatens to crush his spirit... Snippets where Arnacin and Princess Valoretta are teasing each other are genuinely touching while heroics on the battlefield stir the soul with excitement.

In short, this is a great novel for anyone craving realistic fantasy with a dose of spirituality. It is awash with battles, drama, political intrigue, and raw human emotion. Just make sure to save some room on your bookshelf for Esther's next entry!

– **Amazon Customer**

THE ETERNAL STRUGGLE

Ett Wallace

THE ETERNAL STRUGGLE

THE BLACK PHANTOM CHRONICLES
BOOK TWO

BY
ESTHER WALLACE

EMERALD LAKE
BOOKS

The Eternal Struggle
The Black Phantom Chronicles (Book 2)

Copyright © 2020 Esther Wallace

Cover design by Mark Gerber

Cover illustration copyright © 2020 Mark Gerber

Books published by Emerald Lake Books may be ordered through your favorite booksellers or by visiting emeraldlakebooks.com.

ISBN: 978-1-945847-25-7 (paperback)
        978-1-945847-27-1 (ebook)
Library of Congress Control Number: 2020904932

To those who have waited for this book
and those who know the scars
of the eternal struggle

Cast of Characters

Arnacin . . . . .An islander from Enchantress Island.
Ben. . . . . .Husband of Orissy, resident of Minsa.
Brother Channing . .Captive healer of Baulis.
Captain Adhelmar . .An officer in Queen Isholt's navy and master of *Isholt's Revenge.*
Captain Belon . . . .Another of Queen Isholt's navy officers and master of *Pursuit of Justice.*
Captain Xavior . . . .The pirate captain of the *Zedelious.*
Captain Phillio . . . .A renegade captain who deserted Queen Isholt's navy to turn pirate.
Captain Vinn . . . . .An officer of Queen Isholt's navy.
Cayd . . . . .A pirate Arnacin rescues.
Denis . . . . .Captain Belon's suspicious first mate.
Denny . . . . .Grandson of Ben and Orissy.
Duke Nayhuel . . . .Duke Cestmir's oldest son. A duke of Mira.
Firth . . . . .The exiled son of an adopted Miran native.
Hans . . . . .Captain Adhelmar's cabin boy.
Jabril. . . . . .Master of the pirate island, Baulis.
King Navoriche. . . .King of Ursa.
Lera . . . . .Granddaughter of Ben and Orissy.
Lilitha . . . . .An adopted native of Mira.
Lord Carpason . . . .A past lord of Mira, but, while living, a close friend of Arnacin's.

Lord Emroy. . . . . . A lord of Ursa.
Maco. . . . . A captive shipwright of Baulis.
Memphis . . . . Miro's high councilor.
Mr. Butter. . . . . . . One of Xavior's pirates.
Orissy . . . . Wife of Ben, resident of Minsa.
Polion . . . . Captain Adhelmar's first mate.
Queen Isholt . . . . . Queen of Nomacir.
Rosa . . . . Valoretta's step-mother.
Sara . . . . Valoretta's aunt and attendant.
Spyros. . . . . Xavior's first mate.
Tareef . . . . Sailor and compass-maker.
Titus. . . . . Captain Belon's cabin boy.
Valoretta . . . . . . Queen of Mira.

PROLOGUE

Black blow the waves, the crashing waves,
Yet faster than the storm,
Faster and darker than mortal ship be,
The Black Captain's Immortal.

Black blow the waves, the crashing waves,
Whenever is seen the Immortal,
For it rides on air, of its flat-bottomed hull.

Long and sleek, terrible and ruthless,
The Black Captain has stolen its secrets from gods.
Now, no justice can track it, no defender live.

For black grow the waves, the crashing waves,
Whenever is seen the Immortal,
Flat-bottomed, long and sleek, terrible and ruthless,

The Immortal.

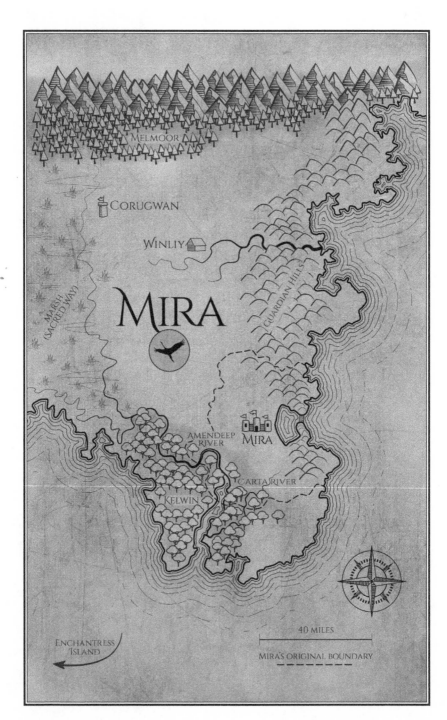

IN THE FIRST BOOK OF *The Black Phantom Chronicles, The Savage War*, a young shepherd boy, Arnacin of Enchantress Island, leaves his home to find fulfillment and honor. Instead, he finds himself assisting Mira, a kingdom torn by war.

There, he befriends Valoretta, princess of Mira, chosen by her father to be heir to the throne. She confides to Arnacin that, not only has the war with the natives existed for as long as she can remember, but she is also uncertain of their victory.

When Arnacin and Valoretta join forces to secure the future of Mira, hope rises. Yet, when the always independent, if extremely loyal, Arnacin clashes with the king of Mira, the islander is condemned to be sealed into a tower to die.

Escaping that fate with the help of Princess Valoretta, Arnacin is caught again but, this time, the king has him exiled. Mira has little hope of their survival in the coming days...

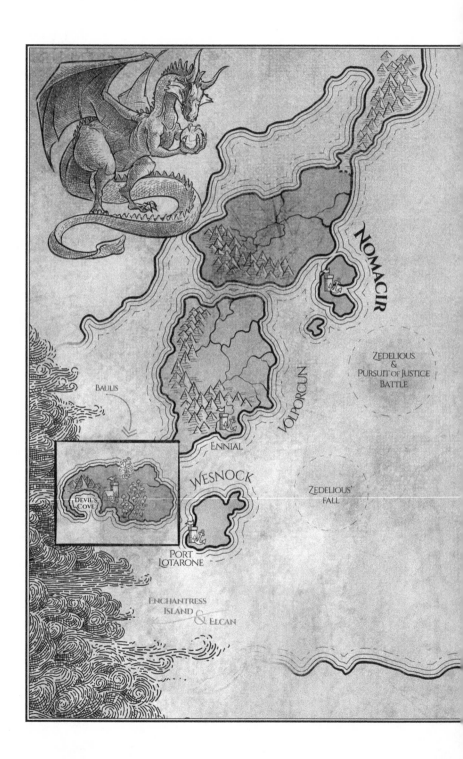

NOMACIR

ZEDELIOUS
&
PURSUIT OF JUSTICE
BATTLE

BAULIS

VOLPORCUN

ENNIAL

WESNOCK

ZEDELIOUS'
FALL

DEVIL'S
COVE

PORT
LOTARONE

ENCHANTRESS
ISLAND
& ELCAN

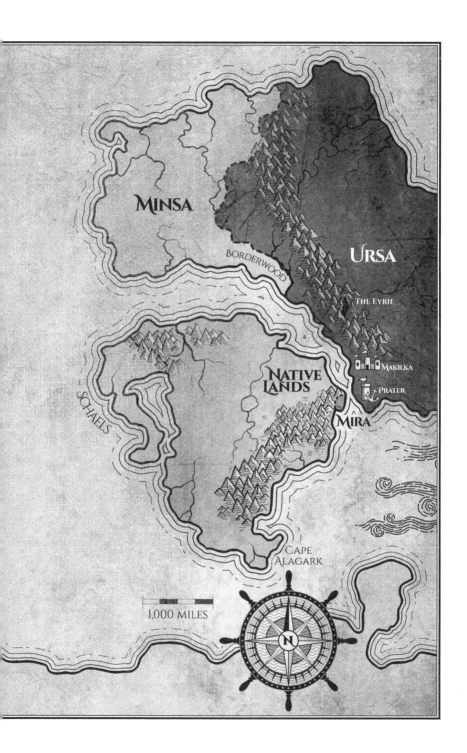

Chapter 1

The Price of Leadership

*S*ILENCE... THE SILENCE OF IMPENDING *death filled the air. No light broke the thick blackness. Not even a chisel of starlight on a moonless night seeped into his tiny, entombed—could it even be thought—coffin. Air gradually exhausted itself in the abysmal space, and Arnacin's uncontrolled shivering, his gasping breaths, the very heat of his body, betrayed him. He sat crumpled against what used to be the entrance, sealed shut out of spite. Already, as he forced sleep away, the pain of airlessness allowed no more movement than the last futile twitch of his fingers in the place a doorway had once been.*

Crack! A flash of light brought the windowless cabin back. Something in the back of his mind told Arnacin the storm bashing against all four walls was reality. His trembling body, however, insisted that the sound was wishful thinking, a last hope granted before he died in darkness.

For hours on end, it was impossible to discern either tomb or storm as reality. Yet, as the world in which the cabin existed stopped rolling on storm waves, Arnacin bolted for the door and yanked it open. He ran until he stood on the far side at the dipping prow in the settling waves. There, as the vision of his tomb dissolved back into memory, Arnacin shivered for another reason—weak relief.

So his life had been since his exile from Mira. Yet, until the storm, he had dreamed of finally going home. At least, he had been traveling in a homeward direction due to the navigations of his heart, not his head. Home was not in actual dreams, for he rarely slept anymore; even when complete exhaustion washed over his thin frame, he could only doze beneath the stars, where the cold permitted solely fitful rest.

Now, in the renewed sun after the passing of the storm, Arnacin looked up at his sail—the sail that would remain limp since the storm stole its brace. Without the wind, his ship could only drift with the current, and neither food nor water would last that agonizingly slow voyage.

There were no alternatives. He was doomed to die at sea, for no one would come across his ship out in the middle of the vast expanses of water and sky. Even if they did, whom would he trust? Even Valoretta had betrayed him. Yes, he had wanted her to keep her part in his escape secret, but she had chosen not to stand up for him at all. Considering her disloyalty, he knew, as he had come to realize these last few months, there was not a soul on whom he could rely.

"My lady," Sara called from down the corridor. "A rider will be here in another moment."

Quickly hiding the rough wooden key in her sleeve, Valoretta met her nurse before the older woman could reach the little alcove where the princess had been sitting.

"I told the gatekeepers to send him to the great hall when he arrives," Sara continued.

The princess shook her head. "I'll meet him in the outer ward." Lifting her skirts, the princess raced toward the outside, wishing to catch the messenger as soon as he rode in. She heard the weary footfalls of her nurse, simply plodding behind with no word of dissent.

Valoretta caught up with the messenger just as he was turning up the keep's stairs. "What word?" she gasped, even as the flushed messenger began talking.

He dropped to one knee. "My lady... I'm sorry. Miro was struck down. His remaining troops sent me back to warn you while they still drew breath, but they didn't expect to live. Those that stood, remained to hold the savages back for as long as they could. This morning, I noticed a false sunrise toward Fort Corugwan while I rode."

"Our last fortress," Valoretta breathed, her skin icy, the perspiration from her mad dash suspended in little droplets along her spine. With a flash of pain, she thought of all those senseless deaths. There was no turning back now though. Looking up at the walls, the princess, now ruler of Mira, calmly ordered, "Go into the city and make it known that it's time to evacuate Mira. Tell the ship captains they must allow our evacuees."

Wearily, the messenger bowed and left to do as bidden. "Sara," the princess sighed without turning around, her gaze returning to the retreating messenger. "Make sure the people know they are to take only what they most need. I will start with the nobility. I doubt we have much time."

"Is that your decision? Have you not thought of another solution?" Sara's tone was beaten, but unsurprised.

Turning to her nurse, Valoretta admitted, "My waking hours have been consumed with little else. This end has been likely for a long time."

"But there is nowhere to go, my lady. No kingdom will aid us. Most are too jealous over our position in the trade routes to wish anything but our ruin, and there is no unclaimed land we can sail to."

"I know... Yet we must go as individuals and integrate into other kingdoms. I see no other way to hope for life."

Sara's gaze flicked to the ground, but she stubbornly asked, "Do you intend to win Mira back someday, once her people are safe?"

"Never, Sara. It should have been evacuated long ago. Mira has proven greedy, unjust and immoral. If and when we find safety, we must start anew."

"My queen," Sara intoned with a gracious curtsy far deeper than Valoretta had ever seen from the older lady. Then Sara hurried off, and Valoretta shook aside her feeling of complete dread and immense loss. Only resolution could pull them through.

"Rosa, take your most important things only. You're leaving on the first ship."

"'You're leaving?'" Rosa—queen through marriage only—repeated. "Won't you be on one of the first ships yourself?"

"So Sara will insist," Valoretta muttered, stepping toward the clothespress and pulling out the young queen's cloak.

Despite her tentative character, Rosa was, unfortunately, shrewd. "You don't intend to comply! Valoretta, as Mira's princess, you have an obligation, far more of an obligation than do I, to leave while you can!"

With a sad smile, the princess threw the cloak over Rosa's shoulders, clasping it for the queen. Then, straightening the folds as the queen looked down in astonishment at the gesture of servitude, the princess softly admitted, "I am needed here, Rosa, until the last man has departed or fallen. It will turn into chaos as soon as I leave and, in that chaos, anyone remaining will be slaughtered."

Dropping her gaze, Rosa whispered, "I'm not leaving without you, Valoretta."

"This war isn't yours. You arrived solely as a tool for Mira. You'll not die as one."

"But you're not queen, Valoretta. I am."

Smiling, the princess quoted Rosa's statement from a year ago, only changing the pronouns, "Mira has only one queen, that title will not be taken from her, and I am she."

"This has nothing to do with their hearts—"

"With all due respect, Your Majesty," Valoretta gently interrupted. "It has everything to do with their hearts. How can you help them in these last days when only love and deep respect will hold them from terror? With that in mind, may I be so bold as to remind you I don't need your assent? I can order you hauled aboard a ship, and I will be obeyed. Understand?"

Both relief and terrible sadness spread across Rosa's face as she curtsied deeply in submission. In honor of Rosa's attempt to live up to her title, Valoretta returned the curtsy before turning away. "Now pack, my lady. Your ship sails in an hour."

As Rosa lifted her chin, tears sparkled in her lashes.

Rosa would not be the only one to raise concerns and, if the princess addressed each one individually, the savages would cut them down while Mira was still in discussion. Deciding to answer all further questions at once, Valoretta called upon the nobility to gather in the great hall, among the blue lapis, opal and gold walls that spoke of Mira's vast wealth. As she entered, someone called, "Hail, Mira!"

"Mira! Mira!" echoed throughout the hall, and Valoretta knew a coronation was pointless. She was Mira, sole ruler of the kingdom bearing that name. As she faced that crowd—most of whom were female, the rest only the very old men, the limbless and the boys younger than twelve—she lifted her chin for their sake.

"I have no doubt you all know where Mira now stands as a nation. It is my desire that everyone departs immediately, carrying only what matters most." At the dull mutter, she dipped her chin in acknowledgment. "Yet I must warn you of the two possible futures facing you. It is folly to think all of us will escape."

"My queen." Young Nayhuel, Duke Cestmir's oldest, stepped up beside Mira's swordmaster, Voninath. Despite his tender age of eleven, he had become Duke upon his father's death. Wars had no mercy. In Valoretta's silence, the boy stated, "We are Mirans. Once we leave her shores, we are no more, whether we still breathe or no. It is against our national pride to flee in her last hours, to lose even our identity. Could we not try to protect that at least, if it must come to a last stand?" He was, as ever, precocious.

Compressing her lips in sick sorrow just briefly, Valoretta announced, "That is something we have all but lost already. Mira's lack of selflessness has caused her to crumble, and those who cannot escape will not face simple death. For our nation's pride, we will resist the enemy until the last minute, and it may be a death far worse than any we have yet known. There will be slow starvation, dehydration, minds will freeze except for thoughts of food and water, humanity will crumble, and only in the very end will the enemy come with their poison.

"Those who are able to escape, however, will find new lives. They will be lives you are not accustomed to, true. You will find lives as farmers or weavers. Some of you might dig in mines or, yes, even attend others as their servants. Perhaps this is why all of you were taught first to serve before leading. I know even with that, you will find it humiliating being forced under other people's authority one way or the other, for even half the farmer's workings will likely be for some landlord. Yet, there will be laughter. There will be festivals and holidays. You will find friends and make new families. In short, there will be life, whereas the last days on Mira will be living death, even for those who remain strong."

"Why is Mira's pride worth that sort of death?" someone in the crowd asked. "Why resist the savages' attack once escape is no longer possible?"

In a soft voice that nevertheless carried to even the farthest corner of the hall, Valoretta proclaimed, "If we are forced to face death, we will stand in the fashion I have described so that Mira will be forevermore the greatest kingdom ever to exist."

Her slowly strengthening voice spellbound the assembly as she continued. "No one will forget it. Memory of it will even haunt the strongest kingdoms in existence. Mira will be the kingdom that stood fast, that never faltered under impossible odds. In Mira's lack of fear and humanity through all that blackness and misery, it will give her an honor she has never had, and it will come through your strength and mine.

"No one person can achieve such a victory alone, to make the memory of Mira light the imagination and call even the lowest wretch to a higher level of life. Therefore, always remember, whether you manage to escape or not, you are Mirans."

After a moment, many bowed out of the room, but a few remained behind. "I will stay until the day you board a ship, Mira," Duke Nayhuel whispered. "For our homeland." As his mother gripped his shoulder in protest, he insisted, "Take the rest of the family now, Mother. I am a duke of Mira and, for my father, I will serve her until death."

"Your Grace," Valoretta interrupted. "With all respect to your commitment and title, I would that the young and old should leave first, or I fear they will be the first to die here."

"I cannot, my queen," the young duke stated with a deep bow. "I am staying with you."

As Valoretta nodded her assent, the swordmaster huffed, "I might as well stay with you until the last. I won't have any life among farmers, and I won't train any man for anyone except Mira."

Despite the muttered retort from somewhere about peg-legs making the best pirate captains, the swordmaster did not budge. As other pledges to remain followed, Valoretta thanked the group and dismissed them.

Miro's councilors had not spoken their minds, however. They entered the great hall with low bows while the queen was planning the best defenses for the evacuees. Seeing them, Valoretta excused the swordmaster, with whom she had been talking.

As befit their training, the councilors waited for her to address them. Facing them, the queen felt her chin rise. "I have no need of your expertise."

"We are here to help, Mira. With the evacuation, it would be unrealistic to swap us for new councilors."

"Indeed." For a just a second, Valoretta paused, aware that there was very little for them to gain by offering their services. They had to mean it in these times. Briefly, she looked at them for the first time as men, capable of feeling fear, duty, Miran pride and love.

Still, she could not trust them. "There is no advice I need for which you have been trained. There are few new choices I must make, and every reason for you to line up with the evacuees. Were times different, I would not only swap councilors, I would try each of you for treason." Some of the councilors paled, others dropped their gazes to the floor. "Have you not tried in every way possible to continue this war? Should your counsel to my father have been less self-seeking, we might still possess a Mira. Now go, and take Memphis with you if he still lives."

Not one argued with her as they bowed deeply and left.

All through the rest of that day, a line of people poured from the city to the quay, where every merchant ship had been ordered to squeeze as many evacuees on board as possible if they wished to be let out of port. As the first night came, with that line still looking as long as ever, Valoretta commanded the destruction of the sea walls to prevent the enemy from conquering them first and thereby blocking escape.

Now watching the ships sailing through those fiery gates, Valoretta heard Sara stop beside her. "They're going to have a comfortable journey," the older lady snorted.

"It will be worth it," the queen sighed.

"You need rest, my lady. Someone can wake you when there is need."

"I need to be awake for the savages' attack."

"You're sure they will come before everyone has escaped?" Sara's tone held no hope.

"As queen, I can't voice my fears."

"I might as well not speak..." Sara paused only a moment as Valoretta glanced resignedly in her direction. "But I wish you would leave now," she pressed. "Politically, Mira's only chance is in your flight. Without that, we have lost already."

Sighing, Valoretta nodded to the streets below where people waited in line for an uncertain future. "That's Mira, Sara. If I escaped and they perished, there would be no more Mira than if I fall to the savages. You must see that."

When Sara spoke, it was a whisper. "Sadly, I do, and I know yours is the right choice, no matter what politics say. Mostly, I just know who is responsible for your disregard of royal procedures, and I don't thank him. He has brought your destruction in his wake."

With a slight smile, the queen dryly stated, "I know exactly who you are insulting, Sara. There's no use in disguising it." Her smile faded as her gaze drifted out to the open seas, and her fingers found the wooden key tucked into her sleeve. "No one could blame him for this, at least not fully. Whether he helped as he could have or not is outside the question. Mira was doomed to die before he came and, without his help, we only would have perished sooner."

Silence was the only answer. Yet, feeling Sara's eyes on her, Valoretta turned to meet that gaze. Awe, pity, respect and sorrow filled her nurse's face, but seeming to conquer her thoughts, Sara curtsied low. "Mira," she intoned before withdrawing to see to their packing, in case they should ever have the chance to escape themselves.

Watching her, Valoretta called her back. "Sara. Perhaps, as my father's sister, you do have an obligation to escape."

Snorting, her nurse reminded her, "I did raise you, Valoretta, and I am just as stubborn. You are my sole ruler and anything you ask of me I will obey without the slightest hesitation—except this. I will remain beside you until my last breath steals me from you. This I swear."

Although warmth filled Valoretta's heart, her stomach twisted. She simply nodded in acceptance, however, excusing her nurse.

As days passed on that still ship in the ocean, Arnacin found nothing to alleviate the despair of approaching death. His journey to Prater to stock his almost-empty ship for the journey home had been in vain. His summer, spent toiling for an outdoor blacksmith to pay for the needed supplies, had been in vain—to say nothing of the fact that his shoulder had made it painfully clear that he was not actually capable of working for a blacksmith.

Trying to survive was pointless and, with the silence of the ship, the ghosts of Mira manifested aboard. Arnacin's only escape lay in the bottle, which he resorted to carefully, knowing the danger of compromised senses at sea. He only needed a little to take the edge off the memories.

It worked until his exhaustion conquered his slight calmness.

Miran houses pressed upon him, their upper floors curving inward as if to crush him. Somehow, he had returned without his consent, but if he failed to find any escape soon, he was dead one way or the other. Yet, he was searching for something, something he could not seem to remember.

Turning a corner, he ran into a slight, brown-haired girl. As she whirled toward him in surprise, he gasped. Valoretta's face met him under the dark hair. Hardly had he recognized her, however, before she dashed away, calling, "Help! The traitor's returned! The Black Phantom!"

Swiftly, Arnacin outraced her, catching her arm. "Valoretta! Do you want me to die?"

Yet, instead of warmth, her eyes were cruelty itself beneath her brown hair. Even as he tried to stop her, the sealed tower—which was a tomb—broke from the ground encircling him, cracking the dirt and swallowing sky and air alike.

Without warning, Arnacin found himself in Mira's great hall, but it was Valoretta who sat enthroned. Yet, like the Valoretta in the streets, she was different: darker-haired, taller, bedecked in gems, her iron crown coldly glinting with stones. In the ruthless power radiating from her, she was an enchantress of legends.

"Your death is written in our laws, Arnacin." She seemed to grow even taller as she stood. Approaching him, she whispered,

"But I can rewrite it. Since the savages trust you, they will submit with you beside me."

As she placed her fingers under his lowered chin, Arnacin jerked away.

The back of his head hit the mast, waking him with a start.

Trembling, he glanced at the wine bottle beside him and then angrily chucked it over the side of the ship. Only overdrinking was supposed to give nightmares, or so he had heard some say. A little bit was only supposed to steady the nerves.

It was clear to him that nothing would control his hallucinations, but at least reality told him Valoretta would never do such a thing. She might have betrayed him, but not as completely as that. Such actions were beyond her capability. Or were they?

Had he really known the princess, who had invented her entire character for foreign ambassadors, who had remained silent when the king unjustly exiled him without even the promised supplies to return home?

Still, Valoretta had rescued him from his entombment...

Yes, but that would never mean anything. Nobles only played political games, when they were not torturing others in the open. Had not Valoretta herself tried to use a prophecy to her own gain, hoping to convince the king he needed to listen to their plans? She had been the one to teach Arnacin politics, to say that anger could be shown but never fear, that outward expressions of love were dangerous, that every action had to be calculated in order to create the best outcomes for oneself out of each opportunity.

No, she was completely self-centered, like all nobles, and a liar. He would never know why she rescued him, and it hardly mattered. He would never see her again anyway.

But his compass weighed against his chest, her gift to him, hidden beneath his shirt. By his own logic, he should destroy it, that close link to her. At the very least, it was a silent mockery every time he told himself he could never concern himself with such a liar again.

Even so, he would always care about Valoretta. Regardless of her actions, he had once regarded her as a sister. Although that made her betrayal all the worse, he would keep the compass in memory of brighter times.

As he spotted three masts rising out of the distance, Arnacin rose, shrinking against his own mast.

"Ship to starboard!" The call carried from the crow's nest of the brigantine, *Pursuit of Justice*. Rushing to the rail, Captain Belon of Nomacir jerked out his spyglass, his heart pounding.

Around him, he heard the murmur, "Pirates? Is it pirates?" What he saw in the distance, though, was not like anything he had expected. There was a ship out there, seemingly dead in the water, flagless, its single sail down, not a whisper of movement stirring its ghost-like silence. Had it been of normal build, it would have screamed, "Eerie." As it was...

The ship almost appeared to be two different things smashed together. The front was an elongated, sleek prow that possessed the deadly beauty of a blade and looked made to act as one, cutting the ocean's waves.

The second part, toward the back, looked like an old, wooden fort cut off at the base. That back had no business being on the water, and yet, combined with that dangerous floating blade, it created a complete enigma of what was, beyond a doubt, some sort of ship.

"Should we approach, Captain?"

For a long moment, Belon gave no answer. Finally, he voiced his thoughts. "It's too small to hold any force that could harm us. Yes, we'll approach. Perhaps someone is still alive in that box."

Upon drawing closer, the captain spotted a thin figure watching them silently. Indeed, the figure was so still, with his back against the mast, that Belon began to wonder if it was not some masterfully crafted statue, wrapped in a cloak and crowned with black hair that swept about in the wind.

"Ship! Prepare to be boarded!" he nevertheless called in the common trade language before ordering hooks thrown over the vessel's rails. As the hooks clattered over wood, the figure twitched, as if briefly thinking of stopping them from pulling his ship closer. Despite his surprise, the captain called, "Stranger, why are your sails down, and where are your colors?"

The stranger said nothing, and Belon leaned over his rail to see the other better. Still, he could not frame any sort of opinion outside of an approximate age in the younger twenties. Between the wind and the length of that black hair playing over the face, the captain could only guess at the reasons for wariness exuding from the youth.

"Is there anything you need?" Belon tried again.

"Four blocks of wood," finally came the response. The voice was husky with lack of use, low in tone as if with uncertainty, and yet marked by a certain authoritative warning.

"Unfortunately, we don't carry any wood we can share, but if you would consent to allowing us to board your vessel, we'll see what we can do."

"Captain," his first mate, Denis, whispered in their native language, "I can tell you now that the only way we can help is if we drag that thing home. None of us would know how to fix it."

"What are you suggesting?" Belon responded in their tongue, equally soft.

"I'm saying we should probably leave him here. I sense a trap and, even if I'm just jumping at shadows, we're wasting precious time."

"I can't sail off if he needs help." At Denis's compressed lips, the captain smiled. "I'm not forgetting the danger. We'll search his ship. What better way than this?"

Without waiting for a reply, the captain called back down to the stranger, again in the common tongue, "Do you consent?"

A spasmodic shiver shook the stranger, and then he nodded slowly, almost begrudgingly.

Scanning his deck, Belon beckoned to four of his men. "I want a thorough search of that ship. Make sure he is the only one on board, and bring any documents you find to me."

One of the sailors finally convinced the rather silent stranger to board the *Pursuit of Justice*. Nodding in greeting, Belon regarded the young man, who watched him as warily as a deer, yet with the alertness of a cat. Aiding the feline image was the lean subtle muscles, the hand lightly resting upon a gold-encased short sword—a nobleman's blade, for certain.

Again meeting the stranger's gaze, Belon held out his hand. "Your weapon, please." He hoped his tone lacked sharpness or suspicion. It seemed the youth was not noble, unless the worn clothes and odd ship were an attempt to disguise. Denis would discard that possibility entirely due to the build and black hair, which closely resembled those of a notorious pirating family.

The stranger's fingers only tightened around his blade, though the rest of him remained still.

Belon kept his palm extended. "I can't assist you if you refuse."

Dark lashes lowered as the stranger's gaze turned to the captain's waiting hand. Shifting, he unbuckled his blade and held it out.

Uncovered, Belon saw a crane stamped into that gold. After staring at it for a moment in his hand, he left the stranger at the rail. Any information from those surveying the smaller ship should shorten his bursting list of questions.

Only ten minutes passed before his first mate entered the captain's cabin with a report. "That ship's bone dry of information. There's no map or even anything resembling a letter aboard. No ship could sail alone without charts or log to guide it. I think some larger ship must have dropped him here, and that makes me very nervous."

"Besides its lack of charts or log, what did you find?" Belon asked.

"There's a bow with arrows. The bow's of superb craftsmanship with a pattern I don't recognize. But except for that, there are only the usual things I would expect aboard a ship—blankets, dried and salted food, several kegs of water, a small portion of medicines, an extra pair of clothes..." He shrugged.

"The medicines aren't marked?" the captain asked in surprise.

"Well... They are, actually, but—"

"What language?"

"I don't know."

"Was it Miran, by any chance?"

Denis paused in thought, then answered, "I don't know what the Miran script looks like. Anyway, don't they use the common trade language now?"

"Unfortunately, I'm not familiar enough with Mira to know," the captain admitted.

"Why do you ask?"

"His shirt is Miran and his sword bore a depiction of a crane, but our stranger himself looks to be of Zedelious's brood."

"And that's the point. His barren ship, his appearance; he's clearly a Zedelious trying to act as something else."

Pointedly, Belon raised one dark eyebrow. "Oh?"

"No one innocent would watch us in silence the way he does or lack all records."

"We'll keep an eye on him, but not all Zedelious's offspring are pirates or murderers—remember that. He might be fleeing his family for all we know. That would explain his distrust at least." He said nothing about the noble's blade—not yet.

After calming his first mate, Belon sent for one of the medicine jars and for a member of their crew who loved to study written languages. Shortly, the sailor and jar arrived. In silence, the sailor scrutinized the writing. Then, he announced, "This is Miran script, but it appears not to be written by a Miran hand."

"How so?" the captain pressed.

"The Mirans have a very specific way they write their letters. Each letter has its own starting point and there is a calculated space between individual letters, words and even angles. Whoever wrote this was very familiar with the Miran letters, but was obviously not taught by a Miran. I can only guess that a foreign merchant sold these bottles on Mira and therefore wrote their labels for his clients' understanding."

Staring at the jar sitting on his desk, Belon remained silent, his face lined in concentration.

Valoretta had ordered that the moment anyone spotted the enemy, the line of people was to break in half–those closest to the docks would board the vessels and those closer to the castle should dash inside the closing gates. She had placed guards in the streets to make sure the orders were carried out. When the attack came, however, no forewarning of the enemy arrived until those in the castle towers noticed a horde of them on the plains. Within minutes, all reason fled from the evacuees.

Mira's queen could only watch helplessly while captains cut the lines holding their ships to the dock. As the vessels floated away from the mass of people now racing, trampling each other in their desperation, some individuals tried leaping for the ships, their fingers clawing for handholds.

Meanwhile, a horde of savages poured into the streets from the hills bordering the shore. From the little rise splitting the city from the valley, more of the enemy engaged Mira's guards, preventing them from trying to restore order. With nothing left to do against the slaughter, the guards inside the castle hauled the gates shut, barring them.

Sara placed her hand over her queen's eyes, and Valoretta did not fight against the pressure turning her face away. Yet no lack of sight could block out the screams, shouts and cries. Nor could blindness remove the crackle and smell of the savages' flames in the city's houses, the clang of metal on metal, and the terrible thud of the gates' latches.

"Mira's death has begun," Sara muttered.

Yes, and she was their ruler. Ripping her eyes away from Sara's covering hand, Valoretta faced the smoke-filled skies with the squared shoulders of a queen. Archers on the battlements sent off volley after volley as savages bodily tried to break through the gates or scale the walls. Even now, dead filled the streets, blood soaking their stones with crimson. Toward the sea wall, the last ship broke for the safety of the open ocean, its intentionally water-soaked sails smoking from flaming enemy arrows.

Slowly, the slaughter lessened as the savages murdered the last of those outside the castle and backed away from the walls, retreating to set up camps beyond the burning city. In their wake, the few ships that had been unseaworthy spewed flames to the heavens. The wood of the dock crumbled into the bay, hissing as waves met fire. Houses blew sparks into the streets, where the dead remained strewn from one end to the other—infant, child and adult alike.

Shakily, Mira's queen turned to her nurse. "Tell our remaining guards to help portion out space in the baileys to the people left, and have someone start calculating exactly how much food we have and how many of us still live. Until death comes, our grounds will be their home." Unable to hide her horror any longer, she left the room. Her nausea would need to fade before she could see anyone personally.

Leaving the royal wing, Valoretta's feet took her to a room that had been left untouched for months. Stopping at the door, she lightly placed her fingers against its wood. For a second, she stood there before she pushed the door open with a sigh, hearing the creak of the ungreased hinges.

A light layer of dust stirred around her skirts as she entered. Closing the door behind her, she rested her back against it as she looked around. The room was as bare as ever, with its single bed covered in the yellow, green and brown quilt where stags and ponies pranced around the edges. Unmissed from Mira's cavern of research, three closed books still sat atop the bedside table. In the candleholder, only an inch of wax remained, a reminder that the room's former occupant had liked to stay up reading late into the night.

The queen shuddered slightly with the eerie feeling that the room's tenant had only just left. She turned her attention to the window, which was still open, and the wall next to it, where maps covered the stonework. As a brief, smoky wind blew in from the ocean causing the dust to swirl in circles over the floor and the parchments to crackle softly as if in conversation, Valoretta pushed herself away from the door.

Closing the window and somberly latching it, the queen paused before those maps, each one painstakingly drawn by the room's previous occupant. There hung the main map of Mira's lands before its smallness disappeared into the vast unknown of the continent. A second, more-detailed map of Melmoor was marked with the individual troops' names, scratched out and rewritten at another location; circles for discovered savage villages and little X's over those circles to state that they were no more.

Next to those two maps hung the one given to Carpason so long ago—the one of the savages' mountain lands—both researched on foot and drawn by the room's inhabitant.

The last parchment on the wall Valoretta could not really call a map, for it was the agreement between the first Mirans and the land's savages, showing the original border of the kingdom. Reading the sworn agreement hanging next to that plan, the queen pushed her forehead against that wall, the wall that shouted: *Where is Mira's honor? Its life?*

No more, followed the whisper at the back of her mind. Controlling herself, she pulled the wooden key from her sleeve. Shaking out its string, she reverently hung it beside the agreement, watching the light dance over it as it swayed to and fro.

"I have unlocked my life, Arnacin," she whispered. "I've made my choice... and all is soon to be over. All the same, I cannot think of much I would do differently."

Chapter 2

Pirates!

Spotting the stranger leaning against the railing in the exact place he had been all the past evening, the ship's cabin boy took over his mending. "Hello. I'm Titus." He held out the ripped sail. "Working always helps a long vigil."

Slowly, a deep breath nudged the stranger's tensed shoulders as his blue eyes flicked to meet the boy's own.

Settling down at the other end of the sail and sharing the thick thread, Titus pressed on. "What took you to sea by yourself?"

He received naught but a slight shrug, yet he remained unperturbed. "A job took me to sea. My mother didn't want me to go." Watching the stranger's features carefully, the cabin boy noticed the ghost of a smile.

"But that's mothers, I suppose." Titus made another stitch before he added, "Did yours object?"

A slight twitch told him no.

"Fortunate, I suppose. The worst of it is that, while she thinks the sea is terribly dangerous, I find the longer I'm out here, the less I can imagine leaving. My short visits home just don't compare with the feeling of the waves underfoot, the constant song of the sea, the chill breeze..." Thoughtfully, he wondered, "Is it the same for you? You're probably too bored to care currently. I noticed there aren't many things to do aboard your ship. No ropes to coil, no endless tasks of sails to be checked. I've never seen a ship so... easily manned by one person."

Glancing at where the mast could be seen behind the *Pursuit of Justice*, the stranger whispered, "It's one of a kind." His voice matched his eyes in that moment, sorrowful and hooded, with just a hint of danger.

Titus easily imagined a wolf sitting there, one that had been captured, abused and only recently freed.

Ignoring the mental image, the boy exclaimed, "I'll say! Do you know the name of the shipwright who made it?"

"My family built it."

"Oh... Then your mother certainly had no objections to your voyage."

The stranger's only reply, as he stared toward his ship, was his silence. But his eyes had grown so distant–sad and old almost– that Titus himself was stilled.

During the afternoon, the wind had died, leaving the sails limp. Now, under the stars, the *Pursuit of Justice* floated listlessly. Despite the lack of wind, the ocean's temperature had dropped in an early promise of the upcoming winter when all ships would return to berth.

Arnacin's deepest wish was that he was among those arriving home, although it looked like he would be wintering in Nomacir instead. As long as they let him go the next spring, he could handle that possibility, if he managed to avoid their cells.

"Stranger." The call accompanied the sound of nearing footsteps. One of the sailors approached, holding out a blanket. As Arnacin tentatively, yet gratefully, accepted the thick wool, the sailor asked, "Don't you ever sleep?"

Danger lurked in every possible answer–hints of his nightmares or intense claustrophobia. At best, they would ask painful questions and, at worst, use his fears to their advantage. He busied himself with wrapping the blanket around his shoulders, making sure it would not hinder him if the need arose. Yet, he could find no answer.

As his silence stretched on, the sailor shrugged. "I'd be in my berth in a second if I wasn't on guard duty, and I sleep during the day."

"Yes," Arnacin agreed at last, "but I'm my own navigator, watch and keeper."

"You mean you are one of those that don't sleep for as long as the journey lasts?"

That incredulous question was also dangerous to answer honestly. Shrugging, Arnacin merely said, "Thank you for the blanket."

Strangely, the sailor accepted the dismissal after a moment.

"You wanted to see me, sir?" Cap in hand, Titus closed the captain's door behind him.

Belon sat with his elbows on his desk, his chin on his hands. "I've noticed you've been spending time with the stranger. Do you think he's dangerous?"

"No, sir."

"Are you absolutely certain?" The captain nodded to the chair across from him.

Dutifully, the cabin boy took his seat. "Fairly certain. Why do you ask, captain?"

"No reason that needs to worry a boy." Straightening, Belon spread his hands along the desk as if smoothing its surface. "Reasons aside, I would like to know what he has said to you and what you think of him."

"Hasn't said that much, truly. I don't even know his name, but I think something terrible must have happened to him, perhaps even to his family. His family built his ship before he went to sea, but he won't talk about them. If they're mentioned, he almost appears to fly out of his body, if you know what I mean. And he seems to distrust everyone."

Standing, the captain strode around the desk, his hands clasped behind him in thought. Then, smiling, he tousled the boy's hair. "You approached him because of that distrust, I know."

Shrugging, Titus replied, "My mother says I don't recognize impossibilities and I hate to see unhappiness."

"Thank you, Titus." Belon's tone dismissed the boy. "Should you see anything other than sorrow and fear, don't hesitate to inform me."

"You wish me to spy, sir?"

"In a fashion, yes. I am told he didn't even sleep last night, and he unnerves the crew." The captain paused. "I should lock him up."

"Please, no, sir."

Turning back to the boy, Belon pressed him for more details. "Why not, Titus?"

"It... He..." Fumbling, the boy crushed his hat in his hands. "It wouldn't be fair."

"For the love of Nomacir, I must make sure he's harmless."

"He *is* harmless, sir. He... His family built his ship."

Smiling, the captain placed a hand on the boy's shoulder. "Titus, you win for now. I won't lock him up yet, but I am commanding that you report on him. It will help our queen."

Bowing, Titus left.

The light shining through the windows of Mira's great hall seemed a little greenish, as if even the sun was shimmering in its last death throes. Alone with the two castle guards Sara had appointed in charge of rationing, Valoretta remained silent while they reported their estimates. "If we make sure everyone receives balanced meals—albeit smaller—we will last only a month, Your Majesty."

Standing in front of what was now her throne, the queen thoughtfully fiddled with the crane on her necklace. At her silence, one guard admitted, "If we kill every single animal—horse, dog, cat, all—we might make it to one and a half. At best, we have two months."

"Stretched to the maximum?"

"Two months, but at such a small amount of food, we'll likely go insane or turn on each other. Of course, that doesn't even take the water supply into consideration. With so many more people using them, our wells might dry up before we run out of food, despite your order to use it only for drinking purposes. We can catch rain in buckets and barrels, but like the wells, the quantity is unreliable."

For a long moment, the queen said nothing. Then, with a defeated sigh, she replied, "Even should we ration the food with the least amount of pain initially, it will hurt all the more when the real torture comes. Leave the falcons in case we can safely send them out to hunt without the savages shooting them, but kill the other animals, so long as you don't force anyone to surrender their pets. And if you can, train us into starvation slowly. Hopefully, when the worst comes, we will be ready for it."

As the men bowed, Valoretta added, "Is there a way to slaughter the animals without needing to use water to clean afterwards?"

"We could perform it outside and hope rain cleans it, but the smell of death might attract rats in the meantime. If that happens, we could lose most of our food to them."

"Hold off on the butchering then until a day when it looks like it will rain."

"In the meantime, the animals will eat. And what if rain doesn't come before the end?"

"Then it won't come. There is nothing more we can do." As they bowed, however, she said, "See if there is a way to parley with the enemy and put someone on digging tunnels. If we can, we'll try to slip around the enemy, at least for supplies."

"What would we ask them, Your Majesty?"

"If they would allow anyone to join their tribes."

With nothing left to do, Valoretta returned to the royal wing and the spare room she had been occupying while she watched over the evacuees. At least there, she could stand outside on its balcony, feel the unhindered breeze and hear the murmur of Mirans below. Voices would cease all too soon, and the breeze would mean nothing when the real pain began.

When she entered the room, however, it was no longer sparse. "Sara!" she exclaimed. Instead of the bed standing stripped against the wall, she saw her bedclothes adorning it. The furniture had been freshly polished, and her nurse was hanging the last of the queen's dresses. "No one's supposed to do any hard labor!"

"This was not hard labor." Sara shut the bureau's door with a snap. "You have not been in your own room since this whole mess began. You need rest, real rest, and if you like this room better, then I will move your things in here." At Valoretta's drumming fingers, her nurse added, "I left all your furnishings in your own room, since you forbid anyone from moving heavy objects."

Running her hands along her nose in exhaustion, Valoretta relented. "Honestly, Sara, I already miss baths. I'd love the heat."

"I know, my lady," Sara whispered, and the queen looked up as hands settled lightly on her shoulders. "I have thought of that, but as you have wisely outlawed baths, I have warmed your nightdress and the bedcovers. It's time you slept for at least a night. There's no telling when you'll be able to do so again."

As only happened when she was entirely spent, the queen meekly allowed her nurse to change her, brush out her hair and tuck her beneath the warm covers, with wonderfully cool pillows against her cheek. After nearly four days of only dozing when able, she was asleep within seconds.

Although Valoretta slept deeply at first, dreams eventually came—spawned by the guilt that had plagued her since Miro's departure. In her dream, her father stood before her, telling her again of Mira's last hope.

"Valoretta," Miro sighed, placing himself on the window seat beside her. "I don't usually discuss battle plans with you, but I'm taking all our remaining men and attacking those marshes. I don't expect any of us to return, but it's our only chance. I hope some of us will return in the end."

Coldly, the princess dropped her gaze back to her embroidery. "I'm ready for the responsibility, sire."

Instead of speaking, Miro took her hand, fixing her attention on him. "I'm telling you for another reason. I intend to accept Onstantin's proposal of an alliance through your marriage to Prince Yohannce. The wedding will take place there."

As Valoretta leapt to her feet in horror, her father continued. "It is a fairly good kingdom, and should Mira stand, Yohannce will make a strong king—"

"No!"

"Valoretta, it will take you out of danger and strengthen Mira, if there's any hope of that at all. I'm sorry it steals your sovereignty."

"Out of danger?" Harsh laughter escaped the princess. "I refuse to live in slavery just for your mistakes. You destroyed Mira! Don't ask me to pay for it! If Mira falls and I escape, I'll sooner marry some foreign peasant!"

"Is my desire to keep you safe asking you to pay? I love you."

Through her uncontrolled laughter—high, wicked laughter—the king tried to recapture her hand, yet she ripped it away. Some part of her knew how she sounded, yet in that moment, she wanted nothing more than to grow long nails and slash them down his face. "Love!? From you!? Where was love when you silenced our proof that a wall would work, or when you attempted murder, or exiled your victim when he escaped death? Don't speak to me of love."

Rising, Miro turned away, saying only, "The letter goes with their ambassador this afternoon. I'm leaving with the troop first thing in the morning." Meeting his sister's pale gaze, he added, "Sara, when the ship returns for her, make sure she is on board."

Sara bowed, and the king left closing the door with a snap. Throwing herself against it, Valoretta screamed, "Die out there!"

As her own horrible words echoed in her mind, Valoretta woke abruptly, then buried her head into her pillow. Thanks to her deep sense of betrayal, she had made her father's last moment with her a curse and, in her actions to make sure no marriage plans were ever made, she had even betrayed his last wish.

Yet there was no going back. Mira was dead. And in her monarch's death, Arnacin's view that nobles' lacked love was proven. All the same, it was Valoretta's task to see that Mira's end was one worthy of praise. With that thought, she rolled out of bed.

Six days from home, those aboard the *Pursuit of Justice* again heard the dreaded cry. "Ship approaching off the main bow!" the lookout called from the crow's nest.

"What colors?" the captain hollered back.

"None, captain!"

"Pirates, captain!" Denis exclaimed, appearing at Belon's elbow. "I knew it! While we're busy defending ourselves, that rat will massacre us from behind." He nodded toward the stranger still sitting at the railing Titus was busy polishing.

"There's no way he could have known we'd come by," the captain reasoned.

Turning, he ordered his men to the alert before striding over to his cabin boy and the dark-haired foreigner who had already slid off the railing. Looking at his rigid stance, the captain knew the stranger sensed the same thing–an attack.

"Titus," Captain Belon whispered as he stopped beside them, "take cover in your cabin."

Nodding, the boy retreated to the smaller door next to the captain's cabin, and the captain approached the stranger. "Can I trust you to protect him?" he asked, holding out the confis-cated blade.

"Why do you ask?"

Belon hesitated for only a moment. "If the ship is a pirate ship, it will not be your fight. Furthermore, I would like someone inside to protect him if an attacker does break through. You seem differ-ent around him. I hope that would remain true during a battle."

Glancing swiftly toward the approaching ship, the stranger stammered, "I can't... I... If you want him defended, you must leave me on deck. I will keep any attack away from his cabin."

Sensing the stranger's fear, the captain stated, "I am willing to give you a certain amount of trust, whoever you are. Will you not respect my request in return?"

Cool blue eyes regarded him darkly for another moment, and then the stranger dipped his chin slightly. Without another word, he retrieved his blade and slipped off to Titus's cabin.

With no retreat now, Captain Belon turned back to the unmarked ship still sailing toward them with a white flag now rising into the air.

"Captain!" Denis called, holding out a telescope. "Their prow!"

Rushing over, Belon seized the instrument and trained it on the approaching ship. Two wide-set, red glass eyes marred its prow—two eyes lit by the giant torches behind them. By legend, that was the sign. The *Zedelious*, the monster of the waves, was declaring war.

In the stillness of the cabin, the first sounds of battle echoed outside the slightly open door by which the foreigner was leaning. Trying to muffle it and thereby muffle his fear, Titus admitted, "There are times I wonder why I agreed to go sailing."

Dark eyes flicked toward him and, self-consciously, the cabin boy shrugged. "My father was a rope maker for the queen's navy. He died after a pirate attack on our harbor, and my mother and I spent several years finding small jobs to feed our family. When I was eleven, I asked one captain if I could serve as cabin boy since it paid better than anything I could find. Mother needed the money, yet she was right. It's more dangerous than I ever expected it to be."

"Why did they even take an untrained pup on board ships that exist only to track down pirates?" Intense resentment sounded in the stranger's voice.

"I'm not on one of those ships." Titus winced as a thud sounded much closer than the other sounds of fighting. Why did the stranger not lock and blockade the door? Pirates could break in any moment, and their defense was weakened by that open crack. Yet the stranger did nothing to shut it.

Rubbing his sweaty palms together, Titus continued, "Since my queen rules alone, everyone deems her weak. Pirates openly defy her, swarming her waters with their ships and baiting her into attempts to punish them. Other kingdoms hire privateers and attack her shores. As strong as she is, she could not hold up to the barrage thrown against her and, without trade, she is completely ruined. Yet all merchant ships sink after only a day at sea–" He stopped abruptly, glancing at the stranger in sudden wariness.

"So, you carry the goods on navy ships in order to disguise them," the stranger finished all the same.

The cabin boy briefly narrowed his eyes, yet there was no point in pretending when the stranger knew anyway. "And to protect them. We were on our way home after a successful trade." He smiled apologetically, "I'll need to tell my captain you know."

He was sorry the second he said it. A darkness he had not seen before entered those deep blue eyes–but at that moment, the door swung inward. Without the stranger ever seeming to move, his blade slid between the attacker's ribs. The thud of the body as it hit the floor spurred Titus to yank out his own short blade as another pirate attempted to thrust himself through the doorway. He also fell due to the boy's unlikely protector.

Jumping over the fresh bodies, a third attacker grabbed the door, yanking it toward himself and then slamming it inward to catch the stranger in the shoulder. In the ensuing rush through the open doorway, Titus was forced to defend himself. Strangely, he never had to do any of the killing, for his opponents would all drop as the stranger found time to dispatch those attacking the boy.

Still, the number of pirates inside the cabin grew.

Then it happened. Titus was stepping back from four advancing pirates, when cold, sticky fingers seized his ankle, yanking his foot out from under him. As he landed hard on his back, a knife pressed against his throat. Above him, a heavily wounded pirate sneered. From the edge of his vision, he saw the stranger whirl toward them and freeze as the pirate hissed, "Another move, mate, and this brat feels it."

Titus dared not look at his companion, fixing his gaze instead on the large amount of blood soaking the pirate's shirt from a wound in his side. Apparently, the dying pirate saw something, as he snapped, "I meant it! Drop that blade if you wish him to remain alive. Ah, sure, you'll likely kill me, but you won't save him."

There was not a breath of air in the room, as if all waited to see if the stranger would succumb. Titus's heart pounded in that stillness, pleading silently to the heavens to let him live somehow.

A dull thunk attracted the boy's gaze in time to see the pirates swoop upon the stranger for the easy kill. A nasty cackle sounded from the pirate with his knife against Titus's throat. The boy's gaze shot upward, meeting his killer's murderous eyes.

With a sharp pain, the blade bit into his neck.

Hot wood cracked, releasing spurts of fiery rain. Flames smarted the captain's eyes. The smell of burning timber and flesh clogged his lungs. Black smoke nearly blinded him, yet his attacker, a sturdy man with sharp, cruel eyes, appeared immune to it. Instead of suffocating, he was breathing it in like a dragon, and only his eyes were affected—the hatred growing brighter with every inhale, lit by destruction.

Against his opponent's rising ferocity, Belon was forcibly pushed back. He retreated too far and, with the searing pain of the flames burning his leg, his defense faltered. Giving a triumphant leer, his attacker slipped through, driving his weapon into the captain's sword-arm.

His face only an inch away, the attacker ripped his blade free and brought it up to the captain's throat. "Surrender, captain?" Even his tone was filled with mocking hatred.

"Death first."

"As you wish." The attacker shrugged and pulled his sword back an inch. In that tiny space, Belon retreated into the flames, switched his own sword to his left, and batted away his attacker's thrust. Regardless, Belon was too slow. As his attacker once again slipped through, his good arm was caught and the hand-guard of his opponent's blade struck his head.

Belon awoke as water splashed his face. He was tied to one of the masts of the attacking ship. Before him, the *Pursuit of Justice* spewed flames into the sky. In that crackling roar, he saw a mast snap and fall to the deck with a loud crash. There followed the sizzle of dropping cinders.

With horror, he watched his remaining men forced back into the flames as they tried to escape to the attackers' ship. Wood had fallen in front of the cabins, blocking any flight Titus might have attempted. Bitterly, he noticed the small ship was no longer tied to the back of the *Pursuit of Justice*. Perhaps Denis had been right in thinking the stranger a pirate.

"All the treasure's aboard, Captain Xavior," someone said. Belon looked over to see the man who had defeated him earlier. Beside him stood a tall, one-eyed man in a richly tailored coat, his hair black, his nose sharp—the pirate captain, richest of the Zedelious line.

"Shove off," Xavior commanded, emotionless. A few last cries of desperation shrieked from the *Pursuit of Justice* as pirates cut the ropes lashing the ships together. Answering those cries, Belon struggled against his bonds, his face screwed up as his injured arm ridiculed him while course fibers scratched along it.

After a minute, he opened his eyes to see Xavior watching him maliciously. "Behold your ship, Belon of Nomacir." The pirate captain extended his arm toward the burning ship, now too far away for rescue or flight. Smoke curled to the far reaches of the sky above its fire-blackened carcass.

"Worm!" Belon cried. "You could at least have had the decency to kill all the men yourself instead of burning them alive."

"You should know I have given them the chance to try to put it out."

His eyes blazing, Belon continued to fight the ropes. Indeed, the pirate was right. Anyone still alive aboard the *Pursuit of Justice* would be struggling for that last futile chance of survival—knowing all along that it was pointless, but also knowing they had to try nevertheless. And Xavior had purposefully created that scenario.

Darkness came before the smoke in the distance disappeared. Then, Xavior's pirates dragged Belon down into the hold, which was filled with barrels. Iron rings sprouted from several of the kegs.

Shoving Belon against one of them, they secured him to the rings with the promise, "Don't fret. We'll 'ang you fast enough."

Belon lacked the desire to fight his captors, but in the light of the small lantern they left him, he reviewed his options for escape. His gaze rested on the only other occupant of that stuffy hold.

Bound just as tightly to a barrel several lengths away, the dark-haired stranger trembled as if with cold, his eyes glassy and remote.

"So, you live." Belon's accusation received no answer but that hissing breath of fear. In the silence, the captive captain regarded the stranger he had asked to guard his cabin boy. Although there were no scratches on what Belon could see of his skin, blood was splattered on the young man's cloak, shirt and pants.

"Why aren't you dead? What happened to Titus?" the captain tried again, still to no reply. Abandoning the attempt to engage his fellow prisoner, the captain returned to surveying the hold and testing the ropes that held him, all the while willing his heart to stop thumping in dread. Finally, as the stranger's shuddering breaths seemingly began to echo in his thoughts, Belon voiced one question, "Are you afraid of death?"

Again, nothing changed in that blank façade. Painfully, the captain whispered, "We'll hang. At least I will... But to speak with the honesty of looming death, I'll go insane long before I die without some distraction. I know they want that fear." At the lack of reaction, he tried anew. "Were you born on Mira?" Waiting a little bit, he continued, "I've heard there is no richer city, that the temperatures are always mild, almost always perfect, with just enough chill or heat to aid the greenery. Have you found it so?"

Something seemed to flicker in those eyes, yet it was not until Belon pressed for a description that the stranger growled softly, "It's just like any other city out there, and it only likes to pretend otherwise."

"There must be some difference."

A long silence followed. The captain was just beginning to think he would hear no more, when the other captive whispered, "It has a school of politics for its peasantry, so they may speak for their own kind."

"Did you study there?" Belon received a dark look. "You have that authority and knowledge about you."

With no reply forthcoming, the captain asked, "Are you familiar with Zedelious?" he waited a second and then explained, "the highly successful pirate, who had an infinite number of children through his dallying? He's the father of Captain Xavior and the original owner of this ship, which bears his name."

Still, no answer came. Belon let them again drop into silence until a soft whisper reached his ears. "Are you?"

"Am I what?"

"Afraid of death?"

The captain paused only for a moment. "At their hands, in their time, terribly so. Are you?"

The stranger swiftly turned his face away, but the hissed, "Fear is for spineless worms," caused the captain to snort.

"I must disagree. It is inhuman to lack fear. You are tough, stranger, yet I believe you possess more fear than many of us."

"That belief changes nothing."

For a moment, the captain studied his fellow prisoner before probing, "So, you dub yourself a spineless worm?"

Dark lashes closed without confirmation or denial. Just as his thoughts were starting to drift away, however, he heard, in the barest of tones, "Black blow the waves."

"Black blow the waves?"

"The *Immortal*."

"The *Immortal*?"

Softly exhaling a sound of defeat, the stranger turned his depthless eyes back to the captain. "The Black Captain and his ship, the *Immortal*, used to plague Mira in its youth. As far as anyone knows, he was never caught—yet he disappeared. To this day, there are rescued sailors who swear they had spotted the *Immortal* before catastrophe struck their own ships, hundreds of years after the *Immortal* disappeared."

"So, a legend sprang up?"

"I think the legends were already circulating in the taverns."

"What do the legends say?"

A slight shudder passed through the stranger. "You don't want to ask."

"I'm curious."

In the voice of a practiced storyteller, despite long disuse, the stranger surrendered. "The last time the Black Captain appeared was his victorious theft of all the gold meant for the building of Mira's capital. That night, the *Immortal* sailed away much faster than all that weight should have allowed and, mostly for that reason, Mirans deemed the ship demon-possessed.

"What tales say afterward is that the gold spoke to the crew, fanning every individual's thirst for sole ownership of the wealth. Every one of them knew the captain possessed the deadliest skill, and they knew they needed each other in order to satisfy their desires. Therefore, the crew mutinied as a group, overpowered the captain and fell upon the treasure trunks. As a ghost, the captain returned for his revenge. While the crew dug among the treasure, he beheaded every member before any noticed his transparent presence.

"Now, as a ghost, the captain keeps his own form and retains his crew as shadows to do his bidding. They quiver at his power and delight in nothing more than the commands he gives to murder other ships' crews. A ship that spots the *Immortal* now is breathing its last."

Thoughtfully regarding the storyteller, Captain Belon commented, "Strange. I see you as this Black Captain—nameless, mysterious and dark in many ways."

A sigh escaped the stranger. "I'm just Arnacin. I don't even belong at sea."

"Ah! A name... What brought you off Mira, Arnacin?"

"Mira?" Arnacin repeated with bitter sarcasm. "Everything in the world."

Meeting the spark of rekindled fire in those haunted eyes, the captain nodded.

Any amount of time could have passed. No real light showed in the pirate hold. The only mark of time was their growing thirst, for no one came with any water, and still the pirates let their prisoners sit.

After their first conversation, neither spoke. Belon's dry tongue adhered to the roof of his mouth. His companion appeared to have lost consciousness, his breathing raspy, as if very sick. Not only that, but he trembled without stop, feebly struggling from time to time against the ropes pinning him to the barrel.

After a considerable amount of time, a heavy step sounded on the stairs. Wrenching his gaze from its fixation on Arnacin, Belon looked up and groaned inwardly. "Captain Xavior."

"In person," the pirate captain muttered, his gaze only briefly flicking in Belon's direction. With a sinking feeling, Belon realized the reason for the pirate's visit—Arnacin. Whatever the stranger had done to keep himself alive was about to bear rotten fruit. Looking at the build and hair color of Zedelious both the captain and prisoner shared, Belon suspected he knew what had rescued the stranger from immediate death.

In contrast, Arnacin remained oblivious to the pirate's scrutiny—oblivious to all but the demons that plagued his mind.

His eye narrowing more, Captain Xavior kicked Arnacin. When that barely received a response, he turned to Belon. "What disease afflicts him?"

Unable to unglue his own tongue, Belon smiled slightly.

Xavior smiled in return, yet nastily. "You'll answer, if you wish for an easier death."

Struggling to coherently string a complete sentence together, Belon rasped, "It will be the same either way."

"Am I not a pirate of my word?"

"In *words*, we have never known you to lie," Belon was forced to admit.

"Then you have no excuse. Did you and your upstart queen hire him?" Belon remained silent, and Xavior growled, "Would it matter to you that he is not Miran?"

"What?"

"So, he lied to you?"

"No..." Belon trailed off, and the pirate laughed.

"There are no people of dark hair in those waters. Therefore, of what relation is he to the nobility there?" He fingered the gold sheath at his side, Arnacin's sheath, the one engraved with the emblem of a noble house of Mira. Belon only shrugged.

"Is he, or is he not, sworn to your queen?"

"Your intention is to make him a pirate."

"It matters little. He's so touched with fear. Those types are easy to control. My only question is about his honesty."

"You'll have to find out yourself."

"We shall see," the pirate hissed, slowly drawing that Miran blade. "A slight flaying won't kill you."

Pressing himself into the barrel he was bound to, Belon admitted, "You waste your time. I only met him stranded at sea a few days ago, and he's highly secretive. He's only just told me his name's Arnacin."

"Very well. I will learn myself." Despite that assertion, the pirate drew the blade under Belon's chin threateningly. "A Nomacirrian knows better than to lie."

The captive captain boldly met the hate-filled, green-specked eye opposite an eye patch. After a second, Xavior turned away with a dismissive shrug.

As the pirate reached the bottom step, Belon forced himself to ask, "Does Mira have a school to train the peasantry in politics?"

Xavior shrugged. "I have never been inside their sea wall to know."

Chapter 3

Xavior and Zedelious

Arnacin's awareness of blackness and intense thirst was fading. Pain, dizziness and fear were giving way to death when fleshy fingers touched his arms. Someone was unbinding him.

As that realization roused him, he felt the dampness of his mouth and throat—the dampness of water recently passing through.

"'e's comin' 'round now," a voice sneered above him.

"He was practically dead!" someone snapped. "Can you not even have the decency to leave him alone, or must you do such wretched things twice?"

"Oh ho, Cap'n," another voice mocked, less uncultured than the other. "No one would pull him off your ship simply to let him die of dehydration. As a Zedelious, he at least is entitled to choose his own form of execution." After a short pause, the same cultured voice ordered, "Carry that one. He won't revive enough to walk."

None of those words meant much to Arnacin until he felt a vise grip on his ribs. As he weakly kicked out, blackness descended.

Wonderfully cold wind across his face was the next thing he knew. This time, he was able to open his eyes, but the world swayed and blurred around him with no focus.

"Aye, 'e a carcass already," a voice said in his ear.

"We'll fix that," another voice commanded, "enough water to keep 'im dancin'." Swells of laugher erupted about the islander, sounding almost like evil seagulls.

Someone jerked Arnacin's head back. Alert enough to fight, he choked on the water sliding down his throat. Above him, the world righted itself. The hazy blue coalesced into the sky, blocked only by white sails, rigging and a few masts. More sound returned, bringing the swish of the ocean and the snapping of the flags far atop those masts.

Hands yanked him to his feet. Before him, other pirates were tying the captive captain to a mast so his back faced them. His shirt had been slashed open from behind and, in two pieces, it dangled off his arms, revealing fine, flawless muscles and skin. Arnacin had never personally witnessed a flogging, but he knew that was about to change.

As he closed his eyes, the less cultured of his captors slapped him across the face. "By orders of 'e cap'n, ye need t' be lessoned. If ya refuse, we'll just leave ya in 'e 'old until yer turn." A brief vision of the black, stuffy hold stilled his resistance, though his insides churned as one pirate unrolled a long, many-headed, black whip.

The captive captain simply straightened his shoulders as the first lash fell, but Arnacin noticed his teeth grinding into each other behind the shield of his lips, the whiteness of his clenched fist.

Lash after lash fell on that back and, as they did, the captive captain weakened, pain grew obviously visible on his countenance, his body slumped forward against the mast, his face paled. Still, that whip continued snapping through the air, across the back that was hidden by rivulets of blood. The victim's breathing started to sound cut off. Cringing, Arnacin guessed the pirates meant to lash their enemy to death.

Unexpectedly, they stopped, and the pirate in charge stepped near the tortured man. "Now, mate, you have the captain's solemn word that your pain can end now *if* you tell us the best way to cripple Nomacir. If not, we'll have ourselves a bit more fun."

Glassy eyes barely saw the speaking pirate. After a moment, however, the captive hoarsely coughed. "I would repeat this death a thousand more times for my queen." The croaked sound did nothing to degrade the sentence's indomitable loyalty.

"Fool," scoffed the pirate, stepping back. Guiltily, Arnacin agreed with him. "Well then," the pirate continued, beckoning another torturer forward, this one with a long rod, red with heat. "We took this off a slave ship."

He nodded once, and the new torturer thrust the rod against the victim's cheek. A low moan escaped Belon as the smell of burning flesh blew on the wind beside the instrument's steam. It caused a sick knot to tighten in Arnacin's stomach, but after seeing the slaughter of children, the amputation of injured limbs and executions of the guilty, that knot and his blanched face would be the only signs of his weakness.

When the pirates pulled back their branding rod, a bright pink S glowed against the captive's cheek. Snorting, the pirate in charge said, "'Slave?' I rather think it stands for 'stupid' or 'scum' in this case."

His victim remained silent, muscles quivering in pain beyond control.

Unabashed, the pirate leaned closer to the man dying against the mast. "It was my desire to remove your arms next and then send you back to Nomacir as a lesson. Captain thinks you would still manage to be dangerous, but I would rejoice knowing you lived like this."

"I would find a way, *pirate*," the captive forced out, "to see every last one of you hanged."

The pirate simply snickered and, from somewhere above, another dropped a thick rope. Arnacin's breath stilled as the pirates looped that rope around their victim's neck, tightening it.

Spots drifted into the islander's vision, overlaying reality with that tomb of a Miran tower. His sudden trembling or panting must have betrayed him as the cultured pirate holding him whispered in his ear, "Oh, you're seeing a real treat. See how his legs kick, his face turning purple, his eyes squeezing up like that? Believe me, his head wants to burst off. Every fiber of him is working for air he can't grasp and, the harder it works, the more it screams–"

"Stop!" Arnacin snapped, writhing in his captors' grasps. The present blurred with the past. He could hardly even see the pirates anymore, nor the ship or the sky. Blackness, like fog, was settling around him. His own breathing became a struggle.

"We'll do, if'n ye joins up," someone whispered. "Cap'n promises yer escape from hangin' if'n ye do."

Those words ripped through Arnacin's panic, yet weakly, he could only pull against his captors. "'e's decided," came another voice. As a rope slipped over his head, that black tomb burst into reality. *Only one pinprick of light shone through a single air-hole, from which scraping noises emitted. Someone was sealing it with clay.*

There came no tightening of fibers around his neck, however, as a new voice growled, "I will offer one compromise. Swear to remain here peaceably, and you will be given some freedom."

Panic licked at the edges of his mind. As the rope tightened around his neck and his lungs burned in agony, he heard himself cry, "I'll stay! I'll stay! Let me go!"

"Swear," that hard voice hissed. "Swear to remain, with no aggression toward any pirate."

Trembling, Arnacin breathed, "I swear."

"As a pirate?" the voice pressed his advantage.

That question caused the tomb vision to tremble, shaking, laughing almost, as something far older and stronger than the islander's great fears clenched around his heart. "No," he weakly forced out.

His eyesight returned to see, of all things, a black-haired pirate's single eye fixed on him, hard and scrutinizing. The pirate nodded in acceptance. "Keep your oath, where you have given it. That is a rule not one of these pirates spurn, not even myself." It was a low hiss of warning, and then the pirate turned away after ordering Arnacin's release.

The noose disappeared from around his throat, and the pirates grasping him stepped away. Too weak to hold himself up, Arnacin dropped to the deck, watching as one pair of feet and then another—some booted, others not—wandered away to return to work.

The islander did not even budge as a hand patted his back and a wheezy voice soothed him. "Ah, pirating ain't so bad, s'long as ye don't kill personal-like. It's jest a way of livin', see?"

As the last feet disappeared, the islander squeezed his eyelids shut over hot tears. He wished for nothing more than a blade at hand, a blade to end all feeling. The splash from the pirates releasing the dead captain's body into the ocean only made it worse.

The sky turned pink and lavender before Captain Xavior sent his first mate, Spyros, to rouse the still form on the deck. Rubbing his chin, the captain watched how easily Spyros grabbed the captive by the back of the neck and jerked him to the ship's galley. If this Arnacin was as spiritless as he seemed, Xavior might as well give up.

As the silence stretched, Xavior shifted. Perhaps his first mate had been a little too eager to stir some life into the captive.

Then, a crash sounded from the galley, and the captain smiled victoriously. A boom was followed by an angry outburst. Grinning wickedly, Xavior started toward the galley.

Inside, the floor lay strewn with overturned kegs. The table had a new notch in it and, on the floor, Spyros knelt on Arnacin's back, a knife inches away from the captive's neck. "Spyros!" Xavior snapped. With an evil grin, the first mate leapt to his feet, kicking his victim in the ribs.

"Ah! He must learn to defend himself sometime or he's extinct," Spyros stated with a shrug.

Behind him, Arnacin weakly rose to his feet, staggering around to the far side of the table. Both pirates turned to watch him. Removing the gold-covered blade at his side, Xavior considered him. "I think you're right," the captain mused. "He'll never survive without a defense."

Spyros's gaze latched covetously onto the blade Xavior shoved across the tabletop toward its owner. Arnacin, on the other hand, only glanced at it before his attention returned warily to the pirates.

"Now, drink some water, boy, or that blade might find a home in your side instead," the captain ordered, knowing from the light in the captive's dark eyes that the uncompromising fire that had nearly exhausted his crew on board the navy ship had returned, fatigued though that fire might be.

"What do you really want?" The captive's breath and tone were ragged, emanating a pain deeper than the physical. "I won't give you anything."

Studying the captive, Xavior asked instead, "What connection do you have with the nobility of Mira?"

"None!" It was too vehement to be believed.

"Answer, boy, unless you wish for trouble."

"You can beat me to death for all I care."

"Indeed," the captain murmured. Beside him, Spyros licked his blade. "You're not Miran. This I know. Tell me how you came to be of such importance that you wear one of the noble emblems on your blade, and why you left with so much wealth at your fingertips."

"What wealth?"

As the captain's glance went sarcastically to the gold sheath, the captive added, "The sea has more to offer than that pit called 'Mira.'"

Switching tactics, Xavior demanded, "Who were your grandfathers?"

"What?"

"Was one of them Zedelious?"

After a pause, the captive breathed, "Abilom and Yulcer."

Simply nodding in acceptance of that answer, Xavior grabbed his first mate's arm, leading him out of the galley. Shutting the door behind them with a snap, he drew out a key and locked it. For now, he would wait and see what he had spared from hanging.

"So," Spyros asked after the captain had unfolded all the intricacies of his plan for Arnacin. "Why do you want him?"

"Because he's capable of making a very skilled pirate. Because he's likely a Zedelious, and there needs to be one to inherit this ship."

Spyros huffed, and Xavior said, "You must understand the subtlety here. Manipulative molding of a creature is a glorious art."

"Arnacin seems very unstable to me."

"On the contrary, Arnacin is ripe for the picking. He has apparently suffered greatly. The signs of that are in his fears, his sudden swings from lifelessness to fervor. If we can identify his hurts and his cares, we can make sure he sees things our way. He's obviously passionate about what he views as right and wrong. It is our task to slowly whittle away at that mindset and free him from such shortsightedness... That's where your magnificent part comes in."

"How?"

"Take, for example, how he apparently views piracy as a terrible evil. I agree, sometimes, it can be—but is it wrong to take a stance against tyrants, to tell them that you can't pay tribute to their corruption and will protect others from falling into their traps? Well, is it?"

With a cruel grin that sliced across his face, Spyros laughed, a sound of delight. "Of course not."

Xavior grinned back.

Early the next morning, Xavior let himself into the galley and abruptly stopped. The captive was gone, along with his blade. Indeed, except for the yawning port that opened onto the ocean, nothing had altered from the prior night. Yet, if Arnacin had jumped out the window, he had committed suicide. His only possible escape that way was if he had found a rope and had the strength to use it.

Without wasting a moment, Xavior ordered his crew to search the ship, as well as the smaller one they had taken from behind the *Pursuit of Justice*. A shout from the deck of the smaller vessel informed the captain his quarry had been found. Striding to the poop deck's rail, he saw one of his men frozen, having just dropped from the rope to the deck. The captive was only a few feet away, short sword drawn, crouched beside coils of rope where he had obviously been sheltering.

"Boy!" Xavior called. "Did you not swear never to draw blade against my men?"

"This is purely self-defense," returned the low growl.

"Is it now?"

"Since the time his foot touched my deck. Any intrusion on this vessel is a physical attack against me. I never promised not to defend myself. Is that understood?"

Without argument, Xavior called for his crewmember to climb back onto the pirate ship. Turning, he allowed himself a wicked grin. Oh, yes, he understood. He understood the ability to twist sworn promises to fit desires. That ability could go a long way over time.

As Valoretta had predicted, the old and young reacted to the rationing first. Infants were not the only ones to wail at the top of their voices. Even six-year-olds did so, and parents took turns sharing their water and food with their children.

Slowly, the piles of dead bodies rose while the swordmaster informed Valoretta of the savages' grisly attempts to instill fear in the besieged and their refusal to parley. Even the idea of a tunnel had failed when, seeming to sense its presence, the savages had begun digging to meet the Mirans at the other end. When the Mirans discovered they'd been found out, it was safer to collapse the tunnel than continue digging.

The queen's heart burned in her chest in response.

"No hair accessories today, Sara," Valoretta softly ordered as her nurse pulled out a box filled with pearls.

"You're queen, my lady," Sara lightly admonished. "You will look like you've given in if I leave your hair plain."

"Then, please, put flowers in it, not the…" She could not think of the words to finish her thoughts, and she instead shook her head slightly, compressing her lips.

"Real flowers?"

"Yes, real flowers, Sara, with the beauty and sadness of life, short and so fragile. I believe it will give our people more strength than any bejeweled nobility."

Curtsying, the nurse departed. She returned half an hour later with flowers cut from the courtyard, which she proceeded to thread through the queen's rolled hair.

Once done, Sara whispered, "There, my lady." Quickly swiping at her eyes, the older woman nodded to show she was satisfied. "May they indeed see your honest compassion through it."

Valoretta had only just left her room when one of the girls who'd been tasked with distributing water approached her. "My lady, Duke Nayhuel is not well."

"Has he had his morning's ration of water?"

"It didn't do much good." The girl lowered her voice still further. "It revived him just enough to give him strength to try stealing the rest of the water from me. His mind seems to be gone, my queen."

Her shoulders sagging, the queen commanded, "Give me my ration." As a small cup was filled, Valoretta asked, "Where was he?"

"In his rooms. Be careful, Mira."

Nodding her thanks, the queen covered the precious cup with her hand and headed to the indicated place. The young duke sat curled up in one corner, his eyes glazed, his breathing shallow. He took no notice of his queen until she hitched up her skirts and knelt in front of him, holding out the water. Instantly, he snatched it, gulping it down.

"That's all I have, Nayhuel," Valoretta whispered as his desperate eyes returned to her. "There will be more later, but not before."

Slowly, those eyes focused and his cheeks turned red. Dropping his gaze to the cup clenched in his hand, he said in a weak, shaky voice, "This was your ration."

"I'm fine for now," the queen soothed.

Yet the boy trembled. "I can't, Your Majesty," he softly moaned. "I can't think of anything but water..." He trailed off miserably, and the queen touched his arm.

"It's alright."

"No, it's not! I'm failing Mira. I'm one of her examples! Yet I can't do it."

"You must," Valoretta insisted, now squeezing his arm. "Try harder. If you're thirsty, think of something else. Go assist someone, *anything* to help you until the next ration comes."

Nayhuel shook his head, his eyes filling with terror. Pulling away from Valoretta, he yanked out his knife, shooting to his feet. Striving not to appear alarmed as he now towered over her with blade brandished and madness in his eyes, the queen slowly rose. "Can you not stand by your own decision?"

"That's just it, Mira," the boy croaked. "I know I'll never make it and, if I try, they'll know my weakness. I'll ruin our chance for glory."

"How do you intend to change that?"

The boy turned his blade toward his torso and, as he did, he softly begged, "Please, don't let anyone know. Please, Your Majesty. I died of dehydration. Please?"

The queen quickly grabbed his hand to stop it, yet strong muscles tensed beneath her fingers, the strength years of training had given him, the strength desperation had temporarily returned to him.

Unexpectedly, the boy did not pull away. Yet his eyes beseeched her. "Please."

Staring into those wide pupils, Valoretta saw all his fears, saw that his worst dread was dying after betraying his home. In those eyes, she saw there was no point in living, no life beyond more torture—slow torture—and complete loss of pride. Could she, as his queen, condemn him to such a death when his youth could not permit him to live for the final cause?

Slowly releasing the boy's knife hand, Valoretta dropped her gaze to the floor. "If that's the way you feel, Nayhuel, I promise they'll never know." The queen's voice was beaten, and she looked away as he plunged the blade into his heart. Out of the corner of her eye, she saw him slump, heard his last broken gasps and slowly turned back to face him.

As his eyes glazed over in death, Valoretta dashed into the adjoining room, yanking the covers off the bed. She ripped off a portion of cloth to wad around the wound then gently wrapped his body, tying it off so as not to come undone. Slowly exhaling after guaranteeing that no blood incriminated the boy, she pushed herself to her feet to find someone to remove the wrapped remains.

Beyond the great hall windows, dew sparkled in the rising sun outside the castle wall, outside Mira's prison. Knowing Sara watched her in concern, Valoretta smiled grimly without turning away from the brightening morning view. She now knew how Arnacin could once have stood still for so long.

"Your Majesty?" The call, accompanied by the sound of the doors opening, caused the queen to turn at last. Two guards escorted one of the men responsible for guarding the food at night inside. "We caught him stealing food from the larders."

"Is this true?" Valoretta softly asked the culprit, whose eyes remained fixed on the flagstones at his feet.

"I won't lie to you, my queen," the man finally replied. "I did take some bread."

"Was this the first time?"

"No."

"Do you realize you have betrayed all those trusting you, condemning some to die even faster, condemning them to endure torture sooner?"

"Mira, with all due respect, the sooner this torture ends, the better. Why bother prolonging it? We stood while we had to. Nothing will leak out of this tomb now. No one will ever know if we all stabbed each other, ate each other or not."

"The savages will know!" Valoretta retorted. "Are they not still human—capable of feeling awe, of potentially changing themselves? Even if they aren't, we'll lose entirely to them, entirely, if we surrender our humanity. If you can't feel love, feel enough hatred of them to stand to the last!"

"What is the use of love or hatred? Our death is still the same."

"Indeed, it is, but we have not lost even in death, unless we first lose ourselves. Have you so lost your very being?"

"I would sooner die, my queen, than continue."

Valoretta compressed her lips. "Very well then. As a traitor to Mira, you are condemned to death through beheading, this very moment."

Sinking to one knee, the culprit whispered, "Your command is my desire, Mira."

Discarding political strength, the queen turned her back as one of the guards raised his sword into the air. As the body's soft thump sounded behind her, she called to the second guard. "Manni, you will take his watch in the larders."

"My queen, please," the guard begged. "Ask someone else. I doubt I could stand it any better than he. The sight of food weakened him, tormented him. Truly, who could stand?"

Whirling to meet his eyes, Valoretta insisted, "You will. Your empathy will prevent you from doing likewise. Manni, I do not order this lightly. I know the torture it will be, but if you do not help watch... I cannot describe the horrors I fear from more than just thieves. As difficult as it is for me to order someone to accept an agony I cannot share, I must."

Bowing deeply, Manni submitted, "You burden yourself with the most agony, Mira—responsibility for everyone's misery. With that in mind, I can withstand the portion you feel fit to deal me."

That night, Valoretta sat motionless on her bed while Sara brushed her hair and massaged her scalp with oil. "Remember when you used to fight me while I did this?" her nurse softly asked. Despite the fact that it had only been a few months since the last one of those fights, it indeed seemed like another lifetime.

When Valoretta neither moved nor responded, Sara breathed, "You were so troublesome. I could only hope you would someday learn your mother's dignity, but it seemed to have missed you entirely." She paused before whispering, "In certain ways, the foreigner made it worse, but I can't deny he made you grow up in other ways. I wish you would still fight, though. I'd worry less."

She halted, and Valoretta turned to glance up at the older lady. Sara stood there, staring off into space, yet her face held the still, alert look of someone who has sensed danger.

"What is it, Sara?" the queen asked, straining to hear. Floating in from the balcony came the sound of singing—beautiful, peaceful singing. She could not say it was happy, yet the peace was other-worldly, almost eerie.

Pulling a shawl over her under-dress, Valoretta crept toward the balcony and looked down into the bailey. The sound came from a group of people huddled around the low fires—embers really. From a distance, the queen could not see faces, but their emotions flowed through their melody. Yes, longing trickled throughout, yet it sounded to her like hopeful music, a song of fulfilled wishes in a dark time.

"Sara," Valoretta softly called. "Join them and then tell me what they're singing."

She heard the rustle as her nurse bowed, turned and softly left, gently closing the door behind her. The queen did not look, however—spellbound by that wonderful music.

It ended too soon, and Valoretta dragged herself back to her bed. Sometime around midnight, Sara returned. "It's the island-er's influence, I can tell you that," her nurse scoffed. Although Sara said no more, Valoretta noticed she left whenever the sing-ing started during the next few nights. That knowledge brought a slight, if brief, smile to the queen's face.

Captain Xavior had no trouble reading the captive's tempta-tion to escape in the fingers that fiddled with the rope binding the two ships together. He could also guess at the reason for the hesitation and, with a cruel smile, he made sure to use it.

Stopping beside the captive in the dusk of one such evening, Xavior commented, "I should think locking you up or sinking your ship would be unnecessary. You're already a wretch due to your cowardice. Could you live with yourself if you became one of these sniveling, grubbing souls who give their word in fear simply to break it after?"

Hatred flashed in the captive's eyes, yet he continued staring at his ship, otherwise unresponsive. Xavior was used to no less. Turning around to lean his back against the railing, the captain dismissively baited, "I know your thoughts. Since your ship cannot sail, you intend to sink it with yourself on board. But that reac-tion isn't brave. It's just another form of animal terror. How low can you sink?"

"You're playing with things far beyond your understanding," the warning hiss finally came.

"What am I playing with?" Xavior pressed tauntingly.

"In the first place, my honor. Why else would you haul my ship around?"

The captain opened his arms innocently. "Because it's your ship. Can you not tell I care? All you must do is accept our mission of freeing the world of enslavement and all my wealth is yours, your ship included."

With a dark glance, the captive simply left, and the captain leered in triumph.

Arnacin did not go far, retreating to the niche behind the galley where all the kegs stood. Plunking himself against the wall, he stared out to sea, Xavior's all-too-true taunts ringing in his ears. He was a wretch, and his only possible escape was to become more of a wretch.

Whirling toward the nearest keg, Arnacin kicked the drum over with one swift, brutal strike. The spigot broke off and rolled around the deck. Red wine gushed from its container, seeping across the wood, running over the side of the ship. Glowering, the islander watched it bleed into the floor.

When Xavior ordered Arnacin to clean the stained deck, the islander obeyed. At least, the task occupied some of his thoughts for an hour.

As Arnacin was emptying a bucket over the rail, however, Spyros sauntered by. "So, a Zedelious…"

Facing the first mate, Arnacin let his hand drop to his hilt. "I'm not."

"Your appearance testifies against your protests."

"I'm an islander."

His eyes widening in dramatized surprise, Spyros gasped, "That's your surname?" He shrugged without waiting for a reply. "Still… That means nothing. For all we know, your mother cheated on her husband."

Arnacin's eyes flashed, yet Spyros ignored it, continuing, "Between us, Islander, I'd love to prove you're no relation to our cap'n." He paused, regarding the captive. "I might have a deal for you. Tell me all you know of where you grew up and your family. We'll see if there's anything in there to prove you're not a Zedelious and, if so, we'll take it to the cap'n."

"I have a deal for you," the islander growled. "Leave."

Spyros grinned. Yet pulling his forelock as if it were a hat, he mockingly bowed. "Have no fear. I won't fight with you, at least for now." Chortling, he turned back to the main deck.

"My queen, this is the last of the food. I think the well's fairly deep, though."

Accepting the morsel of meat from the girl distributing food that day, Valoretta nodded. "Continue giving people water. That's all we can do." Her own voice was hoarse, dead, but no one acted with contempt at that sign of weakness. It was as if they heard some strength she could not.

Bowing, the girl gave Sara her portion and then departed. Once the great hall's doors shut again, Valoretta spoke softly. "Sara, if they don't attack soon, our corpses will stretch from the outer bailey to the keep."

"Then that's how it will be," her nurse whispered.

Before Valoretta could reply—before she could even express the thoughts that caused the heat in her face—a call rang out, even through the closed doors. "Your Majesty! Mira!" Whirling toward it as the doors banged inward, Valoretta met a lady as bony as all of them were by then, who grabbed the queen's hand as she neared. "They're after my nieces!"

"Who?" Valoretta gasped, letting the woman lead her.

"Please! They plan to eat the children!"

Paling, Valoretta ordered, "Run! I'm right behind you."

Within the outer bailey, five hunger-driven madmen had just laid hands on a squirming, screaming toddler, intent on snapping its neck. Fighting against them, the toddler's mother and siblings kicked, bit and screamed as loudly as their hoarse voices permitted. Along the edges of the scene, starved men and women simply watched, too ill to care one way or the other.

"Stop!" Valoretta commanded, striding into the center of the fray. Even were the sight of her not enough, the guards behind her brought everyone to an abrupt halt. "This is the action of animals, not men—certainly not Mirans."

The steel and strength in her otherwise dead voice caused four of the five men to drop their gazes in shame, yet the fifth crossed his arms. "What difference does any of that make? We're all dead anyway. There's already nothing left to eat."

"We are dead," Valoretta snapped. "What difference will it make, turning into beasts that prey upon the weak? You'll simply prolong your own torture, and you'll die without even pride left to you. If you can't stomach this battle, kill yourself! No one will stop you from ending it now if you lack the strength to persevere. That goes for anyone who can't continue anymore. But the rest of us will stand to the end, as Mirans."

For half a minute, the men stared at her. Then, without a word, they dashed to the battlements. No one stopped them from throwing themselves from the outer wall of the castle. In the ensuing silence, Valoretta returned to the keep with her guard.

Throughout the rest of the day, the queen saw others follow the example of those men by throwing themselves off the battlements.

Eventually whirling away from the sight, Valoretta dropped beside her bed to bury her head in her arms. As her shoulders shook in her misery, she barely noticed Sara stroking the top of her head.

She had offered them false hope in the absurd idea that their last stand would make a difference, that their slow death was worthwhile. So, she had condemned herself as a liar. Not only would they die victims of terrible, prolonged torture, but no one would ever know anything other than that Mira was destroyed forever. The journals some had been commanded to write would burn in the savages' fires.

If they were smart, they wouldn't turn into beasts—they'd all slit their own throats while any strength was left them. Yet, the torturer she was had painted a cruel picture of divine purpose, a glorious death in sticking it out, dying from the lack of food, or

for those who somehow survived the longest, from the natives'
poison. And that death was all Valoretta's fault.

Chapter 4

The Last of Mira

THE QUEEN DID NOT SLEEP that night, despite Sara's imploring. When Valoretta again heard the soft strains of singing, albeit no longer melodious but husky, her nurse whispered, "Come, my lady."

When the queen remained sitting on the edge of her bed, staring at the floor, the older woman insisted, "You should come. They'll help. I know."

"I can't, Sara," Valoretta finally breathed. "As queen, I'll disrupt it, if not put myself at risk. You go. It seems to strengthen you."

Sadly bowing, Sara departed. Valoretta returned to staring blankly at the moonlight shining across the floor, her thoughts as numb as her parched tongue and salt-dried eyes.

It was not until dawn began to change the colors of the polished wood beneath her feet that Sara returned. Oddly, when Valoretta finally turned to her, the older woman's eyes lacked all weariness, though the sorrow remained.

"My lady," Sara whispered, stopping beside the queen. "Lilitha... the mother of the attacked children, wishes to see you."

"Are they all right?" Paling, Valoretta forced herself to her feet, swaying as she did so.

Catching her queen's arm, Sara nodded. "As much as anyone can be." Her gaze now on the arm trembling in her hand, she mumbled, "My lady, we all know death is very near. In reality there is no such thing as being 'all right' as long as we're here. I believe, though... there is hope after death."

"Sara, please," the queen protested, tugging her arm away. "I don't want to hear about spirits right now."

"This isn't about–" The nurse quickly broke off at the look she received. "Is that the real reason you won't go, because you fear native superstition?"

Valoretta simply stared at her.

When a moment passed, Sara shook her head. "Lilitha waits."

Lilitha was as terribly skeletal as the rest of them and, next to the equally parched ruby flowers in her hand, her skin was horribly colorless–but her green eyes held a strength that Valoretta could not explain, even knowing that the young mother was of savage descent, judging by her name.

As the woman sank to her knees, Valoretta courteously asked, "Are your children well?"

"In all honesty, Mira, they are soon leaving this world for a better one." Lilitha held out the flowers in her arms. "I wanted you to have these, though. I saved them from my garden in the hopes I could take a bit of home with me if we should actually escape." Her already hoarse voice cracked, and she paused for a second. "They'll spare the flowers in your courtyard a little longer, I hope."

"I couldn't..." the queen breathed, yet her words trailed off.

"Please, Mira. It is the only thing I can give."

"Why give anything? I'm torturing you to death."

A slight laugh escaped the woman. "You have given us time, Mira. An extremely precious gift, if we could all learn the best ways of using it. Sadly, many of us never do–but my family has been spared by your rule. Please, wear these roses. They were planted and kept in love. Now, with love, I give them to you."

"I don't think you're going to succeed with this Arnacin Islander," Spyros said. In the dim candlelight, he and Xavior discussed plans inside the captain's cabin.

"On the contrary, it's going very well." Unrolling a map, Xavior spread it over the table. "He is now at the point where his emotions have settled... enough, anyway. He hates everything to do with life, including himself, and he hates even more all the high standards to which he clung. They are naught but lies. All I must do now is open the door for some sort of purposeful life, and he will jump through."

Skepticism shone on Spyros's face, but all he said was, "What door is that?"

Grinning wickedly, Xavior placed his finger over a port on the map.

"Ennial." Spyros laughed, looking at it. "With the rowing slaves."

"Of course. Ennial's government enslaves the men, we liberate them, and they happily become pirates."

According to plan, Xavior spotted the islander watching the next day as the pirates conquered the Ennialian ship that had attacked them once they sailed too close to harbor. Quickly, the pirates went about freeing the men shackled to oars, passing out water and food, and for those that joined—thankfully, all of them did—a little bit of money on the spot.

Arnacin stood aloof, yet his dark eyes flickered over the line of gaunt, weakened men with their many scars and open lashes on their backs. Xavior wasted not a second before joining his captive. "It's a shame what governments do to anyone they can lay their hands on."

Those eyes cooled, the usual fire licking at the edges, yet only silence followed. Shrugging, the captain added, "This kingdom leaves their own peasants alone by raiding others and turning free men into slaves, many of whom die within a week."

"I know all about the treachery of kings," Arnacin growled. "There is nothing new with monarchs."

Smiling, the captain cajoled, "See how much happier those men are. Do you not wish to help liberate such men from the tyranny of governments?"

"You would know nothing about that, yourself."

"Don't I? Come, in all our raids, we lessen kings' strength. Village raids are only for supplies, but the real stuff is in the navy and merchant ships." When his captive only turned his face away, Xavior whispered, "You can help free the world and give those fiends everything they deserve, with the wild waves as home and not a soul to torment you."

Arnacin abruptly turned to him. "Join the nobles in that fiery pit! There is nothing even worth 'rescuing' out there, as you put it. The lower classes have no more morals than the rest. They don't have the power to torture anyone, but just give them that power and they'll misuse it!"

"You know you are no different," the captain pressed. "There comes a time when all honor must fail. How can you, in this troubled world with your own survival to look after, keep something so pure? Your only hope is to act as if you can—as if you can give that honor to others and find some pride in yourself for at least trying."

Fire now filled those eyes. "*You* don't try. You use that excuse to pardon your greed."

"Why are you alive then, if I don't care? Why do I allow you a blade?"

"Answer your own question!"

"Because there's something in you, boy, something worth saving. Do you not believe I wish to help? You can live without anyone being able to harm you on the ocean—"

Yet Arnacin strode away, yanking his hood up as if he could disappear. Permitting himself a smile, Xavior returned to his cabin with a satisfied step. Whether his captive admitted it or not, that conversation would haunt him.

As the singing again started, more hoarsely that ever, Sara stilled. "Is it spirits, my lady?" She finished slipping the night dress over her queen.

Valoretta sighed. "I'm glad you found hope, Sara."

"My lady—"

"No, Sara. Spirits only betray. They might give moments of peace for some great sacrifice, but even for that peace, I know too much to give it. Yet, if I go, I will have no strength to resist their offer."

"All He asks—"

"Sara, listen. We're all going to die. Even the adopted natives, who so faithfully followed their gods, will die. They will be trampled by the very spirits they serve. And don't bother to tell me the god Arnacin believed in is different. Arnacin was also betrayed."

Sara stepped around to face her queen. "Please allow me to speak."

"I'm sorry, Sara. I don't have the strength. Please don't convince me Arnacin's god is real. I'll only hate Him all the more."

Her eyes downcast, Sara wordlessly took Valoretta's hand and gently squeezed it. Although disappointment shone in every line of her nurse's worry-creased face, she dropped the subject.

The *Zedelious's* crew, Arnacin had discovered, was motley. Their speech was as widely different as their intelligence and appearances. Yet, beneath their differences, he found them very alike except for Mr. Butter. Dedicated pirate and deadly swordsman though he was, the stocky Mr. Butter rarely visited taverns and never dallied with the ladies. Instead he worked on the ship, sewing or knitting, while the others enjoyed their merriment. His relative honor, however, was as much a tool for recruitment as his skill with a blade was for slaughter.

As for the rest of the crew, they were completely abominable. With delight, they looted shores, sank ships, built their treasure hoard and molested females, some of whom they forced aboard for brief periods.

Arnacin avoided the crew, but such solitude led to the acute awareness of his own inner depravity. On a beautiful night, one in which he would have once gloried, his hatred of himself lit like a bonfire.

He passed Mr. Butter, sitting at the rail, and stopped. Moonlight reflecting on the water stretched before the ship. The waves held the same soft whisper they had shared with a boy so long ago on a night when the sea's calling forever lured him away from his nymph-like sister.

With that memory, a voiceless scream slashed through Arnacin's heart as hot tears slid down his cheeks. He could not live with himself if he chose to break faith with Xavior, but he could no longer live with himself if he did not.

He could never go back to a more innocent life nor could he return to the island, but he could pierce through the *Zedelious's* hull at water level and then make sure his ship sunk with it. To not alert the pirates, he could destroy their ship from the outside.

As the waves promised the freedom of death, Arnacin pulled himself onto the rail—but at that moment, strong hands seized his shoulders. "Don't, Islander!"

Cursing himself for failing to realize the proximity of Mr. Butter, Arnacin pulled against the pirate, however futile the attempt. Starved, dehydrated, sleep-deprived, with a shoulder that had never fully recovered, he was no match for any fit adult male once they laid hands on him, and he had foolishly allowed one to do so. Trying to unsheathe his sword would accomplish nothing. Mr. Butter would feel the movement.

"Arnacin." Mr. Butter's tone was now a sad whisper, although his grasp remained firm. "Don't do this. Ya have too much to live for."

If he had been cunning, the islander could have easily played along until out of range of the pirate's grasp, but those words stirred deeply in his heart. "Like you would know anything about worth!" Hating the raggedness in his breath that betrayed his torment and the cracked voice that revealed his tears, he yanked loose to stand beside the pirate. His temporary desire for suicide had dwindled away, although his pain remained.

Pulling himself up to sit on the rail, Mr. Butter peered at him. After a moment, he asked, "Are ya drunk, man?"

"With what?" Arnacin hissed, pulling his cloak closer about him.

The pirate shrugged. He waited a moment, then said, "Worth, ya say? Well, ya don't see me throwing meself inta the jaws of the ocean. That must be some understandin' of worth."

With an ugly suspicion that Xavior had told Mr. Butter to be there, the islander looked away. "You're just here to convince me to turn to piracy."

The pirate sighed with a half-groan of weariness. "Look, I told ya before, if ya don't take it personal-like, it can be used for good. Now, I know there are some baduns, but ya've the makin's of a cap'n, and no mistake. I'm here to convince ya of nothin', but if ya would take me advice—and I know ya won't—agree to piracy, learn under our cap'n, and then ya can make yar own crew. Free the world if ya like! Tell ya mites them honorable rules of yars—"

"You can't free a world through murder."

"Murder, Islander! Ya only kill them that's deserving of it. That's what I do."

Arnacin could not control his snort of sarcasm. "Well, that's just about everybody. The whole world deserves to die, and those killing others are no better. The only reason you can sit there and say that is because you're the dumbest pirate on board. The rest all know they're murderers, but they're too drunk on blood and money to care. You just sit there and swallow the most basic of demonic lies."

Mr. Butter straightened on the rail. "Look, mite...!" Pausing, he shrugged. "I know I can't be cap'n of anything. I don't have all them skills. But I know one thing: me dear mother never lied, and she told me the world had a place for me. The only place I've found

that's not wantin' me head is the pirate world. So, I will start here
and help liberate people like me. This is the only freedom they'll
have in this world."

The depth of Mr. Butter's conviction revealed itself in his voice.
As it caused the pain in Arnacin's heart to burn again, he turned
away, heading toward the sanctuary of his own deck, and the
shelter he had set up there behind coils of rope. "Your vision is
not worth the living," he nevertheless mumbled as he left. "You
should have let the first man kill you who could... before you found
out a truth far worse than death: the longer you live, the more
monstrous you become."

Somehow, Mr. Butter must have heard him, for he called out,
"Oh, now... Don't take on so! Ya'll be drowneded next!" When
Arnacin simply continued treading away, the pirate added, "There's
a place for ya! Worth, as ya call it! Remember that!"

Closing his eyes, Arnacin felt another hot tear drop past his
lashes for the unmeant lies in that call, lies in which his parents
had always believed: the promises whispered to their doomed son.

Valoretta could no longer keep track of the days. Each seemed
an eternity of misery with nothing to ease it. Eventually, weakness
took over the nights and, despite her pain, sleep would lighten
hunger and thirst for a few hours.

"Mira, my lady." The soft whisper pulled Valoretta out of the
blackness of sleep as Sara's hand ran down her cheek.

As consciousness returned, intense pain gripped her ribs,
stomach and head. Weakly rolling onto her back, Valoretta felt
as if the room had started tipping wildly. "Sara," she moaned, the
sound coming from her throat an unintelligible croak.

Sara smiled sadly. Meeting her nurse's eyes, the queen became
fixated by them. Though Sara was equally gaunt, she wasn't shaking in weakness and, like the half-Miran Lilitha, her eyes, though
filled with deep sorrow, lacked despair.

"Come, Valoretta," Sara cajoled, placing a hand as steady as the rest of her under her queen's shoulder.

Gasping now from the effort staying conscious took, Valoretta slid away. "Don't. Just leave me here. I can't go on... can't go..."

"You *must* go." If Sara had shouted, her fervor would not have been any less intense. For a second, the queen merely stared at her.

"I've nothing left, Sara," Valoretta finally whispered. "I don't have any strength."

"You're queen."

"And when I die before they do? If there's nothing to stop..." She shook her head. "I'll just die."

"I have faith you won't." Taking the queen's arm, Sara succeeded in helping the weaker woman to a sitting position. Valoretta leaned into that support, trembling. "Come," her nurse gently commanded, "I'll dress you."

Just as Valoretta succeeded in standing on her own and Sara slowly backed toward the wardrobe, a boom sounded through the castle, resonating through every wall. The savages were pounding on the front gates.

"The attack has come, Mira," Sara said, picking the first gown that came to hand and pulling it over Valoretta's head. "Just live a few more hours."

"If that," the queen agreed, sliding her arm through the bodice sleeve held out for her. "Just do me one thing, Sara. Don't mess too much with my hair. There won't be time for that."

"Yes, my lady, but our queen will not be slaughtered in her under-dress."

So, Sara dressed her queen, while they heard the continual *boom, boom* of the savages' attempts to gain entrance. From where she stood, Valoretta could see the swordmaster rallying men for the battle to come. She knew without looking that all heads were turning toward the gates, all the weak, all the possible defenders, all those who could move and even those who could not, hauled themselves to meet that enemy with everything they had.

Meanwhile, Sara threaded flowers through her queen's hair.

Watching with helpless horror as the enemy breached the walls, Sara's heart wailed as those savages easily cut down everyone remaining in the outer bailey before turning to the inner walls. There, the screams of death continued.

Casting a look at Valoretta, Sara nodded sadly. The queen simply stood against the balcony doorframe, mercilessly thin and dehydrated, yet appearing calm, awaiting the death that no Miran would escape. She did not tremble, pace, throw herself from the keep, stab herself, nor plead with Sara to end it before the savages did. Only the brightness of her eyes spoke of the pain writhing inside her.

Had she been male, she would have been in the first few cut down but, for the good of her people, she had to hold out hope, even if she must view the entire annihilation of her beloved country before her own death. Thus was Valoretta, Mira, sole ruler of the land bearing that name, condemned from birth alongside her kingdom.

After what seemed like several lifetimes, they heard feet in the corridor before the hated enemy appeared in the doorway itself. With a surprising laugh, they slammed the door shut. Sounds of heavy things scraping across the floor followed–then retreating feet and silence.

Meeting the fear that had finally appeared in her lady's gaze, Sara wondered aloud, "How much more do they think to torture you?"

"Sara," came the very weak groan of protest as Valoretta slid to the floor. Only a moment later, her nurse realized that the queen was no longer conscious. For a second, Sara thought her dead; then she noticed the rise and fall of the queen's chest through the changing light in the tiny ruby eye of her crane necklace. That necklace, the signet of Mira, appeared almost dulled to Sara's gaze, yet its eye burned in defiance, an unbroken zeal to survive. Not that it could. Mira was dead. Even Valoretta was breathing her last.

Within a few minutes, Sara turned at a scraping sound, and she noticed a plate of water had been shoved under the door—a whole plate. That sight drove both excitement and fear through her heart, for while her body craved the substance held in that vessel, she feared the implication that the savages wanted at least one of them alive.

Drawing in a shaky breath, she decided not to wake Valoretta. Yet as she took some of the water, telling herself that she would need it to guard the queen to the last, she could not shake the guilty thought that the real reason for her actions was something she would not dare voice even to herself.

The water's taste was not normal, as if they had mixed something in it. Sara hoped it was poison, but for the first time in her life, she truly wished that the islander could be there to tell them what was in the liquid. Regardless, she drank all of it.

Sometime later, the nurse heard the items blockading the door shift, and three of the savages walked in. Protectively, Sara stepped between them and Valoretta's still form. One of the men simply shoved the frail woman aside, and the three of them surrounded the queen.

Although they proceeded to force water down Valoretta's throat, their mannerisms, the tones in which they spoke words Sara knew nothing of, and the ways they touched the queen caused Sara's heart to clench. In a flash, she knew how they planned to finish the very heart of Mira and, with renewed force, she shoved herself into their midst.

"Leave," she croaked.

To her surprise, they stood. "Until it revives," one sneered in Mira's tongue, "you take care of it." He tossed a waterskin at Sara's feet, and the three departed, laughing.

For a long moment, Sara stared down at her precious queen, knowing what lay in store should she live. Yet, the older woman knew that if she refused to do as their captors bid, much rougher hands would do it instead. As Sara continued to hesitate, something someone had said echoed in her mind. Was it only a few days ago?

...*time, Mira. An extremely precious gift, if we could all learn the best ways of using it. Sadly, many of us never do—but my family has been spared by your rule.*

Indeed, time was an extremely precious gift, the final one she could grant her queen.

Sinking down beside Valoretta, Sara pulled her queen close and carefully drizzled water through those parched lips. As she looked down at Valoretta, no longer the girl she had raised practically as her own daughter, her gaze was again caught by the signet—the signet that seemed to be whispering to her.

Earlier in the week, Xavior had tossed a blanket onto the smaller ship. Where it went, he knew not, but he would try a different tactic.

Turning his key, he unlocked the door of the ship's treasure room. Here, he kept half of the Zedelious family's fortune in the cabin that used to be his as a boy. The porthole was boarded over, with treasure expanding to all sides and hardly any space for an occupant.

From a small chest, the captain chose a palm-sized bag of gold coins. Before leaving, however, he glanced at the porthole. Although improbable that any of his crew would dare pry the board away, he always checked for tampering. Satisfied, he locked the door.

Islander was standing at the *Zedelious*'s rail when Xavior joined him with the comment, "Money is something you need in this world."

The captive ignored the proffered bag, instead watching as the sunset cast the calm ocean into flames of color.

"Zedelious's family must stick together in this dark world, you and I." When Islander remained unresponsive, Xavior dropped an arm over his shoulder.

It was as if life had leapt back into a corpse. Islander threw the captain's arm off and jumped back six feet. "Stay away!"

"Arnacin, you can't go through life alone."

"Yes, I can! And I will!" A shudder passed through the captive. Xavior had finally managed to break through that shield of hatred, yet it was horror and unyielding stubbornness that he found there. "There isn't a single person who actually cares for anyone unless they want something, so don't tell me I can't!" With that, he fled.

Hearing exuberant cries emitting from the ship's galley overhead, Mr. Butter slowly roused from sleep after his night shift. Feet thumped and the thunk of a cup followed by a splash of liquid jerked the pirate fully awake.

Someone had broken into a keg of rum at off hours! Well, he better not miss out. Throwing his legs over the side of his hammock, Mr. Butter made to rise, but then paused.

Xavior could find them... But what of it? Even if their captain did give them a few lashes, it would be worth it, right? They just had to make sure not to drink themselves into an unworkable condition, so that their punishment would be less. And there was that excellent batch they had just stolen from the mayor of Brums. It was unlikely the crew would taste that stuff at all unless they stole it. They would be stuck with watered slop to ensure their sobriety.

With that thought, the pirate leapt from his hammock.

True to his deductions, someone had broken into the liquor. However, that someone was forcing it down Islander's throat while Spyros pinned their victim against the wall, which meant Xavior was aware of their actions and was pretending otherwise for the time being. Slippery as he was, struggling as he was, Islander was no match for his assailants, and they rammed his head back, pouring liquid down his throat.

Exhaling, Mr. Butter straightened his shoulders. Then he stepped into the group, putting a hand on Islander's arm. "Leave 'im alone, mites. Ya've done enough."

Oddly, Spyros nodded to his assistants and they backed away. Freed, Islander's hand went instantly to his sword hilt, yet his movements were shaky.

Mr. Butter grabbed his arm. "Come on, mite. Ya need freesh air."

It might have been only because he was no longer fully sensible, but Islander heeded the light tug on his arm, allowing the pirate to take him outside and to the railing. Pale and shaking, the captive hunched over it for support.

Releasing his light grasp, Mr. Butter waited. He had never seen Islander take a drop of alcohol—although judging by the wine in his hold, the captive had in the past. Still, the stuff forced down his throat was no doubt picked for its strength with the full intention of humiliating him, since killing him was not an option.

As the captive retched, Mr. Butter asked, "'Ow did they nab ya?"

Islander's hand trembled as he wiped his mouth. "I didn't look up. Spyros jumped on me from the poop deck above." His voice was rough with drink. As he jerked back over the railing with another spasm of his stomach, the pirate shook his head.

"Ya should eat more. It might've helped now."

The captive's fingers dug into the railing, tightening in anger. Looking at the marks left on the wood, Mr. Butter noticed that Islander's nails were short. Considering that he did nothing to take care of himself, that smoothness could only be because of friction. The pirate would have to look closely for more nail marks along the Zedelious's railings.

"I'll kill them." That whisper brought the pirate's attention back to Islander's blazing eyes—a bit unfocused perhaps, but no less filled with hatred.

"Ya 'ad that option," Mr. Butter reminded him.

"No! I'm serious. I'll cut out their hearts and force them to eat them. Xavior's first. I'll hand them their precious gold and shove it down their throats, watch them strangle to death on their treasure." Islander spat the last word out with the utmost hatred.

Horrified, Mr. Butter remained silent, yet his gaze again dropped to those skeletal fingers digging into the railing's wood. If they were claws, they would look no different. In the following silence, interrupted only by Islander's ragged gasps, the pirate pressed his previous assertion, "If ya meant that, ya would 'ave done it. I don't doubt ya could 'ave at least killed some of us."

"I do mean it!"

Reason was lost on him. Throwing up his hands, Mr. Butter tried anyway. "Then what's stopped ya?"

Only the snap of sails answered at first, but slowly, gasping, Islander appeared to regain at least some of his composure. With a moan, he sunk against the rail, curling around his stomach. "Honor," he whispered at last. "A false honor, yes, but you wouldn't know. How can you cut your last strings to life of your own free will? Would you throw your gold overboard, your shiny trinkets?" His head twitched in what might have been a dismissal. "Neither can I discard the last drop of honor left to me. Still, it will happen."

His voice lowered further, and Mr. Butter knew he had no idea he was speaking aloud. "When my promise has turned old, when I'm sick of the stench of death on this deck and the blood dripping from my own fingers for not stopping them sooner, I will bring justice. I'll give them the death they deserve, burn both ships to the bottom, send them into damnation... and jump into that fire after them." Slowly, his gaze turned to Mr. Butter—a gaze that was scared and hollow, stripped bare by alcohol. "I will. Eventually. I gave my word to remain."

Staring at that ball of misery with those drawn, tortured features, Mr. Butter shook his head. "Ya're drunk, mite. And it ain't pretty."

The only response was a spasm of muscles as the captive pressed his face into his palm, angrily flattening his nose while his fingers again curled into claws, this time digging into his own forehead.

Gently, the pirate tried again, tentatively reaching out to grab that self-wounding hand. "Sleep it off, mite. I'll keep watch."

Unsteadily, Islander pulled his hand away and it fell back to his side. As his head rested against the *Zedelious's* wall, Mr. Butter knew there was no reason to speak again. The alcohol itself would compel sleep in another few minutes.

Perhaps there was no reason for the pirate to feel the sympathy he did, not after that rant, but somehow Islander had moved him. He would keep what he had just heard secret and see what happened. Hopefully, the captive would someday recognize the potential in pirating, before it was too late. Hopefully.

In the days that followed, Sara found that she was allowed to leave the room if she insisted that she must watch the savages prepare anything to do with her lady. Once, she would have tried to smuggle poison in to Valoretta, but no longer. And she knew that with her queen nearly well, her own time was running out.

Therefore, a few weeks after their capture, Sara again insisted on watching the savages prepare the food they intended for their captives. Escaping her captors while they were cooking dinner over a fire, she raced to the falconry room where the savages had temporarily left Mira's birds.

Choosing the closest falcon, she tied a previously penned note to its leg with Mira's signet twisted through the string. As her pursuers' footsteps pounded up the stairs, she grabbed the bird around its body and launched it out the window. "Take the note out to sea, to anyone who will help Valoretta, please."

At that moment, someone grabbed her by the arms. Something struck her over the head and darkness descended.

"Sara." Valoretta's voice woke the nurse. Sara found herself in the queen's bed while the queen herself mopped the older woman's brow. "What did you do?"

"I wrote a note, my lady," Sara whispered, pushing herself up. "One of the birds has it."

"And what good will that do?" Valoretta's voice held a touch of bitterness, and Sara's heart broke at the sound. "The only people on this rock are savages, and that's where the bird will have settled."

"I hope it will go to sea. All of our hunting birds came from our trade with other kingdoms. It might return to its original home. The note says that Mira has fallen, but they have kept you for a troph–"

The door flew open and Valoretta paled as five muscular savages entered. Sara lurched to her feet. No one would touch her queen while she lived.

Some of her defiance must have shown in her eyes, for, with wicked grins, the savages' blades appeared. Sara barely flinched as one savage abruptly lunged, running her through.

Watching the pirates unload treasure from an enemy ship, Arnacin stopped along the forecastle's rail. Although the current valuables came from a ship, they stole from every land they passed. A chartable trail could be marked from the origins of their wealth.

It would be an interesting study despite the fact that he had no way to replace the porthole's board once he pried it open. Still, the distraction from his misery would be worth death if Xavior chose that punishment.

Therefore, as the sun set that night and the deck quieted, the islander slipped over the side of the ship, breaking through the treasure room's sealed porthole.

Shadowy shapes cluttered the floor and swung from the ceiling. Carefully moving toward the door, Arnacin rolled his cloak against the bottom crack before lighting one of the lanterns. In the light, locked chests glittered, some inset with costly stones. Atop one large chest was the name of the ship, stenciled with a care uncharacteristic of Xavior. Kneeling beside it, Arnacin began teaching himself the art of lock-picking.

He did not succeed in one night, but he returned the next and accomplished his task. Slowly opening the large chest, Arnacin's breath caught. Gold coins glittered before him. A few goblets protruded from the mound, decked in sapphires, rubies and more. Very carefully, he pulled a cup out, wincing as each coin tinkled while sliding off. No markings revealed its homeland, and he gently replaced it.

As silently as possible, he probed each chest, uncovering a dragon's treasure, from gold coins—millions of them—to goblets, plates, jewelry and even medals. Captain Xavior was an extremely successful and dangerous pirate, or he had inherited this endless treasure.

A few of the items bore inscriptions. Most were beyond understanding, perhaps even for the pirates themselves. A few had the name of the ship and some even bore Mira's script in both newer and older languages. Lifting an inscribed medal from the top of one chest, he read the name Captain Mildrod Damkin. As he began to turn the medal over, he froze, then hastily flipped it back. A closer look caused his hand to tremble. His native script formed that name.

Rapidly, he scanned the back for any mention of a land he might recall, yet the only place the captain was honored as having served with valor meant nothing to him. All the same, if the pirates raided places as close by as Elcan, if they knew anything about that landmass...

Over the following nights, he searched through the rest of the treasure. Although he came upon other usages of his island's script, he found no indication of where the pirates had obtained such articles.

Relocking the last chest in defeat, he stilled at the sound of movement on the ladder outside. Hastily, he slipped back out the porthole and onto his ship.

When night came again, the islander crept toward Xavior's cabin. Since the treasure was too large to yield answers, Arnacin turned his focus to the captain's own documents.

On trying the door, Arnacin found that it wasn't just locked, but barred from the inside. He barely paused. Looking over his shoulder toward the crow's nest far above, he once again slipped over the side of the ship and then through the cabin windows.

Xavior slept with the hilt of a blade sticking out from under his pillow. Looking at him, Arnacin felt his fingers clench around his own hilt, practically squeezing it.

Not daring to breathe too loudly, the islander nevertheless released his boiling hatred and looked about the room. It was sparse for a captain's cabin, and there were very few places capable of holding the information he wanted. Regardless, Arnacin's silent search revealed nothing and, with nowhere left to look, the islander approached the oval table nailed to the floor in the center of the room.

Crafted from stained mahogany inset with a gold border, the table seemed to lack drawers, at least in the moonlight. In surrender, Arnacin ran his fingers along the underside of the table in the hope of discovering a secret compartment. Without one, the only way of finding Xavior's maps would be to take apart the entire ship, which was out of the question.

He was just about to give up when his index finger found an irregularity in the pattern, a slight gap. Exploring it produced a drawer stuffed with parchments. Swiping the entire pile, Arnacin took them to his own deck to review, hidden behind the coils of rope.

As expected, there was nothing recognizable as far as scripts went, yet all of Xavior's maps were marked with constellations. Those, the islander pored over, striving to place them all, remembering through the fog of time how his mother carefully taught him to tell the season and travel by the stars. And then, he spotted it: LinArial, his island's spring constellation. It was with some relief that he saw Elcan and its islands were missing from where they should have been on the left corner of the map, but from these charts it was obvious that each spring, the *Zedelious* sailed only leagues away from Elcan. If ever it strayed, for any reason...

Silently, Arnacin returned the charts to their secret compartment. Instead of leaving, however, he stood there for a moment. As he glanced toward the sleeping captain, his heart clenched, his eyes lit with wrath.

His captive stood in the darkness of his cabin, framed in the light of the moon, his eyes glowing yellow in hatred. Slowly, he drew his blade...

His eyes snapping open, Xavior scanned his empty cabin. Nothing seemed out of place, yet he could not shake the crawling feeling along his spine that his dream was at least partially true.

Curled tightly around herself in the farthest corner from her room's door, Valoretta crushed her back against the walls as the doorknob rattled. With a gasp, her chest began heaving. Sweat erupted along her skin beneath the blanket she had yanked around her bruised and naked body.

One of the native women stepped in, her wisps of gray hair tied at the base of her neck. Over her arm, she carried a native dress. With her heel, she closed the door behind her and then stood there, appraising her people's captive.

After a second, the native shook out the garments draped over her arm and held them out. Petrified, Valoretta made no move to accept them.

"Protection," the woman finally explained in a husky, accented voice. When the queen only twitched her head—the sole movement she could make—the native tossed the clothes at the queen's feet. She then mimed pulling the gown over her head. "No need for a dresser."

Slowly, Valoretta stretched out one shaking arm and yanked the dress beneath her blanket.

Still only a few paces from the door, the woman settled herself on the floor. "I was picked for my good language." A second passed in silence. "Live, queen. Defy them."

Valoretta's heart skipped a beat. "What?" Could a native actually have said that?

The woman's gaze left the captive's face and dropped to the floor. "We won when all your forces attacks the Sacred Way. Some say we should just force Mira's survivors into our tribes so you can never rise against us. They was tired of bloodshed. Our mediums say the gods demand all of Mira's death. We must finish it.

"I did believe them until they do this to you. They want to see Mira quit. When you refuses before, they think to win through you. Don't let them. Prove your strength and their terrible weakness."

Beaten, Valoretta shook her head, pulling her blanket tighter about her shoulders.

Compassionately, the woman grimaced in pain. "Mira Queen, I refuse asking. The gods would throw down the sky to kill me as a traitor else. I will say, though, you know some power, some god, we don't. Through siege, you stand. You sings nightly, sings in love and hope while your bodies dying in... your word, agony.

"We was terrified, cajoled, others hate-filled. Our gods could do nothing and they angry. They own us, their slaves, but don't quit now. Don't let them win because they think they men. They think there nothing human fears more than this abuse." She nodded toward Valoretta to stress her meaning. "That they can trample you, and Mira, beneath their feet. Some of us think you invincible. Show them you can't break, no matter what. Let them kill you after they quit. They not win."

Valoretta simply stared at her. Biting her lips, the native woman pulled herself to her feet. At the door, she turned back. "Not all our men monsters. Some argued against touching you, but we slaves of the gods. None wish to seem on the side of the gods' enemies, so after a while, they be quiet. One saved your friend when she run to the birds."

After a pause in which the captive only shifted uncomfortably, the woman continued, "Don't hate. You don't win that way. They make sure you fed and watered. Find your strength for the rest." With that, she stepped out.

For some time, Valoretta distantly gazed at the closed door, but as the blood orange of dusk heated the flagstones at her feet, she gripped the gown until her knuckles turned white. Then, remembering Arnacin and Sara, she shakily pulled it over her head.

Chapter 5

BAULIS

DAYS PASSED. THE TEMPERATURES DROPPED and supplies began to run low with no plans for restocking, which Arnacin learned from Mr. Butter meant the *Zedelious* would return to a safe berth soon. Unfortunately, the ship did not reach its destination before the pirates ran completely out of food and hourly squabbles among them began in earnest.

One evening, they stopped along what the islander considered not much more than a cliff on a sand-spit, where a tavern nestled into the rock wall. Xavior quickly ordered all of his men, but Spyros, ashore to help restock enough to reach their destination. Arnacin was another story.

"Do not expect me to enter a tavern simply to witness your gluttonous thirst for alcohol and females!" Arnacin snapped.

"Get in the boat, Islander," the captain growled. "No one stays on board except for the first mate."

"Can't you make an exception, Captain?" Spyros chuckled. "It would be very interesting with just the two of us." He licked his blade.

Stepping into the gig at last rather than tempting his honor more, Arnacin hissed, "When you wish to die, just ask."

"Rather, it will be the other way," Spyros muttered as the gig lowered.

A glare creased Xavior's forehead, yet there was no need to reply.

The tavern sitting on the edge of the sea proudly bore a sign, void of letters, in the shape of an overflowing chalice. The red liquid it dripped all over the depicted table was the only color next to the bare wood of the rest of the sign.

Arnacin hated the image at first sight and hated even more the sound of raucous, coarse laughter, stamping feet and off-key music flowing from the lighted windows and open doors of the place.

With a glare toward the pirate captain, the islander spun back toward the beached gig. Xavior seized his arm, jerking him in the direction of the tavern's doorway. Abruptly, the music broke off, those in the middle of the floor pausing in the midst of their artless dancing as Arnacin tripped on the lintel. Laughter broke out, however, as Xavior entered like he owned the place.

Not wanting to draw anyone's further attention, Arnacin stepped aside as a middle-aged man bustled before the captain, bowing. "Captain Xavior. How many rooms do you require?"

"I'm not staying the night." Xavior's gaze did not flicker from his captive's hate-filled eyes.

With a swift glance toward the islander, the man welcomed them, "Take a seat, sirs. We'll take care of all you require." With that, he turned away.

Still staring at his captive, Xavior drew out a chair, positioning himself at a table right next to the door. Following his example, the *Zedelious*'s crew spread out around the doorway. Trapped, Arnacin turned away and dropped down by the open fireplace, opposite a chair occupied by an aging man.

Within a short while, the tavern keeper had served all Xavior's crew tankards, and Arnacin covertly watched those closest to the door.

His gaze would occasionally lock again with Xavior, but a tingle along his neck told the islander someone else was also watching him. Twisting, he met the coy smile of the tavern maid as she swished back toward the kitchens, her skirt tucked up to her bare calves.

She was back a few minutes later, giggling as she avoided a drunken man's pinching fingers. After distracting him with another full tankard, she placed her tray on the table closest to the fireplace, asking with buttermilk sweetness, "Did you not wish to join the merriment?"

Arnacin pretended he did not know whom she addressed.

"I know better than that," she pressed. "Can I be of service to you?"

Had Arnacin just come off Enchantress Island, or possibly even Mira, he would have assumed she was asking if there were any drinks she could serve him. As it was, after a few months of forced observance of pirates, the no-longer-innocent islander knew better. "You may continue to remain out of my sight."

"That might not be so easy," the girl said, retrieving her tray and brushing past, close enough that her skirt slapped his ear. Arnacin ground his teeth.

"I'm afraid you just offended my granddaughter." The shaky voice came from the man sitting in the chair before the fireplace. "In some places, it would be only right for me to toss you out."

A slight, wicked grin spread across Arnacin's face. "Should I continue?"

Taking a long pipe out of his mouth, the man nodded to the doorway, where Xavior was now engaged in a game of dice with another captain. "Is Captain Xavior attempting to train another heir?"

"Another?"

"His own son was hanged a couple years ago. I gather you're of Zedelious's brood."

"No, I'm an islander from a shepherding 'brood.'"

"Ah, that doesn't mean a single thing. Most of his brood were simple folk, grown up with other..." he paused, chewing in thought, "fathers," he finished. "Ah, Zedelious loved his women, hundreds of them. No one knows how many descendants he had, not even him. Course, the only one he carried away to marry gave him Xavior before she died in labor, but that's the way it goes. Aye?"

"I don't care what he did—there is no possible way they are of any relation to me."

The man gave him a sideways glance. "Would you like me to prove it for you? I'm a soothsayer, you know. For a copper, I'll be able to tell you all you never knew."

"I don't own a copper, nor am I interested. I've had quite enough of that."

"For free?"

"One more word and you'll be prophesying about your missing tongue," the islander warned

"Oh, ho! No humor, this one," someone cackled as chairs scraped on the floor. Glancing in the direction of the voice, Arnacin saw three men, the lust for battle in their eyes. He sprang to his feet right before all three men lunged for him.

"No bloodshed!" the older man screeched as blades flashed out, Arnacin's leading the rest. "I'm warning you again, for your own sakes. The first person to spill blood dies by his own cup. So, I have cursed this tavern."

Stillness followed. Then, slowly, everyone except Arnacin sheathed their swords. The islander simply stood there, watching the men who were surrounding him with cool readiness. Yet more pirates joined the circle, and he heard even more creep up behind, including some from the *Zedelious*'s crew. He knew their thoughts as he saw them slip around him. He could read their faces. They wished neither to curse themselves nor to be murdered by their captive.

As one, all the islander's attackers moved in to grab him, and Arnacin knew he would only have the time to kill one before they overpowered him—one, murdered solely for the islander's hatred. Even now, that thought was daunting.

In that split second of decision, Arnacin sheathed his blade before he was seized by an army of hands. Instead of the beating he expected, he was yanked back before the old man.

"I cannot understand what you would fear in this art," the man huffed, heaving himself to his feet in order to grab the islander's wrist.

"It's not an ar—!" Arnacin's protest was cut short by the large, alcohol-perfumed hand that clamped over his mouth.

"Yes, hummm," the man mumbled, taking no more notice of Arnacin's obstinacy as he ran his finger over the islander's palm. "That takes no gift to know. I see a great darkness that threatens to take over inside you. It is growing, boy, dangerously. Beware, else it swallow you." He ignored the muffled sound of fury, nodding his head. "I do also see the hope of glory. Here is a chance that you will be the rescuer of hundreds—thousands possibly."

A blazing heat was beginning to rise up Arnacin's captive wrist as the man continued, but it was as if their skin had melded together, and he could not so much as twist inside that grasp.

Still the man pressed on, engrossed in his imagined predictions. "Yes, many lives hang on your choices—" He froze, his eyes widening, fear dazzling their color. "You're—" Gurgling, both his hands shot to his throat. Horrified, Arnacin stood there. Before his gaze, the man dropped to his knees, struggling to breathe. Then he stilled.

"Grandpa!" The sound of two pairs of feet accompanied the feminine cry, as the tavern maid and keeper dashed over to the fallen man. As the maid took her grandfather into her arms, the tavern keeper ran back to the kitchen. In seconds, he returned with some water, which he proceeded to flick in droplets over the old man's face.

With a sudden gasp, the man's eyes snapped open, but he continued to stammer without real words. Swiftly, his grandchildren helped the man into the kitchen. In their absence, Arnacin finally looked around. All gazes were turned warily on him. There was at least twelve feet between him and the closest pirate. Only Xavior still obstinately blocked the doorway.

Absently rubbing his hot wrist, Arnacin returned to his spot on the floor.

"I saw—he's a nobleman!" the old man finally gasped out when his grandchildren entered his bedroom after seeing their last guest retire.

"Grandpa," his granddaughter complained. "You don't need to continue the hoax for us. We thought it was a marvelous performance. The idiots will be flocking back here for years."

"No, no, I saw it... the emblem—his eagle—rise into the sky beneath the king's, and above both of theirs was another emblem, one that shone as the sun, blindingly, a king above them all. I saw it, yet when I tried to speak, a hand seemed to clench about my throat. It ripped out my tongue for hours."

"Grandpa," his grandson attempted this time, "don't be absurd. There is no possible way that pirate is a nobleman."

"He's the prince of Mira," the old man declared. "The only prince they'll ever have."

"Good night, papa," the other two wearily replied before softly shutting the door behind them. "The dream will straighten itself out in the morning." So they told themselves.

Mounting his horse outside his hunting lodge north of Ursa's capital, Makilka, Lord Emroy winced as a bright light flashed into his eyes. He looked up to see a falcon circling overhead. Something metallic had caught the sun's light along the bird's leg—the cause of that blinding flash.

"Boy," the lord commanded the page standing at his steed's head. "Find something that will lure that bird."

"That bird, my lord?" the boy asked, glancing upward.

"Of course! Something's on its leg."

"I'll bring it for you." Bowing, the boy slipped off into the nearby trees.

Impatiently tapping his thumbs on the reins, the lord waited, yet the boy was not gone ten minutes before the falcon dove into the trees. Almost immediately, the lord saw it rise again, seemingly unencumbered.

"How did you do it?" he demanded as the boy reemerged from the woods.

"He was hungry, my lord. It was fairly easy." With that statement, the boy dropped the item into his lord's outstretched hand.

Peering into his hand, the lord saw a bedraggled piece of parchment with a gold chain dangling off it. Carefully opening the parchment with barely a glance at the necklace, he stopped. Mira's letters stared up at him. Hurriedly pulling the pendant onto his palm, he gasped. "I must see the king!"

Without another word, the lord kicked his steed into a run. He would need to quickly gather supplies, but that would be his only stop.

Two days of riding brought him to the capital, where he hurriedly presented the note and necklace to King Navoriche. "It's Mira's own signet, sire!"

"Yes," the king growled in thought, reading the note. "But it's not much good. Everyone thinks the princess dead. No one would believe otherwise, which gives us no claim over anything."

"Would we even want an annihilated kingdom?"

"Of course. Our trained soldiers would easily kick those barbarians back out, however horrifying, and show them what power really is. But that's where we need unquestionable rights to the kingdom. If someone thinks we stole Mira, they would feel obligated to try the same."

"So, how can we obtain the rights if the signet is not enough?"

Fiddling with his thumbs, the king slowly mused, "If we spread word she is alive—a trophy of the savages—when the time is right or we find a good enough look-alike, we can say that we rescued her and she married one of our nobles... The signet will satisfy curiosity. Yes, I think that will work."

"But if someone does rescue her?"

Navoriche flicked his wrist dismissively. "Impossible. She's dead already. This had to have been sent at least a month ago."

"You mean it's *likely* she's already dead. But what if she's not?"

"That is such an absurd thought. She's dead. It's so unlikely she's anything else, it's laughable."

Bowing out, the lord muttered, "If it's that improbable, who's going to believe us?"

After another few days, Xavior sailed into a bay, one all the pirates clearly anticipated with eagerness. Even the captain stood against the starboard rail. Standing only a few paces away from him, Arnacin knew the pirates would never attack in their captain's presence. Like all the rest, the islander's gaze traveled over the land before them.

A village nestled along the edge of the dock, chimney smoke wafted into the air from little houses, a mixture of straight white-painted ones and others plastered in clay.

Many other ships already lay in harbor against the wood planks. Rising to the left of those watching on the *Zedelious*, a mountain towered above the bay, falling into a red-tinted cove at its feet.

Xavior nodded to the lagoon. "Devil's Cove, where all the dead are thrown. A fresh body must lie there even now, seeping the last dregs to the sharks." Arnacin looked sharply at him, and he laughed. "Yes, sharks. I'm sure you saw their sharp fins, circling as we approached. Don't think there is escape off this rock, Arnacin Islander. One girl tried it when she thought her captors' guard had slacked off. She slipped overboard, and the last ever seen of her was the circle of crimson on the surface of the water. Your blood would also turn the water a lovely shade."

Arnacin's unresponsive gaze remained fixed on the red water trickling into the bay from the cove.

"Heed this warning, Islander. Until you accept us as family, you may go wherever you like here on Baulis, but if you step on a ship, my crew will stick a bolt through you."

"And if I'm just fixing my ship?" Though the words were low, they were a challenge.

"Fix your ship. But cut the line, and it will be the last thing you ever do." Xavior received no answer.

As extensive as the pirate city was, Arnacin did not stop there once Xavior granted his men liberty to wander. Instead, the islander meandered through the milling city just long enough to reach the other end without suspicion and then ran for the wild. Ascending every incline he found through a forest mainly of ash trees, over a few patches of loose rock formations, Arnacin sought for a place to view the scope of the land.

Upon a pinnacle of rock, the islander stopped. Below, woods clambered down the slope toward the shores of a pathetic island, only about two miles wide in any direction. Forcing his rapid breathing out in a loud puff, Arnacin dropped to the rough, mineral ground. Honestly, he had expected nothing else, and yet the hard lump in his chest thickened with another layer of stone at the sight—the sight of an inescapable blot in the ocean.

The wild terrain was altered only by geysers bursting into the sky from a flat portion of rock and, in the opposite direction, by a lone city by the bay and a single mansion surrounded by guarded, high hedges, sitting over the cove. For some time, Arnacin sat watching the geyser jets without interest. Had they not moved so uniquely and frequently, they would not have captured his attention at all.

It was not too long, however, before his turmoil forced him back to movement. At the edge of the geysers' pool, he stopped, looking down into the steaming, foaming, boiling water not an inch from his dampening toes.

Hearing rustling behind him, Arnacin jumped away from the pool, whirling as a group of twenty leering pirates, one of them from the *Zedelious*, hauled another struggling pirate into the clearing.

"Ah, Islander," the *Zedelious* pirate cackled. "Is this where you dragged yourself? Good choice. I hear it's an excellent day for a swim." Around him, everyone else burst into laughter and proceeded to lift their whimpering captive over their heads.

Glancing swiftly to the geysers, Arnacin snapped, "Stop!"

Without paying him the slightest attention, they threw the pirate into the middle of the boiling water. As a short, hair-raising scream filled the air, a pirate snickered. "I dare anyone to try cheating me again."

Instead of staying to watch the rest of the slow cooking, Arnacin hastily retreated. As he did, the *Zedelious* crewmember called, "Wish to give it a go, Islander? I'd like nothing better."

"If you wish to take a dip yourself, try." Arnacin's hand dropped to his blade. "I hear it's an excellent day for it." With that, he disappeared, ignoring the stomach-churning popping sounds coming from the pool.

Known as Maco the Shipwright, the middle-aged man kept his shop with as much pride as possible, although he was no more than an invaluable captive of the pirates. He was fortunate if he was paid the right amount for his hard labor on the ships that frequented the city's harbor and sometimes his dry dock. Still, he managed to survive, if only with the grouchy assistance of his only friend, Brother Channing, the city doctor, captured long ago for the same reason as the shipwright—his usefulness.

If ever that usefulness ended, he had long ago been warned by their ruler, Jabril, that he would be tied to the bottom of his dry dock's framework before they flooded it again.

A week after Xavior's arrival on Baulis, while Maco sanded a board outside his back door, he looked up as he felt eyes on him.

A young, black-haired man stood appraising him, darkness exuding from the folds of his green cloak.

Without flinching, Maco met those cold eyes, not even sure of their color. "How may I assist you?"

"What type of ships have you built?" The answer, spoken in the common tongue, came with an unknown accent, closely akin to that of Mira yet unique unto itself. Pirates were acquired from all around.

Without pause, Maco shrugged. "Full-rigged, sloops, galleys, any warship you like. Back home, we had triremes and galliots. I can show you some of my drawings."

"What about single-sailor, single-mast ships?"

Remembering the only ship to fit that description, Maco properly scrutinized the pirate, "The small thing Xavior brought in? It's been here a week. I finished all the repairs on the *Zedelious*. Why are you here only now?"

"I didn't think you would be foolish enough to pry."

Quickly straightening, Maco replied, "No, I have not worked on that sort of ship, but it should be about the same as all the rest–wind, oars or tiller, balance, weight, so forth and so on. What part needs my attention?"

Those shudder-inducing eyes regarded him wordlessly for a long moment. Not only could Maco not decide their color, he found it impossible to read their darkness. They did not shine in hatred or scorn, nor did they reveal pain or sadness. They were simply black holes, yet those alone spoke of millions of thoughts swirling below the surface, none of them pleasant.

"My mast and sail," the pirate finally voiced.

"In what way?"

"I am looking for someone with more experience to help me think of a simple way to easily raise and lower the sail. My solution failed."

Looking askance at the pirate who dared admit failure, if in an extremely dangerous tone, the shipwright asked, "Will you show me your ship?"

Without another word, the pirate turned away, yet the order to follow shouted like the sun shone, unmistakable.

Maco noticed they were closely watched as they walked down to the quay. Any questions he had vanished as he stepped aboard the smaller ship he had noticed behind the *Zedelious* earlier that week. Unlike most ships, which rocked gently side-to-side, it hovered up and down with the lapping waves. Instead of the normal coverage of ropes and thin walkways, a clear, open deck appeared to stretch out forever, perhaps due to its thinness, clearness and lack of forecastle deck. In fact, no ropes existed, except for the black-streaked ratlines arching proudly to the top of the mast far above.

"What a ship," Maco breathed, staring up at the mast. "It's flat bottomed *and* perfectly balanced." He dropped his gaze back to the pirate silently watching him, one arm around one of the ratline ropes. "Who designed it?"

"Enchanters."

Maco paused, yet no leer, twitch or twinkle betrayed the pirate's thoughts. "How many people were intended to sail it before you tried adjusting it?"

"We thought two when we built it."

"You built it? From scratch?" His disbelief died after another look at the depths of the pirate's eyes. Shrugging, he nodded upward. "May I take a look?"

The only answer was a movement away from the rigging. Accepting the wordless invitation, Maco approached the mast where the top bar of the sail was oddly lying against the bottom bar. A strange crevice ran up the mast.

Shimmying up it, Maco discovered an intersecting channel three-quarters of the way around the top. It took the shipwright a moment to understand the function of the design. The crevice and channel were slides for the sail, allowing a single person to manage the sail and turn it sideways to cut into the opposing wind.

"In the first place, the channel actually weakens the design," Maco informed the pirate, drawing a loose sketch in the dirt floor of his shop's backroom. "Sooner or later, something will break, whether it is the attachment to the sail's arm or, worse, the mast. You were fortunate neither happened. That aside, in its simplest form, your idea is a good one. If you like, I will make a few sketches myself and, a day from now, I'll see what you think of them."

Wordlessly, the pirate accepted the dismissal, pausing at the door. "What will you take in exchange for your work?"

"I gather you are not intending to pay me in money?"

"I have none, but if you offer your assistance, I'm willing to give you mine in whatever jobs you would trust to me."

"Who are you?" Maco asked in astonishment.

Dark eyes remained empty as they stared at the shipwright.

Clearing his throat, Maco said, "The first job: the delivering of a name. I prefer to call no one Pirate or Black Pirate or Silence, or whatever else you can conceive."

"The pirates call me 'Arnacin Islander.' It will suffice." With that, the pirate vanished, the last sight of him being the end of his green cloak whisking around the corner of the door.

Maco was not sure he had ever met such a pirate before.

Only one idea would work, Maco knew. A hard clamp would lock around the top of the mast and slide smoothly down once loosened. But the first step was to replace the mast.

After drawing his idea onto parchment the next morning, he showed it to Arnacin Islander. After a second, the pirate asked, "How much would this clamp weigh?"

"On average, twenty-two pounds."

"What type of wood do you intend to use to replace the mast?"

"Here, I use alder, typically several alders per mast, but your ship is small enough we might not need to put that strain on it, if we can find the right tree."

Without even nodding, the pirate scraped Mira's numeral for ten into the floor with his foot. Maco watched amazed, as he soon had intricate number problems scrawled across the open space of the shipwright's floor. Finally, the pirate seemed satisfied and, stepping back over the temporary designs, he wrote his results in their proper places along the plan. At least according to Maco's estimates, the plan now included the exact weight, height and placement of the new mast along the actual length of his ship.

"Were you a shipwright originally?" Maco dared to ask, looking at the pirate in a new light. At the sardonic glance, the shipwright nodded. "Yes. You built your own ship. Well, you'd make one fine shipwright if ever you tired of piracy."

He was not sure, but for a split second, he thought he caught a bitter grin pass those features.

Whatever Arnacin Islander's story, he helped with the rebuilding every step of the way–the only assistant the shipwright ever had. Though they were watched by a pirate named Mr. Butter aboard the *Zedelious*, they were left alone.

Meanwhile, the shipwright provided the conversation, chatting about wood quality, the ship history of which he knew, the main similarities in all the vessels harbored there, the way of life on the island and whatever else came to mind. Only once in the following days did his companion speak, in order to tell him he made too much noise.

"Well, someone needs to supply the smiles around here," Maco had said with a shrug, unintentionally ending that conversation.

It was clear after the first day that the pirate was Miran, not just from the diluted accent but from the clothing, the Miran emblem on his–likely stolen–sword's sheath and the fact that he wrote in their characters when they made notes on Maco's new plans of the ship. Other than that, the strangeness of Arnacin Islander far outweighed the clues into his persona. What had led him into piracy? What type of pirate was he? Was he actually a pirate? What could he be, were he not a pirate? The shipwright spent many futile hours puzzling over those things.

A week after meeting Arnacin Islander, Maco received an answer to one of his many questions.

One sunny day, as Maco returned from working on Islander's vessel, ship-owner alongside him, sudden screams caught the shipwright's attention. In the center of town, officials were flogging a pirate.

Nodding grimly, Maco simply continued on, until he noticed the alert stillness in his client. "That," the shipwright explained, nodding in the direction of the flogging, "followed by two days shackled in the stocks without water, is our city's official punishment for thievery on the rare occasions when pirates don't take matters into their own hands."

Those dark eyes flicked toward him, though Islander did not stir otherwise. His gaze was, as ever, indecipherable. Guessing at the thoughts behind it, Maco nodded. "Yes, there is a government here, of sorts. The master might like to remain anonymous to increase fear, but even those who know him know he's deadly if the need arises. Otherwise, the whole island would likely be naught but a bloodbath."

"It *is* a bloodbath." The billow of Islander's cloak as he strode past, leading the way back to the shop, emphasized his dark tone.

Contemplating Arnacin Islander's words, the shipwright followed. It was an interesting piece of information.

He had more to consider the next day, as he emerged from his shop to see Arnacin Islander shove through the guards around the stocks to pour water down the culprit's throat. Instantly, a guard lunged toward the one guilty of disregarding their law. Yet, so swiftly and smoothly no eye could follow it, Islander blurred, and the guard dropped to the ground, clutching his bloodied weapon arm.

The waterskin lay trickling its contents into the dirt, and Arnacin Islander stood outside the ring of guards. "Don't move if you value your existence."

No one questioned his ability to carry out the threat. In the stillness, Islander walked away, wiping his bloody blade on the end of his shirt, seemingly indifferent to the guards' further actions. Everyone who watched knew better than to dare assume such a thing, yet Maco knew it was not the end of the commotion. No one could attack an official without being punished.

"You want me to spare him?" Jabril, the master of Baulis and owner of the mansion overlooking Devil's Cove, turned to Xavior. Below the mansion's upper porch, the officials forced Arnacin into the stocks.

"That is, unless you want someone incapable to inherit the *Zedelious*? Spyros would be quite glad."

"Of course, I want the *Zedelious* to stay in the family. Yet is this Arnacin Islander really the Zedelious you want?"

For a long moment, Xavior stared at the top of the black head below them. "He has all the skills required."

"Yet he interferes."

Xavior shook his head. "That was a complete surprise. He hates them."

"Surprise or not—"

"Listen, I want to see what another year at sea will bring. Some freedom here will allow him to settle. By spring, he should be ready for real training. If you care about our family pride, let him keep his life and health."

"On one condition... He agrees not to interfere with this government again."

Xavior grinned. "He doesn't care enough about anyone to interfere again."

"What did they do?" the shipwright asked when Arnacin Islander returned a few days later.

Islander, however, merely glanced at the shipwright, taking in the reason for the question, and then pulled his sleeves back over the angry red shackle-marks on his wrists.

"Brother Channing, our city healer, has ointment for that," Maco said. Yet looking into those dark eyes, he knew no help would be accepted.

All the same, he visited the healer-monk that night to procure some of the ointment and left the little bottle on his own backroom table, where Islander could not fail to see it. It was never touched.

Once they finished Islander's mast, the shipwright accepted the pirate's offer of odd jobs as payment. At first, Maco requested his shop's backroom be cleaned, where things had become somewhat disorganized. As far as Maco knew, Islander did not even sleep for two days, during which time the backroom was transformed. The shipwright did discover that the pirate had removed his back door, though. Shaking his head, Maco decided not to ask why it was leaning against the opposite wall.

"If you would like," the shipwright said after inspecting the room, "many of my plans need redrawing and preserving. I'm sure you saw the condition of them."

"Does it matter? As long as you keep enough for anyone's inquiries into your talent..."

As the pirate trailed off, Maco explained, "Many of them are actual plans of the ships in harbor, either now or later. Until those ships are no more, it saves much time to have detailed drawings of them at hand, and time is of the essence. If I cannot meet the demands of even one pirate, my value to them will drop. Too much of that, and they'll drown me."

"What a pity," Arnacin Islander scoffed. Nevertheless, he dropped to his knees by the chest of drawings.

Surprised at the pirate's act of trust, it was a moment before Maco commented, "I am, of course, assuming you can draw details with perfect accuracy."

Dark eyes flicked upward. "If you want a technical drawing, I am practiced in them."

"Well, then... The ones that are still in readable condition, you can just coat with this," he instructed, holding out a bottle. "Naturally, if you need to redraw them, you coat them afterward as well."

As he expected, no response came. The shipwright hovered around long enough to guarantee the pirate's skills were adequate. Observing that they were, he left to see to other tasks.

A week after starting the job, Arnacin paused as a shout echoed into the backroom. "Fix the tiller! I want to be out of here in another four hours!"

"Captain Phillio, you just sailed into harbor." Maco's voice replied. "I–"

"The *Zedelious* is here! If he realizes I'm in port, Xavior will not waste a moment to rip every Nomacirrian on this island to shreds by nightfall. The tiller holds for now, but it's weak. My crew's emergency repairs won't last another voyage. Open your dry dock! I'll have the ship sailed in. You have four hours!"

Clomping sounds indicated his departure. As Maco wearily stepped into his backroom, Arnacin passed him the ship's plans marked with Captain Phillio's name.

The shipwright paused, staring at the plans for just a second. "I shouldn't need it for a tiller, but thanks. It still might be useful once I see the exact problem." Grabbing his essential tools, he slipped past the islander and out the door.

With only a second's hesitation, Arnacin followed, pulling his hood over his hair.

He caught up to them as the captain was growling, "Make sure your work is satisfactory. I have my hands full with just Xavior and that high and mighty queen of Nomacir. I can't safely put into any port, at least until the spring, but if that rotten ship isn't gone, you can bet on warfare right here. I've had enough."

Casting a glance at the captain, Maco licked his lips. "You're not connected to the queen, captain. Why are you so certain Xavior will hunt you down?"

"Ha! He only sees that I'm from Nomacir, and he'll leap at any excuse to steal my gold! I'll tell you something, if I ever come across any of Zedelious's family, I'll burn them alive before Xavior stumbles on them. His son's death was lucky, I say."

The islander tugged his hood more closely about his head, yet the shipwright engaged the captain's attention with his muttered question, "Have you ever considered surrendering to Queen Isholt and apologizing? She might return you to a better position than you're in now, running for your life."

Clenching his sword hilt, Captain Phillio warned, "Another suggestion like that, slave, and I'll run you through. That queen is everything I hate—deceitful, arrogant, covetous, complaining and stupid. I'll sooner become a privateer for the backstabbing Ursans!"

Arnacin could find nothing to criticize in that. Even Maco only nodded as they stopped before the massive *Queen's Head*.

Within three hours, the *Queen's Head* had sailed for the open ocean. Wearily, Maco returned to the back of his shop. He had just put his awl away when a quiet voice asked, "Why is there a feud between Nomacir and this family of Zedelious?"

Looking at the pirate who sat, seemingly completely involved in copying every line with precision, Maco inquired, "I would think you knew. You are a Zedelious, are you not?"

When no response came, the shipwright almost doubted hearing the question. Yet, shrugging, he turned back to the railing he had been working on before Captain Phillio's interruption. "There used to be a ship, *The Red Dawn*, that sailed into harbor every summer for three years. The captain of that ship was Captain Xavior's son, an extremely successful pirate despite his young age. Rumor has it he secretly sold his services to almost every single country at once, backstabbing and lying when two tasks conflicted. Whether any of that is true or not, you can imagine that with their dislike of pirates, Nomacir would not be on that list of money brokers and, with an unmarried queen, they would be the target of many.

"Really, no one has any idea how he acquired wealth so rapidly, but it is considered a fact that he plagued Nomacir without ceasing. If that is true, it is only natural that Nomacir finally caught up with him—and, with him, there was no such thing as being 'found guilty.' He would've announced with pride how many ships he sent down during his short reign. An outrageous quantity, I can assure you.

"On Nomacir, the punishment for piracy is near death through flogging and then the rope, I'm told."

"I've seen it."

"Well, you likely know that Xavior has hunted Nomacirrians down ever since. I suspect he'll go to his grave still doing so or..." Glancing at his companion, staring motionless out the open door into the night, Maco breathed, "Or commit suicide the day he wins. At that point, he'll know there's nothing left—such is the path of vengeance."

In the stillness that followed, the shipwright heard the low hiss, "Is that meant as a warning?"

"If you wish it so." Maco shrugged. "I always hope no one needs that warning, that they know better intuitively. As an interesting example of how ridiculous vengeance is, if Captain Phillio expects to enact his threat, he doesn't know that the richest, wealthiest pirate alive is not Captain Xavior."

Dark eyes fixed themselves on him, and Maco laughed sardonically. "Do you want to know who shoddily upholds the laws on this island, who receives a 'safety portion' from every captain once a year to keep Baulis a pirate haven, who those pirate guards bow to for the easy, safe money granted them, a pittance though it is? Zedelious's son by his secret second wife, whom he never took to sea. His mansion is the one that sits on the steps leading to the cliffs of Devil's Cove, and do you want to know why Captain Xavior has not been seen since arriving? He's up there himself, with his three mistresses who await him there every year."

Disgust wrote itself across Arnacin Islander's face before he turned away. Maco returned once again to the railing.

The days stretched on. In the shop's peace, Arnacin's thoughts seared all the more torturously. His time as Xavior's captive had gone on too long. The pirate cooked in the geyser pool particularly plagued the islander as atrocities happened daily, just within his view. He knew, if no one else did, that he had to change something or the insanity that awaited him would finally completely claim him. Even alcohol, if he turned to it, would not protect him from such a breakdown. He knew it was just a matter of time before something happened—and so it was.

Spotting a girl in disarray duck around the wall of the house facing the shipwright's yard, Arnacin paused. The girl's wide eyes looked twice their normal size, so much did they shine with hysteria.

As she quickly glanced around the corner, Arnacin shoved aside his work. "The cellar, quick!" he ordered, pointing to the open door in the house she was hiding behind.

The girl turned her wide eyes toward him and tried to dash past. The sound of pounding feet, however, told the islander of their lack of time. Quickly, he grabbed her. She struggled in his grasp and, as he heard those feet halt suddenly, he knew they had been seen.

Dropping all attempts at gentleness, Arnacin shoved the girl into the cellar and spun to meet the attack.

"Fetch the girl," someone said. As the islander found himself facing two attackers, there was nothing he could do about the pirate who slipped around him into the cellar.

Chapter 6

BROTHER CHANNING

MACO RETURNED TO HIS SHOP after affixing a new helm to the *Dawn Beer*. Hearing some commotion outside the back door, he quickly strode through his shop, noticing the absence of his temporary assistant as he passed.

Outside, a ring of pirates jeered and shouted at some fight in their midst. Expecting a simple brawl, Maco's breath froze when one of the pirates forming the circle stepped into the middle. Through the brief hole, the shipwright saw the body-strewn ground, blood-tinged sand and the target of the many attackers—Arnacin Islander. Judging by the way he staggered before parrying the new opponent's blade, it would not be long before the pirates obtained their goal.

"What is this?" Maco barked.

"Stay out of this, shipwright," one pirate growled, standing farther back with two other pirates who held a whimpering girl between them. "This is a matter of justice."

"All the same, I demand an explanation! Are you so bloodthirsty you choose death before conversation can settle it?"

Surprisingly, stillness fell over the ring. The same pirate spat, "Islander dares to steal my wife! You do not need anything more."

Looking again at the bawling girl, Maco asked, "Arnacin?" In answer to the charge, Arnacin simply flicked his damp hair out of his face, his chest heaving with every breath.

Despite his silence, however, the girl hysterically screamed, "I fled! I won't go back! I won't! I'll kill myself!"

With a disgusted glance at her, Arnacin finally growled, "You ought to thank me for stopping her from throwing herself off some cliff."

"Thief! I won't thank you for nothing until I see your body in the cove," the supposed husband spat.

"Yours first."

"All right," the shipwright interjected, "Take your *property* and leave him alone. Only gentlemen like you would charge someone with thievery for helping an abused girl."

"Are you questioning what I can do to my own property? You'll be a lot easier to kill than that brat!"

Arnacin's blade lifted a little higher. "Who'd die, I wonder."

"Enough!" the shipwright snapped. "I notice, sir, that although he was 'stealing' from you, you stand outside the fight."

Without another word, the pirate grabbed the girl's wrist and dragged her away. Slowly, the rest took their leave, casting withering glances at Arnacin's bloody sword. Once the last had disappeared down the street, Islander gasped in pain. Turning to him, Maco watched him shakily clean his blade on his thigh. "Are you alright?"

Islander only limped back into the shop.

Without asking, Maco fetched some water. Yet as he handed it to Arnacin and turned away, he heard a soft splash. At the islander's feet, a quickly dissolving puddle soaked into the dry dirt floor.

The shipwright suppressed his frustrated growl. "You're not the easiest man to live with, Islander."

"You don't have to. I'm leaving soon."

"Why sail with them? We could find some way for you to remain here, out of Captain Xavior's reach."

"And within yours. I refuse to be anyone's slave, war machine or anything else, and I am returning to sea. When his ship sinks in the next storm or is burned beneath the waves, I will be on it, owned by none."

Softly, the shipwright said, "Only you have the power to make yourself a slave. To the pirates that shelter here, I am one, but would you deem me so?"

"You don't wish to hear what I deem you."

"Perhaps I do."

Turning away, Arnacin took a minute before replying. "Anyone with any sort of decency would leave this place. They would never stand for what you just allowed, nor dare call a person, however revolting, 'property.' Interpret that as you will."

"And why don't you leave? You have a superb vessel, which is now fixed." When no answer came, Maco insisted, "I am not here to protect everybody. I keep peace when it is possible for words to stop the bloodshed. Unless all their captives revolt, there is nowhere to hide her, and rebelling would likely mean all our deaths, not escape. Most of us who aren't pirates are females, and none of us know half as much about weapons as do our captors. I called her property only in disgust at how they view women."

"Tell that to someone who's dumb enough to believe it." With that, Arnacin shoved himself to his feet, swayed for a second, and then left.

Maco waited only until he knew Arnacin Islander would not hear him, then hurried to the shack of his sole friend, Brother Channing. Here, injuries were often roughly cleaned and stitched before the victims were kicked out. The shipwright found his friend in the back, bottle-feeding a goat where pens kept the injured or sick animals.

"Channing," Maco panted, receiving little more of a response than if he had still been with Arnacin.

"These goats are just like their owners, injured day in and out from brawling with each other. Then, of course, they're still so violent I need to drug them, forcing me to feed them all like babes."

"Channing," Maco insisted. "Speaking of violent pirates–"

"They were all fighting a few moments ago, I know. What's your interest?"

"Arnacin Islander."

With a sarcastic humming, the healer huffed to his feet. "He's half the city's interest, I must say–the most effective killer on this rock, and that's saying something. They all say he cheats. Thankfully, that means I don't have to patch up any of his victims."

"Channing, I think he could be dead very shortly if we do nothing."

"Is Captain Xavior going to blame you or something?"

"Channing."

"He's just a pirate–"

"Channing!"

"Fine, answer this and I might help: why do you care if he breathes or not?"

"Because he's Arnacin Islander. I know that means nothing to you. I can't even put a name to it, but I feel if he's just given the chance... he's meant for something, Channing..." Pausing in exasperation at the words he could not express, Maco pleaded, "Trust me. Help, please. I'm guessing he headed to the creek. I'm also guessing someone will trail him."

Moaning, the healer grabbed his bag. "If you insist..."

The pain in Arnacin's shoulder caused the world to spin. A small part of him called himself a fool. He desperately needed water, and it was far more dangerous to travel in his current state than to accept Maco's compassion.

For just a second, he had almost taken that water, but as he looked into its depths, he recalled how he had once readily accepted Carpason's hospitality. That image was replaced with thoughts of his last hour on Mira. He heard Valoretta's silence, and Miro's... everything about Miro.

Should Maco stand aside for Baulis's officials to converge on Arnacin–if he had not already done so–the islander's heart would feel no pain, unless he cracked open that door to his trust. Never again could he allow anyone inside his shields who was not from Enchantress Island. The potential for pain and the extent of the agony were too high to risk.

Twice, he stopped on the way to the nearest creek in the woods, unsure if the footsteps he thought he heard, under the influence of fear and pain, were just normal forest sounds. Yet both times, he heard nothing unusual.

Once at the creek, he halted again to listen. Yet the forest's peace sounded complete. Knowing unconsciousness was near should he not relieve his thirst soon, he crouched by the water. He had not taken so much as a sip before he heard movement behind him and whirled toward the pirate rushing him.

Had his arm listened like it should have, that threat would not have taken another breath, but he moved too slowly. Fire burst in his shoulder as he forced it to swift movement. In that split second, the pirate seized Arnacin's sword-arm. Dark spots burst like fireworks as the pirate viciously twisted it.

His focus faded in and out as the pirate taunted him, "I knew you leave the city for water. Know better than to steal from the wells—what with the possibility of arsenic and all. Don't worry, I'll give you water."

Arnacin was not aware of the pirate jerking him around until water closed over his head and instantly filled his lungs. Brief panic broke through his state of semi-consciousness, yet even temporary full awareness could not summon air as he gagged on water.

Freezing as Maco seized his arm, Channing looked to where his friend was pointing. Between the trees, he saw a burly pirate strangling the one he recognized as Islander. While shipwright and healer watched, the attacker, one arm around his victim's throat and the other restraining his weapon arm, shoved his motionless, gasping victim to the ground. There he pushed the black-topped head beneath the water.

"Channing," Maco hissed. "Pretend you're out here picking herbs. Everyone knows they curse themselves if they kill another in your presence. Hurry."

"He's dead already," the healer huffed. Nevertheless, he stepped to the water's edge, looking at the plants growing alongside it as he closed the space between himself and the struggle without appearing to hurry.

Halting abruptly, he gasped, "What's this?"

The burly pirate froze, looking up at the healer in disgust.

"You better halt," Channing continued. "I can see the gates of death opening beneath you already."

Fear conquered the pirate's gaze, and he sprang to his feet. Kicking his victim into the creek, he growled, before stomping away, "I don't see why I'd be killed for meting out justice."

"You can come back to it later."

Huffing as the pirate disappeared into the thicker forest, Channing yanked up his habit and waded into the creek to grab the floating form by the hair and drag him onto dry land. No gasp of air or choking cough stirred the sopping heap. Shaking his head, the healer dropped down to push his linked hands below the rib cage.

"I frankly still don't know why you bother," Channing said, placing his instruments inside his bag. "This pirate certainly has not bothered to make any companions."

Sitting in the small, dim living space above the shipwright's shop, Maco looked at the sleeping form from whom they had emptied all the excess water before the healer checked him over to make sure the attack had left no lasting damage.

"I think that's part of it," the shipwright whispered, his gaze traveling from Arnacin's slightly furrowed brow to his blood-stained, still slightly-damp clothes, which they had left on to tend to their patient. "I've seen him sit for hours downstairs while I work around him—times when he has made no effort to change the fact that he's easy prey should I decide to attack. Somewhere, I know he trusts, but only when trusting doesn't take conscious thought."

Channing snorted.

Smiling slightly, Maco commented, "That bitterness ill becomes a man of the church."

"Ha! There were men with worse attitudes in the holy of holies." With that, Channing stood. "His arm still seems to be in its socket and there's nothing wrong with his lungs. Leave him alone. He'll wake when he's ready."

Sitting in the silence of the room, Maco watched as Arnacin passed from deep to light sleep. The difference was marked by a gradual increase in restless movement.

Watching tears trickling past the confines of dark lashes, Maco wondered how long it would take before his own breathing would alert Xavior's captive. Part of the shipwright hoped it would take quite some time, for he saw in that moment, as the dark, bitter shields were lowered, some of what lay beneath the hatred and distrust.

As those black lashes flickered a second later, however, Maco quickly feigned sleep.

If not for the mattress's rustle as Arnacin slid off it, the shipwright would not have known the other man had moved. That sound cued his pretend yawn, and he lifted his eyelids in time to see Arnacin recoil warily.

"Do you wish to tell me why you won't simply escape? Your ship is seaworthy once again." Maco asked.

"They would shoot me the minute I cut the rope," Arnacin whispered, closing his cloak about himself. "You yourself know Mr. Butter guards both ships almost ceaselessly."

"He has never struck me as being so bloodthirsty."

Arnacin only made to slip out the door. Hastily, Maco volunteered, "Arnacin, I'm willing to be your shield. They'll only have one shot and, if they hit me, you're free."

Xavior's captive stilled, yet the glance he threw the shipwright was like flint, a refusal to believe the offer, at least without more of a reason.

"I've lived long enough, here in particular," Maco explained. "But if you wish to know the honest answer, once upon a time, you weren't who you are now. I know," he quickly added before Arnacin could interrupt, "that could be said for everyone on this rock, but they are far beyond recovering their former selves. Anything can happen, of course. But your past self lies just beyond reach. I have spent years trying to bring someone a little good. If I could help you avoid the shark jaws looming before you, my wish would be fulfilled."

Bitterness blazed in Arnacin's gaze, yet through it, the tiniest amount of hope flickered. A long moment passed. "It's a pity I don't believe a word of it," he eventually said. As he made to leave, however, Maco boldly grabbed his arm.

"What don't you believe?"

"Everything!" Arnacin struggled to pull his right arm away. "You yourself admitted you're tired of staying here and that there are not enough captives to escape. Only a fool wouldn't believe you were going to reverse that 'shield' at the last minute and use your knowledge of ships to escape yourself."

"Your distrust blinds you, Arnacin," Maco whispered.

With a lift of the chin, Arnacin stated, "I've seen enough manip-ulators to know better. So, don't lie to me."

His shoulders sagging, the shipwright let him go.

To Maco's surprise, Arnacin was back in his shop the next day, resuming work on the shipwright's maps, diagrams and ship plans. Shaking his head, Maco tossed the remainder of the seal hide he had been applying to the bottom of a gig. "You didn't have to come back. I'm sure any amount of trust you possessed is gone." He heard the note of bitterness in his own voice and looked away from the indigo gaze that flicked upward.

"How much more work will it take to pay for your labor and supplies?"

In surprise, Maco met his companion's gaze. "Why should it matter? You've paid me ten times my usual recompense."

Arnacin simply returned to his work.

Involuntarily, Maco smiled. "Oh, Arnacin." He shook his head. "You would honor yourself straight into the hangman's noose."

"I already have." The soft, serious whisper carried across the backroom, fixing the shipwright in place with the depth of defeat behind it.

A day later, Maco looked up as someone stopped in the doorway. It took a second for him to recognize the hazy figure rimmed in pink from the sun setting behind him. "Channing! What brings you here today?"

Coming around the counter, the healer settled himself onto the shipwright's workbench with a huff. "I never leave an unfinished job. Are there any signs of injury now that he's up?"

Smiling, Maco put down his work. "You can't fool me, friend. You're interested." When Channing only folded his arms, the shipwright shrugged. "Islander's working. He seems to be fine."

In response, the healer only pursed his lips. But in the silence, Maco inched closer, admitting in a whisper he hoped would not carry, "I'm concerned, Channing. With how he is, he's never going to accept help. He'll die before he does, or Xavior will kill him. He himself insists it will be so."

"Maco, why do you think I have no belief anymore in all that meaning and purpose stuff? You can work yourself into the grave, and everyone does exactly what they please with no desire to change."

"But you can't deny that Arnacin is different."

With a snort, Channing rose. "That doesn't mean you can do anything to help him. He's still content to damn himself. Let him, since he's so determined."

Grimacing, Maco picked up his tools. "Only a part of him is determined. I want to find the other part before it's too late."

"I think you're a fool to try and I can't help you, but if you think he's physically well, I'll come back tomorrow. Something might have changed by then."

Shaking his head, Maco smiled grimly. "I know better, Channing. You're not really the least bit afraid of missed injuries."

Without making any answer, the healer left.

Ships sailed off the island as spring approached. However, the *Zedelious* did not. Meanwhile, Arnacin grew ever more restless. With growing frequency, he would leave Maco's shop after the mornings to wander through the forest, especially now, with Channing's visits becoming ever more common. Yet, even long walks were no relief from the prison of that island.

While shuffling despondently to the woods one evening, Arnacin paused after hearing raised voices and pounding feet headed up the street toward him. As the islander stepped out of the road, a pirate stumbled headlong past him, purposely knocking over anything that could fall into the street as he flew by.

The shouts grew louder. "Cayd! Rat!" Pursuers came hard behind with blades drawn and eyes glinting. Beholding those faces—faces that matched those of the pirates by the geysers months before—Arnacin's heart burned with hatred. Yet for a moment, he did not move as he watched the crowd disappear into the woods ahead.

He cared little what they did to each other. Every single one of the pirates deserved the backstabbing they received. And yet...

Relenting, Arnacin yanked his hood up and disappeared into the woods on the trail of the hunters.

Following the shouts and snapping underbrush, Arnacin shadowed the pirates to the geysers' edge. There, the pursued pirate, Cayd, jerked to a halt and turned. Now that he was unable to run any farther, the horror and fear on his face quickly gave way to defiance as he confronted his leering opponents and drew his blade.

Slowly, the victim's attackers closed in, but Arnacin did not give them the chance to strike. Like a wolf, silent in the hunt, he charged the nearest pirate.

Only a brief gurgling scream as the Tarmlin blade sank through that pirate's abdomen alerted his compatriots. "Islander! Islander!" The hate-filled cry rose into the air. Many pirates whirled to face their new enemy, only to find they were in the middle of a two-front attack.

In the confusion that followed, Cayd broke through, dashing into the woods. After finishing off his current assailant, Arnacin followed.

He heard the pirates give chase with angry shouts and their crashing through the underbrush. Yet he lost them in the woods. Pausing only long enough to mark the position of the fleeing victim by the softer sounds of cracking branches and rustling leaves, the islander took off in the same direction.

Catching up with Cayd, Arnacin jerked him behind a thicker tree. "Follow every move carefully and as softly as possible," he hissed.

Meekly, the pirate nodded, and the islander set off on a zigzag flight.

Until darkness overshadowed them, they led their pursuers in circles about the woods. Then, as Arnacin heard Cayd falling behind in the dark, he slowed the harsh, twisting pace.

"They're not that far," he whispered, stepping aside to avoid collision with the night-blinded pirate. Torchlight flickered forty paces away. If they were quiet, the lights might pass by, but counting on that was insanity. "Do you have a hood?"

"On board me ship. Cap'n won' be pleased, 'ough."

"I'll find you something. Lie down close to a tree and stay still." So ordering, Arnacin slipped off.

Even cloaks would not be able to hide them should anyone see beneath their hoods, and the palpable nervousness of Cayd shifting beside Arnacin under the lantern of the healer's door made it more likely someone would find them. "Do not even look," Arnacin breathed. "Not back, not to the side. Pretend someone in your crew needs a doctor—that is all."

"And if theer righ' be'ind us?" The pirate quivered.

"Stop trembling and you should hear them." Yet Arnacin knew they were being watched. He sensed it.

Just as Brother Channing opened the door and Arnacin shoved Cayd nearly into the healer, burning pain shot up the islander's left arm. His haste carried him forward, and he slammed the door on the charging pirates. Only then did he glance down to see a knife hilt protruding from his upper left arm.

Someone struck the door from the other side. "'ealer!" An angry voice demanded. "Send them two out or we'll come in!"

Brother Channing simply ignored the demand, quickly closing the space between himself and the islander. Arnacin ducked away. "No! I can take care of it."

"Is it through the bone?"

The islander shook his head. Yet as he made to grab the hilt, the healer snapped, "Don't yank it out!"

Sending Brother Channing a baleful glance, the islander proceeded to inch the knife out. All the same, the slowness made it even more agonizing. Arnacin could barely control his sharp hisses every time the blade moved slightly.

"Theey'll come in!" Cayd's outburst captured the healer's attention, as if in sudden recognition of his existence and of the continued demands from outside.

Rummaging in his supplies, the healer coolly stated, "They know they can't harm anyone under this roof."

"Oh, yes," Arnacin hissed through his torment. "It's cursed. What terrible endings befall them here?"

As the room swayed, thick wool pressed beneath the blade. The islander jerked away, yet Channing seized his injured arm with the warning, "Don't move." In a softer tone, he commented, "Islander, why would you put yourself to such trouble for him?"

"For him?" Arnacin scoffed despite gritted teeth. "I'm just saving myself. Nothing can save them from where they're going."

"Sure, you are... By making enemies of every captain and crew-member in existence? My, my..."

"What am I gon' do?" Cayd spoke up again.

Struggling through the pain, Arnacin gasped, "The *Dawn Beer* sails tomorrow morning. Do yourself a favor and be on it."

"In the meantime," Brother Channing added without looking up from the ever-darkening red cloth, "you may take yourself into that back room and sleep. I swear, nothing will attack you while you are here. Men of my sort are able to curse their enemies as they see fit."

At the dangerous tone in the healer's words, the pirate shuf-fled off in submission. Arnacin watched him leave before weakly returning his attention to the man holding his arm, who had finally freed the knife from the wound. "I don't suppose you have ways of proving that."

"You don't believe, I see. Why ever not?"

"You should be grateful most of them are a superstitious lot. I am not."

"Then you also won't believe that I know some magic tricks that are enough to convince them." Sitting back on his heels as he lit a candle and held a needle above it, Brother Channing asked, "Would you like me to wash the blood out of that shirt when we're done here?"

Flinching away, Arnacin asked, "Does this shirt look like I care about bloodstains?"

"You don't want me to say what that shirt makes me think," the healer quipped without looking up.

It was almost amusing how wrong Channing was, how his suspi-cions protected the truth that Arnacin was actually hiding the massive scar over his right shoulder. Yet... the healer was right.

Miro had murdered Arnacin of Enchantress Island and Xavior had finished whatever was left.

As that thought wiped the slight grin from the islander's face, silence fell in the room. Outside, the voices drifted off as the pirates left. While the healer stitched the wound through a wide rip in the sleeve, Arnacin held his breath.

Only when Channing finished binding the wound with herbs and clean linen, did he say, "I would suggest wearing a sling for a few days or the stitches may break."

"Oh, yes, as if that's a fear when a sling will just shout, 'He's injured. Attack!'"

"I did not suggest leaving this house, Islander."

Arnacin's gaze darkened. "I'm not staying here."

"Islander," the healer warned, "you can't go through life trusting no one. If you never trust, there will likely come a day—such as this one—when you have no choice. To choose not to trust is to choose death. You, yourself, admitted that a sling will be an invitation for everyone on this island to end your days. Yet without one, that wound will open and infection could set in. If it does, you will die without help. I think I have enough experience to know. Must I further convince you?"

When Arnacin remained unresponsive, Channing added, "You may not trust me, Islander, but in times like this, you do have someone to trust. He will not allow your death until your time."

His gaze flicking back up to meet the healer, Arnacin breathed, "You're assuming something."

"I doubt you would feel duty-bound to rescue criminals unless you acknowledge His presence. No one else, no other god, would spare them. I know your trust doesn't go beyond that knowledge, but my strongest advice is for you to change that. He might help." He said no more and just sat there, as if waiting. Arnacin ignored him, though his heart tightened.

Surrendering, Channing whispered, "Rest, Islander. You can be sure no harm will come to you under this roof."

As if his words held some spell, Arnacin's eyelids grew ever heavier, despite his resistance. In moments, sleep conquered him.

An hour before dawn, Cayd left without a word. Channing sniffed in disdain, yet Arnacin Islander showed no sign he even noticed. Glancing at his remaining guest, the healer returned to rolling his linen bandages.

Although Islander was still curled on the floor, his head pillowed on his right arm, Channing noticed his left fingers rested over his hilt. It would have been terribly unwise, however, to mention how idiotic it would be to draw the blade with that hand.

Finally, Channing inquired, "For curiosity's sake, Islander, how are you saving yourself by inciting the hatred of three thousand pirates?"

He expected no answer and for some time he received none, yet he felt those eyes studying him. Then, softly came the reply. "You call yourself a healer. Can you live with yourself when everyone around you tortures and kills one another while you watch and do nothing?"

Such answer gave Channing pause, and he appraised Arnacin Islander anew. Eventually, he shrugged. "There is nothing to do to stop it. I'm here to take care of wounds, that's all."

He dropped his gaze back to his linens. A second later, his attention snapped back to his companion as Islander breathed, "Then you've lost as much meaning as I have."

Those blue eyes were shuttered again, but the healer replied, "It doesn't matter what you do, nothing changes. They *like* to kill themselves. And who believes in meaning as something that can be lost, if it's there at all?"

"An islander's parents said every worm is born with purpose, although it is easily destroyed." Islander's words were even softer, as if he was talking to himself.

Silence again fell in the shack.

"You are stalling, brother," Jabril growled, his fingers tapping on his arm. "It won't gain you what you want. Islander will not become a pirate."

When Xavior only shifted against the column, Jabril insisted, "I don't care that he's killed as many as he has. It is the island's policy to allow individuals to seek their own justice unless the captain protests. That way, everyone but the dead is happy, the population is never too large, and the island's location is a secret they'll all keep, since they'll want the safety from—"

"What are you trying to say?" Xavior snapped. "If you mean that I should remove Islander's weapon since he is a captive, you're mistaken. He'd be dead within a moment. And on board the *Zedelious*, he only attacks when he has to defend himself. As far as I'm concerned, the fear the crew has of him will be useful if he ever becomes captain."

"Ah ha! You say *if*. Then you also realize that he is the enemy of every ship's crew because he's not a pirate and they know he'll never be one."

Xavior only looked at him. Angrily, Jabril threw up his arms. "For Zedelious's pride—the pride of our heritage—I am willing to execute him in private. He will simply disappear, and no one will know what happened."

Compressing his lips, Xavior turned away.

"I want him dead, Xavior, because I can only foresee him destroying our heritage. I know that not only is he a Zedelious, but his appearance reminds you of your dead son. Yet I look at him and I see death in his face—not greed or power—death. You failed to train anything else in him. He is the Black Captain manifest. Do you know that poem?"

"Yes," Xavior whispered in defeat. "You know Father insisted the Black Captain was our ancestor. He used such fear to his advantage." For a long moment, he was quiet. Then, turning back to his half-brother, he admitted, "I sail within the week. Islander goes with me, and I hope he finally surrenders. But if he does anything similar to his actions here, I will make him pay. No one refuses a Zedelious without losing more than just his life."

A week later, Islander was absent from the shipwright's shop. Knowing what it meant, Maco shuffled out to the dock. Channing also stood there, watching Xavior's crew bustling about on the deck and in the rigging as each sail dropped and furled.

Teasingly, Maco inquired, "Suddenly like this ship?"

"It's the gold," his friend huffed to the shipwright's amusement. "There goes the wealthiest ship in port."

"Funny you never knew that before." The healer made no reply, and they dropped into companionable silence.

Before them, the *Zedelious's* anchor rose, and the ship turned toward the open ocean. As it did, a dark figure could be seen leaning on the aft rails of the smaller ship towed behind.

"Oddly, he's challenged my thinking," Channing muttered. "The first person in eons to do so. I hate to admit this, but you were right. Perhaps he was the reason we're here: to help him rediscover his ordained path."

Softly, the shipwright said, "You know he'll never have the chance unless a miracle happens and he escapes his captain's grasp."

"Well, it's out of our hands now. We'll see what comes next year."

"I hope he takes my advice and escapes."

As Channing began chuckling, Maco glanced over. "Fancy such advice coming from you," the healer said. "I dare say I wouldn't take it. You're not trying to escape."

"You and I are the only men here that are not pirates, and one ship or another is always here, no matter the season. I don't have much choice, do I?"

"Sure, mate. You and I could become pirates or privateers for that matter. Pick some country out there, sink all the other pirates... Why not?"

"Like the pirates would believe we intend to do that."

"They would believe me. My kind are forced to keep our words on pain of death."

"Sure," Maco huffed. "Go ahead, lie to God."

"The reason they won't let us off is because we know too much and could turn them all in—but if we were pirates as well, our own necks would be in the noose."

Laughing, Maco slapped his friend on the shoulder and headed back to his now-lonesome shop.

Chapter 7

ADHELMAR AND THE FALL OF THE *ZEDELIOUS*

THE *ZEDELIOUS'S* CREW AND THEIR forced companion returned to the ocean. Arnacin kept close watch on their position, knowing only a few leagues separated the *Zedelious* from Enchantress Island. His heart burned in the dark as he stared at the very familiar constellations in the west–homeward. How easy it would have been to escape, especially with his ship freshly stocked from Baulis. Yet, as it was their closeness to Elcan that fanned the impulse to escape, so did it hold him.

If he did flee, he feared the *Zedelious's* pursuit would make the pirates stumble upon that continent and its island. He could sink the ship, but that would be the height of betrayal after his promise to Xavior.

Then the *Zedelious* successfully attacked a village on the edge of their route. With that victory, half the pirates went ashore.

They returned several hours later with a captive girl, likely no older than sixteen. Laughing uproariously, the pirates shoved the whimpering girl back and forth among themselves.

"There's a dandy for you. Oh, those gold curls will be lank before we're through with her."

Gritting his teeth, Arnacin forced himself not to draw his blade. Yet as one pirate pulled the girl to him, forcefully placing his lips against her cheek as she vainly tried to yank herself away, the islander positioned himself at the pirate's elbow.

With a cackle at the girl's protest, the pirate turned to push her into the next waiting arms. Spotting Arnacin, he froze. One look at his hate-filled face and the hand on his hilt brought all the pirates to a nervous halt. The islander knew they might take advantage of him when he was caught unawares and the captain was not present, yet they shivered under his gaze.

Clearing his throat, one of the pirates said, "Ah, tie her below. We'll decide tomorrow who takes her first." Arnacin gave them a cool nod, then watched as one pirate threw the girl over his shoulder to take her below.

Though the islander made it a point to avoid the pirates' attention, he watched the crow's nest and sky over the next few days, waiting for the weather to give him cover.

Not a week later, the sky was completely overcast and blackness covered everything. Only thin patches of light from the cabin lit the ship. Carefully, the islander slipped below deck with a preparatory inhale. The girl's sobs were his guide in the darkness, and he crept silently closer. That was, until he ran into a keg.

"Who's there?" A scared gasp ended the sobbing. Cursing, Arnacin felt his way around the obstruction without answering the question, until it was repeated.

"A ghost," he growled. "Not another word."

"Who are you?"

"I told you," the islander whispered, moving toward the sound of her voice.

"The ghost of whom, then?" This time, a different tremor of fear touched the voice, and the impishness that had once characterized Arnacin flared up. Yet that feeling, so distant, had no power over the islander's newer, humorless darkness. He simply did not answer.

In obvious terror, the girl ceased speaking. Without a guide in the darkness so thick even a hand in front of his face was invisible,

Arnacin had no idea how far or near he was to his goal—until he tripped over trembling legs, landing with a thud beside the captive.

Stilling, Arnacin strained his ears for signs that his fall had alerted anyone. None came. "I guess no one stands guard over their prize."

The girl's legs shuddered beneath his ankle. "Don't use that word."

It was an easy matter to slice through the ropes that held her against a keg. Although the cut rope left an obvious sign that she'd had help escaping, Arnacin could not bring himself to care. The pirates would know of his actions regardless, and death would follow. For his own pride, he would not shrink from it. And for his island's safety, he would not flee with the girl.

Once back on deck, they lowered a gig into the water, equipped with supplies and oars. "Keep to the northeast, and you'll hit land in two days," Arnacin whispered at the girl's shoulder, aware of the pirate in the crow's nest far above.

"Which way is northeast?" the girl asked in panic.

Sighing, the islander studied her shadowy figure. Then, reluctantly, he drew out his compass from under his shirt. Looking at it, he informed the girl, "The needle points north. Keep the compass always in front of you with the needle before your right eye and you will make land, unless a storm knocks you off course."

As she shivered, he pushed his compass into her hands. When she continued to stand there, he hissed, "Move. Dying at sea is nothing in comparison to what awaits you here."

Outlined in the dark, she looked up. "May I at least have a name?"

For just a second, Arnacin paused. Although a part of him understood the rationale behind the girl's request, he hated speaking a name that was no longer his own. Arnacin. Arnacin of Enchantress Island belonged to a boy murdered by time, nobility and his own choices. It was as much a lie to use it as to invent another.

Furthermore, names helped exact revenge, although it was unlikely the girl would seek revenge on a person who had rescued her.

All his thoughts passed in a flash, and he shook his head minutely. "Nothing of interest."

The figure still did not move in the darkness, and he surrendered. "Arnacin. Now go."

With that, the islander helped her over the edge. Only his keen ears caught the sound of muffled oars dipping through the water.

His sole regret in helping her lay in the empty place beneath his shirt—he no longer had his compass. Forcing himself to exhale, he dropped his arm back to his side and turned to the line attaching his ship to the *Zedelious*.

"Captain!" came a cry from one of the pirates the next afternoon. "The girl's gone!"

Xavior had only one short, furious order. "Bring him to me." The crew needed no help in knowing he meant Arnacin Islander. They looked over their shoulders to the middle of the ship, where their captive was scrubbing the deck.

Islander might help wash the deck, test knots or polish rails, yet the crew had long ago learned it did nothing to slow him if they chose to attack. Before they were three yards away, he would sense their intentions, and the first attacker would be wounded, disarmed or both. If that attacker was exceptionally persistent, he would often lay dead a short time later. Knowing all this, they shifted uncomfortably.

Since their captain had mandated this attack, however, they had no choice but to engage. They grabbed nets—yet, as they turned, striving to appear casual, they saw their victim dive over the starboard side of the ship.

Rushing to the edge, they looked over the rail, yet they saw no black head break the surface. As Captain Xavior joined them, one pirate asked, "Did 'e jest drown 'isself?"

"Watch for him," their captain growled. "He'll return, and when he does…"

Everyone knew that the ledge beneath the ship's bow could not be a permanent hideaway. For one thing, there was no sustenance there and, for another, should the water become choppy, the ship's increased movement would throw any stowaway into the ocean since no handholds existed.

Because of that, it made a perfect hiding place, at least for a time.

Sitting there with his right shoulder against the hull and his feet up beside him, Arnacin shivered in the cold wind, his wet clothes weighing him down, watching those foamy waves toss below. It would have been such a blessing if he drowned. Yet, there he stayed, for as long as he could.

Finally, as dusk fell on the second night, his body trembled and pain attacked behind his temples. It was no easy feat to climb back aboard, dehydrated as he was, with his swollen tongue stuck to the top of his mouth. When he reached the water-butt behind the ship's galley, he nearly lost consciousness.

However, he managed to fill a waterskin and disappear into the space he had found long ago between galley wall and rail, where someone on the deck above could not see him. There, he waited for the dizziness to subside before he attempted the inching scale along the ship's side.

It was a few minutes before he realized the dizziness was only increasing. The more water he sipped, the faster his unusual symptoms worsened. Blood drained from his face in the horrifying realization that Xavior had tainted the water.

If it was poison, it was over, but he feared it was only drugged. Arnacin knew the pirate captain too well to really hope for a simple death, and he had just walked into the captain's hands. He could either throw himself overboard or let Xavior finish it his way. The islander shuddered at the memory of Belon's end.

As large black spots appeared in his vision, Arnacin stubbornly pulled himself to the railing. He would sooner fall beneath the waves in an attempt to escape back into hiding than surrender. Yet it was too late. Feeling his head slam into wood, he wished he had thought to attempt the beer or wine.

When Captain Xavior heard the gleeful sounds of wicked jeering early in the morning, he knew his crew had found Arnacin Islander. Judging by the complete lack of fear in that sound, they had found him unconscious. For once, the pirates could approach, and even assault him, without dying.

The captain unfortunately could not let them continue. Hurrying to the spot from where the sound emitted, Xavior put a stop to his crews' victorious abuse of the still form at their feet.

Looking contemptuously down at those ashen features so akin to the whole Zedelious family, the captain commanded his crew to bind the captive between two of the table legs in his cabin. It was an ideal place, both to make sure the islander could not escape and to ensure his physical safety from the others. To further guarantee Arnacin could not free himself, as unlikely as that was, the captain tied a cloth around the islander's eyes once all of the crew had left.

For hours into the next night, the captive remained unconscious, "safe" behind the locked cabin door. Then, just as the moon disappeared for the night, he stirred weakly, semi-consciously pulling against the ropes holding his wrists above his head. Watching him, Xavior grinned in triumph, anticipating the panic to come.

The fear, however, did not seem to appear as full consciousness returned. Arnacin's only movement lay in the subtle flexing of numb fingers.

Laughing, Xavior approached. "You've tested me too far, Islander, and anyone who tests me loses. Don't think you're special enough to be an exception."

He wrapped his fingers tightly around his captive's throat. The neck muscles tensed in anticipation, and the captain chuckled. "By now, Islander, you should know I would deem strangling you too easy a death, yet you are right—I have finally decided what to do with you. It's not death, oh no. If you refuse to aid me through your talents, I can find other ways to use you. Tell me, Islander, where do you think we are going?"

He received no reply and pushed gleefully onward. "It will soon be Ursa's trading season in Heamra, the largest market since the fall of the old trading route, and there they sell..." He paused for emphasis, running his free hand along his captive's arm. "Slaves," he finished, grinning at the sudden, brief stillness beneath his fingers. "You would bring in a large sum, I am sure, and if you think it will be dangerous for me to deposit you somewhere so close to a government, it won't be. You see, there, they remove the tongues of slaves."

A low scream of fury escaped Arnacin as he struggled. Xavior simply laughed.

When the captive was forced to subside, the captain stood. "Learn what it means to cross me, boy."

He turned away, yet the angry whisper halted him, "You're wrong if you think anyone will pay more than a pittance for me. My shoulder's too ruined for that."

Throwing himself back on the captive, both hands around Arnacin's throat, Xavior warned him, "If you think of being wise..." He trailed off, his temper cooling as he contemplated his own words, and then settled back on his heels. "There will be nothing you can do about it. Do remember, slaves never speak there—not before they lose their tongues, certainly not after. When one attempts speech, no one listens. You hanged yourself when you decided to release the girl, and now you'll pay. There is no alternative for you."

Arnacin's response was silence.

Captain Adhelmar looked up as a knock sounded on his cabin door. "Enter."

One of the newer crew members stepped inside. "There's something you should see, Captain."

Outside, in the fog of morning, only the hazy outline of Port Lotarone was visible. It was the last port before the great blackness that Nomacir knew to mark the edge of the western world.

A century ago, sailors had returned saying the western sky was blacker than that of the underground, starless on what had been a cloudless night. In disbelief, other ships had sailed beyond the known world. Some never returned. Others did, with the same scary story of no sky or stars.

Very soon, everyone deemed that darkness the ocean's warning of the world's edge. Not even Xavior would sail beyond Port Lotarone—the last haven before the world's end. Therefore, Adhelmar's western hunt for the Zedelious and the hidden pirate city stopped there.

His watch never faltered, however. This close to the edge of the world, it doubled, in fact. At the starboard rail, a watchman called him over and passed him a telescope, pointing toward the open ocean. A small, hazy gig bobbed in the waves. It looked empty. Lifting the glass to his eye revealed a girl occupying the craft, motionless, her upper body slumped over an oar.

"Bring her aboard, quickly," Adhelmar ordered.

As men rushed to their own rowboat, the owner of the telescope asked in a hushed tone, "Do you think she's dead?"

"I have no idea," the captain whispered, "but something happened. That's not a vessel meant for sailing across any ocean."

It soon became clear that the girl was alive, for as the navy's gig bumped against the girl's, she jerked upright with a scream. Watchman and captain shared a look as the girl proceeded to fight the sailors. Her screams drifted toward them on the wind.

Somehow consoling her, the sailors managed to bring her back to Adhelmar's ship, Isholt's Revenge—named after his queen. Trembling, the girl climbed the ladder ahead of the sailors. Meeting her at the top, the captain soothed her with a bow. "We mean no harm, young lady. Is there anything you require before you tell us your story?"

Obviously too afraid to speak, the girl swiftly shook her head.

"Some food and wine, perhaps?" the watchman suggested. "You appear on the verge of fainting."

Although the girl stepped back in fear, her head nodded of its own accord. In a few moments, she sat wrapped in a blanket at the captain's table, while he thoughtfully watched her eat. Finally, he asked, "So how is it that a girl, obviously with no sailing background judging by your sunburn, is sailing a gig across the ocean—if I may ask, Miss...?"

Tentatively pushing limp curls out of her face, the girl whispered, "I'm Mary from Lennai."

"That's quite some distance," Adhelmar exclaimed. "You went all that way in a rowboat?"

"No," Mary breathed, her eyes dropping back to the table. "I've only been in that vessel for two days. It was terrifying, but perhaps not as..." Meeting the captain's gaze, she confessed, "I was captured by pirates."

Trying to appear calm for her sake, Adhelmar inquired, "Where is it headed? Do you know?"

"On the first day of captivity, one of the pirates said if I was very good, they might release me in Ursa."

"Is that where they are currently headed?"

"I believe so. They were talking about the market season."

"I see." The captain nodded, then as another thought emerged, he pressed her, "You escaped before then?"

Mary turned red and then slowly slipped something over her head from where it had lain hidden beneath her chemise. "One of the pirates helped me escape."

"One of the pirates?" Adhelmar repeated incredulously, taking a closer look at what the girl held in her hands, the object of her fond smile. Inspecting the strange, beautiful compass, which must have cost a pretty amount for the original owner, he wondered, "What sort of pirate?"

"I don't know. He said his name was Arnacin."

"Arnacin?" The name matched with none of the pirates currently known to Queen Isholt's navy, yet that meant nothing. New pirates sprang up like weeds and crewmembers changed constantly, although a pirate with a penchant for rescuing girls would likely find his name well known. "Who was the captain of the ship, or what was the name of it?"

"I don't know the name of the ship. I heard a few pirates refer to a Cap'n Xavior."

"Captain Xavior!" Adhelmar could no longer remain calm. Flying to the door, he threw it open and called, "Polion, take this lady ashore. You will have to stay there. We are leaving immediately, but we will come back for you. Hans, send your trained birds out. We need every ship between here and Ursa to be ready. The *Zedelious* is on her way."

A battle cheer went up at that pronouncement. Instantly, men were hustling about the decks. Turning back to the girl as Polion joined him, the captain stated, "You must leave quickly. As soon as the sails unfurl and the anchor is raised, this ship will not stop."

"You're going to sink them, aren't you?" Mary whispered, clutching the compass in her fist.

"Yes. Although, it is my hope that Captain Xavior at least is not let off so easily."

As Polion gently took her elbow, the girl held out the compass. "Return this to him, please. To Arnacin. It's his."

Bowing, the captain promised, "I will." Looking down at its glass surface, he muttered, "If I must bury it with him."

"Cap'n! Cap'n!" The urgent call rang across the *Zedelious*'s deck. Three ships bore down on them from the portside to the north, and Xavior cursed softly upon spotting them.

"It looks like the Nomacirrian navy," Spyros growled, also leaping to the rail.

Cursing Nomacir's queen, Xavior whirled back to his crew. "Tack her southeast! We'll outrun those skivers."

Watching the pirates shimmying up the ratlines, the captain's gaze fell on the fluttering raven skeleton on its black background. "And take down our colors! Once we are far enough, put up Nomacir's!" Whirling back to watch the enemy ships, he hissed, "With any fortune, it will make other ships hesitate."

Throughout that day, they stayed ahead of the navy. As darkness added cover, Xavior commanded them to tack back east, raise Nomacir's colors and keep all lights extinguished. Once those tasks were completed, he turned back to his cabin, where only a small candle burned behind heavy curtains.

As dawn came, it appeared they had lost their pursuers, but Xavior remained uneasy. In the late morning, a seagull swooped over the mainmast. That far out at sea, Xavior instantly knew its purpose and snapped, "Shoot it down!"

The crew scattered to find shelter from descending bolts as one pirate arrived with a crossbow, whose aim was true. The bird dropped to the deck, where one pirate picked it up, ripping something off its leg. "What's it read?" the pirate exclaimed as Xavior snatched it out of his fingers.

"'They've moved east,'" Xavior growled as he read the note aloud. Crunching it in his fist, he heaved the message across the deck.

The color washed from some of his crew's faces. The one holding the bird's carcass whispered, "What d' we do?"

Spotting the mast of Islander's ship poking into view behind the poop deck, the captain barked, "Turn the ship into the wind."

"What?!"

"Do it, unless you want your heads adorning some ship's yardarms! Islander's precious junk-heap can cut through the wind! We'll have it pull us. That's the end of it!"

Within seconds, five pirates slid down the rope attaching the smaller ship to the larger. Within a few minutes more, it was cutting into the wind, chained to the forecastle deck of the *Zedelious*, its unfurled sail sideways, while the *Zedelious* dropped its sails. It was slow work, for as swift as the smaller ship was on its own when the wind was on its side, it had barely the strength to pull the larger ship—yet move they did. To help it, pirates ran below deck and rowed as fast as their arms allowed with the long poles stored there. When one tired, Xavior swiftly changed them out. Perhaps it would have worked, if not for the four ships traveling in the opposite direction.

At the speed those ships bore down on them, everyone knew they could not turn the ship again. "Allow them to meet us," Xavior directed. Turning to Spyros, the captain said, "Ready for battle. Light the eyes."

With that, he stormed inside his cabin and roughly unbound his captive, growling, "Move, Islander. Battle is on its way." His eyes glinted. "I wouldn't want you to be unable to defend yourself."

Pushing himself slowly to his feet, Arnacin angrily accused him, "You simply don't wish them to free me while I appear to be a captive."

Crimson flashed in the captain's eye. "It hardly matters, does it?"

"And if I simply leave?"

Seizing the islander's arm, Xavior softly replied, "But you won't, will you? Oh no, you would end any honor you possessed by doing so, and honor is the only thing dear to you in the universe. Think of breaking your vow simply for fear of what may happen to your hide. Oh, how pirate-like, indeed."

As Arnacin jerked furiously away, the captain added, "Besides, I would just like to see you try to undo the chain holding your ship without the key." He would see to it that Arnacin Islander would hang with them if the *Zedelious* sunk. The little traitor deserved no better.

Had the lock not been on the *Zedelious*'s deck, Arnacin would have escaped regardless of "honor," yet he remained closely watched until he descended to his own deck. Then the ships were on them—mammoth ships. Even climbing his rigging to drop his own sail, the top decks of those ships were still far above Arnacin's head as they sailed right against their prey, their painted names shining brightly against their mahogany sides: *Isholt's Revenge*, *Bane of Immorality*, *Ocean Sword* and *Pirate Skinner*. Arnacin himself was forced to shudder at the destiny those names proposed, while the *Zedelious* groaned and cracked beneath the onslaught of grappling hooks.

On Xavior's orders, fiery arrows flew into the navy ships' sodden sails. With a thunderous hiss, the fire went out in billows of steam, blocking the sky from view.

"We don't have time for this," Xavior hissed, watching his crew on the main deck, already struggling against the many grappling hooks snaring the *Zedelious*. "Take your torches and board them," he ordered his crew of archers. "We'll light them up from inside. The first one to step foot on their deck will be paid double!"

"This must be a nightmare," Spyros muttered beside him.

"Quiet!" the captain snapped as he spotted the name of the ship crushing into their starboard side, practically smashing the two ships' masts into one. "Find a way to slip onto that *Ocean Sword* and split open her hull. I don't care how! If you succeed, go to the next one."

Without a word, Spyros left as the *Ocean Sword*'s crew dropped from ropes onto the *Zedelious*'s deck. On their port side, the *Bane of Immorality* struggled against a wall of pirate defenders.

Quickly, Xavior drew his blade. A mass of navy men surged in his direction, as the *Zedelious*'s crew could no longer stem the flow of attackers climbing over their ship from both sides.

In the flurry of battle, the pirate captain found himself facing one of the navy officers. Still in the prime of his life and around fifteen years younger than Xavior himself, the tawny-haired officer had the upper hand. His movements were skillful and quick, but Xavior hung on with his greater experience and cunning.

For a considerable amount of time, they battled back and forth. Then pain shot up the back of Xavior's upper sword-arm from another attacker. Someone had stabbed him from behind. The saber tip in his flesh withdrew, yet in that brief second, his tawny-haired opponent used the flat of his own blade to slap the pirate captain's wrist, causing Xavior to drop his sword.

The navy officer then slammed Xavior into the rail, placing his sword against the pirate's throat. Xavior's other attacker stepped off the rail from behind. It was another navy captain, much to Xavior's contempt.

"Order your crew to surrender!" the first attacker snapped, pressing his blade harder against Xavior.

"Or you'll slit my throat?" Xavior scoffed. "Pray tell, why should that scare me now? If they manage to cut down most of your crew, I'll be pleased."

"Command their surrender or, I swear to God, I will make sure your end is long—portion by tiny portion, if I must."

For a second more, Xavior pierced his opponent with his gaze. In those stormy eyes before him, he saw no lie, no weakness, and every ability to order as slow a death as he deemed deserved. Forget a swift execution. This officer would make that death last months.

"Lay down your swords, swine!" the pirate captain shouted into the consistent clash and ring of battle around them. "Refuse, and I'll give you worse than they!"

In the sudden silence of battle, the clatter of many blades echoed around them. "So, the worst of Zedelious's brood has finally been brought to justice," chuckled the officer with his blade at Xavior's shoulder. "Where did you stumble, I wonder?"

"We spotted the *Immortal*," Xavior growled. Then a slow, wicked smile spread across his face. "I do believe you're next, gentlemen."

"I am afraid I have no idea what you mean," the officer at his throat said.

"Pirate superstitions, no doubt," another navy captain commented, joining his comrades around Xavior. He, at least, had sheathed his own blade. "If the *Zedelious* houses half as much treasure as is rumored, we should divide it along with the captives and split up. That way, if one of us sinks, something will still reach the queen, and such wealth will go a long way in helping her."

"You wouldn't dare," Xavior barked. "That's been *Zedelious's* for generations. It goes down with her."

"I'm sure," the tawny-haired officer muttered, looking to his nearest crewmembers. "Bind the captives and divide them amongst our ships' holds. Put Captain Xavior in mine, and don't forget to blindfold them—we don't want any escape attempts near a rail or anything." Meeting Xavior's glare, he stated, "You're all going to face justice and stand trial."

He stepped aside to allow other men room. Xavior did not tarnish his dignity by fighting them as they pushed him away from the railing, twisting his arms, injured or no, behind him. He ground his teeth, however, as the tawny-haired officer said, in a tone not meant to carry, "Divide whatever you find useful to Her Majesty among your ships and take the fastest winds back to Nomacir. I have to retrieve one of my men, and I am hoping extended fear will weaken some of the pirates enough to pull information on their havens from them."

"Careful, Adhelmar," another voice cautioned. "The last thing we want is for Xavior to escape. He's one of the deadliest pirates in existence, yet his capture doesn't entirely remove the threat of pirates in our waters."

"I know, and I would suggest you take him with you, but he knows the most. Considering how quickly he surrendered, prolonged fear of death might change him."

"You think he'll break?"

"I'm hoping. I promise, if I think we'll lose in some attack, I'll have him beheaded. I will use every last breath to do so, if I must."

Now blindfolded, Xavior could no longer see as he was turned around and led away, hearing only, as the conversation grew too distant, "We don't want any of them escaping, you know."

As the light of the sun disappeared into the darkness his captors pushed him down into, Xavior could only promise himself he would not break. Perhaps that Adhelmar *was* foolish enough to run into the Black Captain and all the dark mystery that would drop him into the depths of the ocean before the *Immortal* again changed hands.

Xavior would only cheer. And if he were able to escape, that would indeed be the end of Nomacir.

Chapter 8

ARNACIN ENIGMA

AFTER XAVIOR HAD BEEN LED away, Captain Vinn sheathed his blade. "Alright, so he won't escape, but why do you think any of them will break by giving them longer to live?"

"They already know what awaits them." Adhelmar shrugged. "Their imaginations will increase their fear as they wait in darkness for that moment, particularly with our orders to keep them all blindfolded so that they remain docile. Living with prolonged terror has changed many a man. However, if you doubt it will be enough, I can have their guards chat about other pirates' similar death sentences. Their conversation will be natural since it's the obvious thought process."

"Wha–"

"There's another one that won't surrender!" Hans, Adhelmar's grown cabin boy, came running toward them. "He's on the ship below–one of Zedelious's brood, I think. He's covered by Captain Vinn's best archer, but we're awaiting your orders, sir."

"Let me see." Adhelmar turned once more to his companions, "Go find that treasure, and hurry. The longer we stay, the more nervous I become."

Sight of the uncooperative pirate, who stood tensed for an attack at the small ship's rail, caused Adhelmar to freeze. "We hanged him several years ago."

"I don't think that's Xavior's son," Hans laughed grimly. "For one thing, he appears too young, at least at this distance."

"I hope you're right."

"Don't tell me you believe in ghosts now."

Ignoring him, Adhelmar spoke to the archer standing with his bow drawn taut. "Order him aboard and, if he doesn't obey, make sure he is aware of your prowess. If he still does not listen, shoot him. I only want one shot wasted, but I do want him alive and unharmed if possible."

"If I must shoot, I can subdue him without killing him," the archer suggested.

"And bring him up?"

"There are ways."

"Very well. I leave it to your discretion."

Stepping back, Adhelmar watched as the archer called, "Surrender, pirate! I've been given orders to shoot for the kill should you refuse again!"

Time appeared to stand still as the pirate considered his options, but it was less than a second before he abruptly dove aside and the arrow flashed downward, disappearing into his side. Or so it appeared.

To Adhelmar's amazement, the pirate halted, yet moved without injury as his hand shot to his unscathed side. The archer, however, laughed in cold triumph. "Need I do that again, pirate, or are you now convinced that lack of compliance means your death?"

To the archer's right, a sailor warned, "That miss was no mistake. He could do it again and worse. He's the best archer the world has to offer."

For some reason, that brought color and life to a countenance that had previously looked gray and shallow. "I contest that. Without all the world's best archers present, there's no way you can prove it."

"Yet you couldn't disprove it either..."

"I might."

Although the archer's eyes lit with the enjoyment of the challenge, he only said, "I see no reason it should be the least bit important to you one way or the other, pirate. I can shoot you with ease."

"You want cooperation? Wager your skill and I'll be willing to wager my freedom."

While Adhelmar snorted, Captain Vinn's archer declined. "A part of me wishes to accept your challenge, yet I submit fully to my queen, and it would be her choice to allow such a thing. Now, climb up before this arrow finds whatever it pleases me to find."

For just a moment longer, the pirate did not move. Then, defeat washing across his thin frame, he started climbing up onto the *Zedelious*'s forecastle deck. There, whether because of the arrow trained on his heart or for some other reason, he allowed Hans to remove his sword while the other sailor shackled his arms behind his back.

Adhelmar stared at the carved gold sheath of the sword passed to him. Returning his attention to the captive, he took a good look for the first time at the thin features and unreadable eyes.

"Amazing," the captain whistled after a moment. "You're not who you look to be from a distance. Who are you, Master....?"

"I don't give my name freely."

"A name, boy, or our conversation is through."

Begrudgingly, the pirate complied. "Arnacin."

The captain paused, looking again at this rescuer of females. "Just Arnacin?" When no more came, he asked, "You apparently helped neither side."

In the captive's silence, the captain's eyes went to his shirt. "Miran craft." His fingers followed his thoughts toward the frayed embroidery at his captive's chest. Stopping when Arnacin drew back as far as the two men flanking him would allow, Adhelmar commented, "It's likely the last we'll ever see of it too."

"Why?"

"Don't you know? Mira's natives flattened her. They left not a person alive."

"No one?" The captive's question was a horrified breath.

"Well, it is rumored that the princess lives, but if she does, I pity her." The captain paused, again studying the captive, whose shroud of bitterness—momentarily parted by the mention of Mira's fall—had returned full strength to his eyes. "Again, who are you and where did you obtain the craft of the noble houses of Mira?"

"I'm no one but a captive of the pirates you just conquered, and I wear what was made for me, nothing more."

"Am I supposed to believe that tale?"

"I stayed on Mira for a short time."

"In the castle?" Adhelmar heard the doubt in his voice.

"My ship needed repairing before I could again set sail, and they lent their support."

"Why? What was a random sailor to them?"

Arnacin, once again, gave no response and the captain nodded. "Very well—there are ways to test your story. Many of the traders that used to gather on Mira still roam the sea. If your ship was there at any time, one of them should recall you. If you speak true, you will be free to go with your ship. If not, I shall assume what I must, and you will return home with us to be hanged. Does that seem fair?"

"I don't know why you ask. You wouldn't change your decision if I said no."

"You are shrewd and cool for a common pirate, if you are one—that is for certain." The captain nodded to the men behind the captive. "Put him with the rest of Xavior's crew for now." As one of the men drew out a cloth, binding their captive's eyes, the captain dipped his chin. "My apologies in advance if you are as you say, but my orders are to let no one escape."

With that, Adhelmar stepped aside, watching as his men led the captive over to *Isholt's Revenge* between sailors laden with confiscated plunder.

"There is the chance he is telling the truth about being their captive," Hans whispered at his elbow.

"Why do you say that?"

"There are rope burns on his wrists and ankles."

Turning to Hans with some surprise, Adhelmar reminded him, "Yet he was able to free the girl, and he didn't leave with her. If you saw recent marks, it is likely due to some punishment for rescuing her." From his pocket, he drew out the helm compass, shaking his head. "There must be some other way to prove his words and, besides Xavior, I think this is the best place to start."

"How?"

"Hans, you have never seen a compass like this, have you? It's not only a tool but someone's art, someone who leaves their signature. Hopefully, this person is well enough known that the search won't be too difficult."

"And if it is difficult?"

Adhelmar shrugged. "I'll hang him as a pirate. I have no other lead to go on."

"Doesn't that feel like lying, to say you will find proof and then hang him if you can't locate any?"

The captain had no answer as he watched the compass twisting slowly around on its cord.

A week after sinking the *Zedelious*, Adhelmar ordered Xavior brought to his cabin on the *Isholt's Revenge*. As expected, the pirate, though heavily shackled, stood defiantly, his gaze scoffing. Knowing Xavior had not broken in the least as soon as their gazes met, Adhelmar decided to save his interrogation for other pirates. Instead, he demanded, "The smaller ship you were hauling... Tell me where it was built."

With a slow, evil grin, the pirate rasped, "We steal things—we don't inquire into where they were made, even if it turns out to be the *Immortal*."

"Then from whom did you steal it? What sea were you in?"

"Yours." At Adhelmar's frown, Xavior's smirk grew wider. "From behind the *Pursuit of Justice*."

Adhelmar did not so much as blink, but after a second, he growled, "Surely you thought something of its strange design.

Moreover, I'm sure you searched it, as you would any ship, for valuables. Did you not think it strange there are no maps, no documents, no logs, no scripts anywhere? Or did you remove them? I'm sure you asked Captain Belon before you tortured him to death. What did you find?"

"Tortured him?" Xavior repeated with false indignation. "I ripped his hide off and hanged him. How is that torture? After all, Nomacir did it to one of my own."

The cabin descended into silence. Finally, Nomacir's captain dared whisper, "You killed your son yourself, Xavior. Had you even once thought of him, you would have found somewhere he could live free and at peace. Certainly, he would not have been lacking the funds to do so."

"Ha, there is nowhere freer than the wild ocean! What place is there where any wealth would not be bled out through some upstart's tax? None, I tell you! The sons of Zedelious have never groveled before anyone, and so it will stay. No, I gave him the best life imaginable. Dare you say otherwise?"

Twirling his quill pen around, Adhelmar asked instead, "Speaking of 'the sons of Zedelious,' from which branch did Arnacin come?"

Xavior's wicked smile returned. "Whichever one you like! It hardly matters, does it? It only matters that Arnacin Islander is a son of Zedelious."

"Did he ever live on Mira?"

"If his possessions and clothes are any indication, you already know the answer."

"He's a pirate. He could just as likely have attacked a Miran ship, particularly during the days of its evacuation, when it was in panicked flight."

"He could have."

"Let me change that—*you* could have. Where were you those days or any time before?"

Xavior's eyebrows rose. "In your seas."

"Then you did not find Arnacin on Mira?"

"No!"

Adhelmar jumped slightly at the vehemence of the answer, yet he quickly smoothed over his surprise. "Where did you meet him?"

For just a moment, the pirate remained silent, then he hissed, "At sea."

"I have no doubt the two of you are related," Adhelmar fumed. "Answer me at once! Under what circumstances was he integrated into your crew?"

"The circumstance of your captain's hanging," Xavior snapped back. "He nearly begged to remain aboard the *Zedelious* afterward."

"Why then? Was that where you met him?"

As much as Adhelmar pushed, however, Xavior was done talking. Even a reminder of the consequences for lack of cooperation did not loosen his tongue.

"Very well." Turning to the guards, Adhelmar ordered, "Give him five lashes and then return him below. I'll try again tomorrow."

As the door shut behind the prisoner and his guards, Adhelmar pounded his fist into the wall.

Xavior remained silent the next day as well, yet despite his defiance, Adhelmar did track down the compass maker after retrieving Polion. Anchoring farther than usual from shore, the captain took Hans with him and rowed to the docks.

His quarry sat inside a seaside tavern when Adhelmar walked up. "You have very fine work, Mr. Tareef."

"Iendeed." The carver winked, holding up his current hunk of wood, almost formless except for the hole he was whittling out. "You ien need of a fine compass?"

"Actually, I've been hunting for you, and I was told I would find you here." Drawing the compass out of his pocket, the captain let it dangle and spin on its cord before its maker. "This has your mark. Do you remember it?"

Tareef's eyes widened as they flicked back and forth between the navy captain and the compass shooting light off its surface every time the sun hit it just right. Finally, he croaked, "Weere'd you find fat?"

"Is it actually yours?" Adhelmar passed it to the carver for closer inspection, but after staring at it as if paralyzed, its maker still said nothing.

"Was it stolen?" the captain pressed.

Quickly, the sailor shook his head. "The Preencess Valoreetta purchased it."

"Did you make more than one?"

"It be one o' ah kind. People want larger compasses fan fis one, but I fought it a fine design."

"If the Princess Valoretta bought it," Adhelmar began slowly, "this must be a fake."

"Nope," Tareef pronounced, and the captain's eyebrows rose. "Fis be the one Valoreetta placed around Arnaceen's neck. I've purposeful notches I carve ien things so fat I know."

"Arnacin?"

"Arnaceen of E'chantress Eeland. He was treasured by the preencess during the two years he leeved on Meera. Ien fact, he was her chosen king. She announced it to the world by placing fis very compass around hees neck." The sailor could not have looked more pleased with himself.

"What did he look like?" Adhelmar's voice cracked, and he attempted nonchalance as he coughed to clear it.

Tareef shrugged. "Black hair, dark blue eyes, tall, fin. You'd never forget heem once you saw heem. Now, me turn. Weere'd you find fis?"

"Arnacin," the captain puffed in complete breathlessness.

"You've seen Arnaceen? Arnaceen of E'chantress Eeland?"

"Um, I have a captive pirate going by the name of Arnaceen." Adhelmar quickly corrected himself. "Arnacin."

To his further surprise, Tareef burst out laughing—high, roaring, hysterical laughter. "Captured Arnaceen! You captured Arnaceen! Fer piracy!"

Adhelmar tried to ignore the sudden stares they were receiving from everyone in the establishment.

Wiping tears from his cheeks, the sailor exclaimed, "Listen, Cap'n. I don't know how you came by fat compass, but you can't have Arnaceen of E'chantress Eeland. And if you fink you have a pirate, fat's all the more reediculous. Meera's Black Phantom would drown ien hees own blood before he turned to piracy, and no one, *no one* could ever catch heem if he did."

Striving to make some sense of it, Adhelmar simply asked, "Did he die on Mira?"

"Of course not."

"What happened?"

"No one knows. He came on the weends of a storm, aided Meera for two years, and fen he and hees ship took off, never to be seen again. Of course, fere's all type of stories. Some who are jeelous say fat Arnaceen tried to keell the king and ien love, Meero only banished heem. Some say he foresaw the end of Meera and fled ien cowardeece. Ofers say the king grew jeelous and entombed heem ien a tower, fat seelors saw only hees ghost leave. Hees bones lie forever on Meera. Still ofers say he seemply walked frough fose sealed walls of hees tomb and escaped."

Rubbing his pounding head, Adhelmar asked, "What do you believe?"

"Me, huh..." Tareef grew silent for a long moment, running his fingers thoughtfully along the compass. Finally, he confessed, "I fink I'm wif Meera's adopted natives. Arnaceen of E'chantress Eeland, feir Black Phantom, be the son of gods. Fey sent heem to aid Meera and rescue eet from eets end. When Meero refused fat aid, the gods called feir son back. Had Preencess Valoreetta been queen, she would have leestened. Alas, she was not."

Skeptically, Adhelmar reminded him, "Then how do I have the compass?"

"I don't know." Sadly, Tareef passed the compass back. "Mayhaps the gods told feir hero to leave fis as advance warning fat your queen will also receive, or has received, her aid, and she should pay close atteention before she goes the way of Meera."

Snorting, Adhelmar nevertheless thanked the sailor before stuffing the compass back into his pocket.

After wasting time hunting down more information about his prisoner, Adhelmar returned to *Isholt's Revenge*. With the wind now blowing against her sails, he asked Polion, "How is Xavior's crew handling their captivity?"

"Tuh," Polion huffed. "They're not handling it well at all. They shiver, moan and scream in their sleep. The rare time they appear completely conscious, their only interest is in kicking each other to make more room for their legs."

"They are likely cramped." Scratching the back of his head, the captain said, "Bring one of them up tomorrow. We'll see if they're ready to give us anything helpful to Her Majesty."

"Why not today? They're not likely to be that much more broken in just an extra day."

"I have in mind someone else to interrogate," Adhelmar growled in frustration. "How's Arnacin faring?"

Polion crossed his arms as his gaze traveled to the open sea. "Starving. Purposely. I don't know what goes on in his mind, but either he hates us so much he has to give us as much difficulty as he can, or he's just that determined to die. All the rest of the pirates, including Xavior, just meekly let us feed and water them. Not him. He tries to break our knee caps, smash our toes, anything he can."

"He's both blindfolded and shackled, right?"

"Ha! Of course. He attacks us with shoulders and feet, as soon as he senses us near. We've learned to descend on him en masse, and he's even ripped out his own hair when we try yanking his head back."

Coughing back his laughter, Adhelmar pressed, "And when you're not down there, trying to make sure he lives?"

"He's about the same as all the rest, I suppose. Restless, shivering, passing from one nightmare to the next."

"Are you sure about that?"

"Well, why wouldn't he be?"

The question gave Adhelmar pause. "If he's actually innocent, I don't see how he could be tormented by nightmares. We don't hang innocent people."

"Ah." For a minute, Polion was silent, then he shrugged. "But depending on what they've done, he might anyway."

"True," Adhelmar sighed. "It could be a hint, though."

"I really have no idea. He's just one of the pirate crewmembers down there. I'm not close enough to know. If you asked about Xavior, I'd be able to tell you."

Adhelmar smiled sardonically. "You stand right in front of his cell door for all your guard shifts."

"That's why I'd know." Polion nodded. Turning to his captain, he asked, "Why is it so important to you to find out? He's probably guilty of something, the way he acts. You should rest easy about his death."

Softly, Adhelmar spoke. "My cousin was unjustly executed."

"How?"

"He was covering for a friend."

Staring out to sea, Polion was silent. Then, he shook his head. "You don't actually think he's innocent, do you?"

"Arnacin? I have no idea." After a second, Adhelmar ordered, "Bring him up to my cabin."

Nodding, Polion slipped off, taking some other crewmembers with him.

Even considering the length of time fetching a prisoner took, it was a while before Adhelmar heard Polion's knock on his cabin door. Sitting at his desk with his feet resting on its mahogany surface, fiddling with his quill pen, Adhelmar's eyes went wide as two of his crew led their blind, trembling captive inside the cabin.

Arnacin had been gaunt the first time the captain had laid eyes on him, almost a month and a half ago. Polion had not exaggerated his attempts at starvation.

As the captive's rapid, short breathing cut off, Adhelmar remarked, "My, my, Arnacin. You should allow them to feed you more. You are beginning to look like nothing but a stack of bones with skin stretched across it and cloth hanging over that to hide the fact."

That image was aided by the strange beardlessness of the prisoner. Despite his long imprisonment, not even a shadow marked his upper lip. Whatever blood strain created that unique trait, it did not come from Zedelious. Xavior's beard had grown thickly during captivity.

There was no response. Yet as Polion untied the blindfold, Adhelmar studied Arnacin's eyes as they focused. Unlike Xavior, there was no defiance, pride or disdain in those dark blue eyes. Nor was there fear, despite the earlier trembling, which might have had more to do with weakness. The only readable emotion was intense distrust, but there was also a stillness that belied a guilty conscience. Regardless, it was not what the captain would have expected from someone Mira had claimed as king.

Then again, the captain did not really believe this was Mira's Black Phantom, Arnacin of Enchantress Island. It was time to see if he could prove that. "How long did you say you were on Mira?" Adhelmar asked, sliding first one foot off its perch and then the other.

"I didn't say." Arnacin voice came out in a low, scratchy whisper.

Again contemplating his captive, Adhelmar demanded, "Then how long were you there?"

"Two years." The words sounded dragged out, yet the voice was strengthening with use.

"Two years," the captain eventually repeated. "Close to the royalty?"

"If you wish."

"I don't wish, Arnacin! I want to know," Adhelmar snapped, shooting to his feet. "If all you say is true, why did you ever leave? Why are you not dead on some Miran field, and why are you found unfettered in the company of *pirates*?"

Had he shouted the last word? The captive's eyes lit up with that much more temper and scorn. For a long moment, however, he remained silent. Then, he hissed, "Cowardice."

A slight note of victory stirred in Adhelmar's chest. "You deserted Mira in her hour of need because you saw it would not survive?"

"No," Arnacin's response was sharp as his chin rose. If he truly was Mira's Black Phantom, Adhelmar could now see a resemblance. "I was with the pirates due to cowardice. I was betrayed on Mira and exiled."

"Ah, so you were charged of a crime you had not committed by a jealous competitor and the king believed it."

"Jealous?" Arnacin scoffed. "There was no one with whom to compete."

Looking down at his desk, the captain slid out a drawer. "I have heard otherwise." With those words, he held up the compass by its cord, dangling it before the captive, who paled as if realizing some treachery. "So, you recognize it?" the captain mused.

"What did she tell you?" Arnacin breathed, his gaze fixed on his compass as it slowly twisted around.

"She asked me to return it to you, and I agreed to do so... if I had to bury it with you. However, I think you stole it. You see, I talked with the artist, its creator, and he told me someone else purchased it." Adhelmar stared closely at his captive, though he kept his face turned toward the compass. "How do you explain that?"

"She purchased it for me." The words came forth with a shudder.

"She?"

"The Princess... Valoretta." Those words broke painfully, and Arnacin dropped his gaze to the ground, trembling as he finished.

Momentarily, Adhelmar studied his captive, the one who not only remained unscathed by the trap, but actually sounded like the Miran princess's death hurt him. Exhaling, the captain lightly dropped the compass onto his desk and, at its dull *thunk*, Arnacin looked up.

Staring into those masked eyes, Adhelmar resumed his seat, resting his elbows on his desk. "And you still say there was no reason for jealousy or competition?"

The mask flew away as fire lit in the captive's gaze. "Only an ass would feel jealousy toward someone blind enough to think a *noble* cared. They're rot to be trampled, all of them."

"Yet you apparently want your compass returned to you, a gift from 'that rot?'" No reply followed, yet the captain saw those dark eyes close in pain even as the captive appeared to study the carpet. "Do you know what I think, Arnacin of Enchantress Island?"

Arnacin's head shot upward as if slapped, and the captain smiled grimly. "Yes, I know of the title. After all, I found all I could about you–and believe me, I did not glean much except that you are considered akin to a god or spirit. One sailor thought it was the most absurd joke that anyone could have you held prisoner anywhere, much less arrested for piracy. Let me say I learned nothing from him, except that he considered you to have vanished back into the clouds from where you came, never to be seen by mortal man again. I contemplated that one."

The torment across his captive's lowered face made all thoughts pause. "Is the pain new or has it been there long?" he softly inquired.

The anguish vanished from those features, leaving the cold bitterness the captain had expected as that gaze again rose to face him. "Whatever happened on Mira was every inch deserved by her rulers. What pain could it cause me?"

"Much. Enough to push you to the edge and turn to piracy."

"What?" Arnacin asked in horrified disbelief.

"Yes. From this conversation, I think you left Mira internally wounded from the king's supposed betrayal and, as that wound healed, you swore to rid the world of like filth, turning to piracy against every and all royal ships. I have come to the conclusion that you were with those pirates because you knew you could not continue alone and needed a crew. What better way than joining another crew until you could gain control?"

For a long moment, Arnacin simply stared at the captain, while Adhelmar repeated, "'They're rot to be trampled, all of them.' Did you not just say that moments ago?"

"They trample themselves."

His eyebrows rising, the captain asked, "What proof can you give that my conclusion is wrong?"

Dark eyes glittered. At last, the captive breathed, "None I will say."

"I see." The captain's thumb flicked up and down in troubled contemplation, and then he laced his fingers together, leaning forward. "You have put me in a hard place, Arnacin. I should fail my queen if I were manipulated into allowing a pirate to sail free across her shores, yet I fear hanging an innocent man by mistake. I find you have yet to lie to me on most things, though I wonder."

The captive gave no answer, and Adhelmar considered him. Either Arnacin was playing a very skilled game and had no proof, or there was some reason he actually refused to speak. Would threatened torture pull it out? From someone who purposely starved himself to death, it seemed unlikely.

A gentler approach and a closer watch might be the only things to loosen that clamped tongue. Leastways, Adhelmar had no other ideas. "This is what I'll do, Arnacin. For now, I'll offer you my hospitality until I can determine whether my assumption is true or not."

"I've had your hospitality," Arnacin quipped. "I don't care for it."

His lips quirking upward slightly, the captain said, "If that is considered hospitality, Arnacin, I'll remember to decline yours, if ever the chance arrives."

The captive's only response was the darkening of his eyes.

Finished, the captain inclined his head to Polion, who stood against the closed door.

As soon as Polion touched his chained wrists, however, Arnacin tensed. Stilling, Polion leaned forward to whisper, "I'm going to relieve you of these. Don't make any sudden moves, or I'll leave them on."

Unobtrusively gripping his knife hilt beneath his desk, Adhelmar raised his eyebrows when Arnacin only studied the captain warily once released, while he slowly rubbed his right wrist.

His attention drawn to that movement, Adhelmar noted the sores. "Polion, call someone to bring some food and then fill a tub in here with seawater."

Polion grunted, turning away. Still keeping his hand on his hilt, the captain nodded to the captive. "Salt water may not feel good, but a bath in it will help, and I have a good soap that will make you feel better."

To his surprise, Arnacin recoiled. "I wish to be left alone."

"Are you still denying hospitality? Come, take your compass. Food will be here in a moment…"

"That you made," the captive muttered as his gaze returned to his compass. Slowly, he inched toward it as if it were going to strike him. Once he reached the desk, he made no move to reclaim the compass, staring down at its glass surface.

Just as Hans entered with a plate of food, Arnacin glanced up at Adhelmar. Studying the captain, he abruptly snatched his compass, closing it tightly within his fingers.

Staring into those eyes that now resembled those of a wild deer, Adhelmar softly pressed, "What's the compass to you, a gift from that rot?"

It was as if some spell had descended on his captive. Arnacin trembled, yet he only pressed his closed fist against his chest, the black cord of his compass dangling from it, and retreated back to the center of the room.

Glancing at him appraisingly, Hans placed the food on the desk. "I'll be back with the tub, Captain." As he made to leave, however, he switched to the Nomacirrian language. "I think, whatever else happened, he's deranged. That's all there is to it."

With a shrug, he left. Adhelmar nodded toward the food. "He thinks you're deranged, Arnacin. Why don't you act sane and eat like a usual starved person would?"

"He'd make himself sick if he ate like that," Polion muttered from the corner.

Adhelmar barely smiled, waiting for a response. The only movement from the captive, however, was his thumb running around the edge of his compass. Then, his gaze dropped to it and his shoulders fell in defeat. Silently, he accepted the food.

Not so with the bath half an hour later.

If Arnacin's protests were due to a strange amount of modesty, Adhelmar could not fathom it, and if it was a clever ruse to gain some time alone in which he could escape, that could not be allowed. When Arnacin first drew his cloak about himself, saying he wanted nothing to do with a bath, Adhelmar considered allowing him to stay dirty, but the sight of those raw wrists and blood-splattered clothes and hair convinced him otherwise. He simply stood aside with Hans as Polion wrestled Arnacin into the tub, soaked clothes coming off only afterward.

To everyone's shock, the captive submitted once submerged in water, except that he never allowed Polion to pull him back out. Still, he permitted all but his torso to be attacked with soap and water, including his scalp.

Once he was done, he shot into the clean clothes they offered, as if afraid to leave his skin exposed to air for even a second. Compressing his lips, Hans tapped the side of his head and slipped out with the dirty bundle of clothes to be washed.

Chapter 9

The Black Captain

EVENING CAME BEFORE ADHELMAR COULD attempt any more conversation with his obstinate captive. Writing his review of the day, the captain glanced up at his silent clean prisoner.

Arnacin sat in the large chair he had been offered, his heels tucked up onto the seat in front of him, his gaze fixed on one flickering candle hanging in its lantern. With his arms resting atop his bent knees and his thumb brushing his lips, he appeared quite oblivious to any movement around him, his breathing as ragged as his shivering implied. Although wrapped in a blanket, he still trembled.

Aside from a few moments when the sound of his breathing cut off strangely, nothing changed. Glancing from the figure in the chair to the two guards on each side of it, Adhelmar thought not so much of a watched prisoner as an ailing king protected by his attendants.

Shaking his head, the captain softly inquired, "You have not told me what caused your cowardice amidst the pirates, Arnacin."

For quite some time, no answer came. The captain was beginning to think he had not been heard when Arnacin whispered, "I should be brainless to do so, after telling you the power it apparently has over me."

"If it's what I think it is, it doesn't seem all that strong."

Those dark eyes finally turned in Adhelmar's direction. Yet, unlike that morning, they told him nothing, those still pools of depthless indigo.

Striving not to end a conversation that could lead to an answer, the captain confessed, "I also interrogated Captain Xavior. It was difficult to make him speak of you, although he gloated about what he did to our Captain Belon. He did let me know you agreed to remain on his ship just after that. If your agreement lay in cowardice, Arnacin, would your fear be of death at the hands of others?"

Arnacin's gaze simply flicked downward, and the captain tried again. "I know what controls pirates, what can make them agree to drink poison to avoid it, but what about you? Are you also fearless about the possibility of death while in the midst of battle and then a coward when you must wait for that punishment?" He waited, yet no answer came. "Because frankly, Arnacin, I know you're thinking you know what's coming, and I haven't heard any sound of a plea or bleat for it to be otherwise."

The captain finally sparked a brief look of scorn, yet it reverted to the silence of before. Shaking his head, the captain searched for a different angle. In the silence, he did notice the sudden disappearance of his captive's heavier breathing. Looking back up, he eventually tried, "Is Enchantress Island a real place or was it a title given to you?"

"I wouldn't tell you either way."

"In that case, what type of place would receive such a name?"

"If it isn't a place, how should I know?"

Briefly looking heavenward, the captain gave up on that angle. "What were you blamed for on Mira?"

Again, those dark eyes turned to him, smoldering in their depths and, in the cabin lit only by the flame of candles, the captain could not shake the feeling that he had roused a dragon from rest. Shivering, he resumed his writing, hoping he was not moving too hurriedly. When he looked up a moment later, however, the captive had returned to staring through the wall.

Clicking his tongue, the captain asked, "Very well, Arnacin. Perhaps you would like to present a topic for tonight's discussion?"

After only a second, Arnacin spoke with the same distant softness that marked everything he had said that night, "Where is this ship headed?"

"To its home port." The answer brought a jerk of alarm, and Adhelmar added, "The queen will be awaiting word with growing concern."

"You will release me before then." It was half-question, half-order, and the captain grinned in spite of himself.

"You might as well not quibble. I hear your ship needs a replacement or two before she is on her way again. Therefore, you must land in some port."

"My ship is ready to sail this minute."

"Then we shall simply await the queen's decision." With that, Adhelmar returned to his journal. The sound of hissing metal and swift movement made him look up again to see that the captive had shot to his feet—and in reply, one of the guards had drawn his blade, resting the tip against Arnacin's back.

"Sit down, Arnacin," the captain advised, contemplating those rage-white features. "There is nothing for you to do, other than whatever pleases me."

Ignoring both the order and the blade, Arnacin whispered, "If whatever pleases you is to bring me back to your country to hang or worse, you will find only death will bring me there."

Reminded once again of a king, albeit a captured one, Adhelmar remarked, "It looks very likely, but I have not said once that I intend to play with you in any form. If I was hoping for that to happen, you would still be below. What I need to know, Arnacin, if you would be so kind as to actually assist, is whether or not you have ever committed an act of piracy."

Head raising, Arnacin stated, "I told you."

"In words only. Where is the proof of that? You refuse to tell me anything that will help me make a decision." In frustration,

Adhelmar slapped his hand against his journal. At the snap of paper, he exhaled. "What brought you to sea?"

Slowly returning to the chair, Arnacin buried his head in his arms. Still, the captain waited. After long, ticking minutes, a muffled voice breathed, "You don't want to hear about anything before Mira. It doesn't have any answers."

"Then what do I want to hear?"

"Why I yielded to Xavior."

Yet Arnacin had refused to reveal that piece of information. Asking again would likely bring the same answer—fear of what Nomacir would do with that knowledge.

Softly, Adhelmar tried anyway. "Why would we use that information, Arnacin? What do you really have to give us—your bondage? Nomacir has no extra strength to keep slaves in line even if we wanted them."

The top of that black head only rocked back and forth in refusal. If there was something special he could give, perhaps no one could blame him for keeping the secret, despite anyone's frustration.

Rubbing the quill along his nose for a second, Adhelmar returned to his writings.

With his right ankle chained to the creakiest bunk in *Isholt's Revenge* and guards posted nearby, Arnacin found no chance to escape. For the first half of the night, a candle burned while guard and captive watched each other. When the candle burned out at last, Arnacin lay there, feverishly striving to keep his visions of sealed tombs at bay while he waited for the deeper, even breaths of his guard.

Finally, the awaited sound came. Cautiously, Arnacin raised his head and winced as the bed creaked beneath him. Abruptly, the guard's breathing changed. Even in the dark, there was no doubt he was awake.

Sighing, the islander rolled onto his back, feeling his compass tap lightly against his chest as he did—the compass Valoretta had given him.

Valoretta. He could still clearly picture her as he last saw her a year ago—regal, pale and silent to the injustice transpiring before her.

Even so... Pulling his compass out from under his shirt, he tightened his fingers about it. Once they had laughed and teased each other in Mira's library. In sharing their deepest concerns and dreams, he thought they had become family. But by her silence that fateful day, she had proven otherwise.

As if in contradiction to his hurt, the princess's last words to him seemed to echo in the dark. *Come out by noon, Arnacin. Don't die before you can.*

Birds circled around a muddy dell, where a bundle shivered. Approaching, Arnacin's breath stopped. Valoretta lay there in a curled ball, covered in dirt and blood, her tangled hair sprawling about her face and the ground, a thin shift hardly even covering her skeletal legs. Whether she was conscious or not, even the birds knew it was only moments before her last breath.

Abruptly, Arnacin stood on the edge of a rock tower rising out of the sea.

"How are you here?" The snap was Charlotte's, as she glided downward to land beside him, her ebony eyes flames burning beneath her skull.

Retreating a step into the grasping waves, Arnacin quickly shook his head. Yet, his horrific sister pressed onward. "You're here solely through the death of someone else! You've betrayed us all, brought dishonor on yourself and your family, abandoned your rescuer to her death—"

"Charlotte, every sane person knows she's likely dead. It would be foolishness to return to Mira!"

"*Coward! Can you live with yourself for not personally finding out?*" With a curl of her scarlet lips, his sister circled him. "*Besides, who said you're a 'sane person?'*"

As that condemnation struck like a dagger, Arnacin woke. Tossing his blankets to the bottom of the bunk, he released a long exhale. Since he had heard of Mira's fall, his nightmares continually grew ever more insistent and condemnatory. No longer could he deny that, regardless of Valoretta's betrayal, he could never return home without first going to Mira. If she still lived, he could never leave her to die like some of the pirates' female prisoners. And if she was really dead, he had to know.

Yet Adhelmar would never release him. Had the officer intended to do so, he would have already. Arnacin's only chance was escape, and he had limited time for that before he was sentenced to the gallows.

Early the next morning, before the guards allowed Arnacin back on deck, Adhelmar asked Polion to bring up a pirate for questioning. If the selection was made by levels of fear, a better choice would not have been possible. As soon as the small, thickset pirate was allowed to see, he dropped to his knees, trembling.

"Please, Cap'n, sir. Grant some mercy. I never attacked Nomacir personal-like."

"But you attacked it."

"Nothing else enabled me to eat, see?" As pathetic as this pirate was after Arnacin and Xavior, he was a relief.

Releasing his frustration in a long breath, Adhelmar asked, "What's your name, pirate?"

"Mr. Butter, Cap'n."

Adhelmar's eyebrows raised. "Mr. Butter?"

Hastily, the pirate nodded. "They calls me that 'cuz they thinks me too soft. It's a jibe against hows I niver like the dallying, Cap'n, nor drunkenness. It's disturbing, not being in yer right head."

"Then what is your real name?"

"No, Cap'n. I've always been called No until I was Mr. Butter. Some think it's short fer Noel, but no one rightly knows. It's just Mr. No Butter."

Shaking his head helplessly, Adhelmar controlled his quirking lips. "I see." His tone revealed the opposite but, continuing, he said, "Does Mr. Butter also mean you're spineless?"

"No, Cap'n. Not to me reckoning, but me neck's especial."

It was just the right opening. "You may save your neck some if you tell me where the pirate haven is and the best way to demolish it."

To the captain's surprise, Mr. Butter simply studied him for a minute. It was as if he had sealed a lid over his fear. At last, he whispered, "Would that I believed ya."

Irritably, Adhelmar growled, "If you can believe Captain Xavior, 'a man of his word,' you can believe me. My queen will likely spare your life in exchange for that piece of information."

The pirate remained kneeling. Another moment passed, and finally, he whispered, "I'll think about it, Cap'n. Becoming a traitor is a hard thing, no matter the need."

Strangely, Adhelmar was reminded of Arnacin in that simple statement. Muttering, "Yes," he forced his attention back to Mr. Butter and asked, "What do you know of Arnacin? Did he commit any act of piracy?"

Mr. Butter cocked his head, his brow furrowing. "Arnacin, Cap'n? I couldn't say. He's a clam, he is. If'n he did murder someone, ya'd never read it on his face, but he hates hisself for some reason. No, I couldn't say either way."

"Of course not," Adhelmar breathed, but there was nothing else to ask.

"With fortune, we will be back in our own waters by tomorrow," Hans informed Adhelmar as they stood on the forecastle three days later. Below, Arnacin wandered the main deck, free to enjoy the wind and sky as long as his two guards stood on either side of him and he remained on *Isholt's Revenge*, not aboard his own ship, which was trailing behind.

"Good, I'll—" The captain cut off as a taunting voice drifted toward him on the wind.

"Oh, hail the king as he passes with his entourage."

Quickly Adhelmar whirled just in time to see his captive squarely punch the outspoken sailor, Silas, in the jaw. In wrath, the sailor, who loathed everything to do with the *Zedelious*, swung back, just as one of Arnacin's guards attempted to grab the prisoner. A snort of amusement emitted from Arnacin as the two Nomacirrians hit each other, since he ducked at the last second.

Instant chaos ensued. Impressed in spite of himself, the captain watched as Arnacin engaged the whole ship in the brawl within seconds, always seeming to avoid the mayhem himself. When the sailors' tempers flared and they turned to attack each other, Adhelmar sprang to life.

"Attention!" He ordered. Below, everyone halted, some in mid-strike, as heads turned to their captain. Glaring toward Arnacin, who was fighting a grin even as the guards seized his arms, Adhelmar reprimanded his men. "I would never expect such contemptible and undisciplined behavior from the lot of you. You are sailors in Her Majesty's navy. Act like it!"

Low mutters of apologies and shame arose from the men below. Turning his attention to the real culprit, the captain stalked down the stairs to stand directly in front of Arnacin. "And you," he growled. "How dare you attack any of my men?"

For a second, only an unflinching stare of triumphant victory answered his fury. Yet when Arnacin spoke, lifting his chin, his voice was low with bitterness. "He dared to call me a noble."

Biting back the reply that Silas spoke the approximate truth, Adhelmar warned, "Whatever the cause, do that again and I will see you back in the hold without any intention of asking the queen for a pardon. Is that clear?"

The captive made no reply, not even altering his expression. Turning on his heel, the captain snapped to his guards, "Keep him in the cabin for the rest of today."

Although his captors roughly pushed Arnacin into the cabin, they never thought to check his sleeves, never thought to question his given reason for starting a brawl. With any luck, that taunting sailor failed to notice his missing dagger. Or if he did, hopefully, he thought it fell off in the skirmish and was lost somewhere.

With that metal pressed against his forearm, however, Mira seemed much closer. As the guards shut the door behind them, the islander's control of his fears slipped. The cabin of *Isholt's Revenge* melted into a black tower room.

On the other side of the thick stone, he heard Miro's voice, and he whirled toward that wall—perhaps it was thinner.

Fingers seized his upper arm. "Where are you going?"

He had no answer, no awareness of space. *His lungs were closing, his muscles twitching in weakness.*

Someone was speaking nearby, on his side of the wall, but he could no longer understand.

Then, water was trickling down his throat. Something in that sensation brought reality back. He was seated in Adhelmar's large chair with the captain himself staring down at him, eyebrows raised.

Despite his warming cheeks, Arnacin was glad Adhelmar's expression was completely devoid of understanding. At the least, it appeared no one would put the pieces together. At best, the dagger was still lying against his forearm.

Without asking anything, however, Adhelmar turned to his desk, sitting on the edge of it. Arms folded, he continued to stare at the islander for a moment longer, then turned to some papers beside him. Apparently, he was as tired as Arnacin was, but if he thought patience would bring answers in time, he would keep waiting.

Closing his eyes, the islander rested his head on the back of the chair, striving to focus on the draft blowing under the door, the scratch of the quill pen—sounds and sensations that were far removed from Mira's tower room. If he were to survive that night, he had to keep his thoughts away from the dagger that would enable his return to the land of his exile.

He had no real notion of time. Paper crackled and the quill kept scratching. Abruptly, however, Adhelmar asked, "What is your mission, Arnacin?"

When the islander simply looked at him, the captain stated, "Your guards tell me something drives you near to insanity. By day, your gaze is frequently fixed either westward or eastward. Why is that?"

So, the captain *was* chronicling everything. Drawn to a world map mounted behind the desk, Arnacin shuddered. Mira's mass seemed to cackle at him, but on the parchment, the westernmost sea was marked by blackness. Unable to read the Nomacirrian lettering, the meaning was unclear. Still, it agreed with his observations of the sky.

Without conscious thought, he whispered, "The sun rises in the east and sets in the west. Yet it's a lie, for the sun rises where it sets and sets where it rises."

Adhelmar's glare was apparent even without looking. "I have also heard that someone overheard you talking in your sleep."

Paling, Arnacin's gaze fixated on the captain.

With just a twitch of a victorious smile, Adhelmar continued, "If you remember anything of this dream, what does 'Not Mira' mean or 'Not her'? Who? Princess Valoretta, by any chance?"

Heart beating hard, the islander waited. Was the captain toying with him? Was there a reason he had ordered Arnacin kept within his cabin—to prove his suspicion?

Finally, Adhelmar continued, "Of course, it was only heard at a distance, and the attempt to move closer woke you instantly. Maybe you didn't say that."

"I don't... I don't remember a dream at all." Arnacin's voice cracked, and the captain's stare bored into him, searching.

With a shrug, Adhelmar asked, "Nevertheless, what is your mission?"

"To go home."

"Again, where is that?"

The islander's gaze drifted to the map on the wall, to where the sky turned black and the ocean tipped off into nothingness, where his island fittingly sat. Finally, Arnacin whispered, "Over the edge of the world."

"If that means you intend suicide, don't think I will oblige you. Yet, if you would tell me where your home is, I might be inclined to drop you off there once all this is over."

"You most certainly will not."

"You try my patience! Once and for all, what could my knowledge of your home harm?"

"Perhaps I simply don't wish anyone to know my whereabouts, particularly not someone devoted to a queen."

"And what difference does my loyalty to Queen Isholt make? Has it not occurred to you that it is her goodness, mercy and greatness that causes such loyalty?"

Adhelmar had unwittingly barreled through Arnacin's shields. Pain, disgust, memory and rage roiled through that crack. "So your queen plays," the islander finally said. "The world views her as weak. How would she survive without devoted servants? What could she do but pretend all those things in order to ensure absolute worship? And worship you do, for she—so good, so great, so beautiful—is also so defenseless, and she knows it. She will rise to her own power and glory, not through the force of kings, but through the cunning of the grave, and while she purrs in gratitude by day, she shrieks with glee behind closed doors, glorifying in how she enslaves men to her whims.

"That in itself would be enough to execute her, but to keep her mask of helpless perfection, she must make sure to rid her army, navy, lands of all who see through her. But she can't do it openly. No, instead, those *dangers* 'betray' their country in some fashion and are quickly removed. Beware when comes the day you are no

longer necessary to her, or you may find yourself sharing Captain
Phillio's story. I know better than to allow her anywhere near me."

"You've met one of our captains who turned to piracy,"
Adhelmar breathed.

"Turned or was forced?"

Shaking his head swiftly, the captain snapped, "I will not be
poisoned, *pirate* of an islander. Those men were snared by love
of gold, and yes, they fled trial, but they were not *forced*. I have
no idea what you've heard from the traitor, Phillio, but I know my
queen and I knew him.

"Captain Phillio was a proud, arrogant man. He was continually
asking why, since we were the actual defenders of Nomacir and
not the queen, why we delivered all the gold to her. Should we not
be the ones to judge how much we needed and how much should
go to support the other needs of the kingdom?

"When he left to guard a precious shipment back to Nomacir,
we were dispirited, but not entirely surprised to hear he ran away
with all the cargo and killed those of his crew unwilling to turn
traitor. Whatever he said to you, you can be sure it was a self-ab-
solving lie."

Folding his arms, Arnacin glared. "The names of your ships
swear against you, to say nothing of your butchery of criminals."

"Our ships are named to incite fear so that, maybe, we can
spare more of our men's lives! And the punishment is to—"

"To prevent others from trying the same," the islander interrupted. "Then kill them immediately and hang their carcasses
along your city walls. Otherwise, you torture for sport or hatred
on your queen's orders and then try to proclaim her goodness."

Adhelmar leaned back, cocking his head slightly. "You feel
compassion for them? Were you or were you not their prisoner?"

"You drift from the point to hide your doubt. Your queen is a
liar and you know it."

Pausing for only a second, the captain asked, "Surely you realize there are good rulers and bad?"

"Hardly. By your own words, simple, *devoted* men are 'snared by love of gold.' What does the glory of a throne, combined with its tenuousness, do? It corrupts."

"So, you would be one to deny possessions, for it corrupts even the innocent?"

"Innocent!" This time Arnacin could not keep his voice level. "Humans are born with self-glory as their mission."

"Ah, including yourself? Or are you about to tell me all those superstitions are correct–you're not human."

Words lodged in the islander's throat and he could only look away.

After a moment, Adhelmar finished, "One or the other is true, Arnacin. Either there are people who don't fit into your *beastly* description or there aren't. Which one is it?"

"I once thought there were," Arnacin finally breathed.

Dropping his attention back to his work, Adhelmar growled, "Someday, you will come across someone who can gain nothing for their deeds, nothing, and then you will know righteousness exists. I hope it does not come with too much cost to you."

"There seems nothing I can lose. You insist on dragging me to the 'mercy' of your enthroned hag."

His head jerking upward, Adhelmar snapped, "One more word like that, and I will do what I've considered doing for days."

"Kill me? Good riddance."

"Absolutely not." Standing, the captain approached the islander. Putting one hand on each arm of the chair to trap Arnacin, he whispered, "If you insist on knowing, I was thinking of chopping off your legs at the knees and leaving you on whatever island you choose. In so doing, I wouldn't be forced to execute someone innocent of piracy, and I would know you could never return to threaten Her Majesty. In retrospect, I should consider removing your tongue as well. After that, suicide would be entirely on your head!"

Horror prevented the islander from remarking on how such cruelty would only prove Nomacir's guilt. Although he bit his tongue, he refused to tremble, darkly meeting the captain's stare.

Pushing himself away, Adhelmar resumed his seat on the edge of his desk and folded his arms.

Arnacin remained silent. Yet Xavior had ruled through his fear. That thought again stirred him. "You can't use that to force me to succumb to your every whim."

"Ha!" Adhelmar exploded in sarcastic laughter. "If it could force you to do even one thing I wanted, it would be a miracle. My every whim? Incredible!"

Finally back in Nomacirrian waters, Adhelmar kept extra watch for enemy ships, fearing every additional moment spent at sea with the captives. He had wasted far too much time on Xavior's Arnacin Islander. Since it seemed no solution was forthcoming to that enigma, the captain was nearly ready to quit when they arrived home. Heaven forbid an actual audience with Queen Isholt. That wretch would slam her into the wall just with words.

And yet, if he truly was Arnacin of Enchantress Island, Mira's chosen king...

Seeming to echo his thoughts, shouts sounded through his cabin's walls. Dashing to the door and throwing it open in the expectation of some sneak attack or escaped pirates swarming from the hold, Adhelmar groaned in exasperation. Approximately a third of the ship's crew leaned over the poop deck's rail, while others lowered the sails of the *Isholt's Revenge*. Behind, the small ship had been freed and now floated alone, already some distance away.

"Where is he?" Adhelmar snapped. A few of the sailors shifted aside at their captain's approach to reveal the culprit, his arms once again shackled behind him and a darkening bruise on the side of his head. Only one of his guards stood there. The other one leaned over the rail, holding his ribs as he gasped in pain.

"What did you do?" the captain demanded of his captive, receiving only silence.

It was the remaining guard who supplied a knife that obviously belonged to one of the sailors. "He was just standing here, as he does every day, when this appeared in his hand. Before we could stop him, he had sliced through the rope mooring his ship. We both went to grab him, and he jabbed Quentin under the ribs with the hilt and avoided my lunge. He almost slipped over the side…" He showed his left fist, where a long slash went across the knuckle. "If Silas hadn't arrived with the pole, those sails wouldn't be furled on his ship now."

Glaring at the captive, who denied nothing, Adhelmar swiped the blade, turning briefly to the nearest sailor. "Retrieve the ship." With that, he whirled back toward the cabin. "Bring him."

Once inside with the door shut, the captain dropped the knife onto his desk before turning to regard Arnacin. "Where did you obtain that?"

"From the sailor I punched." It was said matter-of-factly, without the slightest gloating.

Pressing his hand against his forehead, Adhelmar sank into his chair. "Why do I have the feeling it wasn't for wrath you hit him?"

"Perhaps because I didn't."

For a minute, the captain said nothing, dropping his hand to again study his captive—it seemed he had to do so constantly. "You're something else, Arnacin. Do you *wish* to be hanged?"

"I've been told it's my highest ambition."

"I highly doubt it. You would honestly prefer hanging to an audience with the queen?" The following silence spoke volumes Adhelmar did not actually want to hear. "What is it really that makes you think so little of her mercy?"

"What mercy?" Arnacin said. "I don't think so little of it—I don't believe her to possess it."

"I think she would spare you, if you would only behave."

"That would not be a mercy, and therefore I would not accept it. I would sooner believe a water snake of simply keeping me warm in its coils."

Adhelmar's face grow hot, but before he could reply, a sailor dashed in, calling, "Captain, pirates northbound!"

The captain's gaze locked briefly with the captive's. After a second, he rubbed his forehead. "Very well, Arnacin. Help against the impending attack, and I will pardon you myself for service to Her Majesty." When Arnacin made no reply, he only waited.

Finally, Arnacin relented. "Fine, I'll aid, but only in this, and on the understanding that I am free afterward."

"Curious," Adhelmar vengefully said. "With all their talk of Arnacin of Enchantress Island, I never pictured him so selfish." He gained nothing but a lift of the head, and the captain nodded to the guard to release their captive. Pulling Arnacin's blade from a locked drawer in his desk, Adhelmar cautiously relinquished it to its master.

Without taking his gaze from that blade, watching every small movement as it was returned to its proper place at his captive's side, the captain told the messenger, "Send Polion in here. Tell Hans to order additional sails. We'll outrun them as long as we can."

As the messenger departed, the captain again contemplated the captive. "It's likely to come to a fight, since they spotted us first. Under those circumstances, I want you to board the pirate ship as soon as possible. Be the first one over, if you can."

A cruel smile spread across Arnacin's face. "The first one over is often the first one dead."

"Hang you, Arnacin! I don't trust you on this ship while we're engaged in battle!"

"I agreed to help, did I not?" Before Adhelmar could reply, the captive pressed on. "If you do engage, I would suggest you weaken your own resistance, at least visibly. Don't let anyone actually board the pirate ship—"

"You agreed—!"

"Build their confidence until it kills them! The first thing you've done is attempt to run. Use it."

Although Adhelmar saw Polion enter out of the corner of his eye, he did not turn from the glaring match for another precious second. Then, he snapped, "Polion! As needed as the men are, take a whole bunch down into the hold and stay there. Take fifteen and guard those prisoners. I want you to personally stand by Xavior. Let no one down there and, if even one pirate slips by your men guarding the stairs, run Xavior through."

Glancing toward Arnacin, Polion asked, "Would you not want me by—"

"I will rue the day if I actually do need you. But go. Hurry! There are others here to help with him."

Opening the door for Polion as Arnacin's two guards closed in on the captive, Adhelmar whispered, "And, Polion, tell Hans to weaken our resistance until he can taste the attackers' confidence in the air."

Nodding, Polion ducked out.

"Come," Adhelmar ordered the remaining three in his cabin. He saw Arnacin untie his cloak, throwing it over the desk before leaving between his guards. Considering that the captive wore his cloak like a shield, never removing it, Adhelmar lifted his eyebrows before exiting himself.

Standing beside guards and navy captain while the *Isholt's Revenge* vainly attempted to outdistance the ship bearing down on her, Arnacin overheard—and ignored—the soft whispers between the sailor, Hans, and the captain.

"Why ask him if he'll help?"

"It's his only chance," Adhelmar hissed back. "To my reckoning, he actually is Mira's Arnacin of Enchantress Island—but I still don't know if he's a pirate. So, if he returns with us, I'll lump him in with the rest. Our queen's peace of mind depends on it. Hang me if I guess wrong, but somehow, I wanted to give him one last opportunity to spare himself."

"If you guess wrong, none of us may be around to hang you," Hans muttered. Nodding, he returned to the main deck and his command post.

For the most part, Arnacin remained still until the pirate ship had succeeded in snaring the navy ship. Then, as the sounds of battle erupted from the surging mass along the rail, the islander moved, dropping to the main deck, out of reach of his grasping captors.

"Pirate!" one of his previous guards snapped.

"What are you doing?" Adhelmar's suspicion sounded over the fray.

"You wished me to be the first one over, Captain?" Arnacin mocked. "As you command."

With that, he raced to the rail alongside the enemy ship. Dispatching those who attacked, he quickly placed his bloody blade between his teeth and vaulted over the rail, catching the pirate ship's side ladder right before he hit water. Hanging there for a second while bodies splashed around him, he climbed up one rung before starting on the slippery, tarred clamber around the back of the ship and through the first bay window.

Dropping his blade back into his hand, he crept out of the cabin. Standing right on the stairs to the main deck was the pirate captain, a squat, round-faced man of dark hair. Currently, his back was to the islander as he urged his crew forward.

For just a moment, Arnacin paused, loathing to strike anyone unaware. Yet in that split second, the pirate must have sensed his presence. Ducking as the captain's blade whistled overhead, the islander stabbed upward, running the captain through the stomach.

In the captain's death cry, Arnacin sensed, more than saw, the pirate crew look up. A shout of victory rose into the air as Adhelmar's sailors swarmed over the rail in the brief hesitation.

Over that, a voice shouted, "Fight, idiots! The *Isholt's Revenge* is ours for the taking!"

Scanning the crowd for the speaker, Arnacin kicked the body of the captain into the pirates swarming up the stairs. Pounding footsteps to his left alerted the islander, and he whirled to meet the attack.

"You'll find me a harder captain to defeat," the second-in-command growled, taking a full step back, baiting him.

With pirates clambering over the body at the bottom of the stairs, the islander was forced to accept that bait—and win fast. Charging, he sidestepped at the last minute, driving his blade through his opponent's side, and whirled on his heel to meet another sword lunging for his shoulder blades.

But the second-in-command was not yet dead. Sensing the dying pirate lunge behind him, Arnacin dodged, wincing as metal scraped his side.

Gasping, his two current attackers ran each other through. Three more reached the step below him, and he clashed with them.

For some time, Arnacin faced one attacker after another. Then, a shout rang out. "The *Immortal*! Ur damnation's 'ere!"

Should Nomacir lose that moment of fear, it did not seem like they would win. Quickly dispatching his current opponent, the islander commanded with cold authority, "Surrender now, while the option remains open to you!"

"Kill them!" The shout forced the attack on. "We'll simply be hanged instead."

"I'll burn this ship to the bottom of the ocean!" the islander warned. "Then, meet the burning furnace of eternity!" As Arnacin whirled back toward the cabin to carry out his threat, he heard several yells and then the thudding of weapons dropping to the deck.

Still, many pirates refused to surrender, and the navy sailors pressed their attack. Lighting the cabin in flames, Arnacin then joined the fray on the main deck, carefully staying out of reach of the navy.

Finally, as the aft mast crashed to the deck, amid the choking black smoke and flying red embers, the pirates surrendered. Yet the pirate before Arnacin growled, "Kill me now, Zedelious. If you possess any mercy, run me through."

Without answer, the islander turned away. He heard the warning rustle and he whirled, sinking his blade into the pirate. Watching the body crumple to the deck, he whispered, "There's your mercy. Little good it will do you."

Stunned silence filled the vessel, yet not another pirate gave the navy sailors trouble while Arnacin stood there.

Chapter 10

Return to Mira

SAILORS LED PIRATE AFTER PIRATE over from the burning ship. There was no sign of Arnacin Islander, although Adhelmar heard quite a bit from those reporting. The reports were enough, however, to make him think again about the character of the captive.

Then, he spotted Arnacin step onboard, bent forward slightly, his hand pressing into his right shoulder beneath his shirt. A red-edged slash rent through his shirt's side, shining dully in the sharp light of the setting sun. Adhelmar also spotted scarred slashes over Arnacin's right forearm, where his rolled sleeves no longer hid them from view.

Before Adhelmar could even inquire about injury, however, the islander glanced once around the *Isholt's Revenge*, as if to confirm the captain's victory, and then instantly turned toward his ship, tied to the larger vessel.

"Arnacin," the captain called, "where are you going?"

Without even turning around, the former captive quipped, "To haunt natives."

"Do you trust me so little that you will not even give me a brief report before you leave?"

This time, Arnacin whirled around, dropping his arm back to his side. "Had you released me when you knew I had spoken true about Mira, as promised, I might think differently."

"You never answered what I really needed to know!"

The only reply was a cold dip of his chin as the islander again started toward his escape.

Adhelmar dashed into his cabin, snatching up the cloak the islander had left there before the battle. "Arnacin," he called as he rushed back to the deck.

Slowly, as if some ingrained politeness battled with his bitterness and distrust, the islander turned back from where he had just touched the railing. The captain tossed the cloak to him. Catching it in surprise, the islander nodded in wordless acknowledgment and disappeared.

Mere minutes passed before the sail on the small ship rose into the air and, filling, drove the ship through the waves like a low-flying arrow. As Adhelmar watched the dark, quickly shrinking form begin to descend the ratlines, he whispered in contemplation, "I thought they were simply superstitious when they called him the Black Phantom."

"Captain?" He turned to see Hans watching the disappearing ship.

Nodding to it, the captain finished, "Seeing him in action, I can only agree. He is nothing, if not a *Black* Phantom."

His course had been set for Mira for three days already, and each new day brought an increasing desperation to turn back. Open air no longer kept that tomb away.

The mammoth tower rose out of the ocean's morning fog and floated on the waves like a giant whale surfacing to swallow him, ship and all.

Yet for some reason, Arnacin kept sailing toward it, trembling with feverish terror.

For that reason, it took him a moment, as he sat curled up against his mast, to realize that he could hear the strengthening swish of waves striking against something other than water or his own vessel.

Shooting to his feet, he saw a black-flagged ship bearing down on him, already almost within boarding distance. Spinning around, Arnacin scrambled up his rigging as fast as possible. Without wasting time looking at the position of his attackers, he reached the top, loosened the sail's clamp and swung it to cut into the wind.

With a lurch that nearly cost him his footing, his ship tacked away from its attacker. Looking up just in time to see several figures splash into the ocean as they missed his aft deck, Arnacin grinned in bitter triumph.

He waited only until he saw the enemy ship turn in a new direction, then shifted wind again. That ship, many-sailed though it was, could not keep pace with the little twisting one. Eventually, now leagues away, Arnacin watched the ship turning in resignation.

Sighing, the islander waited until sight of the ship vanished over the horizon before fixing his course back toward Mira. Slowly, he descended to his deck.

In the absence of danger, however, his thoughts returned to Mira and its king, who haunted him worse than any ghost. If the islander was forced to again enter that keep, he could already guess that specter would lurk around every corner, waiting to gleefully order entombment.

As his fingers whitened around his gold sheath, Arnacin sagged against the rail at his ship's prow.

The soft whisper of feet over wood sounded behind him. Whipping out his blade, he stopped the attacker's sword an inch from his throat. Gloating, green eyes met him on the other end of those briefly locked blades before Arnacin pushed his attacker away, giving himself a second to escape the trap of his rail.

Mid-step, the attacker lunged. Caught at just the right moment, Arnacin twisted closer, knowing he could not prevent that blade from piercing his skin. Instead, he chose where it would go, painfully allowing it to sink through his upper left arm as he shoved the Tarmlin blade through his attacker's chest.

Now pinned to Arnacin, the attacker's skin paled. His weight increased as his knees gave way. Carefully, the islander lowered himself with the body to the deck.

With a last, choked gasp, the attacker stopped breathing, leaving Arnacin to slowly free himself, squeezing his hand over the holes in his upper arm. He stayed only long enough to slide his own blade out with his free hand, while bracing a foot against the pirate's body and standing up.

Stopping in the doorway, Arnacin kept his blade drawn. Nothing moved. No other attackers hid aboard. The only thing amiss was a black bundle sitting on his bed.

Cautiously, he approached the bundle the pirate had obviously left behind. Ripping the cloth away, he gasped. An uncut stone, the size of a child's head, lay there. The light from the open door skittered across its surface, bringing forth blue, green and purple iridescent rays from the depths of the stone.

So, this was why his attacker had waited until after his own vessel had left—he had wanted to steal the islander's ship to make away with his fortune. Many a man would kill for the mesmerizing beauty of that stone.

Even on Enchantress Island, it was said that dragons had come to the island with stones of this size, making the enchanters give chase.

Hastily, Arnacin rewrapped the stone, shoved it under the bed, and closed the cabinet doors. If he were intelligent, he would toss the troublesome thing overboard with the pirate's body once he was done stitching his arm. But when had he been intelligent?

Nearly a year after Sara's death, Valoretta still paced her room. For days, she had not rested. She neither dressed for the morning nor undressed for the night, instead staying in the light linen gown and black fur mantle the tribal woman had given her. Despite its natural waves, her hair hung limp and dirty, the flowers she had asked Sara to weave between its strands long since dead.

In their complete looting of her home, the natives had thrust all Mira's business writings at their captive without explanation—perhaps to remind her of all she had lost, hoping she would crack.

Yet, between their physical attacks on her, the room grew cold and silent. Her only possibility for much-needed warmth lay in the pile of papers before her, taunting her. Reading through them one last time, she committed them to the flames—all of them except for the parchment she had slipped inside the gown she now wore.

Although it strengthened her in a painful way to cleanse her homeland of its folly, her will to survive was slowly crumbling. Each second chipped away at her resolve and only pride mixed with her memory of Arnacin's indomitability had fueled her for even this long.

Just as Valoretta passed the door for the twentieth time that night, a wheezing, barely audible gasp of air reached her ears. Whirling to face the door, she backed against the wall, her own breath cutting off. The door did not budge, however. Jerking away from the wall, she realized the sound had come from the room's balcony. Standing between two doors, she knew there was no escape, or even fight, against a two-sided attack. In the dark of night, when the fear of the hunted came naturally, her weakened heart raced near to rendering her unconscious.

It was a few seconds before she noticed that no other sound followed. Nothing approached her. Slowly, the meaning of her name returned to her and she edged toward the balcony. Just that second, however, something appeared from around the corner. Involuntarily, a squeak ripped from her throat.

"Quiet. You'll only call more horrors upon us." She knew the accent of that angry hiss as if it were her own, and she threw her arms about him. Hardly had she touched Arnacin, however, before he shoved her off—but not before tensing beneath her arms.

Looking at him, she felt a slight shiver run down her spine. Beneath his cloak, every inch of him was locked with a darkness that matched the shadow of his lowered hood. His bitter anger seemed to have quadrupled since the day he had faced her father.

Through his coldness, she recognized terror and her heart was stabbed with guilt. "How are you here, Arnacin?"

Arnacin only turned back to the balcony, where a rope hung from the railing. Glancing at it, Valoretta wondered how he had scaled the wall. It had clearly been tied from the top. "Do you know how to climb down?" the islander demanded.

Tossing her head back without reply, the queen grasped the rope, swinging her legs over the railing. Sliding more than lowering herself, she winced as the sawing fibers burned her skin. Halfway down, the rope gave a twist, and she looked up to see that Arnacin had also started the descent, carefully and skillfully. Stumbling upon reaching the cobblestones below, Valoretta glanced at her hands, now smeared in her own blood.

Wordlessly, the islander dropped beside her. Seizing her wrist, he jerked her toward the gates. The baileys stretched before them in the moonlight, deathly silent, long black shadows seeming to follow them.

In the blackness beneath the inner gate, Arnacin paused abruptly. As the queen bumped into him, he whispered, "Except for those inside the keep, they're all along the mountains and the city's remains, watching the bay. Someone must have attempted battle recently."

"There were ships that attempted to sail into the harbor. Ursan, I believe. I can't remember how long ago."

Silently, Arnacin jerked her into flight across the outer bailey. Once beneath the outer gate, he paused, briefly looking back at her. She nodded once in understanding, knowing from her balcony viewpoint that a camp filled the area before them. They would need intense stealth.

"Pull your mantle over your head, keep to the walls and crawl," Arnacin ordered, stepping behind her. "That way." The direction he indicated led toward the forest of Kelwin and the marshes, but now was not the time to question anything.

Obediently, Valoretta yanked her mantle over her head and dropped to the ground, stuffing the folds of her skirt into her mouth to enable her to crawl. There was nothing she could do to stop the scuffing sound she created as she inched forward. It was only a slight relief to hear Arnacin behind her, not much quieter than she was. Still, casting a quick glance over her shoulder, she barely saw him amid the shadows. He drew the darkness in as if he belonged to it, and the queen quickly turned back to her own progress, her heart hammering for the freedom just beyond.

Deafened by her own thudding pulse, rushing blood and loud breathing, she was stunned when she reached the end of the castle's wall and no shout had rung out yet, no sign that they had been seen or heard. Ducking around the corner, darker on that side due to the position of the moon, she waited for Arnacin to join her. As he slid around the edge, he slowly pushed himself to his feet. Pulling her up, the islander pointed to the nearest tip of Kelwin's trees, an eighth of a mile away from them.

Her heart quailed at the open distance in full moonlight, a moon that had to be full on this night of all nights. Arnacin never gave her time to think, however. Seizing her wrist, he jerked her to full flight across that treacherous ground.

Sprinting through the night, they headed toward Kelwin in an arc that would leave them in the castle's shadow as long as possible. Valoretta did not complain as she was dragged along, one hand captive in Arnacin's tight grasp, her other hanging onto her mantle in their flight. Although she expected one any second, no cry of alarm followed. Somehow, they remained unseen.

It was a relief all the same when, under the shelter of the trees, the islander released her, slowing due to the underbrush.

Still, their progress was not much slower. Stumbling in an effort to keep up with him, the queen's foot slipped on a rock. Tiny stones impacted her bottom in a trickle that could hardly even be considered a brook. Grimacing, the queen glanced up.

She expected her companion to have missed that she had fallen behind. Not seeing him, she pushed herself to her feet. As she tripped again, however, he returned to where she was struggling.

His hood had slipped off, and his familiar expression of wicked laughter was just visible through the light in the trees.

"They'll find the rope by morning," Arnacin warned, again grabbing her wrist. "You have to hurry."

"Oh, and I just fell by walking carefully," Valoretta huffed, flicking water droplets at him. "You would think you were of the tribes with the ease you possess."

"I was born and raised around a wooded mountain," he hastily replied, starting off again, this time with her wrist captive in his guiding grasp.

Not much farther away, she spotted his ship resting serenely in the thin, shallow place where the river Carta almost died before it fell into the larger river, Amendeep, and from there rushed into the ocean. A fallen tree rested against its bow, along which they ran onto the ship's deck. While Valoretta stood below, Arnacin clambered about the mast. He completely turned the sail around, hanging it at the aft side. Though he raised and tightened it, it continued to hang limply, and she saw him nod, as if expecting no less, before he started down.

"Was that supposed to help?" Valoretta asked, feeling the ship drifting slightly beneath her feet.

"If the wind was blowing, it would," Arnacin snapped softly. "Right now, we have only the weak current to rely on and that's not strong enough to push us back into Amendeep."

"If." Valoretta nodded. "What brought you on such a suicide mission? It appears to me we are dead except for a slim 'if,' as you put it."

For a minute, Arnacin said nothing, glancing back up at the limp sail. When he finally looked at her, cold hatred filled his face. "Unfortunately, I gave your father my word—"

"A vow that was fulfilled the second he banished you!"

"No. I promised my service until the end of the war."

"Well, it's over."

"There's still a loose end," Arnacin bit out. "Until you are dead or free, my service is not over, although he refused my keeping of it."

Studying him, wondering why he had returned for her despite his hatred, Valoretta inquired, "What is your word, but a spoken sound? You promised your help to him—you certainly will not honor him by keeping it now."

"Honor *him*! That was all the swine ever thought about. I'd be proud to *dis*honor him. Maybe it's about my honor to myself, although you'd little understand." He paused, regarding her as penetratingly as she studied him. "While we're asking for reasoning, what about you? What was your motivation for assisting my escape from the tower, when you knew the price you would pay at the hands of your father for such treachery?"

"Treachery?" Valoretta laughed humorlessly. "Is it treachery to save him from his worst mistake in life or are you admitting that you committed some disloyalty that caused his attack?"

"With pride," Arnacin hissed. Valoretta could not decide if that was bitter sarcasm or not—his tone would likely be the same. Yet she little cared as he continued, "Nobles deserve nothing more than disloyalty, nor do they create anything more."

"Is that what you think of me?! That I only helped you for the sake of some political game, perhaps one in which I inherited the throne?"

He merely leaned against the rigging, yet it seemed even in the dark his eyes dared an answer.

"Let me tell you something, Arnacin, son of Bozzic of Enchantress Island. In the king's death, I would receive everything, male or not, and I had no wish to inherit that responsibility faster. Were you going to suggest that I hoped, in your righteous anger, you would murder him?"

"Perhaps," the islander whispered. "If you waited long enough, there certainly might have been challenge to your birthright, a son of Rosa's, a husband for you." Before she could answer through her enraged shock, he finished, "You certainly have been silent about what your actual purposes were."

Glaring at him, Valoretta opened her mouth, snapping it shut again just as quickly.

As condemnation glinted victoriously in his gaze, she wondered if she could simply alert the tribes to their flight and, before she died, confirm that she had wiped the oh-so-knowing expression off his face.

Even as she thought of revenge, her temper dissipated. Down deep, she knew she would never do it even if he betrayed her three times over—for she did love him, deeper than any love she had ever experienced. In him, though clearly buried, existed faithfulness, love, honesty and even trust. Those virtues, so desired by her and once so deeply ingrained in him, she would protect and fight for until her last breath. That she knew, however he treated her at the moment.

"It had nothing to do with that," she finally whispered, dropping her gaze. "But I cannot tell you why, and I know you cannot guess—for if you could, it would be no secret." There was a soft rustle before her. Looking up, she saw him land on the ground and disappear into the forest.

While watching for pursuit from the natives, Arnacin spent the rest of the night searching for wood they could use as poles to push the ship through the mud. If he did find something sturdy and of the right length, he also had to ensure it was lightweight enough for him to carry back, making his task almost in vain. Still, he labored at it in desperation.

As the breeze picked up, he heard the faintest rustle. Glancing in that direction, he saw them: dozens of tribesmen, some with their gazes on the ground, tracking, others with bows ready on the hunt.

Watching dawn creep across the sky while she waited for Arnacin's return, Valoretta gasped as the ship suddenly moved beneath her. In the turns of the river, it would likely run aground without guidance, and then they might never escape. However, the current guided the ship ever true, and her thoughts turned to the islander.

If the river took her out to sea without Arnacin... She did not even know where he had gone, nor why. Had he seen his ship move? Could he keep pace if he had? How could she stop it?

Before she could decide what to do, she heard the cries of men in pursuit of their prey. Whirling, she saw the islander break from the woods downstream, near where Carta joined Amendeep. Yet the waters of Amendeep had now seized the ship. It flowed rapidly downstream, and the queen thought it unlikely that anyone could keep pace. Arnacin seemed to come to the same conclusion, yet he rarely quit. His flight slowed just enough to calculate the ship's speed, and then he took off along the bank. Somehow, his pace almost matched the ship—almost. Little by little, he was losing ground.

"Arnacin! How do I stop it?" Valoretta ducked as an arrow whipped over her head. In her movement, however, she caught a glimpse of Amendeep's mouth, pouring into the open sea, and the blood drained from her face.

Abandoning her shelter in that moment of desperation, the queen shot to her feet and, leaning as far over the ship's side as she dared, she stretched out her hand. Thankfully, the ship was not that tall; if not for the speed of the vessel and the expanse of water between them, she could have easily brushed the islander's head. "Arnacin! Jump!"

Out of the corner of her eye, she saw the savages skid to a halt to aim as their quarry ran out of ground. Just as the ship brushed by the last of the land, Arnacin leapt. Valoretta gasped in pain as he caught her hand, jerking her shoulder in so doing, yet she hung on with all the strength she lacked. Both of their lives depended on it.

The islander's hold slipped, and Valoretta tightened hers. Oddly, he lacked the strength to clamber up. With horror, she noticed the red color of the water the ship was now dragging the islander through. Jerking her gaze back to those closed eyes and ashen features, the queen drew in a deep breath and pulled.

Somehow, straining her own muscles, Valoretta managed to heave her rescuer aboard. There, they both collapsed, sprawled across the deck while the ship sailed onward toward freedom.

Valoretta let herself rest for only a second, though, before she pushed herself up. Arnacin was a trembling heap, only a few inches from her feet. Otherwise, he did not move.

Urgency spread through her like a drug as she took in his stillness, the shaft protruding from his calf, his flushed face and slightly twitching fingers. In a flurry of action, the queen stumbled over to him, tripping constantly on her skirt in her haste, and ripped the arrow out. Blood quickly pooled over the deck.

Jerking convulsively, Arnacin stirred for the first time. "Leave it alone. It's nothing."

"Nothing!" Valoretta repeated, as white as him. "You know they slather poison over their arrow tips. You likely know that better than I, and you're showing every sign of those fevers!"

He neither replied nor moved.

"Arnacin, you can't die! I'll be stuck with a ship I know nothing about, in the open ocean, without any idea where I'm headed. This ship isn't even natural!" Her desperation grew as she took note of how his breathing was slowing. "I may as well be lost in a labyrinth if you die on me! Arnacin!"

In horror, she shook him viciously. To her surprise he responded, muttering as if from a great distance, "That's nice."

He had not heard a word she said. He was gone, and there was nothing she could do about it. In her desperation, as she mentally cast about for something to do, one of their old conversations rose to her mind. *Valoretta, I promised to return... I have to.*

With nothing left to do, Valoretta leaned toward his ear, her hair brushing his cheek as she whispered words on which she hated relying. "Arnacin, what will your family think when you never return, when you break your promise?"

Backing away, she watched, sure that it was a futile move. But to her astonishment and relief, some color gradually flooded his face. Shifting, Arnacin dragged himself to his knees. Valoretta dared not intrude as he reached for the rail, using it to haul himself to his feet. For just a second, it seemed he was going to simply pitch over, but then, little by little, he limped toward the cabin and disappeared inside, shutting the door with a soft thump. That sound was no less horrible for its softness.

Chapter 11

Once There Were Friends...

For hours, Valoretta remained where she sat, staring at the still-shut cabin door. It was her thirst that roused her first. The deck was devoid of anything to hold water, but in spotting the blood-tipped arrow on the deck before her, she seized it, tossing it overboard. That small venting of her frustration opened a well and, ripping the mantle from around her shoulders, she threw that overboard as well with a low scream. Exhausted by her own temper, the queen lay back on the deck, staring up at the red-tinged skies.

She knew her own death was near. At sea, her only hope lay in Arnacin, who was likely already a corpse inside his cabin. Valoretta had been betrayed by almost everyone and was now deserted in her final hours. For a year, she had expected no less. What she had not expected...

Slowly pushing herself up, the queen turned toward the cabin. Carefully opening the door, Valoretta felt her pulse quicken as she pictured the horrific sight she might find. In the light cast from a glass-encased candle, she did not find what she imagined she might. Indeed, reality was better, if messier.

A dresser stood against one wall, its top drawer on the floor, its contents rolling or smashed, littering the space around where Arnacin lay. He was crumpled in a ball, shivering in fever. Blood drenched the wood by his injured calf—not from the original wound revealed by his ripped pant-leg, but from a long, clean slash above it. If he wasn't dead yet, he must have somehow conquered the poison.

Her thirst temporarily forgotten, Valoretta knelt down beside the islander, gently touching his shoulder. Glassy-eyed, he looked up at her, and she knew it was with only partial consciousness. "How may I help?" she asked softly, hoping he both could answer and would not shove her away.

His gaze moved to his leg, where blood still oozed from the wound. At first, there was no response. Then, hardly audible, he rasped, "It has to be wrapped. There..."

His voice trailed off as his eyes closed. Looking around, Valoretta spotted a cloth still halfway in the drawer. Although her experience in binding wounds was limited to the occasional observance of another's work, she nevertheless seized the cloth, wrapping it as firmly and as smoothly as she could around the open wound. The arrow injury, she noticed as she worked, had been covered in some type of paste that had hardened like a scab around it. That, she left alone and open, not knowing if she was supposed to do anything.

Minutes ticked by while she pressed her hand over the cloth and watched it turn red around her fingers. Finally, however, it seemed to stop and she slowly straightened, sitting back on her heels. Arnacin continued to shiver in fever, but otherwise did not stir.

Without thought, she ran the back of her hand down his flushed cheek. "I've never been happier to see anyone, Arnacin, whatever the outcome."

Although she wished to help more, she feared her lack of knowledge would harm.

Unsure what to do, she turned to the items spilled about the floor and gathered everything that remained intact, restoring them to their former location. After a sip from the wine flask, she returned the drawer back to the dresser before pushing the remaining glass fragments into a small pile with her foot.

Arnacin's unoccupied bed seemed to call her, yet the thought of taking another's bed without permission unsettled her. Instead, she curled up against the wall, using her arm as a pillow, and drifted off to sleep.

Valoretta jerked awake as a weak moan sounded nearby. Her breath caught with the brief recollection of savages, yet the gentle feel of bobbing brought her back to the present. The glass-encased candle must have burned out during the night, and only a small shaft of light fell down the short flight of stairs from the crack under the door to strike the wooden floor below.

Stiffly pushing herself to her feet, the queen groped her way to the door, shoving it open. Cold wind from a clear sky blasted into her face, and she hastily stepped aside.

When she turned around, she saw that Arnacin had pulled himself to his knees by the bed's edge, though every inch of him was aquiver from the struggle. His forehead rested against the thin mattress.

"You're not well enough to do anything, Arnacin." Valoretta knew she advised him in vain, yet since it was the truth, she spoke anyway. "Tell me what you need and where to find it."

Though gentle, her words were an order. But as ever, the islander ignored authority. Sighing, the queen tried again. "Where do you keep the candles? It's too cold to keep the door open."

"Don't close it!" The urgency in his tone caused the queen to hesitate. "The day will warm as the sun strikes the water."

Wrapping her arms around her body for warmth and wishing she had kept her mantle, the queen settled herself beside the invalid. "As you wish. Do you have food and water in here?"

For a long moment, Arnacin remained silent, though he tilted his head to the side to look at her. Alongside the pain still glazing his eyes, distrust lurked. Yet Valoretta saw the thoughts turning back there, saw the stubborn promptings of reality forcing him to some decision he clearly disliked.

Eventually, he rasped, "Help me onto the deck." His voice trembled.

It took all of Valoretta's strength to haul the islander onto the deck and then to the stern. Though he obstinately attempted to carry his own weight, he instead hung from her shoulder like an oversized cloth doll. A few times, the queen even felt his head slump against her arm and wondered if the strain had caused him to lose consciousness, yet he always took that next step.

They reached the ship's stern just in time for Valoretta's waning strength, and she was able to carefully let the islander slide off her arm, propping him against the rail. Arnacin's eyes had closed but, rubbing her shoulder, the queen realized his fever had also left with the night.

"Arnacin," she asked, slipping down by him. "Where are the supplies?"

His dark eyes slowly reopened, yet he only glanced from her to the hold's hatch a few paces from them.

Staring in defeat at the heavy, double-braced wood between her and their survival, Valoretta turned back to Arnacin. "How far back?" she asked. "And what am I looking for?"

A ghost of a smile brushing his face, Arnacin hoarsely whispered, "It depends on what you want. There's water in a keg in the back, wine bottles in a crate somewhere, salt blocks and potatoes in sacks, and dried, salted meat in a keg nearer us."

Knowing it was up to her, Valoretta stood. Lifting the hold's hatch caused her back to protest sharply, even using the pulleys Arnacin told her how to set up. She dropped the hatch the rest of the way back and, pressing her hand into her backbone, she jumped lightly down. The space was not tall enough for her to stand, forcing her to her hands and knees. Finding a glass-covered candle nearby, she lit it. Then, shoving the hem of her skirt in her mouth, she pushed the light ahead of her on the floor and crawled forward.

As the light from Valoretta's lantern disappeared beneath the deck, Arnacin painfully shifted. With the wind taking his ship

south, he could ill afford weakness. No sane sailor but his once-un-
trained self would travel into the stormy seas and harsh cold by
Cape Alagark.

With the fresh air to help, the islander forced himself, dragged
himself, on one knee and his two elbows to the edge of the hold,
where a bucket sat below. By flattening himself, his fingers just
brushed the bucket's edge. Letting himself slide farther into the
hold, he grasped it.

By the time he succeeded in pulling it up, he had only just time
to send it rolling in the direction of the cabin before Valoretta
reemerged with some dried meat, water and a tiny bit of very
stale bread. She took one look at him, only an inch from her, and
shook her head. Yet she said nothing, only blowing out the lantern
before pulling herself up to sit beside him.

Arnacin remained unmoving until she touched his shoulder.
He jerked away, slowly pushing his legs in front of him. Using his
arms, he scooted back to the rail.

"What have I done to earn your distrust, Arnacin?" Valoretta
asked, passing him half her meager rations.

After a second, Arnacin answered, "You're Miro's daughter.
That's cause enough."

The queen's chin rose. "I defied him."

The islander's eyes lit as his unanswered charge from the other
night rang through the air. *Why had she defied her own father?*

Valoretta apparently heard it as well. "If you wish to complain
about that, 'with pride' hardly answers my own inquiry. I'm not
demanding information from you, but I dare you to charge me
with any crime simply because I lack a good justification."

"You don't lack one. You're hiding something."

"Likewise," Valoretta tossed back. With a last glare, Arnacin
let it drop.

In their silence, the sun did its work. Throughout the rest of the
day, Arnacin involuntarily dozed beside the queen under the brilliance that warmed the deck. As evening came on, he woke when

Valoretta's head slid onto his shoulder. A sigh forced itself from him as he looked down at her while she shivered in her own sleep.

"Valoretta," he whispered. The red hair on his shoulder shifted, and the queen jerked upright.

"Go sleep in the cabin. Take the bed if you want it."

"What about you?"

Although Arnacin's wicked grin flickered at the sudden wariness in her tone, he only said, "I never touch it."

"Won't you freeze out here?"

"I haven't yet, for over a year."

Valoretta's gaze dropped guiltily to the deck. "Since Mira," she breathed. Arnacin refused to admit it. She knew. That was already too much.

Without a reply, the queen rose, disappearing into the cabin.

Waiting only until his body would obey his will, Arnacin used the time during which she slept to shift their course and quietly scrub the blood off his deck and cabin floor. Although Valoretta stirred in her sleep, tossing with the fitful memories of all she had endured, she never fully woke.

Pausing whenever she shifted, Arnacin made slow progress, hoping the breeze through the open door would not wake her or cause her dreams to be worse should she realize his presence. Undoubtedly, she would react to that similarly to his response when inside.

A few hours before dawn, he finished. With another drink of water, the islander curled up on the deck beneath his spare blanket and cloak, ignoring the shooting pain from his leg.

When Valoretta woke, it was with the sensation that it was late. Rolling onto her side, she looked at the strip of sunlight on the floor. Its width and brilliance informed her that it was sometime around midday, and she pushed the covers off her legs. While lighting the candle she had left nearby, she froze in sudden realization and then shot to her feet.

The cabin floor was clear of the bloodstains that had blemished it just the night before, and a bucket sat on the bottom step, a cloth draped over its side. For just a split second, terror seized her at the horrifying thought that the islander had been in there while she thought she slept in complete safety.

Yet that was absurd. It was Arnacin, and was it not his cabin anyway? No one could deny its need for cleaning as soon as possible.

Calming herself, the queen picked the bucket off the stairs before leaving the cabin. Even salt water would feel better than not washing at all.

On deck, however, Valoretta paused, spotting the apparently sleeping form atop his blanket, cloak thrown over him to protect his head from the noon sun. Softly, Valoretta turned back to the rail and lowered the bucket. It was hard not to cause noise as she pulled the full container back up and then shakily carried it to the windowless cabin. Tottering under its weight, she wished she could have been her mother's handmaiden like all other princesses.

Although her dress was easy to pull over her head, she dared not take it off. After scrubbing her scalp, unfortunately without lather, she only ran water up her sleeves and along her legs with her hands.

As she took the gritty water back out to dump, she noticed Arnacin shift painfully from time to time, as if he were fruitlessly striving to rise. She left him alone momentarily, returning the bucket to the cabin and snuffing the candle. As she re-emerged, however, she found he had moved to the rail and was fiddling with the cloth around his leg.

Hiding her smile, the queen cautiously approached. Some things, she knew, never changed. She remembered how Arnacin used to complain about the castle physicians during the times he was forced under their care. He would bleed to death before he surrendered to his wound, and she knew any word of caution on her part would be unwelcome.

"Do you know where the wine is in the medicine drawer?" the islander asked as Valoretta stopped beside him. Red was staining the cloth again. Nodding, the queen returned to the cabin for the wine, which she herself had put away.

Back on deck, she handed him the flask, glancing down as she did so. Parts of the scab had ripped away, whether during the cloth's removal or before, she knew not, and blood trickled down his leg. Ignoring it temporarily, Arnacin soaked the cloth in the wine before once again wrapping it tightly around his leg. Even he could not prevent his grimace as the alcohol came into contact with the open wound, and Valoretta hoped she never had to know what it felt like.

"Arnacin, what was the paste you used against the poison?"

"A gift from a native."

"So, they did know a cure."

Arnacin's mouth stayed closed while he carefully tied the bandage. Stillness descended between them, and the soft swish of the sea captured Valoretta's attention. Finally, the queen turned back to her companion, who also stared out over the waves. "What did you do out here for a year? I thought you went home. Wasn't it torturously lonely after... what happened?"

"Lonely?" Arnacin repeated skeptically. "Out here?"

As she folded her arms, the islander added, "Unfortunately, no one is ever alone, not with...."

"A god?" Valoretta guessed the ending of his sentence. "Alright, Arnacin, tell me why I should believe that. You were expelled, Mira flattened. Prior to that, storms sent you to a land that took you down with it. Would you not stick to your word more if you actually believed in such a being?"

Looking away, Arnacin said, "I always keep my word."

Laughing, the queen snapped, "Not its heart." His shoulders straightened in what she had long recognized as the erection of emotional walls, and she laughed in reply to that silent protest, that condemning self-righteousness. "You are the type any king would instantly seize, fetter and lock up to starve, and still, they would feel that it was too good for you."

"Naturally," he whispered, cold pride in his voice.

"And you are proud of it?" Valoretta exclaimed.

Turning back, Arnacin eyed her darkly before answering, "Like anyone would rejoice at the devil hating them."

Those words struck like a blade of betrayal. Shrieking in fury, she leapt at him. Coolly, however, he caught her wrists, shoving her away. Tripping over the back of her skirt, Valoretta landed on the deck. There she sat, panting in temper while he warily watched.

A moment later, Arnacin broke the silence. "And you thought you understood love."

"Perhaps I only thought of your handsome looks!" Valoretta shot back, paling as her thoughts caught up with her mouth. Time seemed to freeze as Arnacin also appeared unsure of that comment.

"What do you mean?" he finally demanded, and the queen smiled coyly.

"I could remind you of your own words, Arnacin of Enchantress Island. For no one who understood love would call another the devil, as you just did." Picking herself up, the queen whirled away and slammed the cabin door behind her.

Except for one occasion when Valoretta emerged to fetch more food from the hold, leaving some on the deck for him, Arnacin did not see the queen for the rest of that day. He refused to ask what she had really meant and told himself he was unbothered by her hibernation.

Yet the next day, as Arnacin half-sat on the rail, mending a new run in his cloak, the queen approached, determination in her stride. "I can sew," she stated, reaching his side.

Looking up at her, the islander wondered, "When was that in question?"

"I mean, I need something to do." Valoretta's voice trembled just slightly. "I need something to keep my hands, if not my thoughts and heart, busy."

"Outside of volunteering to crawl through the hold from time to time, you mean."

The queen only waited, it seemed, and Arnacin looked around at his little, easily manned ship. As he glanced at the decks, however, he shrugged, trying to appear unconcerned as a wicked thought stirred his mind. "Well, I haven't scrubbed the deck in a while."

He had anticipated her frown as she caught on, but she apparently little realized what such a job required, as she nodded regally. "Very well. Tell me how to do it, and I shall."

Quickly dropping his gaze back to his cloak, lest she see his face, the islander stated, "The bucket that should still be in the cabin had a cloth inside it. Just fill it with salt water and use the cloth as your scouring tool. Start in the bow, and the rest is common sense." As she turned toward the cabin, he warned, "Just remember to take out the cloth before you lower the bucket or you'll be using your nails."

Throwing him a glare over her shoulder, the queen headed to work.

Afternoon came while Arnacin procrastinated over his sewing so as to give himself an excuse not to end his sport. Sitting now on the edge of the poop deck, Arnacin watched as the queen labored on hands and knees, pausing only briefly, either to refill the bucket or to stretch her aching shoulders. The whole front of her dress looked like she had gone swimming, and the end of her auburn tresses dripped water from the continual dunking as her hair trailed in the bucket every time she emptied or refilled it.

For just a second, their eyes met. It was as if years had been stripped away. Her gaze had that determined, slightly frustrated air of recognizing his act, and he knew pure teasing delight shone in his. It only lasted a second, however, before Arnacin quickly dropped his gaze, returning to his cloak in earnest.

It was not until Valoretta had finished the main deck that the islander agreed to finish the poop deck and suggested she change into the clothes she would find in the fourth drawer of his dresser until her dress dried. As she did as he suggested, Arnacin heard the latch on his cabin door fall into place after she disappeared inside.

When she reappeared, self-conscious in the oversized pants and shirt from Enchantress Island that Arnacin had outgrown, she proceeded to tie a line from the ratlines to the poop deck's ladder, threading it through the armholes of her dress along the way.

Only when he took his rest later, looking at the female practicality now added to his ship, did Arnacin again smile slightly, pulling his cloak farther over himself under the bright sky of the ocean's night.

When Valoretta insisted the islander show her how to do the various jobs on board, Arnacin did not gainsay her demand. Instead, he showed her how to check the lines and knots, patiently teaching her to tie the complicated ones herself. She learned how to pull the ropes tight, how to gauge the forthcoming weather, and how to check the ship's speed and direction.

The queen had once destroyed him by showing him her political world. Now, he showed her his, and it was one of hard work, of endless but good pain. Slowly, the blisters on her palms hardened and her back became a constant mass of aches. Although Arnacin never volunteered to help ease her pain, and she would not have accepted it if he had, she gloried in the work, in the freedom it brought. Now she knew what it meant to not feel alone at sea. When everything was done, her mind held only a weary pleasure and blankness as she stood at the rail, watching the foam's patterns alongside the ship.

Finally, she felt strong enough to release some of the hardened wall around her own heart. Standing beside Arnacin at the rail while the sun set on the horizon, the queen whispered, "You were right, you know."

When he only glanced askance at her, she relayed her story. "Mira was lost. Even my father knew it. One of the first things he did was to agree to a request for my hand in marriage. I was furious, but he told me then that the union was not for a stronger Mira, but to guarantee that I was not there when it fell. All the same, I commanded Sara to steal the letter before it was sent to sea. She did, and my father never knew—too involved with the country's only chance to survive.

"Then he went to war personally, intending to burn every square inch of the marshes. We could not wait any longer with the enemy encroaching ever closer to our city. I remember standing on my balcony at night, watching the sky glow blood red. I didn't know then..." The queen's voice trembled for the first time, but mastering it, she continued in a flat tone, "Most of the harbor had emptied when our king went out, as if it was a sign—all the traders, foreign ambassadors, they all left our harbor. Even some of our own ships had departed on any excuse they could find. Then, a messenger came racing from the northwest with such urgency his horse died from the flight. He told us... he told us Fort Corugwan had fallen and the savages were on the march without fear of pursuit.

"King Miro had taken his entire army into battle. Except for our castle guards, we had no fighting men. Everyone knew that signaled our doom.

"Sara wanted to send me away... But I looked around... I was queen, Arnacin. Before I could evacuate Mira, the enemy overtook us. I tried to plan for everything beforehand, but it failed. Some people were racing toward the ships, setting sail as soon as enough men were aboard, while other men hung off the edges, still hoping to escape. Others—families—had to halt on the quay, watching their last chance desert them as the savages shot them down and burned the few ships still in harbor.

"I had the gates shut. I might as well have ordered them to throw themselves on their own blades. Over the next weeks, the savages delighted in performing every horrifying, grisly, bloody act before us, from dead animals, to cannibalistic feasts, to... We grew insane with starvation and thirst. Those who seemed to do better became the hunters. Adults murdered—"

She broke off as Arnacin's trembling hand briefly touched her arm, but it was as cold as it was comforting, an order for silence as much as an expression of sympathy. His next words only proved it. "It's the way of this twisted world, Valoretta, and no amount of tears will change it. You might as well learn to deal with it."

"Oh yes, dealing with it has done you wonders," she scoffed. Then, shoving her anger away, she reminded him, "Light exists, Arnacin. Once, you came to Mira with it. I see the darkness of this world has chiseled it away through its greed and selfishness, but Arnacin, that light's still there for you to find and retrieve. Just go home and leave the evil behind."

Turning to face her for the first time, the islander stated, "I intend to, but when I do, I will leave every inch of this world behind."

Fully understanding the meaning behind the words, Valoretta jerked her gaze back to the open sea. After a long pause, she tried again. "I don't want anything, Arnacin. I just want healing, a place I can feel... renewed myself."

"Yes, and that's all," Arnacin huffed sarcastically.

"What is that supposed to mean?" the queen snapped, whirling toward him.

"And after your supposed renewal, what happens when that perfect spot is no longer any use to you?"

"I know what selflessness and love are—"

"Oh, nobles know what love is, all right. They 'love' just as long as they can take something from that love, and then they behead whatever remains. I was told nobles would kill their own children if the child displeased them in any way."

Studying her companion, Valoretta asked, "Memphis's words?" For a second, Arnacin's blue eyes flickered in surprise, and the queen shrugged. "Not much happened in the castle that I didn't know about, Arnacin. I would hazard a guess that Sara and I were the best-informed people dwelling there. I saw things even my father never did, since he was blinded by his pride and fear of appearing weak."

Arnacin only looked away. Yet after a brief pause, he muttered, "I never doubted your insight."

"Having never doubted *your* insight, I'm surprised," Valoretta shot back, receiving the expected glare in return. "Yes, nobles know nothing of love, you say. You, of course, know everything, and yet, as you stand there and scorn us, you deny that. By your own words, you said that love would force you to forget wrongs and trust that a person is really good."

"I never said I loved you."

Flushing, Valoretta hissed, "It doesn't matter. When you spoke of it, you meant love in general. Otherwise, nobles could know love as well, just not for their subjects. Oh, no... They know nothing as the hypocrite that you are reminds us, simply because they attack people who displease them, whom they never loved. However, you know so much, are so good at everything, are honorable, loving—"

"Those rules never included the devil's fiends."

Almost shrieking in humorless victory, Valoretta exclaimed, "So we're not even human! I've already attacked you once, Arnacin of Enchantress Island. I won't do it again. We're less than animals? So parrot all murderers, justifying their deeds. Mira had savages. Other countries have mindless thieves, and what does our islander have? Demons. So, you hide your squirming conscience behind such excuses, enabling your revenge and hate, all with the certainty that it's honorable. So say they all."

Arnacin no longer faced her as he stared out at the endless ocean. Leaning forward, she whispered, "And you cannot even deny it. But tell me I'm a liar, stating these things only for my own manipulative reasons. Tell yourself whatever you like, but I know you know somewhere that Arnacin, son of Bozzic of Enchantress Island, is no more—the one that inspired Mira's last days is no more, and the one that stands here now is all the things he stood against."

Knowing she had won, she whirled away, back up the ladder to the poop deck. Arnacin still had not moved.

Chapter 12

Ursa!

EVENING CAME. SITTING UNDER THE pink sky, Valoretta started to rip apart an old, bloodstained and tattered piece of paper, flinging the bits into the water. A hand closed over her fingers before she had scattered too much of it. Arnacin had joined her.

Angrily, she tried to drop the rest of the paper into the ocean, but the islander grabbed it. "Arnacin," she warned with all the regality of her throne. "I now have the strength to destroy that. Let me do so."

He did not move. His eyes fixed on the inked words in Valoretta's graceful, assured handwriting–half-ruined by water, blood and age. She doubted Arnacin would believe its authenticity, yet she remained silent while the words she had nearly memorized passed through her mind as if she was reading them.

Sire,

When you return, beaten into a last, desperate stand behind your walls, which I know is the only way you will return, I wish a private audience with you, if it will please you. Do not ignore my request, thinking a ship will soon come for me. I ordered the letter burned. I tell you because I have nothing to lose and to let you know I will never run while our people fall before the savages.

Because lying to my king has also plagued my conscience and because I am confessing things already, you should know that I aided the escape from entombment of the one you banished. You may do whatever you like to me, for we both know the savages have won. Your only wise choice, outside of death, is to take all of Mira, attack some unprepared country with the remaining might you still possess, and force an allowance of land out from that country.

I wish to discuss my own desires with you, however. Since you have every right to deny such an audience, I will tell you in short. I still yearn for peace between Mira and her natives. My wish, sire, my only hope for the savages' agreement to let Mira live, is for me to become their peace hostage. If I am queen, they would know it would not be good for Mira if they killed me. All I would need is a trusted regent in the capital to whom orders could be sent, a regent who would uphold the law, protect the country and keep the peace, and who, if the natives ever tried to break their vow by killing me without cause, could carry on his own reign.

You will ask whom we can trust, whom the natives can trust, whom all sides can know will care that the hostage still lives. Once, I would have named Carpason, but he died in battle. Our other option you exiled when we needed him most. I, personally, have no other solutions, and for this reason among others, I wish to speak with you.

Whatever you decide, sire—to perish, depart or step down from the throne before your death— it is fully your choice. You are Miro, Mira's conscience and provider. I am simply and humbly your daughter, but I wish to give you these options. I wish to speak with you as a friend, as your adult daughter, once before we die.

Yours,
Princess Valoretta, the child you named Valor.
Right now, I feel possessor of none.

Exactly how much of that Arnacin could read, Valoretta knew not; however, as his dark eyes fixed themselves on her, she knew he was questioning how it had even survived the savages, let alone arrived on his ship.

She offered nothing until he asked aloud. Then, she said, "The savages dumped every bit of correspondence across the floor. They had no use for it, and they knew it couldn't be used against them. In their spite, they likely knew I needed something to do.

I certainly could do nothing more but cry tears over whatever I found.

"I used sorting Mira's documents as my escape. In the end, I destroyed almost everything in my hopelessness and burned it. This one, this last hope I had ever held, I hated most of all. Yet every time I tried, I couldn't give it to the fire as I had the rest. I've kept it tucked against my ribs as a curse, a useless prayer to no one that time will be reversed and peace will come. I hate myself whenever I remember it."

Turning to the islander, she looked up into his eyes. To her surprise, deep understanding briefly shone in them before the hard wall of ice dropped back into place. "Yet you can destroy it now?" he asked.

"You have convinced me there is no such thing as hope." Vehemently, Valoretta ripped the letter out of his loose grasp and flung it over the side for the salt water to finish its ruin. Neither queen nor islander moved until darkness swallowed them.

After six days of widely skirting coastlines, they were in sight of their destination.

Lowering the telescope he had taken from the body of the pirate who had smuggled the costly stone aboard, Arnacin slid it back into the pouch at his hip. His blanket lay on the deck. With a glance back at the gray strip in the distance, he picked up his blanket and pushed his cabin door inward. There, he paused before warily entering. Valoretta still slept, moaning unintelligible words while thrashing beneath the blanket.

Throwing his own blanket over the foot of the bed, Arnacin studied her for a moment, uncertainly. Her utterances were the husky nothingness of dreams and sweat beaded her forehead.

After all she had suffered, disturbing her might add to her fear, but leaving her in the throes of her memory was hardly any better. Bending over, the islander lightly brushed her leg. "Valoretta."

She screamed, jerking away. The islander jumped backward as the sound echoed around the cabin. As the noise faded, silence settled once more, but Arnacin did not move toward the queen.

Without glancing around, Valoretta pushed herself up, pulling her legs to her chest beneath the covers. Still she trembled, horror like a shadow in her eyes.

Finally, Arnacin spoke. "Land is in sight. We'll reach it this afternoon with the speed of this ship."

Her gaze flicked up to meet his, searchingly. "Arnacin," she breathed. "If you're going to leave me to the whim of others, kill me. It will be more merciful."

"You assume so much from the afterlife," Arnacin stated flatly, turning to the medicine drawer in his bureau. From it, he withdrew the flask of wine, silently passing it to the queen. Her hand trembling, Valoretta took a sip.

Only when her color returned slightly did the islander sit beside her. "I promise, Valoretta, I wouldn't leave you anywhere questionable. I believe this is a place you can trust, but if you have somewhere else you would feel safer, I'll take you there."

Sorrow filled her face and her voice quivered. "You know you are the only home I have. I can't go anywhere else, Arnacin, I'll kill myself first."

Something rang falsely in that. Perhaps her arguments for taking her to Enchantress Island were just too sentimental, too weak for the girl who had vowed to end Mira's vision of powerless queens through ultimate strength.

Regardless, her words conveniently made it hurt to leave her behind. Yet he could not trust her, she who had switched characters multiple times during a royal ball, who had saved him from entombment only to remain silent when her father exiled him.

Honestly, he had little energy to uncover the truth of Valoretta, heir of Mira. Every fiber of his being yearned to run, to flee home and—if he ever made it there—slam the door on all the past years, to try to pretend it never happened, and hopefully forget.

"I told you why you're not going with me, and no amount of manipulation will change my mind."

"You think I'm acting." She spoke in beaten pain, and her gaze flicked to his side and the gold-sheathed blade there.

Refusing to find out what lay behind that quick glance, Arnacin rose. "We both know that Princess Valoretta never shows fear outwardly. It's political suicide to do so." Leaving her, the islander shut the door behind him with a snap.

True to his predictions, Arnacin's vessel ground into a rocky shore carefully wedged between two rocks around mid-afternoon. Since that morning, he and Valoretta had avoided each other. Now, however, the queen exited the cabin with pride returned to her countenance.

Glancing at her, the islander climbed onto the right-hand rock, tethering his ship there. Knowing it would remain there until he freed it, he returned to the deck, dropping a rope over the side. "Would you like to climb down yourself, my lady, or should I help you?" he asked, striving to keep bitterness out of his tone.

Bitingly, however, the queen quipped, "Since I assume if I refuse to leave at all you will simply drag me off, I can descend myself, thank you."

Arnacin just watched as she swung herself over the side of the ship, revealing just briefly that she still wore pants beneath her skirt, and slid down the rope. The gentle splash of disturbed water announced the end of her climb. Pulling the rope back up, Arnacin returned to the rock and started down its slippery sides.

The place Arnacin had beached his ship was wild territory. The little inlet was hidden from land by high cliffs and protected from ships by the reef right under the surface. Only a row-boat or a well-balanced flat-bottomed vessel could find it there.

Valoretta and the islander spent a few hours clambering over barnacle-encrusted rocks before they reached sandy shore and a harbor village.

Far down the coast, an entourage stood around one ship in harbor, their emblems too small for Valoretta to see clearly. The clatter and hiss of blacksmiths and construction, the whirl of pottery wheels—all this reached the queen's ears as she slid off the last boulder after Arnacin and approached the village.

As the buildings grew ever larger and nearer, Valoretta battled within herself. Arnacin disbelieved her desperation or, at least, scarcely cared. She had no strength against him, nor could she have simply refused to leave the ship. No childish fit, command or plea would alter his resolution, and she still lacked the desire or experience to simply fly back to the ship and leave without him.

No, her rescuer was as much her persecutor in this case. Her only choice was to try to find a way of living wherever he deserted her or to kill herself as soon as she could accomplish that without his notice—for as sure as she was of his tenacity, she was equally sure he wouldn't allow her to die.

Yet she had lived, continued breathing, through all the horror and abuse. Why should she quit now? Was it simply because the person she had trusted and loved most had failed her by his inability to retain his original character? She might as well continue struggling, if for no other reason than to cheat the torturer who had written her life.

As in Mira, Arnacin stood out, drawing attention—but perhaps even more than before, for now he not only possessed black hair but had also acquired the dark air of a lord, full of purpose and scorn. Yet Valoretta also possessed a majesty, royalty that she was by birth. Between the two of them, they could have expected nothing other than all the heads that turned in their direction and the working hands that stilled as they passed.

"Arnacin! Arnacin of the Sea!" someone called. Both turned to the blacksmith just leaving his anvil, his hand extended in welcome. "I didn't think to see you again so soon, if at all. You were just here."

"Last year," Arnacin replied, not moving to take the man's hand. Laughing softly, the blacksmith dropped his arm back at his side. "Oh, you're a mass of scars, boy, that you are. I see you have found a lady friend in the time you've been gone."

Arnacin had hardly glanced at his companion before another exclamation broke out. "Princess Valoretta! Burst my sides, she's alive!" Whispers erupted around the travelers and, pale-faced, the queen lessened the space between her and Arnacin. Although she expected him to move away as her shoulder pushed against his arm, he allowed it. His gaze swept the encircling throng, his left hand sitting on his sheath.

"Well, of course!" another shout rang. "She's back with her worshiper. It's no surprise he would drag her back from Hades itself."

As Valoretta's face turned hot, Arnacin only snapped, "Silence."

Although those around them halted, their eyes wide with fear, it was too late. The village's noise had caught the attention of the entourage in the harbor.

Nine horsemen rode near. As they dismounted, the queen's heart stopped. All of them were Ursan nobles, their bear embroidered onto their shoulders. She even recognized one of them as Lord Emroy, once a frequent visitor to Mira.

Arnacin tensed as the lord swept the queen a low bow. "It is our delight to see you alive, my lady."

Suppressing a shiver, the queen replied with perfect court composure. "Your Lordship, are you visiting or is this Ursa?"

"Of course, this is Ursa, Your Highness," Emroy intoned with a smile. "Prater, Ursa, the closest harbor to your homeland. And it would be Ursa's pleasure to grant you all it has in its possession for your rest after what you must have been through."

Valoretta grabbed her companion's arm as his hand shot to his sword hilt. "As generous as that is of Ursa, that shall not be necessary. We were merely stopping by."

Casting the islander a superior smirk, the Ursan lord persisted, "It would be an honor to aid you. We mean no harm."

Somehow, Arnacin had the sense not to speak, yet he drew his blade an inch. Spotting the wordless threat, however, Emroy laughed. "Oh, you don't wish to try that. Harm to a noble on Ursan soil means instant death."

A sinister smile flickered over the islander's face. Making a swift decision as she spotted the other men drop their own hands to their swords, Valoretta agreed. "Very well, we will speak to your king about it and come to an understanding. It seems unfair to judge based only on distrust. Such things have caused unnecessary amounts of bloodshed in the past."

Whether Arnacin understood her tactic or not, he released his sword hilt. For just a second, however, they shared a look—one that meant the same for both of them. If not for the life of the other, they would prefer death in those streets to an audience with the king.

Looking around them, Valoretta saw the confusion on the peasantry's faces, as if they could not fathom the travelers' hesitation. Their reaction little soothed the queen's fear. As she briefly slipped her hand into Arnacin's before he pulled away, it was a small comfort to feel the tremor in his fingers.

Firth, Son of Gagandep, raised his tankard in salute to the fallen Mira as he had every time he purchased a drink since the kingdom's annihilation. Slouching against the sun-warmed outer wall of Prater's tavern, he took a long draft.

Prater was a small port town on the edge of Ursa. Its rulers dictated that only one of every type of business could exist in a single town, ensuring owners a lack of competition—or so they said. More likely, it was a way for them to keep tabs on everyone, particularly the foreign merchants.

Despite his misery at sea, Firth hoped his captain would hurry so that they could leave sooner rather than later.

His captain. Ha! Gagandep's son had rotated captains and ships practically every four months since Arnacin told him to leave Mira.

That thought caused Firth to take another quick pull from his tankard. Many a night, he had lain awake with the horrifying vision of his family, his native father, slaughtered by the pigs of savages. They would have been only too glad to murder one of their own just because he had not run his Miran wife through with a knife. Alongside those images was the one of Arnacin fallen to those same savages before the keep gates, where he would have stood as the castle's last defense, dying for a kingdom he had no obligation to outside of his own commitment.

Tears were alien to Firth, but hatred, he embraced as a friend, a shield. This time, though, it gave him no comfort. Hatred was only good when it could fuel revenge, but there was no longer any possible attack against the savages. They had won. Hatred and revenge rested in his heart without a vent save for the mindlessness of alcohol.

Guessing what his expression might hold in those thoughts, Firth yanked his hood up and finished the last drop of his drink. Done, he stood to go back inside to purchase another. Let this captain release him for drunkenness, as had others. He was tired of them anyway.

"The Princess Valoretta!"

"Princess Valoretta!"

With growing strength, the calls reached Firth's ears. His brow furrowed, he turned back from entering the tavern's doorway and peered down the street.

A large crowd was gathering. People working or talking amidst the street's shops were pausing. From the quay, Ursans were also approaching; their presence opening a wide lane through the throng.

In that gap, the reason for the shouts appeared, and the blood drained from Firth's face. Arnacin stood in the center beside a slight figure, no doubt the new monarch herself. For just a moment, the desires to gasp, laugh or scream curses battled for dominance within him. Gradually, one thought conquered as he clenched his tankard tighter—the savages would never have left their phantom alive, never. There was only one explanation. Arnacin had deserted Gagandep, his family and all of Mira in their time of need.

The crowd dispersed as mounted men filled their place. The horsemen shuttled islander and queen to where an Ursan noble stepped out of a carriage. This high, pompously dressed noble extended his hand to the queen as if to help her inside.

Taking Arnacin's hand instead, she brushed past the nobleman. Even at a distance, Firth could not mistake the islander's murderous gaze before he joined the queen inside. Lastly, the noble jumped in and the surrounding guards snapped the door closed.

Perhaps it was unclear to Prater, but Firth surmised the islander and queen were no more than exalted prisoners, and the former only an accessory. If anyone was going to kill Arnacin, however, it would be Firth, after he rescued them and rang a confession of betrayal out of that closed mouth.

Leaving his tankard on the tavern's bench, Gagandep's son strode after the mounted entourage.

Stone walls, thick and towering, rose on both sides of the tremendous bare corridors of Berns Castle, the larger of the two castles in Makilka. The sound of metal-shod, firmly placed boots echoed from the roof and walls, drowning out the almost silent sounds of Arnacin and Valoretta. At the group's approach, the wide, oaken double doors at the end of the hallway swung open.

Striving hard to ignore his pounding heart and suspicion, Arnacin stepped into the great hall behind the knights who fanned out about the room. A long rectangular table filled the center of the room, and around it stood Ursa's king, marked by his crown, and a few of his nobles. While Valoretta dropped a regal curtsy, appropriate for her upbringing, Arnacin nodded in cool courtesy.

"It is so good to hear, and now see, that the well-acclaimed Miran princess has arrived at a safe harbor," the king's advisor exclaimed after a brief whispered exchange with his master.

Something more than awed respect shone from their eyes, and Arnacin tensed subtly in preparation.

Beneath Valoretta's political smoothness, the islander also heard her own wariness as she replied, "It is complimentary to your character that you are concerned for my safety."

Rolling his eyes, Arnacin felt Valoretta's toe press warningly into his foot.

"You flatter the king, my lady," the spokesperson replied after a pause full of whispering. "And to say so after your ordeal is high praise indeed, but worry no more–His Majesty has supplied quarters for you where you may remain safe from here on." Many pairs of covetous and greedy eyes stared at the queen.

"If His Majesty has no objection, I would be grateful if I were given my own land with a modest dwelling, if I am to stay here at all. With all due respect, I've been far too imprisoned to feel secure behind walls."

"But, dear princess," the spokesman stated, this time speaking without the advice of his lord. "You *are* a princess–a *queen* with your father murdered. It is your duty and honor to win back your kingdom. You must remain here, so that you may receive the proper help you deserve."

"There is nothing there that *deserves* her protection," Arnacin spoke up, ignoring Valoretta's heel, now squashing his toes. "It is fully ruled by its natives, and only more war will reward such *glorious* attempts. The truth is, you wish the possession of her to grant you the right to Mira and its valuable position in the trade routes."

"I would be careful, boy, before you accuse our king," one of the nobles hissed. "Or your impertinence will find you a noose instead of a reward for your valor."

A low, bitterly sarcastic laugh escaped Arnacin. Despite the Ursans' tangible anger filling the hall, Valoretta remained silent and motionless. "I didn't accuse–your eyes stated the truth for you."

In cold reply, the noble tossed his velvet glove on the floor between them. Arnacin merely studied the other guardedly.

Valoretta stepped behind him, and he spared a glance over his shoulder to see her pale-faced gaze fixed on those velvet fingers.

Harsh laughter burst from the noble. "Impudent and dumb—that was a challenge, boy, or do you lack the decency and courage to suitably act?"

"Perhaps I am too smart to be so inflamed over nothing."

"Ha! Insolent cub! What is she to you? She cannot grant you a kingdom, and you should be tired of the monotony of what one woman can give. Take the challenge and you may escape alive."

Arnacin's chin rose in silence. With utter contempt, he responded, "Honor is too great a subject to waste on such as you."

Face burning, the noble yanked out his sword. "Draw, worm, or meet the consequences." Without waiting for a reply, he charged.

Hearing Valoretta flee, Arnacin stepped aside, whipped his short sword out and sunk it into the noble's side in one fluid motion. His attacker kept his feet, however, and as the blade was removed from his side, he twisted, slashing his sword at the islander's neck.

Smoothly, Arnacin again sidestepped and, in one left-handed sweep, decapitated his foe.

The angry shriek of a woman resounded throughout the hall.

Spinning, the islander spotted Valoretta in the arms of a group of knights attempting to haul her away. Already, they almost had her through the doors.

His chin lowering slightly, Arnacin's fingers tightened about his hilt as he stepped toward them.

"Put down your blade, boy." This order came from the king himself. "Dire consequences await disobedience."

The room quieted. Valoretta's skin was sheet-white where she stood in her attackers' vice-like grasps. She slowly shook her head. *Fly*, she mouthed.

The moment seemed to stretch for eternity. Then, Arnacin turned to the Ursan king, tossing the blade toward the high table. Even the king flinched as it clattered on the polished surface.

As knights closed in around the islander, others pulled Valoretta away. With a thump, the doors shut behind them.

Arnacin was forced to his knees and his head was yanked back. "Here's the reward for the murderer of a noble." He heard the hiss of a blade being drawn and welcomed it.

"No." The king's command halted all movement, and the sound of his silk-shod feet approached. "Don't kill him yet. It will be very interesting to see how he fares in one of our *real* challenges." His voice lowered as he ran his flabby hand down the captive's neck and arm. At Arnacin's involuntary shudder, he smiled. "I wouldn't waste such talent and skill by not having a little sport before he dies."

Held as he was, with his head yanked back and his arms pinned tightly behind him, Arnacin could do nothing but close his eyes. Valoretta's order to fly rang tauntingly in the back of his mind, but he also knew that given a second chance to do so, he still would not.

"Take him to the Eyrie."

"You mean up on...?" one knight breathed. The king nodded with a wicked grin.

"Until his death, we must keep the princess apart from such an infidel."

Slowly, they released the captive's head, yet their hold on his arms only tightened as several of the knights moved off. A minute later, one of them returned with a crudely carved wooden cup. The terrible sign of a similar cup, outside the soothsayer's tavern, rose to mind. With that memory, Arnacin sealed his lips—but for all his resistance, its contents were still forced down his throat.

It took only as long as the last drop in the bottom before blackness swirled in, and Arnacin dimly knew he had hit the floor.

Clothed in black robes, this man, if he could be called that, was despised and feared by nearly all who knew of him. He was weasely and beady-eyed, older than most on Ursa, with a constant habit of cracking his knuckles while thinking. Once a doctor specializing in healing plagues, he had turned to other things, of which even the king knew only a little. Many said he had turned to witchcraft, others said to experimentation. All the king knew and cared about was that the weasel obeyed him as master and could force sudden offspring on the unwilling and unaware.

The king's orders that day were simple. "Breed the new prisoners together. A child will give us leverage against the mother, and I would like to add the male's prowess to my ranks."

"Master." The old one's voice cracked with age as he bowed. "Even my *magic* is not a guarantee that a pregnancy will occur, and you have the male slated to die in a week."

"His talents will be a bonus, if it succeeds, but all that is necessary is the rightful heir to the Miran throne. That I will have before the queen is executed, one way or another. The male is too dangerous to be left alive and, the longer he remains, the more dangerous he becomes."

"No man can stand against the Eyrie."

Glowering at the decrepit man, Ursa's king reminded him, "Even your wretched hole up on the Eyrie might collapse against whatever allowed him to slip through Mira and make off with the captive queen. There is the slightest chance he is more skilled, more powerful than anyone could possibly imagine. I would like that skill in a slave, but he himself must die. Even a week may be too long."

"What you request will be done." Bowing, the weasel departed.

Chapter 13

Into the Wild

Valoretta woke on a stone bench in a small cell, a thick blanket wrapped around her. Hastily, she untangled herself and stilled in horror. Her savage gown had disappeared, along with Arnacin's pants. Instead, she was dressed in a long, trailing gown of scarlet velvet that hung only on the very edge of her shoulders. Beneath, were all the proper undergarments, and along her neck was the delicate weight of a thin chain.

Without looking, she seized the pendent, meaning to rip it off, but as her fingers closed about it, she stopped. What felt suspiciously like outstretched wings and a long neck filled her clenched fist. Releasing it, she found the clasp, now hanging on the side of her neck, and slipped the necklace off.

Mira's signet stared at her, the crane's ruby eye as shrewd and cunning as ever. Although she could find no fault with it, she shook her head at the mere thought that it could be authentic. Some savage woman probably had sullied the real crane by wearing it around her neck–the crane that had carefully, lovingly, been recast out of the oversized signet ring meant for a king.

Tightly closing her fingers around the crane, Valoretta pushed her fist against her chest. Even as her thoughts drifted homeward, she believed she knew what Ursa was planning. Pacing slowly now, she hoped against reason that Arnacin had escaped. Even if he had, how could she possibly thwart all of Ursa?

Futilely, she pushed against the door and then banged her shoulder into it in frustration. The loud clang that followed the resultant pain laughed at her, and she released a long exhale.

Just as she finished replacing the crane around her neck, she spotted a shadow coming down the corridor outside her cell. Not a sound followed it as it grew larger. Every fiber of her being alert, Valoretta watched it.

Her eyes grew wide as Arnacin came into view. "How did you escape?"

The islander shrugged, his gaze taking in her gown before resting on the crane.

Looking down at herself, Valoretta shuddered. "It's horrible to think of... Please, Arnacin, just find the keys. I already tried the lock, and the silence is like a tomb in here."

Wordlessly, the islander studied the lock. Looking back up, he licked his lips. "I can open it."

"How?"

Reluctantly, Arnacin pulled a compass from under his shirt with the movements of someone trying to hide an object from view.

Yet the queen could not miss the little spokes between the islander's fingers. With his attention on the compass, Valoretta studied his expression. As remarkable as it was that he actually wore the compass, his face had none of the darkness she would have expected if he knew what it had meant when she presented it, nor what wearing it still meant. Quickly, she dropped her gaze before he noticed anything.

Each of the miniature helm's spokes were tightly screwed into the wheel and, with careful and firm precision, the islander managed to loosen one, using its nail-like end to pick the lock. As the bolt groaned back into the cell door, Valoretta gratefully escaped the cell's confines while the islander replaced the spoke in his compass and hid it again within his shirt.

"You still have it," she could not help but say, her gaze on the almost invisible lump where the compass rested beneath his shirt.

"Never mind," Arnacin growled, taking her wrist and leading her along the passage. "You would think they'd keep more prisoners here, if not more guards."

"I heard them speaking about this place before they drugged me," Valoretta whispered. "Usually, they imprison only the worst of criminals here, leaving them alone to rot."

"I don't wish to know."

"You asked."

No response followed as they crept along in silence. Sometimes they needed to double back as they hit a dead end, despite Arnacin's subtle use of his compass.

Slowly, their fear grew. The proof was in their sweat, in the difference in their breathing. Finally, sick of the feeling, the queen plucked up her courage to ask. "Do you think we shall ever find the way out?"

Arnacin quickly hushed her. Someone would come searching for them eventually, but would it be too late to prevent them from dying? As Valoretta thought along those lines, dying in a closed labyrinth, she looked again at her companion. Was he thinking of the same thing? Or did that fear recall to him his last days on Mira? Sympathetically, the queen shuddered and shifted her grip to squeeze his hand. To her surprise, he did not pull away.

Suddenly, however, Arnacin squashed her fingers together, causing her to gasp slightly in shock. As he did so, he froze like an alert dog, and she stopped breathing herself, recognizing the warning.

"What is it?" Valoretta whispered after a moment.

"Storm breeze," he replied, before jerking her up one of the corridors ahead.

At last, they came to the large, sealed double doors of their dungeon. As hard as they tried to ram those doors open along the weakest point, there was not even a quiver to mark their efforts.

Panting, Valoretta shook her head. "I wish the hinges weren't on the outside."

"As well as the bolt, I shouldn't wonder," Arnacin sighed as they painfully slumped down against it in exhaustion. Far above them, over the giant doors, the fresh air flew through an arch-shaped hole.

Noticing that Arnacin was staring up at it, the back of his head pressed into the door to do so, Valoretta crossed her arms. There was no way she would look at that taunting hole to freedom.

Her companion released a quiet breath that echoed her sentiments. "Those walls are nearly sea-washed in their smoothness."

For a second, Valoretta studied him uncomprehendingly before she recalled that Arnacin had climbed up the outside of Mira's keep. "How high can you jump? Could you reach it standing on my shoulders?"

A sarcastic glance was the only reply.

"I'm not that weak," she quipped. "Not after your ship, especially not with the door for support."

"The door," Arnacin gasped.

Abruptly, he leapt to his feet, pulling out his blade. Reaching as high as he could, he cut a thin slash in the wood.

"You can't tell me they didn't take that from you."

"Of course, they did. I'm a picklock." His dark tone discouraged further questions.

As he continued, the queen asked, "Wouldn't it save time to use me in place of the first few notches?"

He paused, then surrendered. "If you think you can handle it."

Despite her assurance that she could, she almost collapsed in the brief time before Arnacin's weight lifted off her. Looking up, she saw him glued like a spider to the door. Gradually, he hauled himself up, and then he almost disappeared into the hole above. For a second, he lay on the ledge without moving.

She heard him panting a bit as he whispered, "Go back and douse the lights, starting from back there and coming forward. Don't do it the other way."

With trepidation, Valoretta headed back down the passage, hearing a crack of thunder just outside. Walking until she could no longer see the door, the queen extinguished all the lights as she returned toward the entryway. Arnacin had disappeared entirely by the time she reached the last of the lights.

In the sudden deep darkness, she shuddered, waiting.

Slowly, the doors swung outward just as lightning lit the sky in an eerie yellowish green. Grasping Arnacin's waiting hand, she flew down the stone steps beside him and across the ward. They did not stop running until they reached the huge wall surrounding the keep-sized dungeon's tower. There, however, Arnacin took her, not toward the gate, but up the battlement stairs.

At the top, both escapees froze at the sight of what faced them. It could hardly be considered a moat. They stared down into a black, endless chasm. If that had been the worst part, Valoretta would have been relieved, but across that yawning gap stood an ominously lit tower rising out of the pit. It sat perched atop a thin, winding, ridge of cliff. Beyond that, another black chasm opened wide, leaving the tower stranded on an island in the midst of a hole.

"So that's where they keep all their guards," Arnacin sighed, pointing. "Look how they supported those drawbridges."

"Very clever," was all the queen could say, staring at the strange tower with despair. From that inaccessible structure, like two horns into the sky, rose two extremely long drawbridges, supported by many arches of crossbeams clinging to the underside.

A storm wind whipped about them, stinging their bare skin as it passed, while thunder cracked and lightning pierced the sky behind the tower. The islander's gaze remained fixed on their unattainable path of escape, but slipping down out of the wind, Valoretta breathed, "It's pointless, Arnacin. They've won. At least we did more than they ever thought possible."

Arnacin's only response was a low growl, "I'm going home."

"Oh, granted, you are," the queen agreed, "if all you say about death is true." This time, he made no reply. Hugging herself against the cold, she companionably stayed by him. Nothing mattered anymore; it was hopeless.

Some time passed before what sounded like a scream blew toward them on the wind. Valoretta leapt to her feet and, in another moment, saw the light in the tower vanish. With a rumble that could be heard even over the storm, the nearest bridge began lowering. As it touched ground, the bridge somehow caused the large gates of the dungeon-keep to swing open.

As the escapees watched, dark shapes started falling out of a window in the tower. It took Valoretta a second more to realize that the shapes were bodies. Inhaling sharply, she looked away.

"Let's go," the islander ordered after a moment. Once again taking the queen's hand, he pulled her back down the rampart stairs and to the mammoth gates. There, he paused, looking across their only escape route at the relatively narrow, open-sided bridge over the deep chasm gaping below.

Pushing ahead of him, Valoretta took the lead. "They brought us in this way. We'll make it."

"Until they shove us off," the islander muttered, but the queen refused to take notice.

Once on the drawbridge, they both hurried for the break in that frightening path—the tower. At the archway, with its little wooden door beneath, Arnacin grabbed Valoretta's arm, drawing her behind him as he cautiously stepped inside, blade drawn. They entered stables where a flight of stairs led to the living quarters, but although the horses tugged at their tethers, their eyes rolling, perhaps aroused by the awareness of murder, no movement followed the captives' entrance, no step echoed down those stones.

"Well, is it not the Black Phantom and his queen, ghosts from the netherworld." From around one column, a shrouded figure stepped with bow drawn taut. Beady eyes glinted in dark amusement as they briefly fell on the Miran blade in Arnacin's hand. "I'm rather safe from that, don't you agree?"

Arnacin remained frozen. Behind him, Valoretta breathed, "You speak with a Miran accent. Who are you?"

"Ho, no," the figure snorted. "I deserve the answers. Tell me, Arnacin of Enchantress Island, son of the shepherd Bozzic, how you live when all of Mira fell to the sword, when all of Mira was slaughtered ruthlessly? The natives even murdered their own kind who dwelt there—they would never release their Black Phantom, even out of respect for your supposed honor. Did you flee when you realized Mira would never win?"

Tortured pain rang through that scornful tone. Finally sheathing his blade, the islander growled, "I should have."

As Arnacin approached the skittering horses, the shrouded figure demanded, "Did you?"

The islander whirled toward the figure. "You dare ask, Firth, twice-traitor that you are? You, who chose hate instead of allegiance to your country, who now stand in an Ursan tower as if you rule the place. Did money entice you to become a mercenary for such as that cur on the Ursan throne?"

"I, son of Gagandep? You should know me better." A long pause followed, as if the figure's own words made him realize something. In a whisper, he continued, "Yet, were that true, it must go both ways. I should know you better, shouldn't I?"

More seconds passed in silence. Then, the Miran admitted, "I took passage on a merchant's ship. For quite some time, I've been jumping from ship to ship, captain to captain, as soon as one… no longer suits me. The one I had been with set sail this afternoon, but you see, a certain commotion arose in the harbor, and I stayed behind to trail… you. Your black hair is still unmistakable. I came here stowed away on the bottom of the cart that brought you two here."

"And now what?"

Shrugging, Firth said, "I'll just join another merchant, I guess. I'm sorry. Believe it or not, I did come to rescue you."

Arnacin's gaze returned to Valoretta. "Do you know how to ride?"

"No," the queen admitted with a wary whisper. At her companion's disbelieving frown, she explained, "Mother was always scared of horses and didn't want me to ride. Father was more tolerant of the idea until war came."

Arnacin sighed. "Try to find supplies. If there's anyone up there—" His glance flicked to the Miran footman. "Scream."

"The guards are all dead," Firth whispered, yet neither paid attention.

"Do you know much about horses?" the queen asked, remaining where she was, with only a quick glance at the stairs.

"Enough."

With a slight smile, Valoretta said, "Well, good luck."

As the queen crept up the stairs, her hand against the wall, Arnacin slid toward one of the restless steeds, wishing, not for the first or last time, that he had Charlotte with him. After lowering the second bridge, Firth simply stood by, watching him.

Yet, the horse danced away from the islander and trembled with every rumble of thunder. At last, by yanking the beast's head down and twisting one of its ears, Arnacin forced it to stand still long enough to shove a bit between its teeth and yank the bridle over its head. As he released his pressure on the animal, it leapt for the open door, but mastering the beast once again, Arnacin led it over to the stairs. The queen was currently descending them at a controlled run.

"Jump," the islander ordered without preamble. "The minute I mount, it's going to bolt." He knew that simply from the energy seeming to pass from the horse's mouth down through the reins.

The horse nearly took off as Valoretta landed on its back, but by pulling its head to its chest, Arnacin managed to restrain it long enough to turn back to Firth. "You're sure no one will suspect you?"

"Of course." Firth shrugged, just a hint of an impish smile twitching along the corners of his mouth. "Now that I've watched you do it, I can naturally repeat your horse bullying. I'll release it before returning to civilization. Once back in town, I'm just another of the masses." Looking down at the bow he still held, he smiled. "I'll just leave their weapon here to make sure."

Nodding, Arnacin used the bottom few steps to mount in front of the queen. Her arms tightened around his waist, but as he let up on the reins, Firth grabbed the horse's head. "Wait, though! Please! Tell me how you escaped Mira."

"I was exiled for informing the king of his own stupidity," the islander growled.

"Of course. Do you now regret stopping me from assassinating him?"

For just a second, Arnacin paused, and then, kicking the horse forward, he replied, "No."

As Firth leapt aside, the horse dashed through the open door. With Valoretta's arms about the islander's waist, they were flying toward freedom.

As Firth watched the two ride away, he felt an urge to leap onto a horse and charge after them. They were his last connection to his past.

Indeed, it was for that very reason he also wanted to stay behind. If his family was gone, he wanted no reminder. Still, he watched with a heavy heart as they disappeared into the night.

He shivered as another flash of lightning illuminated the colorless sky. Flinging the stolen bow, he turned to one of the horses and placed his palm between its nostrils. Before he had joined the Miran forces, an adopted native had taught him about horses. Now, unlike Arnacin, Firth pulled from the part of himself that still remembered gentleness as he whispered the steed back into submission, keeping his hand constantly on its nose.

The horse succumbed easily enough to tacking once soothed. Mounting, Firth spurred it into the storm, heading it away from Prater. He would pick up a new captain in another port.

All through that ride, though, different thoughts than ships and jobs preoccupied his mind. Arnacin was not sorry for sparing the king of Mira. Either he was completely insane or, buried beneath his cold demeanor, he was still the optimistic believer in a higher authority.

Despite his scorn, Firth truly hoped the islander would regain that buried aura someday. Arnacin had always before been a person to love regardless of faults. It would be a shame indeed if that ever really changed.

The beast careened down the only path through those mountains. Guessing that it led straight back to civilization, however, Arnacin again yanked the horse's head back and, when that did nothing, then around to its shoulder. Still, it was as determined to run as he was to stop it.

"We must be telling it to go on by some signal," Valoretta cried, her voice whisked away by the sharp, cutting storm wind. Another crack of lightning split the sky, and the horse reared in fright. Arnacin felt a jerk as the queen started falling off, unintentionally dragging him with her.

Gasping as he hit the rocky ground, Arnacin rolled a couple of times while hooves pounded nearby. In another moment, the horse was gone.

Slowly, Arnacin painfully pushed himself onto his feet. Valoretta was picking herself up only a short distance away.

Another flash of lightning ripped through the sky and, with a loud crack, the clouds broke. Within seconds of glancing up, they stood drenched to the skin.

"As soon as this path opens up, we'll need to find cover," Arnacin commanded over the howling of the wind and rain. "We're not going to be able to climb these hills safely in this weather."

"Won't the trail be our best chance to find the way back to the ship?" Valoretta inquired, swiping her sopping hair out of her face.

"There is another kingdom to Ursa's northwest..."

"Minsa?" the queen screamed. "We're dead if we stay here on this continent! Crossing the border won't do anything. I only know Minsa by name, but if it's hostile to Ursa, it won't be any better to us, and if it's not, Ursa will contact it about our escape. Even if they don't, if it's *not* hostile to Ursa, I don't want anything to do with it."

"Hopefully, they'll think we put out to sea, but until they assume that, Prater is not safe." With that, Arnacin seized her wrist and continued at a run down the path while she emitted a shrill growl.

Mid-morning found the two curled beneath a rocky outcropping, hidden by a few bushes, some distance from the path. Valoretta remained awake, anger chiseled across her face as she stared up at the cloudless sky. Beside her, Arnacin appeared to sleep, his head resting on his arm and his eyes closed.

Looking back at the sky, the queen left him undisturbed. She found herself watching the water droplets gathering on the underside of the rock. Reflecting the sun, they grew before sporadically dropping, leaving their pearly light with the reforming droplets on the rock. The small sparkle of otherworldly beauty in the midst of that black world caused Valoretta to sigh in beaten surrender.

Turning her head, Valoretta again looked at her still companion. "The rain's stopped, Arnacin."

"A while ago," the islander muttered, otherwise unresponsive.

"Well then, let's move. The sooner we leave Ursa, the better— and anyway, the walk will dry me out, if not warm me up." It was odd to see how slowly Arnacin pushed himself up, odd to feel *she* was the motivator, but as Valoretta gathered her own feet under her, she realized he was almost as reluctant to start the journey northwest as she was, and just as reluctant to wander farther from the sea where his ship waited faithfully.

For a minute, she considered adding weight to his hesitation, but the impulse died almost instantly. He saw through all her attempts at manipulation, even when it did not exist. Trying to persuade him would only strengthen his stance, and he knew her too well to be fooled if she acted like she was supporting a choice she hated. Instead, she stood there silently, mentally screaming her wishes.

He finally glanced darkly at her, as if knowing her thoughts, and set off on their chosen path.

Valoretta had no choice but to follow. It was later in the day before she gathered the courage to ask, "Did you really not know this was Ursa?" Despite her best attempts, resentment filled her voice.

Arnacin did not even glance at her. "Do you think I'd take you here if I did?"

"How could you miss the fact?"

"If you *need* to know, they only referred to the place as 'Prater.' Prater has a good enough economic system. Prater can be cold this time of year, and so forth and so on."

"Prater," Valoretta scoffed. "Yes, 'pray to' anything that will help them."

"Look, its citizens were non-covetous, considerate and charitable, with a freedom unseen in most waters."

"Yes! Because it's Ursa! Unlike most kingdoms, Ursa fits your hatred. It's..." Yet she could not find the words to describe its horribleness. "They take anything they can lay their hands on and hide their evil beneath their peasantry's happiness. They're demons in manipulation, Arnacin! Don't you see?"

Arnacin remained darkly silent, for which the queen was glad.

Sighing, she asked instead, "How could you expect me to be safe in a kingdom you don't trust enough to live in yourself?"

"Because I can't seem to go anywhere without standing out, whereas you're from these waters. You can easily hide among the masses."

"Ha! Admit it, you were just so intent on leaving me behind, you tricked yourself into believing that." When Arnacin refused to answer, the queen snapped, "In that case, if you're going to desert me anywhere, I'll decide if it's safe."

Arnacin whirled toward her. "I gave you that option, and you refused. If you try to use this as an excuse—"

"Excuse!" A long moment passed while Valoretta glared at the islander before her jumbled thoughts landed on anything concrete to say. "I'm the last monarch of Mira, Arnacin. There's little logic in thinking there will be any safety in these waters."

After a second, Arnacin simply resumed their trek, and the queen trailed behind him, staring out over the lonely hills in silence.

Long days followed. Valoretta shadowed Arnacin through the thick woods. Meanwhile, the bottoms of her skirts ripped on thorns and brambles and by simply tripping over them. She was exhausted from constantly swatting small bugs, of needing her companion's hand down slopes, of drawing ever closer to his back during the increasingly cold nights, and even of sharing his cloak.

They only paused to rest a few hours, during the darkest times of night, with leaves and each other as the only warmth. As for eating, they nibbled on their supplies only when most needed, sparing little time to forage.

For four days, they saw no one, yet Arnacin appeared to view that as a bad omen while he picked their trail through the wildest parts of land. Much like on the ship, they existed in silence until a need for rest, water or a bite of food forced one or the other to break the soft sighing of disturbed leaves at their feet.

Every rustle caused Arnacin to pause, and Valoretta knew he was not jumping at animal noises, but was filtering those noises to listen for other sounds.

Relatively early into their journey, a hurried rustle sounded not far from where Valoretta walked. An arm seized her around the waist as a hand clamped over her mouth. She jabbed her elbow into her attacker's side. A stifled gasp informed her she had struck Arnacin. In answer to her raised eyebrows, he placed his finger to his lips as he inched closer to a fallen tree whose leaves had shaken.

Only a rabbit lay there, its open eye blank, four bloody pin-picks through its neck–yet whatever had killed it had raced off in a hurry. "Why did it leave its food?" Valoretta breathed in fear.

"It could have been scared off by us." Arnacin's gaze swept the woods above and around them, then, wordlessly, he reached out to take her wrist. Slowly, he pulled the queen down. Only once they lay covered in ferns did he reply, just as softly as she had asked, "We're not the only ones here." Carefully, he pointed to a tree atop the hill on their left.

Searching, Valoretta made out a green-clad figure astride one limb, arrow and bow held ready as he stared in their direction. Thankfully, trees blocked his view. "Do you think we were spotted?"

"It doesn't appear so."

"What do we do?"

"Stay here." Arnacin had been gradually removing his cloak, and now he slid it over her red dress. "Sleep if you can, it might be some time before we can move safely. If we move, he's likely to take it for an animal and shoot before inquiring further."

"Yet if we don't move..."

"An animal should come along sooner or later and rescue us."

"How nasty," Valoretta muttered, nevertheless sinking her head onto her arm to wait. It seemed hours inched by while they lay there. Although Arnacin dozed, occasionally glancing upward, Valoretta found her heart remained too active to rest, threatening to betray them any second. Her only consolation was that Arnacin seemed not to hear her.

Time dragged on. Then, feeling Arnacin's hand on her arm, she followed his gaze. There, slowly approaching the hunter's tree, stepped the most beautiful doe the queen had ever imagined, snow white, its eyes perfectly framed by lashes.

As an arrow flashed toward the doe, it took off—yet no feathered shaft pierced the ground. A cry of triumph from several voices filled the woods. Men shimmied down trees. Arnacin pushed the queen's head down.

As the sounds of running feet disappeared into the woods, Arnacin pulled Valoretta to her feet and pushed her in the opposite direction from the archers. "Go!"

Without hesitation, the queen gathered her skirts, dashing for the thicker woods her companion had chosen. At the first stream, Arnacin led her through it, masking their trail.

A week passed before the Ursan king ordered a few men to return to the Eyrie and retrieve the dark-haired captive for the "games." The men returned later that afternoon in a panic. The Eyrie was desolate. The gates were already open when the men arrived, and the tower was empty. When the men entered the Eyrie itself, they found only the horses, grazing in the bailey's yard.

No one could check if the captives had died by dehydration or escaped. Only the missing prison guards knew the passages. For the most part, that last bit was inconsequential to the king, except that Mira's heir was among those thirty-two prisoners.

If she lay dead, Ursa could possibly return to the lookalike plan. Now that she had been seen at Prater, it might be easier, particularly if they found her body and retrieved the signet they had returned to her. He had hoped he could stage many witnesses watching her die during childbirth, while they rescued the baby. Without that child, however, that wish was impossible.

But he was diverting from the problem at hand and the men remained standing at attention, waiting for new orders. Who could have infiltrated the Eyrie? It was renowned for its ability to keep prisoners in and everyone else out. No one need speak of the interrogation torture rooms below it to scare captives. Everyone knew that once within those walls, they were only alive as long as the king decreed, and he had never before, not until Valoretta of Mira came along, held anyone there he intended to retrieve.

Had the guards all betrayed him at the same time? The king found that unlikely, but for the time, he ordered his men to go map the Eyrie's passages and discover any clues they might find.

Three days had passed when one of the men returned with word that they had mapped the halls and found thirty bodies of dead prisoners. Their physician suspected the last prisoner died a week ago. As to the Miran, she was missing as was her companion. No trail or hint existed outside of small scratches up the inside of the doors and a few bloodstains in the guard tower, estimated to be over a week old.

"Impossible!" the king exclaimed.

Pale, his spokesman muttered, "Unless her escort's a wraith, or she is. Somehow she escaped Mira."

"Wraith or not, I want her back! Organize all our captains and send them to scour the seas. We will find that ship!"

Licking his lips, the messenger unwisely asked, "What type of ship are we to look for?"

Grabbing the man's collar, the king shook him. "Any that's not connected to a known kingdom! If we must hire privateers to find them for certain, do so, but we'll find that ship!"

As the messenger scampered off, the king muttered, "I want her dead, and a child of hers in our hands. If we lose this opportunity to claim Mira as our own, there may never come another."

After the near escape from the hunters' notice, Arnacin dragged Valoretta into ever-thicker woods. It slowed their journey, yet she knew it prevented them from crossing paths with anyone else.

These woods now wanted nothing more than to catch the travelers in brambles and briars tall enough to force them to use the muddy animal runs underneath. The ability to stand became a rare and wonderful thing. Valoretta might have pressed for leaving those thickets faster, except that it remained warmer on those small trails.

Then, on a rare day of upright travel, the queen stumbled into Arnacin. Without a word, he pointed to where plants twisted around a large stone. "What is it?" Valoretta whispered.

"Those were a foundation of some sort," her companion breathed, causing her to look again. Indeed, she saw now that there were more rocks, all about the same shape, spaced here and there throughout the choking brambles.

"Do you think any danger can come of it?"

The islander shook his head, yet the fact that he took her hand as he started forward told her the opposite.

In all likelihood, they were simply traversing a path along what had once been a home or village and no harm would come to them, yet something in the desolation of the scattered, thorn-wrapped stones caused Valoretta's throat to constrict. The farther the travelers pressed, the more the number of stones increased—some cracked, others completely broken into thirds or halves where gnarled roots and vines had eaten through. As if to echo the desolation, the air grew steadily thicker. Nature's sounds faded away. In its place, the breeze hissed and snickered, as if some unearthly evil had claimed the land as its own.

Without warning, they hit a wall so covered in vines as to be invisible until one stood directly before it. To the left and right, it raced away, before curving back in the travelers' direction, arms prepared to envelop them in a suffocating embrace. With that horrific thought, the walls seemed to gradually pulse inward, closing off escape for all except the trees and weeds that continued to burrow their own holes sporadically into that barrier. Around them, not a breeze moved, the air hardly existed at all, yet the wild grapes swung slowly back and forth among the branches.

Hoarsely, Valoretta gasped as she attempted to unglue her tongue from her dry mouth, yet it was futile. Arnacin himself only took her sweaty hands in his, positioning them around the vines growing up the wall. Bending down, he placed her foot against the stone, lifting his eyebrows questioningly as he did. Slowly, she nodded, for the only way out she could see was over the wall.

The climb was hardly easy. Vines used as handholds gave way, raining damp, decayed-smelling dirt and pebbles over their faces. Arnacin half-steadied, half-hauled Valoretta up beside him, somehow seeming to sense the roots' intention long before they broke on him.

Eventually, they found the top. Dragging herself up to drape over the edge, Valoretta gagged. In the wind, no longer blocked by the ruin, the stench of decay wafted toward her. She bolted upright the next second, bringing her knees under her. Not far away, something chanted in low, hissing tones.

As her horrified gaze found Arnacin's where he stood atop the wall, he shook his head slightly and kneeled beside her to say at the volume of a breath, "The wind through hollows." A slight tremor betrayed him and gave her new resolve.

Helping her up, Arnacin started down the steps into what had once been a city. Broken paving stones led through the streets, opening on all sides onto grotesquely sagging doorways. A step near one of those entrances revealed a reek of the grave so strong as to make Valoretta's knees give way and blackness fringe her vision.

At times, the path forced them beneath arches where that stench clung to the air. Only Arnacin's presence pulled the queen through.

The place felt endless. They could wander forever in such misery without escape.

Eventually, they came to the top of a short flight of stairs that descended into a trench separating the outer wall from the city.

Clunk. Clunk. Clunk. Beside Valoretta, Arnacin dislodged a stone as he stepped near the old stairway, and it clattered loudly on its way down, breaking the desolate silence before it halted with an uncomfortably loud rattle.

Frozen, Valoretta's gaze remained fixed on that stone's final resting place. Just beyond it, she realized she was staring into the empty sockets of a jawless skull peering out from beneath the thick plant growth. Inhaling sharply, she found Arnacin's arm.

With a sideways glance at her, the islander gently pulled her down the stairs to study the outer wall above the skull. Valoretta permitted his guidance, yet she quickly moved to his other side as he stopped before a scattering of bones and spear points.

Running his fingers along several black scorch marks in the stone, Arnacin followed the wall until they came to a place where stones cluttered the ground around a gaping hole. There, both travelers climbed swiftly through, pushing through the unhindered foliage.

Valoretta would have denied it, as she knew Arnacin would, but they fled as quickly as the terrain allowed until, sometime later, they paused to catch some air. There, the islander finally gasped, "Fortune will be with us if the battle that took down that city was a border dispute, in which case, we are near or have already crossed the Ursan border."

"Fortune will be with us if the spirits don't kill us for trespassing," Valoretta panted, receiving his familiar sarcastic expression.

"They won't dare touch me," Arnacin growled, taking her wrist to resume the trek. The queen noticed, though, he no longer insisted they lacked power.

Chapter 14

Never Love

THAT NIGHT, ARNACIN RISKED A small fire—small to keep the heat away from the thick underbrush more than to keep from being seen. He knew they needed it, not so much because of the cold as because of the despair that lingered with them.

Sitting beside the islander with her legs drawn up to her chest, Valoretta sightlessly stared into the flames. Arnacin left her to her silence, but after some time, she spoke in a dead tone. "I'm as afraid of life as of death, Arnacin. Life continues, growing only more miserable, as all die or betray. We're cursed to exist, to wander without hope. If we could even hope for the blackness of nothingness afterward, it wouldn't ease the misery. Yet peaceful suicide is pointless, for what lies beyond the grave? Simply the continuation, without break, of all the dark horrors. It would have been a mercy to have never been born."

Arnacin sat motionless. His own gaze remained unfocused on the leaves nearby until Valoretta finally drifted into a restless sleep. Watching her tremble, the islander sighed. She was right.

Pulling his cloak off his shoulders, he draped it over the queen. If they both died that night, not a soul would care.

Morning finally spilled through the trees onto Arnacin's stiff shoulders as he stared at the fire's ashes. Beaten, he glanced at the queen sleeping beside him. Even now, her shoulders shivered beneath his cloak. Sadly, nightmares were common for both of them.

He turned back to the fire's remnant, which needed obscuring before they resumed their march. Yet as he looked away, he noticed something he had failed to notice at first glance. Whipping his gaze back to Valoretta's face, he took in the perspiration running down it, the angry flush in her cheeks.

Cautiously touching her shoulder, Arnacin felt his breath leave him at the heat beneath his hand. "Valoretta."

Weakly, she shifted, a crease of pain crossing her brow. Without a word, however, she attempted to rise, catching herself as she swayed.

"Are you sick?" The islander reached out to support her.

"No, I'm fine." Yet, the queen pressed the palm of her hand against her forehead. "I just need food."

Arnacin refused to inform her he was already giving her most of what he found; he simply helped her to stand. Tugging her arm away from his hand, Valoretta stumbled forward a step and retched into the dry leaves at her feet. Dropping back to her knees, the queen stuttered with a trace of humor, "I guess that rules out hunger."

Regarding her for only a minute, Arnacin surrendered. "I'll restart the fire."

"Arnacin, Arnacin," Valoretta called him back as he began to leave to hunt for wood. "We have to continue. I can't spare time to be sick—winter will come upon us. It's already in the air."

Dropping down by her and wrapping his cloak about her shoulders, the islander confessed, "We don't have any choice. You can't travel like this, and... I'm not capable of carrying you for long."

Laying back, the queen pleaded, "Then go home, Arnacin. Go. There's no sense in this killing both of us."

"We don't know that it will," the islander soothed, curling up beside her hot body and wrapping his arms about her trembling waist in order to keep her warm. "We can spare a few hours. Go back to sleep. Maybe when you wake, the fever will have passed."

Her shoulder blades pressed against his chest as she sighed, and he pulled his cloak closer about her. Under usual circumstances, he expected she would pull away, and it was foreboding that she did not.

Arnacin could not help but doze also, waking here and there to shrug her hair and sweat off his neck. He dared not stretch his cramped muscles for fear of waking her.

When she finally did stir, her fever had broken, thankfully.

However, the fevers returned over the next few days. Even though she recovered quickly every time, Arnacin feared some sickness beyond starvation, cold and exhaustion. He kept such thoughts to himself. In that cold, there was no other choice. They had to leave Ursa and find shelter.

If she did die or grew so sick that she could no longer move, he would be responsible. Without a companion, the cold would also kill him.

With that thought, his nightmares again increased.

Sun glittered over the snow on Enchantress Island as the lone ship ground ashore. In seconds, the vessel was surrounded by clamoring people: Tevin, Raymond, Bounen and so many more Arnacin remembered playing with once. Some of them, a voice told him, he only recognized because he slept.

Through the tears, laughter and embraces, he finally made it into the village, headed toward home. Not five paces along the main street, however, he froze. An enormous statue dominated the road, a statue commemorating some king that looked like a younger version of Miro, a heavy, twisted crown perched atop his brow. In response to Arnacin's gaping horror, Tevin whispered, "Oh, yes. We were taken over by Elcan. That thing's a monument to the battle fought here."

"But it can't be," Arnacin protested. "That's Miro." Yet no one was around anymore to hear him. He sat by his family's flock. All the healthiest sheep were missing.

The sound of laughter and solitary footsteps caused him to look over. The king who resembled Miro was pulling himself over the last rise of the hill. Arnacin briefly noted his brown hair before Charlotte appeared beside him. It was she who captured the king's gaze and absurd smile.

Fire burst awake inside Arnacin and, softly, he rose, allowing them to draw closer. After another step, the king froze. Without even realizing he had moved, Arnacin closed the gap as pride very much like Miro's flickered in the king's eyes.

"Stop." Charlotte stood between them, her bow ready, though lowered. It was then that Arnacin comprehended the Tarmlin blade in his hand. His sister's voice dropped pleadingly, "For your own sake, Arnacin."

"So we can watch him destroy our home," Arnacin hissed. "He's already stolen the best sheep."

To his alarm, tears glistened in Charlotte's dark lashes. He took another step, and her bow lifted. "Please," she breathed. "He's not like other kings."

Arnacin was sure his scoffing retort shone from his eyes. Now, with tears in her voice, Charlotte said, "I wanted my brother back."

Those words struck like an arrow to the heart. With every added word, she enlarged the wound, even as it seemed she was no longer speaking to him. She was speaking to a stranger, then to a dragonish monster who had stolen her brother and disguised itself as someone she once loved.

Reality whisked back as Charlotte's last words rang in his consciousness, *"Find him."* Her tears were Arnacin's tears, streaming down his cheeks and over the bridge of his nose as he lay on the forest floor. Against his back, Valoretta trembled in her own sleep. Angrily wiping his face dry, he again promised himself such a thing would never happen. Enchantress Island would never know a noble, would never become enslaved to such a demonic being.

Slowly, the woods thinned. Three days after passing through the destroyed city, the travelers reached a river. Watching its gurgling rush of water, Valoretta hugged her arms more tightly. "It feels cold enough. You'd think it would be ice."

"It's still too early," her companion reminded her. "And if we wait for the convenience of being able to walk across it, it will be too cold for us."

"Great," Valoretta huffed—yet Arnacin was already turning down the riverbank. Dispiritedly, she trailed after him.

At last, they reached a place where a great tree had fallen across the water. Knowing it might be the only crossing for miles, Valoretta swallowed her concerns.

She regretted her silence as soon as she stepped onto the tree behind Arnacin. While he clambered across it like a squirrel—if slowly, for her sake—her torn skirts further complicated her crossing. Although she had knotted them up, they constantly tried to make her lose her footing on the slippery bark by catching on jutting branches.

Finally, she gave up, reaching out for her companion's shoulder to tell him of her danger. "Arna—" The rip of cloth and subsequent plunge stole her voice as she tripped and pitched over the edge of the tree. Freezing water closed over her head and poured down her throat.

She thrashed about, feeling the water sweeping her body away. Panic filled her, but try as she might, she could not free herself from the water, even to take a breath. Her lungs already burned, the pain of airlessness and the cold both stabbing like a blade into her chest.

An arm closed about her, lifting her head above the river's angry torrent. Choking, she felt her head reel, for no air could slip down her waterlogged lungs, as consciousness faded away.

She came to, spewing water back into the river. Arms stayed locked around her abdomen for a moment longer as she drew in great shuddering gasps. Then his arms slid away, allowing her to slip gently to the ground, coughing weakly. "Water belongs in the river, Valoretta, not your lungs," Arnacin's teasing voice whispered.

Looking up, she met Arnacin's dancing eyes, but then unconsciousness slipped back over her.

Sharp shaking once again woke her to find her companion offering his cloak.

"Wonderful weather for drowning," Arnacin stuttered through his own chills.

Weakly swinging her arm toward his legs, Valoretta coughed, "I would like to see you swim in my attire."

Her laughter was lost on him as he again offered his cloak, yet she shook her head, "I'll simply soak it in seconds, and it won't do a single thing for me."

"Take your clothes off, rub yourself dry and wrap this around you," Arnacin softly ordered. "You'll freeze as you are in this weather."

"You must be joking," the queen muttered, thinking of herself in nothing but a cloak.

"It's survival, Valoretta."

"My legs will freeze, even if the rest won't. And what about you?"

Her words sparked a smile from him, but she could not tell what he was thinking. He only said, "If you imagine I'll be much warmer, I'll not correct you, but I have fewer layers, and everything's thin with age."

Feeling more frozen with every passing second, the queen surrendered, teeth chattering. "Then I will excuse myself for a minute. You may wait for me."

She could feel his wicked grin on her back as she snatched his cloak and slipped behind some trees to strip her soaked garments off her shivering body. All she knew was that Sara had once told her she was indecent for revealing part of her under-dress. The nurse would have died on the spot if she had known her queen was only wrapping her top in a cloak–Arnacin's cloak–with the desperate hope she could keep it closed about her shoulders.

Thankfully, the islander was tall, if thin, and the back of the cloak dropped to her ankles, though the front only brushed her mid-calves. The problem was that she had to hold its folds closed and so had to kick her discarded garments back toward Arnacin, glaring at the laughter glinting in his eyes.

However, he was good enough to say nothing when she reached him. He simply picked up her clothes and, after wringing them out, threw them over his arm. She could well imagine the sight she made without him commenting on it. Instead, he sighed, "Well, let's continue, at least away from the river. We'll make a small fire once we're out of the open."

Somehow, they both avoided frostbite that night, but they had to remain where they built their fire for a whole extra day while Valoretta's heavier clothes dried.

The next day found them debating again as the queen refused to allow Arnacin to help her lace her gown up the back. After she struggled for five minutes on her own, she yielded, silently cringing as she turned her exposed back to him.

Naturally, she had nothing to fear and, in moments, they again set forth. By that evening, they spotted a village through the trees, quiet with dusk. Warm light glimmered from windows.

"We'll wait until the morning," Arnacin whispered. "When people are out and about, one can assess what sort of village it is much more easily."

Valoretta was too tired to say anything. Curling up for the night, they waited for the morning.

Dawn came. Leaving Valoretta in hiding while he went to collect information, Arnacin pulled his cloak tighter over his shoulders. People were out gathering the last of the harvest. Laughter and bustle filled the town. Children, pushing wheelbarrows of produce down the street at a run, shouted apologies as they barely missed hitting the islander. He could not summon a smile, but simply side-stepped and continued once the danger of stampede had passed.

A man, pushing another barrow behind the children, halted in front of Arnacin with a soft laugh as he held out his hand. "Otto Pampin. Sorry about that. They're young and not thinking."

He dropped his hand back to his side when Arnacin made no move to take it. Uncomfortably, Otto ran his other hand along his mouth. "Are you passing through?" he asked hesitantly.

"Likely," Arnacin finally admitted. "Is this Ursa?" He had skirted the town and entered it from the north and, as he guessed, the man's gaze followed the current direction the islander was headed, toward the woods in the east.

"Hardly," Otto stated, looking back to Arnacin with a sudden, slight glint of coldness in his eyes. "This is the land of Minsa, what *those* neighbors like to call 'Minus.' You need to continue south-east if you aim to go there, toward the ruins of the Ursan fortress of Bruach. Pass that, and you'll be in Ursa."

With a slight smirk at Otto's distaste, Arnacin prodded, "You don't like Ursa?"

Warily, the man appraised him, as if contemplating the island-er's way of standing and the absence of a greeting. "No..." Otto drew out the word, cryptically. "But I don't care to be treated as an inferior, though."

Subtly allowing his cloak to drop open, where his entirely foreign, penniless attire was visible and the folds only hid his sword, Arnacin admitted, "Well, I don't care for Ursa."

"Fairly bold for someone going there, isn't it?"

Shrugging, Arnacin replied, "I've told them as much directly."

Otto blinked, sparking the first real smile from the islander. "Bold?" Otto repeated himself. "Insane might have been a better choice of words. What are you going back for?"

Shifting, Arnacin jerked his cloak closed over his shoulders again and said nothing.

"Well," the man said after a second. "If you're going to continue traveling in this weather, you could likely do with some warmer clothes."

Taking a step back, Arnacin hesitated, "I'm not staying long enough for a tailor."

"It won't take any time," Otto hastened to assure him. "Out here in Borderwood, we all tend to grow bull shoulders when we hit adulthood. My son just acquired his, but you'll likely fit into the clothes he outgrew."

Still resisting, the islander protested, "I don't own anything to trade."

"If you can use it better than the moths, I'm satisfied."

A little while later, the clothes once owned by Otto's son adorned Valoretta. She rolled the pants above tripping length, happily shoved her cold hands down the enormous sleeves, and rejoined Arnacin. The islander sat against a trunk, his gaze turned toward the town visible through the barren trees a little below their small hill.

Valoretta twisted her hair over her shoulder with a frustrated exhale. "It's likely, Arnacin, that I'll only be more noticeable than if I stayed in those velvet rags. I don't look anything like a boy."

A wicked grin passed the islander's face as he looked up at her. "The state you're in, you hardly look human at all, really."

"I have half a mind to kick you," the queen warned him. "You're little more than a mud puddle yourself."

"But I, unlike you, being of *low* birth, am supposed to look dirty."

Tapping her foot in irritation, Valoretta became serious again and seized her large knot of red hair. "I think I'll only pass their notice if I lose this. No female would traipse around in pants, not without attracting looks."

Allowing his own grin to last a little longer, the islander admitted, "I never intended you to enter the town with it." Pushing himself wearily to his feet, Arnacin said briskly, "Kneel, please."

For a moment, the queen froze, her gaze following the islander's movement toward his short sword. Tilting his head in order to catch her eye, Arnacin whispered, "I promise, I won't even scratch you. Back home most people don't own anything like the scissors you used once. We've utilized blades for cutting hair for as long as I can remember."

Valoretta simply stared at him, knowing he was also aware of the real reason why she hesitated. Her trust had been broken as much as his. To kneel before anyone, especially someone holding a blade, scared her. Slowing inhaling, the queen compromised. "I'll sit—you kneel."

For a split second, she thought she saw a sad smirk pass Arnacin's face, but she could not tell for certain as he dipped his chin. Within the next hour, almost all of the queen's hair lay on the velvet folds of her gown.

Running her hand over her scalp, Valoretta expressed her loss with a soft sigh. She found herself turning away when Arnacin rolled the velvet gown around her discarded auburn locks. There, he paused. "Where's Mira's signet?"

"Up my sleeve. Even if it's fake... I need it, Arnacin."

After studying her for a moment, Arnacin shrugged and disappeared to bury the evidence.

She was still dejectedly running her finger over the top of her head when he returned a few minutes later. "Valoretta," Arnacin gently admonished. "You would look like yourself if you were bald."

Acknowledging his attempt to console her, Valoretta pushed herself to her feet. "Well, it's time to discover the lay of this Borderwood and, with any fortune, a hot meal."

Brushing past her, Arnacin warned, "Unless you plan on turning to thievery or can cook it yourself, don't trust a hot meal."

"I haven't trusted any meal prepared for me since Mira's fall," the queen muttered, lengthening her stride to walk at his side. Thus, they entered the town together, Arnacin's hood down in order to hide that he had passed through previously. As the islander gathered many a discreet glance, Valoretta wondered if there were not also other reasons he kept his hood off.

Appraising the townsfolk, Valoretta noted the lack of a market-place, the laughter of children in the streets, the sound of men and older boys in the distance hard at work, building and harvesting. Not far from where the queen and islander entered the town, a large double mill ground away from the hard work of two men and the river's water.

Around the town, chatting women engaged in gardening, pot-throwing, basket-weaving, sewing, carding, milking and what-ever other jobs could be brought out under the autumn sun. Despite the comforting feel of the community, Valoretta feared it, and she shivered from more than just the cold as a breeze blew up from the river.

Skirting along the town's edges, Arnacin encountered an older man painting his fence. "Is there any warm lodging for two coin-less travelers?"

"Anyplace you take a fancy to," the older man answered with a crinkly smile as he turned around to face them. He paused only briefly upon sight of them, took an extra look at Valoretta and then extended his hand. "You may even stay here for tonight if you like. There's room enough for two more. My wife, Orissy, will be pleased to extend her hospitality."

Neither queen nor islander moved. Seeming to read the wari-ness in their eyes, the man stated, "Come on. You two look like you need some warmth and shelter before you die on the spot."

"A barn would do as well," Arnacin finally voiced.

"In this weather? A barn works for animals with winter coats. Neither of you appear to have one. Come on. There's a warm fire and good company; two things all barns lack."

Dipping his chin at last, Arnacin took Valoretta's hand as the man ushered them inside. They entered into a kitchen area, spacious enough that the fireplace had plenty of room to vent without choking its owners. The entire kitchen was partitioned off from the sleeping area by a wooden screen. Its only occupants were the snoring brown dog beneath a stool and the lady kneading dough at the table, who looked up in surprise.

"Orissy," the man said. "These travelers need a place to bunk down for a little while. I've offered them our hospitality."

Behind the man, Arnacin winced and Valoretta squeezed his hand in support, dropping it before either host could see.

"I'm Ben, by the way," the man said. "Lived here all my life."

Hesitantly, the islander supplied his own name, causing the queen's soft laugh as he disguised his own accent with a Miran one. Ben looked at her. Before he could ask, Arnacin stated dismissively, "She's Valor."

"Ah, your sister?" Ben asked.

Saving her companion from the lie she knew he would utter for her sake, Valoretta answered, "My cousin. My dress was so ruined, we left it behind as soon as someone gave him another pair of clothes." Smiling she added, "They didn't think to give him a dress."

Arnacin looked heavenward in response as Ben laughed.

When Valoretta asked Orissy if they could help, the older woman pointed toward the vegetables on the table. "Just chop and throw all that into the broth."

Nodding, the queen looked to Arnacin. As unobtrusively as possible, the islander showed her how to dice vegetables, while Orissy was occupied with making the bread.

"Our fears are absurd," Valoretta whispered to her companion as she dropped the last of the vegetables into the pot he was stirring. "If they planned to poison us, they could just as easily poison the bowls while we make the stew."

Barely audibly, Arnacin breathed, "The choice is up to you. I won't eat."

"Why would they want to poison us?"

"I never leave them the opportunity."

Valoretta smiled sadly. "I'll just pass on the bread, if you serve the stew. If I'm drugged or poisoned, I'll have you to rely on." She saw just the tiniest smile pass her companion's face.

"Both our sons wished to become apprentices in Ursa," Ben told his guests over dinner. When the twosome refused to talk, other than saying they had traveled up from that kingdom, their hosts continued with that subject. "Skills are said to be better there and neither wished to remain stuck in this town. The oldest went when he was of age to learn under a metal smithy. He never finished. When he came back, he told us that Ursa is as lost as it could ever be, and his brother never went at all."

"Ursa's working class doesn't seem so terrible," Valoretta commented. "Are the people closer to Minsa colder?"

"No, they're as relatively pleasant as any Ursan, but they're so... dismissive. There was no talking to them about politics or gods or important things in life. Instead, they speak of their jobs, the girl they're interested in, the food they don't like and trivial, dull stuff, according to my son—all self-absorbed. They said outright that they don't care how the government rules, as long as they have riches and food.

"That attitude leaves their monarchy open to do anything, as long as they're feeding them—though we know nothing about the government itself. Our son didn't have any interaction with it."

Valoretta shook her head, her brow furrowing. Beside her, Arnacin shivered, his shoulders hiking while his elbows rested on the table.

"It's a sad truth," Ben breathed.

"What do your sons do now?" Arnacin inquired, effectively drawing the conversation away from Ursa.

"The oldest became a tailor for another village after marrying a weaver's daughter, and our youngest lives on the other side of town," Orissy explained. "He farms like the rest of us, raises ducks on the side. We take care of his children while he and his wife work, since we're too old to help and our grandchildren are too young, for now."

"In other words, you see him every day," Valoretta whispered, an unintended wistful note slipping into her voice.

"Most days," Ben agreed. His gaze flicked between his guests for a minute and then paused briefly on his dog, whose head Arnacin was pushing off his knee. "I gather you two have no other family?"

Dropping her gaze, Valoretta confessed, "Both my parents are dead."

"Is that why you seem to be wandering aimlessly?" Orissy asked in sudden compassion.

"Indirectly."

"If you two need a family, you're welcome to stay."

"Your confidence in strangers is warming," the queen said, "but we haven't decided anything yet." She tried to ignore the fact that both their hosts were glancing at the dog while she spoke. She hoped they were unaware of the fact that everything Arnacin had eaten came out of their own remaining supplies. The food provided for him by their host now resided safely in the dog's stomach—as it proceeded to remind them with the occasional licking of their hands and pitiful look.

"That may be a better topic for the morning," Ben advised. "It's late, and I'm sure you two are even more exhausted than Orissy and I."

Valoretta ached to the core. All the same, she began to protest, "I'm not actually that ti—"

She broke off as Arnacin touched her arm. "You should, Valor," he whispered as she turned to him. With a quick glance toward where his blade remained carefully tucked beneath the folds of his cloak, she accepted. Her companion shrugged away the offer of sleep.

Leading Valoretta behind the wooden divider, Orissy passed her a long shift, pointing to the bed she could use. Looking at it, the queen commented in surprise, "You own real beds."

"When you carve away the winter, Valor," Orissy laughed, "and you live right next to the woods, anything is possible. You may have noticed the steps to our front door as well. Believe me, I know we live in relative luxury here. Sleep well. In the morning, I'll heat some water for you to wash your journey away."

So saying, she returned to the kitchen. In moments, Valoretta lay curled beneath the warm covers, fast asleep, the crane clasped tightly in her fist.

Chapter 15

An Ursan Child

O RISSY AWOKE THE NEXT MORNING to the sound of her husband's voice. As her mind caught up with her ears, she realized he was speaking to someone. "You have me beat. I can't believe you're still awake. I'm feeling dead at this point. But I guess you have youth on your side."

She jumped as an unknown voice replied with a hint of laughter, "You likely wore yourself out with all your chatter."

Her gaze landing on the young lady still asleep in the other bed, Orissy's memory returned. Sliding out from beneath her covers, she pulled her shawl around her shoulders and crept over to the other bed. Valor's cheeks were flushed against her pale skin, yet she slept peacefully. Therefore, Orissy joined those in the kitchen. It was about an hour before dawn, and the wool curtain they kept over the doorway until the dead of winter, when it was replaced with two bear hides, was pulled back to allow the chill air inside, likely to keep Ben awake, his wife thought at the sight of his glassy gaze.

Running a hand along her husband's shoulders, Orissy promised, "I'll make some tea. Then, perhaps you should think about sleeping." She glanced toward the young man named Arnacin and caught just the fleeting glimpse of his grin.

Oddly enough, he seemed completely alert, although his gaze appeared peacefully distant—unlike the other night, when their depths had contained an approaching storm. Now, the storm had passed, leaving the calm ocean in its wake. For the first time, Orissy dared suggest, "You could likely do with some sleep yourself."

Arnacin said nothing.

Shrugging, the lady moved over to the fireplace, reawakening the still-hot coals—a telltale sign of how long the two men had remained awake. Within a few minutes, a nice fire blazed, a kettle of water hung above it, and the curtain blocked the wind once again.

Not too long after that, Orissy poured three mugs of tea. Softly, Arnacin refused the offered cup.

"Would you like me to drink some of yours first?" she asked with a twinkle in her eyes. At his blank expression, she pointedly glanced at the dog spread out in sleep beneath his chair. Following her gaze, the young man smiled guiltily.

When he looked back up, however, the light of challenge had replaced his smile. "And what else have you noticed that you haven't mentioned?"

Sharing a soft smile with her husband, Orissy sat down. "Have some tea, and I'll give you the list."

Although Arnacin accepted the mug, he left it untouched on the table. Accepting that small submission, the lady began, "Where should I start? Well, your hair is almost down to your shoulder blades, yet Valor's is short. Nor is hers as dirty. My conclusion is that longer hair protected her scalp until recently. Then there's the dress. She said she wears pants because hers was ruined, implying she felt indecent, but it also says you didn't mention her to whomever gave you those clothes or, if they were bought, you purposely tried to disguise her as a boy. Should I go on?"

The young man simply stared into the steam rising from his mug, and Ben picked up the account. "I think the last thing we can definitely add to that list is that you've been hiding a weapon of some sort. You've kept your cloak too close for me to be fooled."

Dark blue eyes flicked upward, and Orissy noticed the storm clouds had returned. "I suppose that is the reason you've stayed awake all this time?" Arnacin pressed. "Because I'm armed."

"Actually, I didn't really think of it," Ben admitted, rubbing the back of his neck in consideration. "It may seem odd to you that I didn't, but we have no reason to fear death and nothing for anyone to want from us anyway. Our point is more that *you* apparently do. I've seen wild animals trust more readily than you two. No, we are not pushing for an explanation. Perhaps we don't even wish to know. But if there is something we can help with, you have our word we will assist."

Darkly, the young man mentioned, "There is no word I trust but my own. Why would you care to help?"

His tone heavy with sadness, Ben said, "Because we see two young adults burdened far beyond their years with sorrows, fears and sufferings. Is that not reason enough for any man to offer help?"

For a long moment, Arnacin only ran his fingers along the rim of his mug. Finally, however, he breathed, "Not in this world."

Although storm clouds hung to the east, the sun shone upon the town that morning. Sitting on the steps, letting the breeze dry his wet and trimmed hair, Arnacin ran his thumb along his lower lip in thought. Below him, people passed, enjoying the brief spell of sunlight despite the cold. Only the children glanced at him in unabashed wonder, yet even they were polite enough to do no more than wave shyly and move on.

Looking up as Valoretta joined him, Arnacin shifted slightly to make room for her. The queen wore a simple brown gown of Orissy's with tucks sewn in several places to fit her smaller frame with a kerchief that hid her cropped hair.

Thoughtfully, she pulled at the kerchief's edge by her ear. "There's something different here, Arnacin, something satisfying and peaceful."

Nodding slightly, the islander agreed. "You can't fool them the way you'd like, yet they let you believe you did. Then they reveal it long before it's useful to them."

"No one stares at you," Valoretta remarked.

Throwing her a smile, Arnacin commented, "Oh, is that all that makes a town feel different?"

"No," the queen whispered. Her gaze disappeared into the distance. "It's in the smiles, the laughter, even the tears."

"What tears?"

"What tears," Valoretta repeated thoughtfully, as if for a minute she was viewing those words in an entirely different light. Returning, she faced her companion. "I didn't ask her why, but Orissy's eyes were moist when she handed me this gown."

Exhaling, the queen returned to her point. "It's not the happiness of the life of ease, Arnacin—it's something more. So much more."

For a long moment, Arnacin stared out over the village, considering her words. Once, he had known a place that fit such description, a place for which he yearned. Home.

Turning once again to her, the islander inquired, "In other words, you would be happy here?"

"No," Valoretta replied without hesitation. "It's a... perfect place, I suppose, but I'm too close to danger here to be able to experience it."

"There isn't a single place in the world that isn't close to danger—"

"Including your h—"

"That place is bordered by a greedy valley. There are things it hopes and prays never leak out for fear of... attack. Why do you think I would never tell anyone its location while I was on Mira? Secrecy and suspicion of strangers are natural traits among us." The islander quickly closed his mouth before he said more; he supposed captivity naturally taught those traits, particularly when enchanters were the captors. Lord Carpason himself had thought it best to keep the island's relation to magic a secret.

"Arnacin—"

"It's time we tell them what happened, enough to know the danger you're in and the secrets they shall need to keep. After that, I'm going home. I've fulfilled my word, and that's all—"

"Of course, that's all for y—" the queen started with heat.

"What more could you want than what you see here? You asked for a place that could provide healing, and you've admitted that you feel it here. Anything else you could say simply proves what I've known all along—you're after some gain, and you're inventing and using the best there is to acquire it."

Once again, Valoretta opened her mouth and shut it. Nodding, Arnacin pushed himself to his feet and turned inside. He heard the queen begrudgingly follow.

Ben and Orissy remained silent during the entire telling of the last days of Mira's war through to Arnacin's rescue of the queen, all the way until they arrived in Borderwood. "Which is why I have to leave," Arnacin finished. "My hair is a trail for Ursa to follow, and... I promised to return to my family."

"Why won't you take Valor with you?" Ben asked, in confusion.

To her own surprise, Valoretta hastily lied, "His home does not allow nobles of any kind."

"They can hardly object to a queen who is no more," Orissy argued, missing or incapable of reading the wary inquiry in Arnacin's eyes as he studied Valoretta.

"A queen who is no more," Valoretta softly repeated, staring at her feet to avoid her companion's gaze. Yes, she was again striving to preserve his honor—his nonexistent honor. Even if he realized what she was doing, however, she could guess he would simply label it as a manipulative attempt to convince him she cared.

Her eyes stung, yet pushing away such thoughts, she continued, "I'm not just any queen, and it's a rule to guard their independence. They don't feel they possess a choice. Furthermore, anyone found trying to break that rule is exiled. Arnacin could lose his family if he tried taking me there."

For a split second, she glanced up to meet Arnacin's gaze, praying he would deny her claim, but there was no shift in his wary expression. Indeed, even if he had wanted to deny it, she knew she had backed him into a corner. If he did care enough to do so, he could not, lest he call her own honor into question.

"Surely they would never know?" Ben asked in the silence.

"They would find out," Valoretta whispered. "Sooner or later, they would find out."

"Well, then." Orissy opened her palms. "When do you plan to leave?"

"That's not the question," Arnacin spoke up, turning back to their hosts.

"*Valor* will remain safe under our roof," Ben promised. "Her secrets are ours."

Bowing with only a dip of his chin, the islander informed them, "Then I will leave this afternoon."

Gasping in exasperation, Orissy left the table, hustling about in a sudden rush to pack food and a few blankets. With a soft smile, Valoretta surmised the lady was very used to boys and their sudden, senseless whims. Ben, however, refused to yield so easily.

"You will need to wait until spring, Arnacin," the man warned. At the stubborn look he received, he pressed, "Winter is here. The last of the harvest was finished yesterday, the trees are barren and the clouds hint of snow. You will never make it. If you brought Valor with you, you still would not make it. Alone, it's impossible— to say nothing about how hard it will be to make any repairs your ship may need in the cold, if it's even still there."

Without answering, Arnacin turned toward the door before stopping in its frame. "Listen." Ben spoke with soft firmness. "Ursa shall be combing the ocean for you, not Minsa, and if you're still concerned due to how much you stand out, there are ways of dyeing your hair. True, it's more difficult to change a dark color to a light one, but it can be done."

Holding her breath, Valoretta felt her heart race in hope, as it had not for what seemed like a lifetime. Without any intervention on her part, Ben had bound Arnacin there, at least until spring.

And, in four months, anything could happen.

Yet, even as that thought flashed through her mind, the queen noted the pillar-like stance of the islander as he gazed out toward the clouds forming ever thicker in the sky. Without trying, she could guess at his thoughts and feelings, and she hated herself for her own desires.

His head dropping in defeat, Arnacin began to turn back, surrender forming on his lips, but softly, Valoretta said, "It never freezes in Ursa. It's never even cold enough to snow." She received the slight satisfaction of seeing Arnacin whirl toward her in shock, yet she refused to meet his gaze. "If you can reach the border within a day or two, you will likely survive."

She allowed herself to look up into his incredulous, probing gaze and knew tears glittered in her lashes. To her right, Ben and Orissy simply watched the silent play between the two travelers.

Arnacin looked away first, seeming to tremble as he nodded in acknowledgment of the information. Galvanized once more, Orissy prepared a sack of supplies in only another few minutes. Neither Arnacin nor Valoretta looked at each other. The islander's nod toward her in parting, along with his quiet thanks to those in the room, was all of their interaction.

With an acknowledging smile, Orissy passed him the sack of food, two blankets and a lantern for the first few nights he could not stop due to the cold.

He had only just disappeared out the door, however, when Valoretta dashed up to it. "Arnacin!"

Three steps away, he paused, turning back. Racing to his side, the queen panted, "You asked, a while ago, why I rescued you, even at risk to myself and despite the betrayal to my father."

Sighing, the islander started, "Val—"

"No," she softly cut him off. "I need to answer. I could never live with myself if I let you walk away thinking that I did it for some political game." Taking a slight step closer, she breathed, "I love you."

Although he froze as if turned to ice, she pressed on. "I always will. If you handed me over to the Ursan nobility or ran me through with a million blades, I'd still love you." Knowing he was betraying her, she slipped her hand into his. "I still love you."

No emotion flickered in his deep blue eyes, and no sound came from him. All the same, guessing that she could not continue without him believing she was once again trying for manipulation, Valoretta slowly backed away until her distance pulled her fingers out of his. Letting go, she whispered, "Goodbye, Arnacin."

The horrible words felt ripped from her throat, but she said them all the same, for she did love him. And so, she released him, sure as she did that he would never return. He might have once before when she thought it impossible, but this parting was of his own choosing.

As if some spell had been lifted, the islander shuddered. Shifting the pack on his shoulder, he softly said, "Find life, Valoretta. It's here." Without another word, he turned away just as the first flurries of snow drifted from the clouds overhead.

Standing there with her arms crossed against the cold, the queen desired nothing more than to call him back, or at least to ask for one last request. In the wind, she heard her own thoughts take flight. *At least promise me, Arnacin, you will never find someone else—then, if nothing else, I shall know that some part of you will always be mine.*

Aloud, however, she only whispered his words back in despair, "Find life, Arnacin." Only the mournful wailing of the wind answered her.

Snow thickened over the day and into the night. Valoretta watched it in glazed surrender—a person whose last strand of life has ended. Nothing the inhabitants of the house said could move her.

By morning, the ground lay covered in white. Though snow no longer blew downward, the clouds remained hanging, waiting above. Nature's stillness finally seemed to stir the dethroned queen, and she turned to her hostess boiling something in a small pot.

"I'm sorry, Valor," Orissy whispered. When Valoretta only looked at the woman, she explained, "Anyone with eyes could tell how much he meant to you. I will never understand how men can only see the insides of their own skulls."

As a low snort came from behind the partition, a brief smile passed the queen's lips.

"Don't let her fool you. Women only see those 'love' things because their heads are constantly up in the clouds where it exists," Ben said, coming out to kiss his wife on the cheek. "Blind bat," he whispered lovingly, and Orissy smacked him lightly in return.

"Yes, put up the act. You'll break her heart."

"Our fun will finally return some laughter to her," her husband protested in the same playful tone as his wife.

"Thank you for trying," Valoretta whispered. "Truthfully, I've known several men who were very insightful and then others who allowed fear to cloud their perception."

Neither Ben nor Orissy replied, only watching her with sympathy.

Perhaps that increased the need to excuse herself after a small bite to eat. When the grandchildren, four-year-old Lera and two-year-old Denny, arrived with all their youthful bounciness, the queen left for the garden.

That afternoon, Valoretta was sitting on the frozen front steps with a mug of a long-cold drink in her hands when her breathing hitched. A figure wrapped in a green cloak was shuffling through the snow, up the street. Had it not been for the Miran shirt that escaped the cloak's protection, she would have dismissed it as some other occupant of Borderwood. Instead, her feet carried her down the steps, and they met in silence in the middle of the street.

She neither asked for his reasons for returning nor welcomed him. His only reaction was a slight nod. Together, they turned back to Ben and Orissy's house.

Arnacin's hair was too dark to dye easily, yet it stood out far too much. After trying unsuccessfully to dye it himself, the islander had to surrender to Orissy's aid. He could not make himself trust Ben's strong hands near.

The lady insisted on cutting the islander's hair first, since it would be easier to work in the pigment that way. Then she proceeded to apply multiple colors with various results that brought smiles to all the inhabitants of the house—except for Arnacin.

Starting with a white to pale his hair, Orissy managed a dingy, bluish gray at which she chirped happily, "Don't worry, you'll be old for only a few minutes more."

With that, she proceeded to rub in a yellow that collided horribly into a sickly green.

"Very becoming," Ben said.

Valoretta could no longer control her laughter. "You might do better just to cut it *all* off."

Orissy only pursed her lips as she said, "Just have patience."

"How much more patience can one possess?" Arnacin whispered, clearly ready to bolt.

"Enough for me to finish," came the reply. Within another few minutes, she had succeeded in turning Arnacin's hair a bright dandelion. Holding out the remaining paste covering her fingers, she said, "Now take care of your eyebrows. I know you won't want me anywhere near your face. Once I tell you it is the right color, leave it for a little while and then wash the extra off your skin."

"Even if you keep it unwashed, I give it a week at most before it fades back to green," Ben said.

Turning to the bucket of water, Orissy admitted, "We might be forced to do this every second night..." She trailed off as Arnacin stilled.

Smiling, she soothed him. "We'll figure it out, but for your own protection and Valor's, your hair must stay yellow. Now, if it were as simple as removing all of it, we would, but we'd still need to dye eyebrows, and those are harder to manipulate than hair. It is my hope that the hair will draw people's attention away from noticing any hint of your actual coloring."

Valoretta watched as the winter lull left Arnacin restless. Sometimes Ben and Orissy's grandchildren settled him for a bit—he would even consent to play dolls and horses with Lera—but sometimes they seemed to make it worse, likely a reminder of his own family. Within three days, he took to long afternoon walks, whatever the weather.

As for Valoretta, she did not regain full strength as she had assumed she would, and she was feverish almost every morning. After a week of living in Minsa, she woke with a horrible suspicion that drained all blood from her face.

Unable to voice it, yet unable to toss it aside, she fell extremely quiet. With concern in her eyes, Orissy seemed to hesitate to say something while trying to rouse her, yet Valoretta's tongue glued itself to the top of her mouth, and she could not even gather the strength to speak when someone asked her a question. Arnacin appeared to be the only one not concerned by it, continuing to guide Denny's repairs on an old water bucket, but Valoretta knew he actually paid more attention than it looked.

When he eventually pulled his cloak over his shoulders, Valoretta finally found her voice and asked if she could accompany him. In a softer tone, meant only for her, the islander asked, "What are you looking for?"

"Please, Arnacin. I need a walk." Surrendering, Arnacin waited for the queen to fasten the short cloak Orissy had handed her. Then they left, heading toward the south.

Watching them leave for the forest, Ben asked, "Do you think Valor's health is up to a walk in this weather?"

Placing her broom against the hearth, Orissy joined her husband by the door. "I don't know, but I know they need some time to talk."

Quizzically, he turned to her. "You know why she's so quiet?"

"She's pregnant, Ben. If I were to guess, she just discovered that herself."

"What? From Ursa or—"

"No, not Arnacin. I can't see that at all." For a moment, Orissy said no more, pulling her husband's arm over her shoulder and resting her head against him. Then she mused aloud, "I wonder if Valor told us the truth about his home."

Ben shrugged. "Why would she lie?"

With a smile, Orissy replied, "She loves him. But if her words are true..."

"You're wondering what Arnacin will do?"

A small sigh escaped the lady. "I have no doubt he loves her beneath that shell of his—not as she loves him. But he's done so much for her, nothing else makes sense. Only love could make him. If she's telling the truth, and she's pregnant... Undoubtedly, he'll want to protect her."

"We'll just have to see." Rubbing Orissy's back, Ben turned her inside.

The snow in the woods was much shallower and would have made for comfortable walking, if not for the cold. For some time, they simply walked in companionable silence. Only after a really strong wind passed, did Valoretta finally speak. "Do you still think my fevers are because I'm weak from travel, Arnacin?"

"You apparently don't think so."

"Arnacin—" The queen broke off, then, forcing it out of her lungs, she breathed, "I think I'm pregnant."

Arnacin stopped dead, his gaze jerking to her. "How is that possible?"

Lowering her eyes, Valoretta said, "Ursa. If I am pregnant, someone must have done it while I was drugged. It's... all too likely they did. I suspected as much, actually, when I found myself in another dress. I don't mean I thought I conceived a child, but..." She could not finish, trembling with both the injustice of Ursa's action and her fear. Instead, she said, "I know what the natives did for certain, but that was too long ago."

Disbelievingly, the islander asked, "You think an Ursan wretch of a noble made you pregnant?"

"A noble, a counselor, a knight or even a guard. Any one of those men could have done it—but Arnacin, that's not the worst of it." She hurriedly finished, seeing his incredulous comment in his expression. "Do you have any idea of the danger a fatherless child of mine creates? If people start talking, and it reaches Ursa... Arnacin... I'm terrified."

For a long moment, the islander simply stood immobile, his own horror reflecting in his eyes as they stared into Valoretta's. Only once did his gaze move down to where her arms were wrapped about her stomach, and the distance in his eyes appeared to increase by leagues.

He whirled away, his expression briefly twisting in pain before he stated flatly, "Don't worry about Ursa. As far as anyone needs to know, I'll be the child's father."

"Arnacin, everyone here knows we're not married. That would simply create a different rumor to spread."

"We'll fix that tomorrow."

It was Valoretta's turn to freeze, although her companion walked on. "You can't," she finally protested. "You still intend to leave in the spring. Do you realize what you would do to yourself... for an Ursan baby?"

"Be quiet and do it," Arnacin growled, still without halting.

Hurrying to keep up, Valoretta protested, "I'm surprised you even believe me."

Coming up short, the islander growled, tears threatening his voice, "If you are lying, Valoretta, I'll kill you myself, because I have no choice but to believe you. By the time proof arrives, it will be too late."

Knowing what he was doing to himself, once again for *honor*, the queen whispered, "I am not your responsibility, Arnacin. You don't have to fix this, not that way."

Whirling back toward her, Arnacin snapped, "If you don't wish for this, why tell me your fears?"

The tears shining in his lashes caught all of Valoretta's attention for a second. "Because I would go insane trying to keep such a fear to myself."

As he took an angry step toward her, the queen retreated.

"The truth is, you do wish for this." Arnacin's tone was warningly low, yet she raised her chin against that attack. "Don't try to make it seem otherwise."

"Do you wish for blunt, harsh truth? Very well, Arnacin of Enchantress Island! If I had to stab my eyes out and cut off my ears to marry you, I would. Don't look at me with that disgust. I would, because that is how desperate I am for a friend who's not going to leave me. Also, I need one from my youth, one who knows the pain of Mira. I have been through too much, Arnacin, to care what condition I was in—if I could find that companionship.

"I need you, Arnacin, but not as you are, not with all the bitterness and the hate. I need the Arnacin I knew. The one who inspired me. Go home unfettered, where you can become him once again. I want you to go home because I want to know you are whole again. Don't sacrifice yourself further, not even for honor. Just go home."

Arnacin's gaze traveled westward, and she knew he was seeing, not the snowy trees around them, but the ocean. And, after traveling that imagined expanse, an island rising out of the waves.

For a moment, he remained there, frozen. Then, with a guilty breath, he led her back the way they had come. There was nothing to say. She knew she had not changed his decision. Tomorrow, they would wed, and it would not come with happiness.

Chapter 16

Union

NEVER HAD VALORETTA SYMPATHIZED so thoroughly with Queen Rosa than the day of her marriage. After the very formal wedding, she and Arnacin were left Ben and Orissy's house to themselves until the next morning. They might as well have attended a funeral for all the pained silence between them that first day and night.

Although her body changed, many months passed before she first felt her child move inside her. Passing the large soup spoon to Orissy with an excited smile, she promised, "I'll be back."

Laughing, the good lady ordered, "Don't forget your cloak!"

Obediently grabbing the indicated article, Valoretta dashed out the door, the dog yapping at her heels. "Just keep exercising, Little One," she whispered.

Arnacin and Ben were not far beyond the first grove of the snow-covered forest, checking their taps for sap when the queen joined them, her hand still pressed against her stomach. Without introduction, she hastily grabbed the islander's hand, pressing it against her side.

Her broad grin faded as he trembled beneath her grip. She looked up into his face, which was suddenly colorless aside from the splatter of cold red across cheeks and nose, highlighted so brilliantly in that moment. His unreadable eyes stared at her stomach as if he could see the child inside. She almost believed he could.

Five steps away, Ben just watched and, lowering her voice, Valoretta sighed, "At least, Arnacin, you can be happy the child lives. You didn't imprison yourself needlessly."

Though his fingers closed beneath her hand, he allowed her to prevent him from pulling away, despite the fact that there was no more movement there. "I never thought otherwise," he breathed, and she knew he was telling the truth, no matter what had been said.

Behind the new partition between mattresses, Arnacin nightly dozed at the foot of Valoretta's bed. Although curled against the wall, he left her the space to sleep peacefully, yet she never did, not for as long as he remained there.

Perhaps her own subconscious scars kept her alert as long as a man remained anywhere near her bed, but every night, he heard her breathing remain shallow without deepening until he left.

Arnacin himself dared not sleep at all, fighting visions of entombment for as long as he remained between walls and partitions. Every time he slipped into a light sleep, his subconscious woke him with urgency. There was no air. Sleep meant death. He must try to escape. And so, it went.

That night, there was a thought that kept imagined suffocation at bay—Valoretta's moving child. She had been pleased, as she should be, as Arnacin himself should be. There, beneath their hands had moved a wonderful innocent life, and it was hers, but it was also the living symbol of the islander's imprisonment.

It was her child, but not his. Even if that had been different, the islanders would never fail to miss the peculiarities of their marriage—he could never speak of the horrors it took to explain everything.

Wiping his cheeks, he slid off the bed, threw his cloak around his shoulders and stepped outside. There, he dropped himself onto the stoop. Moonlight shone from the snow around Borderwood, and a sleepless neighbor had lanterns in their window, assisting the glow.

A soft tread whispered from the doorway. Not wanting her to see the tracks across his cheeks, Arnacin looked away as Valoretta settled beside him, bundled in the bed's blanket. He was glad she refrained from asking questions. He could not rely on his voice to hide the pain of his village's scorn, if they ever made it to Enchantress Island.

So sharply he could picture their rejection, it could have been a painting of islanders whispering behind hands, staring curiously at the small unlikely family—islander, Miran and a child that was obviously not his, all intertwined. Matalaide might even openly press and rebuke him. Regardless of their exact reactions, the island would never seem like home again.

Beside him, Valoretta rested her head on his shoulder. "Are you thinking of your home?"

Suspecting a traitorous voice, Arnacin only nodded.

A soft breath of amusement came from the queen. "From someone as secretive as you, perhaps I should wonder if you're lying."

There was too much guilt and pain to smile with her, but dropping his gaze, the islander sighed, "I'm sorry, Valoretta. I... You—"

"No," Valoretta breathed. "If you apologize, I must also. You've given more than either of us has acknowledged. First, you returned to Mira, a place I know you fear above all others. Then, you were willing to sail even farther from home if it meant finding somewhere safe for me. Instead of being grateful, I've consistently demanded you surrender the one thing you've withheld, although I *never* tried to manipulate."

Taking her hand in his, Arnacin gently squeezed it.

Two days later, thoughts of home forced their way into his mind again. Ben had taken Arnacin out to gather more firewood. The islander was between armloads, stacking the logs to dry, when he heard Valoretta enter the shed. Her steps were growing heavier by the day it seemed, but it still sounded like her tread.

When he finished emptying his arms, he turned to her. Wordlessly, she held out a steaming mug. "Have some cider."

There was something in the gentleness of the queen's order that caused no resistance from Arnacin. Still he quipped, "Didn't you make some for Ben as well?"

Smiling, Valoretta shook her head. "Orissy will take him inside for his. I wanted to speak with you alone for a bit."

With a sip of the cider, the islander waited. In his silence, the queen continued, "When do we intend to start back for your ship? Orissy is pushing me to suggest we don't leave until after the child is born. I fear if we take her suggestion, it will become clear to everyone that the child is not yours."

Drinking warm cider helped him stall for only moments more. With a sigh, Arnacin swirled the mug, watching the patterns its contents made. "If we leave, I intend to retrieve the ship myself, as long as Ursa didn't find it, and sail up this river. I'll hide it beneath the forest's cover and come back here to retrieve you and our supplies."

Valoretta stared at him a moment before repeating, "If we leave?"

Softly, Arnacin asked, "Could you reiterate all that has happened to you again, to strangers?"

Dropping her gaze, the queen shook her head.

"Neither can I. Yet, we're... with a child that will clearly not be mine. Without our explanation, they'll jump to their own conclusions. I doubt you'll ever be accepted."

"No, Arnacin!" Emphatically, Valoretta shook her head. "They love you. Have you forgotten what you told me about their love, their trust? They'll never ask, but they'll support you regardless."

His eyes burning, Arnacin closed them. "They loved Arnacin, Valoretta. You know he is no more." Warm fingers seized his hand, and he startled.

"I don't know what you've been through, Arnacin," Valoretta whispered, squeezing his captive hand. "But I would never have thought anyone or anything existed that could disillusion you so much you no longer believe anyone, not even your own family, knows unconditional love. Knowing the person you were, I cannot believe such an evil lie as that."

He had no idea why he admitted it, but she had stabbed through his shields like a dagger and, in that pain, the truth leaked out. "From what you knew of me... I'm no different from this world, Valoretta. How could they be? And if they are different, how can I introduce my darkness to them?"

The queen drew in a long breath. Pressing her lips together, she looked up at him. "You don't have to be honest with me, Arnacin, but stop lying to yourself. If I may be so bold, I think you have a treasure in the island. You know it's not as faultless as you want, and you would sooner die than face that blemish. When you decided to marry me, you realized there was no escape from the island's faults, but you married me anyway. For that, I thank you."

She took a small step closer as her voice lowered. "I've been there, Arnacin. Despite my feelings, I won't stop you if you choose to quit, but I don't know that you want Ursa to end your suffering for you. If we stay, they will find us here eventually and, if we die beforehand, I have no doubt they will still discover the child."

For a long moment, Arnacin remained silent. Then, unable to look at her, he whispered, "It doesn't matter then, does it? In three days, I'll leave for the ship. That should give us time before the child's born. I also gave my word to return home, and I might as well fulfill it before the end."

"I hope it's not the end."

Grimly, the islander nodded. "It might very well be. I was raised to believe that every human needs a purpose to stay alive. Once all the goals and reasons are finished or discovered hollow, the heart stops beating. With the past years, I believe that more than ever."

"And the reason for your existence will finish as your ship touches the shores of Enchantress Island—a home for me and your promise to your sister." Valoretta's voice was just a breath of air but, tentatively, she brought his fingers to her lips. Temporarily vanquished, Arnacin did not refuse her expression of love.

Three days passed too quickly for Valoretta, but as dawn turned the horizon rosy, Arnacin shouldered the pack they had prepared the night before.

Holding out his hand, Ben cautioned, "It's still very cold out, particularly at night."

His hand still waited and, after a pause, Arnacin clasped it. "Thanks. Take care of everyone."

Smiling, Ben nodded. "We're going to miss you when you take Valor. I mean that. You've both been a great help, even if you're not always the warmest. I dare say Lera and Denny will miss you the most. With them, you were able to play as a close uncle. Although... there are some fears about Denny's introduction to carving."

Dropping his gaze, Arnacin shrugged. "Well, my father began teaching us at that age." With a last nod, he turned to Valoretta. "Give me two months. If the ship's gone, I'll return by foot and start building anew."

"Just promise me you'll be the Black Phantom Mira knew, a shadow that passes through the land unseen. Don't let them find you."

With a smile Valoretta suspected was assumed, the islander turned toward the door, pulling his hood up. "They won't." With that, he was gone. The only sound was the dog's bark as it sensed his departure.

Surprisingly, he returned with his ship within only a month. After two days of hurried preparations and goodbyes, they set sail. For Valoretta, it was into the unknown. Even Minsa was beyond Mira's waters and trade. This was farther still.

As the red of a promising evening arrived that first night at sea, Arnacin joined the queen at the ship's aft rail. For most of the day, she had stood watching land fade into the distance, her heart hollow.

Silently, the islander placed his elbows on the rail. Something in his stance told her he guessed her feelings and she sighed, "I'll never return. Mira's gone, out beyond the horizon. Somehow…"

Turning to her, Arnacin waited. Meeting his gaze, the queen asked, "How many times have you felt this way?"

"Every time since your father exiled me." His words were a sigh of confession. "I watched Mira disappear forever… and then I stared toward home, knowing it was impossible to return there."

Feeling bolder than she had for a long time, Valoretta pressed, "Why? Where were you all that time?"

Arnacin looked back at his hands, but after a moment, he cast her a sideways glance. His lips parted, and then he pressed them shut. "I wasn't home, or I never would've heard of Mira's fall."

The queen hesitated only a moment before gently squeezing his arm. "In the land of torture, obviously. I was also there."

A shudder passed through the islander. "You withstood it far better than I."

Feeling her cheeks warm, she bit her lip. After a second, she whispered, "I wasn't alone, as you were. I had people depending on me to withstand, and Sara… Sara…" Once more, Valoretta stopped, unable to put words to all of what her aunt had done. At last, the queen sighed, "Sara really did all the withstanding. She just forced me along."

Even more softly, she added, "And I had my memory of you, your dreams and ideals. Your example goaded me on, where you had none to follow."

As the time for the baby's birth drew near, Valoretta paled and grew weaker. Worriedly supporting the queen around the deck, Arnacin confessed, "We have to make land. I don't think I have the level of skills needed to deliver this child."

"Is that safe?" Even Valoretta's voice was shaky, and the islander doubted love was the only reason her head rested on his arm.

"The closest port belongs to Nomacir." Arnacin failed to keep the growl out of his tone, but despite his self-rebuke a small smile brushed the queen's face.

"Are they evil or just a normal monarchy?"

Hesitating, the islander turned her back toward the cabin. Nomacir would likely hang him if they saw him, but for her and the baby he had no choice. He had steered their course alongside as much land as possible, and Queen's Isholt's kingdom was unfortunately the closest. Finally, he shrugged. "I don't trust them."

A breath of amusement escaped Valoretta. "They don't sound that bad then."

Arnacin had no answer. It was the queen herself who changed the subject as he lifted her into bed and pulled the covers over her. "Have you thought of a name for the child?"

"Why do you ask? You're the natural parent. You have the right to pick as you will. I'll only refuse if you choose a name after your father."

With a smile, she took his hand. "If it's a boy, what do you think of Tenacity?"

"That should be for a girl."

"Tenacius, then. I want a girl to be named Honoria."

"Honoria," Arnacin breathed in horror. "Why?"

Her sad smile told him all. She intended to name her child after him, in the fashion of Mira. Tenacity and honor; virtues Mira had once thought in him.

Licking suddenly dry lips, he sighed, "Rest."

As he turned away, the queen's grasp tightened. "Arnacin, I love you."

The islander paused and then knelt back beside the bed. "You know something, Valoretta. What is it?"

At first, silence answered him. Then, closing her eyes, the queen breathed, "I am not the firstborn. I am the fourth child of my parents, but all the rest died before turning a week old. My birth nearly killed my mother. Thankfully, she lived through that. But, Arnacin, there is a strong chance neither I nor this child will live. You may return to your island alone after all and bury Mira with the waves."

In the following silence, the islander studied her, her frailness. Despite her courage, strength and heart, she was indeed a delicate woman. All Arnacin could say after a moment was, "Stop worrying."

At last, she opened her eyes with a shadow of a smile. "I just want you to know how serious I am."

When she claimed to love him? Somewhere, the islander knew the answer by then, if he had not long ago, but he finally asked anyway. "Why did you just stand there when Miro exiled me?"

Compressing her lips briefly, the queen again closed her eyes. "So that's why you don't trust me. You were free from Mira, Arnacin. You could sail home. Who was I to stand between you and your deepest wish?"

Nomacir's nearest port lay on their island and not the mainland, which was some relief as Arnacin sailed his ship into harbor. There, however, someone was waving excitedly. His ship had been seen.

Trying to tell himself it was just the night guard who had no knowledge of Arnacin in particular, the islander let his ship bump against the pier.

The man caught the mooring line, tying the ship in place before straightening, a wide smile on his face—Maco. His heart clenching in fear, Arnacin lowered the board he used as a ramp over the side, disregarding his confusion. Nodding once, he turned back to the cabin.

Unsurprisingly, the shipwright followed. "You shouldn't be half as stunned to see me as I am to see you. How did you escape? Mr. Butter told Queen Isholt of Baulis, and we were liberated. But how did you escape Xavior's fate?"

There was no time to reply. Valoretta was curled into a ball from pain when the they entered the cabin, her breathing rapid. Kneeling down, Arnacin asked, "Is it coming?"

Her face tight, the queen shook her head once.

"There's someone here who will help." Carefully lifting Valoretta, the islander cast a pointed glance at Maco.

Wide-eyed, the shipwright nodded. "I know of a family that can help. They helped all of Baulis's prisoners." As he headed outside, he added, "And I'll ask Channing to pray."

Silently, Arnacin followed, carrying Valoretta.

The very ground itself appeared to quake around Valoretta as she feverishly shook in Arnacin's arms outside the home they were shown.

Before them, the door flung open to reveal a middle-aged woman with a rosy flush to her cheeks. With an exclamation in her native tongue, the lady beckoned them inside. Then, she called in the common tongue, "Mr. Makarios! Miss Kassandra!"

Two pairs of hurrying feet responded. "Tica, what is it?" Then a male voice gasped, "A Zedelious!"

"Nonsense," Miss Kassandra snapped, bustling into action. "This girl is *dying*! Tica!" She dropped into the Nomacirrian language to spit more hurried orders.

Tica rushed away.

Still speaking rapidly, Miss Kassandra gestured Arnacin into a side room where the chaise lounge sat before a warm fire.

As Valoretta was placed on it, pain swooped across her consciousness. The only thing she felt certain of was her own death, which she welcomed. Everything else trickled in and out of her awareness as they worked to save both the baby and her— something warm and thick sliding down her throat, her insides seizing up, a baby's howl...

That cry briefly stirred her from her semi-conscious state. Through feverish shifting and foggy vision, she looked at her baby in Arnacin's arms and watched his thumb stroke that fine black hair, and her heart ached for them both. The child was Arnacin's, and glossing over all the painful parts of his past just became so much harder.

Upon realizing that sorrow, unconsciousness finally took her beyond all feeling until a hand against her forehead brought her back to the crackle of the fire in the background.

Arnacin knelt beside the chaise lounge on which she had been placed, stroking her damp hair off her brow.

"Arnacin," she rasped, and he slid his free hand over hers. "Arnacin," she tried again. "Your home is free of nobles. Go... don't make them wait..."

Her eyes closed in pain, but she sensed the islander lean forward, felt his lips brush her skin. For a split second, her heart leapt in exhilaration.

Somewhere nearby, their child complained, but the islander did not move instantly. "Tenacius and I will leave when you have the strength to travel," he whispered, his hand slipping away as he stood to take care of the newborn. "Don't give up, now, Valor."

For the first time in months, her heart struck a real beat and, without any drugs or sudden loss of consciousness, she drifted off to sleep feeling Arnacin's kiss still upon her brow.

Hope and life raced through her, strengthening her. Love had a way of doing that.

Thanks for reading *The Eternal Struggle*. If you've enjoyed reading this book, please leave a review on your favorite review site. It helps me reach readers who might enjoy more of my books.

Subscribe to my newsletter at
emeraldlakebooks.com/blackphantom
to be notified when the next book in
The Black Phantom Chronicles
is released.

Author's Note

I N THE COURSE OF WRITING a series about Arnacin's quest for honor and fulfillment, I am forced to write about the part wherein he fails. *The Eternal Struggle* is that part.

Betrayed by all, Arnacin of Enchantress Island finds himself thrown against a devious manipulator, who desires nothing less than the death of all the islander's morals. Although he refuses to yield, he is powerless without a friend on which to rely.

This story derives mainly from my love of the complexities that make up human nature. Humans' awe-inspiring strength and terrible weakness are among the biggest mysteries in nature. In that mystery, however, is a truth sometimes only hardships can teach us. Honor is not in the laurel wreath, wealth is not in the money, and worth is not in our own worldwide popularity, but in our close friendships.

Arnacin may not search for wealth, but he searches for honor and purpose in a world as regular as many people's daily lives.

Although the third book takes a detour as it returns to Enchantress Island and the struggles there while Arnacin is away, the series is of growing up, of finding truth and, in that truth, finding all the things for which he yearned when he was small.

Arnacin is in his own way the protagonist and the antagonist of his story. It's his choices that bring about the end, good and bad, as I have often found that my own choices shape my life as well. If you are where he is in the eternal struggle, perhaps he'll be a companion to you as you face your own dragons.

May you prosper in your search.

Sincerely,
Esther Wallace

Acknowledgments

I N THE YEAR SINCE BOOK 1 of this series was released, I have found many more supporters and friends. This book is only possible because of you, and I thank you. If your names are not specifically mentioned, I beg your forgiveness. It would take pages and pages to list everyone, but know that I include you with these paragraphs.

As always, I thank Emerald Lake Books for their belief in this series, even without knowing the end. Then, I pass them a manuscript like this one...

My parents and family have also risen in support in ways to make many an author jealous. I have seen posts upon posts of jokes about how authors will keep their profession secret from extended family and bear with the immediate family's dumb questions, such as, "Why don't they find a real job?" I am overly blessed to have a family willing to help in any way they can, even when they don't understand and (mostly) stay quiet about any doubts. Thank you.

I also thank my critique partners and editors, particularly Stephanie Warner who has seen the worst of my writing and has remained supportive of me and Arnacin.

To David Carlson, Chris Upton and those who have taken the time to invite me to author events, I extend my gratitude. I'm terrible at marketing.

I also wish to give a special thanks to those at my local Barnes and Noble. From the managers to the employees, and to those who shop there, I cannot thank you enough for all your support.

Thank you all, no matter where this takes me.

About the Author

ESTHER WALLACE IS AN AWARD-WINNING writer and a freelance illustrator, who holds an associate's degree in graphic design and animation.

Coming from a large homeschooling family, Esther began writing fiction to entertain her younger siblings and share her creativity with them. Likewise, she shared all the most stirring books she read.

Her favorite stories are those that ask the most difficult of questions. She likes it even better when she can encourage other people to discuss those things with her or at least to ponder them on their own.

Esther enjoys hearing from her readers. If you'd like to contact her or invite her to your next book club meeting, visit emeraldlakebooks.com/wallace.

For more great books, please visit us at
emeraldlakebooks.com

EMERALD LAKE
BOOKS

CPSIA information can be obtained
at www.ICGtesting.com
Printed in the USA
BVHW030731190720
584076BV00001B/209

9 781945 847257